To the Devil—A Daughter is a Black Magic story by Dennis Wheatley, who writes: 'I, personally, have never assisted at, or participated in, any ceremony connected with Magic—Black or White. Should any of my readers incline to a serious study of the subject and thus come into contact with a man or woman of Power, I feel that it is only right to urge them, most strongly, to refrain from being drawn into any practice of the Secret Art in any way. My own observations have led me to an absolute conviction that to do so would bring them into dangers of a very real and concrete nature.'

BY DENNIS WHEATLEY

NOVELS

The Launching of Roger Brook
The Shadow of Tyburn Tree
The Rising Storm
The Man Who Killed the King
The Dark Secret of Josephine
The Rape of Venice
The Sultan's Daughter
The Wanton Princess
Evil in a Mask

The Scarlet Impostor
Faked Passports
The Black Baroness
V for Vengeance
Come Into My Parlour
Traitors' Gate
They Used Dark Forces

The Prisoner in the Mask
The Second Seal
Vendetta in Spain
Three Inquisitive People
The Forbidden Territory
The Devil Rides Out
The Golden Spaniard
Strange Conflict
Codeword—Golden Fleece
Dangerous Inheritance

The Quest of Julian Day
The Sword of Fate
Bill for the Use of a Body

Black August
Contraband
The Island Where Time Stands
    Still
The White Witch of the South
    Seas

To the Devil—A Daughter
The Satanist

The Eunuch of Stamboul
The Secret War
The Fabulous Valley
Sixty Days to Live
Such Power is Dangerous
Uncharted Seas
The Man Who Missed the War
The Haunting of Toby Jugg
Star of Ill-Omen
They Found Atlantis
The Ka of Gifford Hillary
Curtain of Fear
Mayhem in Greece
Unholy Crusade

SHORT STORIES
Mediterranean Nights
Gunmen, Gallants and Ghosts

HISTORICAL
'Old Rowley'
(*A Private Life of Charles II*)
Red Eagle
(*The Story of the Russian Revolution*)

AUTOBIOGRAPHICAL
Stranger than Fiction
(*War Papers for the Joint Planning Staff*)
Saturdays with Bricks

it? Only one thing matters. Did you really mean it or not when, just before I snapped the stuff that bound my wrists and smashed the jar with your ring, you called out to me, 'Darling, I love you! I love you!?'

'Of course I did.'

Her big brown eyes shone with happiness as she leaned towards him and whispered, 'Then your own words are my answer.'

Inspector Drouet joined the party at the inn about half an hour later, and he confirmed that Henry Beddows was among the dead who had been recovered from the cave. As Christina was still technically under arrest he discussed her position with Malouet, then agreed to her provisional release on the ex-inspector's stating that he would go surety for her.

Very tired now, John, Christina and C. B. went out to Molly's car, and it was she who drove them home. When they arrived at the villa it was after one o'clock, and John and Christina went straight up to their rooms; but C. B. asked Molly for a night-cap.

Knowing his preference, she mixed him a whisky-and-soda; then made one for herself. He raised his glass, said, 'Chin, chin!', then added in his most conspiratorial voice:

'Can you tell me, Mrs. Fountain, any good and sufficient reason why I should not hand you over to the police on a charge of having committed mass murder?'

She suppressed a start, then asked with a bland smile, 'What are you talking about, C. B.? I'm afraid all this excitement has proved a little too much for even you.'

'No, Molly,' he said seriously. 'You can't laugh this thing off. I saw you drop that Mills bomb on to the heads of those wretched people.'

'Did you?' She smiled archly. 'Well, I don't mind if you did. They were all horrors and menaces to everything decent in life. It is a good thing that they are dead. Perhaps it was a pity about Beddows; but I'm not even certain about that, since he had lived as a Satanist all his adult life. And it ... er ... did the job perfectly, didn't it?'

'Yes, I'm not questioning your act on ethical grounds or

its efficiency. But the thing that troubles me is that someone else might have seen you do it. If they had you would be in prison now, and well on your way to the scaffold. Really, Molly, it's time that you had somebody to look after you."

"Meaning you, C. B.?"

He rubbed his big nose, then looked up at her. "Yes, dear one; meaning me."

She came across and sat down on his knees. Suddenly she gulped. "It was a frightful thing to do, wasn't it?" Next moment she was crying, with her cheek pressed against his, and she murmured, "Oh, you're so right, darling! I'm a horribly irresponsible sort of woman. Please, please take care of me."

DENNIS WHEATLEY'S
other Black Magic novels are

The Devil Rides Out
The Haunting of Toby Jugg
The Ka of Gifford Hillary
The Satanist

All available in Arrow Books

Dennis Wheatley

To the Devil—a Daughter

ARROW BOOKS

ARROW BOOKS LTD

178–202 Great Portland Street, London W1

AN IMPRINT OF THE HUTCHINSON GROUP

London Melbourne Sydney
Auckland Bombay Toronto
Johannesburg New York

First published by
Hutchinson & Co (*Publishers*) Ltd 1953
Arrow edition 1956
Second impression 1959
Third impression 1961
Fourth impression 1963
Fifth impression 1964
Sixth impression 1965
This new edition June 1969
Reprinted November 1969

*Made and printed in Great Britain
by The Anchor Press Ltd,
Tiptree, Essex*

09 002040 5

For our good friends

DIANE AND PIERRE HAMMEREL

With my most grateful thanks for their boundless hospitality and innumerable kindnesses to Joan and myself during our recent visit to Nice; not the least vivid memory of which remains our fatiguing but intriguing expedition (by daylight) to the Cave of Bats

CONTENTS

CHAPTER I

STRANGE CONDUCT OF A GIRL UNKNOWN

MOLLY FOUNTAIN was now convinced that a more intriguing mystery than the one she was writing surrounded the solitary occupant of the house next door. For the third morning she could not settle to her work. The sentences refused to come, because every few minutes her eyes wandered from the paper, and her mind abandoned its search for the appropriate word, as her glance strayed through the open window down to the little terrace at the bottom of the garden that adjoined her own.

Both gardens sloped steeply towards the road. Beyond it, and a two-hundred-feet fall of jagged cliff, the Mediterranean stretched blue, calm and sparkling in the sunshine, to meet on the horizon a cloudless sky that was only a slightly paler shade of blue. The road was known as the 'Golden Corniche' owing to the outcrop of red porphyry rocks that gave the coast on this part of the Riviera such brilliant colour. To the right it ran down to St. Raphael; to the left a drive of twenty-odd miles would bring one to Cannes. Behind it lay the mountains of the Esterel, sheltering it snugly from the cold winds, while behind them again to north and east rose the great chain of snow-tipped Alps, protecting the whole coast and making it a winter paradise.

Although it was only the last week in February, the sun was as hot as on a good day in June in England. That was nothing out of the ordinary for the time of year, but Mrs. Fountain had long since schooled herself to resist the temptation to spend her mornings basking in it. Her writing of good, if not actually best-seller, thrillers meant the difference between living in very reasonable comfort and a near-precarious existence on the pension of the widow of a Lieutenant-Colonel. As a professional of some years' standing she knew that work must

be done at set hours and in suitable surroundings. Kind friends
at home had often suggested that in the summer she should
come to stay and could write on the beach or in their gardens,
but that would have meant frequent interruptions, distraction
by buzzing insects, and gusts of wind blowing away her papers.
It was for that reason she always wrote indoors, although in the
upstairs front room of her little villa, so that she could enjoy
the lovely view. All the same, to-day she was conscious of a
twinge of envy as she looked down on the girl who was lazing
away the morning on the terrace in the next garden.

With an effort she pulled her mind back to her work.
Johnny, her only son, was arriving to stay at the end of the
week, and during his visits she put everything aside to be with
him. She really must get up to the end of chapter eight before
she abandoned her book for a fortnight. It was the trickiest
part of the story, and if she had not got over that it would nag
at her all through his stay. And she saw so little of him.

Despite herself her thoughts now drifted towards her son.
He was not a bit like his father, except in his open, sunny
nature that so readily charmed everyone he met. Archie had
been typical of the Army officer coming from good landed
gentry stock. After herself, hunting, shooting and fishing had
been his passions, and on any polo ground he had been a joy
to watch. Johnny cared for none of those things. He took
after her family, in nearly all of whom a streak of art had
manifested itself. In Johnny's case it had come out as a flair
for line and colour, and at twenty-three his gifts had already
opened fine prospects for him with a good firm of interior
decorators. But that meant his living in London. He could only
come out to her once a year, and she could not afford to take
long holidays in England.

She had often contemplated selling the villa and making
a home for him in London; but somehow she could not bring
herself to do that. When she and Archie married in 1927 they
had spent their honeymoon at St. Raphael, and fallen nearly as
much in love with that gold-and-blue coast of the Esterel as
they were with each other. That was why, when his father had
died in the following year, they had decided to buy a villa

there. As a second son his inheritance amounted to only a few thousands, but they had sunk nearly all of it in this little property and never regretted it. During the greater part of each year they had had to let it, but that brought them in quite a useful income, and for all their long leaves, while Johnny was a baby and later a growing boy, they had been able to occupy it themselves; so every corner of the house and every flowering shrub in the garden was intimately bound up with happy memories of her young married life.

The coming of the war had substituted long months of anxious separation for that joyful existence, and in 1942 all hope of its resumption had been finally shattered by an 8-mm. shell fired from one of Rommel's tanks in the Western Desert. Johnny had then been at school in Scotland, and his mother, her heart numb with misery, had striven to drown her grief by giving her every waking thought to the job she had been doing since 1940 in one of the Intelligence Departments of the War Office.

The end of the war had left her in a mental vacuum. Three years had elapsed since Archie's death, so she had come to accept it and was no longer subject to bouts of harrowing despair. But her job was finished and Johnny had just gone up to Cambridge; so she was now adrift without any absorbing interest to occupy the endless empty days that stretched ahead. Nearly six years of indifferent meals, taken at odd hours while working, often till after midnight, on Top-Secret projects that demanded secretarial duties of the most conscientious type, had left her both physically and mentally exhausted; so when it was learned that the villa had not been damaged or looted of its furniture, her friends had insisted that she should go south to recuperate.

She went reluctantly, dreading that seeing it again would renew the intolerable ache she had felt during the first months after her loss. To her surprise the contrary had proved the case. If Archie's ghost still lingered there, it smiled a welcome in the gently moving sunlight that dappled the garden paths, and in the murmur of the sea creaming on the rocks there seemed to be a faint echo of his laughter. It was the only permanent home

11

they had ever had, and in these peaceful surroundings they had shared she found a new contentment.

For a few months her time had been amply filled in putting the house to rights, getting the neglected garden back into order and renewing her acquaintance with neighbours who had survived the war; but with her restoration to health her mind began to crave some intellectual occupation. Before the war she had occasionally written short stories for amusement and had had a few of them accepted; so it was natural that she should turn to fiction as an outlet. Besides, she had already realized that Archie's pension would be insufficient to support her at the villa permanently, and by then she had again become so enamoured of the place that she could not bear the thought of having to part with it. So, under the double spur, she set to work in earnest.

Very soon she found that her war-time experiences had immensely improved her abilities as a writer. Thousands of hours spent typing staff papers had imbued her with a sense of how best to present a series of factors logically, clearly and with the utmost brevity. Moreover, in her job she had learned how the secret services really operated; so, without giving away any official secrets, she could give her stories an atmosphere of plausibility which no amount of imagination could quite achieve. These assets, grafted on to a good general education and a lively romantic mind, had enabled her agent to place her first novel without difficulty. She had since followed it up with two a year and had now made quite a name for herself as a competent and reliable author.

Molly Fountain's books were set in a great variety of countries, but they were always mystery thrillers with a back-ground of secret service. No one knew better than she that truth really was stranger than fiction; yet she never deliberately based a plot upon actual happenings to which she had been privy during the war. On the other hand, while taking con-siderable care to avoid any risk of an action for libel, she had no scruples about using as characters in her stories the exotic types frequently to be met with on that cosmopolitan coast, or incorporating such of their more lurid doings as the tittle-tattle of her bridge club in Cannes brought her, if these episodes could be profitably fitted in to add zest to the tale. That, subconsciously at least, was one of the reasons for her interest in the girl next door. Everything about this new neighbour suggested that she was the centre of a mystery.

Four days earlier Molly had just sat down to tea on her own little terrace when a taxi drew up in the road below and the girl had stepped out of it. She came from the direction of Cannes. In the taxi with her was a middle-aged man and some hand luggage. From the time and circumstances of her arrival it could be inferred that she had not come south on the Blue Train, but had landed from a 'plane at Nice airport. The man who accompanied her was strongly built, stocky and aggressive-looking, yet with something vaguely furtive about him. His clothes had struck a slightly incongruous note as he stood for a moment in the sunshine, looking up at the villa. It was not that there was anything really odd about them, and they were of quite good quality; but they were much more suited to a city office than either holidaying on the Riviera or travelling to it. He had helped the driver carry the suitcases up to the house, but remained there only about ten minutes, then returned to the waiting taxi and was driven off in it. That was the first and only time that Molly had seen him, and it now seemed evident that, having gone, he had gone for good.

There was nothing particularly strange in that. He might have been a house agent who had arranged to meet the girl and take her out to the villa that she had rented on a postal description through his firm; but in spite of his office clothes he had looked much too forceful a personality to be employed on such comparatively unimportant tasks. It seemed more probable that he was a relative or friend giving valuable time to performing a similar service. Anyhow, whoever he was, he had not bothered to come near the place again.

The strange thing was that no one else had either; nor, as far as Molly knew, had the girl ever gone out—at least in the daytime—and there was certainly something out of the ordinary about a young woman who was content to remain without any form of companionship for three whole days.

Stranger still, she made not the least effort to amuse herself. She never brought out any needlework or a sketching block, and was never seen to write a letter. Even when she carried a book as far as the terrace she rarely read it for more than a few minutes. Every morning, and a good part of each afternoon, she simply sat there gazing blankly out to sea. The theory that she was the victim of a profound sorrow suggested itself, yet she wore no sign of mourning and her healthy young face showed no trace of grief.

Molly had never encouraged her servants to bring her the local gossip, but in this case so intrigued had she become that she had made an exception. Like most women with a profession, she was too occupied to be either fussy or demanding about her household, provided she was reasonably well served; so she still had with her a couple named Botin whom she had engaged on her return to France in 1946. They had their faults, but would allow no one to cheat her except themselves, and that only in moderation. They were middle-aged, of cheerful disposition and had become much attached to her. Louis looked after the garden and did the heavy work, while Angèle did the marketing, the cooking and all those other innumerable tasks which a French *bonne à tout faire* so willingly undertakes. On the previous day Molly had, with apparent casualness, pumped them both.

Louis produced only two crumbs of information, gleaned from his colleague, old André, who for many years had tended the adjoining garden. The mademoiselle was English and the villa had been taken for only a month. Angèle had proved an even poorer source, as she reported that the *bonne* who was looking after the young lady next door was a stranger to the district; she had been engaged through an agency in Marseilles and was a Catalan, a woman of sour disposition who had rejected all overtures of friendship and was uncommunicative to the point of rudeness.

Negative as Angèle's contribution appeared to be, it had given Molly further food for speculation. Why should an English visitor engage a semi-foreigner from a city a hundred miles away to do for her, when there were plenty of good *bonnes* to be had on the spot? It would have saved a railway fare, and quite a sum on the weekly household books, to secure one who was well in with the local shopkeepers and knew the best stalls in the St. Raphael market at which to buy good food economically. The answer that sprang to mind was that a stranger was much less likely to gossip, and therefore something was going on next door that the tenant desired to hide.

Then, last night the mystery had deepened still further. Molly was a light sleeper. A little after one o'clock she had been roused by the sound of a loose stone rattling down the steep slope of a garden path. Getting out of bed she went to the window. The moon was up, its silvery light gleaming in big patches on the cactus between the pine-trees, and there was the girl just going down the short flight of steps that led from her little terrace to the road.

Fully awake now, Molly turned on her bedside light and settled down to read a new William Mole thriller that she had just had sent out from England; but while reading, her curiosity about her neighbour now still further titillated, she kept an ear cocked for sounds of the girl's return. As a writer she could not help being envious of the way in which Mr. Mole used his fine command of English to create striking imagery, and her sense of humour was greatly tickled by his skilful interpolation of the comic between his more exciting scenes; so the next hour and a half sped by very quickly. Then in the still night she heard the click of the next-door garden gate, and, getting up again, saw the girl re-enter the house.

Why, Molly wondered, when she never went out in the daytime, should she go out at night? It could hardly be that she was in hiding, because she spent the greater part of each day on the terrace, where she could easily be seen from the road by anyone passing in a car. The obvious answer seemed to be that she had gone out to meet someone in secret; but she had been neither fetched in a car nor returned in one, and she had not been absent quite long enough to have walked into St. Raphael and back. Of course, she could have been picked up by a car that had been waiting for her round the next bend of the road, or perhaps she had had an assignation at one of the neighbouring villas. In any case, this midnight sortie added still further to the fascinating conundrum of what lay behind this solitary young woman having taken a villa on the *Corniche d'Or*.

For the twentieth time that morning Molly's grey-green eyes wandered from her typewriter to the open window. Just beneath it a mimosa tree was in full bloom and its heavenly scent came in great wafts to her. Beyond it and a little to the left a group of cypresses rose like dark candle-flames, their points just touching the blue horizon. Further away to the right two umbrella pines stood out in stark beauty against the azure sky. Below them on her small, square, balustraded terrace the girl still sat motionless, her hands folded in her lap, gazing out to sea. About the pose of the slim, dark-haired figure there was something infinitely lonely and pathetic.

Molly Fountain knew that she had no right whatever to poke her nose into someone else's business, but she could bear it no longer. Her new neighbour, although unconscious of it, was playing the very devil with her work, and, worse, she would know no peace of mind until she had at least made an effort to find out if the girl were in trouble. That it was not the sort of trouble which sometimes causes young women to seek seclusion for a while in order to protect their reputations was evident, as the villa had been leased for only a month and the girl showed not the slightest sign of pregnancy. Yet there must be some cause for her abnormal conduct and obvious melancholy. Molly was far from being a motherly soul, but she had her fair share of maternal instinct and, quite apart from her desire to satisfy her curiosity, she now felt an urge that would not be denied to offer her help if it was needed, or at least endeavour to animate this woebegone young creature with something of her own cheerful vitality.

There was only one thing for it. On the Riviera it was not customary to call upon temporary neighbours, but the fact that they were both English would be excuse enough for that. With Molly, to make up her mind was to act. Pushing back her chair from the typing table, she stood up. For once a real-life mystery had been thrust beneath her nose. There and then she decided to go out and attempt to solve it.

CHAPTER II

COLONEL CRACKENTHORP'S TECHNIQUE

GOING through into her bedroom, Molly Fountain pulled her linen working smock up over her head. Anyone seeing her at that moment would never have guessed that she was forty-five. Her upstretched arms emphasized the lines of her good figure; her hips had broadened comparatively little since she had reached maturity and her legs were straight and shapely. Only as she jerked off the smock and threw it on a chair did the fact that her youth was past become apparent, from a slight thickening of the muscles in her neck and her grey hair.

From her wardrobe she selected a white, hand-embroidered blouse and a grey coat and skirt. The cut of these, together with her medium-weight nylons and practical, lowish-heeled shoes, did nothing to detract from her real age, since the one thought Molly could not bear was that anyone should have cause to regard her as 'mutton dressed as lamb'. For that reason, too, except when going out at night to a party, she used very little make-up. Yet, even so, the face that looked back at her from the mirror as she quickly tidied her hair would have been judged by most people to be that of a woman still under forty. There were laughter-lines round the mouth and the beginnings of crow's-feet round the eyes, but not a hint of sagging in the still firm flesh, and it was moulded on that fine bone formation that preserves the basis of youthful good looks right into old age.

Reaching up on tip-toe she pulled a battered hat-box from off the top of the wardrobe and took from it a three-year-old straw hat bedecked with cornflowers. Molly hated hats and never wore one if she could possibly avoid it, but she felt that on this occasion a hat should be worn in support of her pretence that she was making a formal call. Securing it on her head at what she believed to be a *chic* angle, she collected a pair of gloves and her bag, then set off on her self-appointed mission.

It was a little before mid-day and the sun was strong enough now to tan anyone who was not used to it. As she made her way down the garden path that zig-zagged among spiky cactus and strange-shaped succulents she saw a little green lizard run up the trunk of a tall palm-tree, and on reaching the terrace at the bottom she made a mental note that enough roses were in bloom in the bed behind it to furnish her with another bowl. Out in the road she walked along under the tall retaining wall of rough-hewn rock that supported both her garden and those of several medium-sized villas situated on the same slope. At intervals along it hung festoons of large-flowered yellow jasmin and purple bougainvillaea. The scent of flowers, mingled with that of the primaeval pine-wood among which the villas had been built, was delicious. For the ten-thousandth time the thought crossed her mind that never could she bring herself to leave it and face another English winter.

By then she had reached the gate to the next garden. Opening it, she went up the steep stone steps set in a narrow cleft of the stonework. As her head emerged above ground level she turned it towards the terrace. The girl had heard her approach and was looking in her direction. Slowly she stood up, but she did not move forward and gave no sign of welcome. Her face had a guarded look and Molly thought she detected just a trace of fear in her dark eyes.

Stepping up on to the terrace, Molly said, "I'm Molly Fountain, your nearest neighbour. As we're both English I thought——"

The girl's eyes widened and her broad face suddenly became animated as she exclaimed, "Not *the* Molly Fountain?"

Molly smiled. Her name was by no means universally known, but during the past two years it had become sufficiently so for quite a high proportion of English people to whom, for one reason or another, she had to give it to ask if she was the author; yet the question still never failed to arouse in her a slightly bashful pleasure, and she replied with becoming modesty:

"I don't know of any other, and if you are thinking of the writer of secret service yarns, that would be me."

"Of course!" said the girl. "I've read several of them, and they're awfully thrilling."

"That makes things easier, doesn't it?" Molly quickly took advantage of the bridge unexpectedly offered by her literary activities. "Having read some of my stories will, I hope, make you look on me as a little less like a total stranger. You must forgive me making my first call on you in the morning, but social customs are more elastic here than at home, and I thought you might prefer it to cards left formally on you in the afternoon."

It was the first time Molly had seen the girl face to face, and while she was speaking she was taking quiet stock of her. Tall above the average, so slim as to be almost gawky, and a slight awkwardness in the control of her long limbs gave her somewhat the appearance of an overgrown schoolgirl. Seen from the distance Molly had put her down as about twenty-three, but now she revised her estimate and decided that nineteen would be nearer the mark. Her forehead was broad and surmounted by thick, wavy, dark-brown hair parted in the middle; her mouth was wide, full and generous. A snub nose robbed her of all pretence to classical beauty, and her complexion was a trifle sallow; but she possessed two excellent features. When her teeth flashed in a smile they were dazzlingly white: more striking still, her brown eyes were huge and extraordinarily luminous.

Molly's reference to formal calls caused her to remember the duties of hospitality, and with only a fraction of hesitation she said, "Won't you . . . come up to the house?"

"Thank you; I should love to," Molly replied promptly. Then, as they turned towards it, she added, "But, you know, you haven't told me your name yet."

"Oh!" Again there was a slight hesitation before the answer. "It's Christina Mordant."

The path between the prickly-pears and oleanders snaked from side to side round a succession of hairpin bends, yet despite that it was still steep enough to require all their breath as they mounted it; so they spoke no more until they reached a small lawn on the level of the villa.

Molly had never been up there before and the lemon-washed house was partly concealed both from her windows and the road by umbrella-pines and palm-trees. She saw now that it was somewhat smaller than her own and probably contained only six or seven rooms including the servants' quarters. As they crossed the lawn she asked:

"Is this your first visit to the Riviera?"

"Yes," Christina nodded, leading her guest through a pair of french windows into the sitting-room. "But I've lived in France for quite a while. I was at a finishing school in Paris until just before Christmas."

"I first came to this part of the world in 1927, and have made my home here for the past five years; so you must let me show you something of this lovely coast," Molly volunteered.

Christina's hesitation was much more marked this time. Her underlip trembled slightly, then she stammered, "Thank you . . . awfully; but . . . but I don't care much for going out."

A moment's awkward pause ensued, then she pulled herself together and added in a rather breathless attempt to atone for what might be taken as rudeness, "Do please sit down. Let me get you a drink. I'm afraid we don't run to cocktails, but Maria could soon make some coffee, or we have delicious orange-juice."

Molly did not really want a drink, but realized that acceptance would give her an excuse to prolong her call, and the longer they talked the better her chance of winning the girl's confidence; so she said, "I'd love some orange-juice if it's not too much trouble."

"Oh, none at all," Christina cried, hurrying to the window. "There are masses of oranges in the garden. I'll pick some. It won't take me a moment. We've lemons, grape-fruit and tangerines, too. Would you like it straight, or prefer a mixture?"

"I always think orange and grape-fruit half and half is the nicest out here, where there's no shortage of sugar," Molly replied; and as the girl left the room she began to take detailed stock of it.

The villa belonged to a café proprietor in Cannes who had never occupied it himself, but bought it as an investment and made a good thing out of it by letting it furnished for short periods to a succession of holiday-makers. In consequence it contained only the barest necessities, and its furniture was of that positively hideous variety favoured by the French bourgeoisie. In vain Molly's glance roved over the monstrosities in cheap wood and chromium for some indication of Christina's personality, until her eye lit on a manicure-set which lay open on a rickety spindle-legged table half concealed by the chair in which she was sitting. Picking it up she saw that it was comparatively new, bore the mark of a Paris manufacturer, and that its morocco leather cover was stamped with the initials E. B.

When Christina returned she came in by the door from the hallway carrying a tray with a jug of fruit-juice, two glasses and sugar. As she poured out, she asked, "Do you live here all the year, Mrs. Fountain?"

"Most of it. I usually spend June in London and have a fortnight in Paris in the autumn; but the cost of living has become so high both in France and England that I can't afford to live for more than about six weeks in hotels."

Christina raised her dark eyebrows. "Really! I should have thought you were terribly rich. Your books must bring you in thousands."

"That's a popular illusion that the public have about all authors," Molly smiled. "Except for a handful of best-sellers, writing is one of the worst-paid jobs in the world; and even in France, these days, a big part of one's earnings is taken away by taxation."

For ten minutes or so she went on talking about books and authors, as Christina was obviously interested, and it seemed a good line for tuning in on the girl's mind without arousing her suspicions. Then, having learnt that she had a liking for historical novels, Molly said:

"In that case it surprises me all the more that you don't make some excursions. This coast is full of history right back to Phœnician times. Fréjus was a Roman town. The streets of the old quarter in Nice are absolutely fascinating, and both Marshal Massena and Garibaldi were born there. Napoleon landed from Elba at Cap d'Antibes and at Haute Cagnes there is a fine old castle that belonged to the Counts Grimaldi. When I was your age I would have given anything for the chance to visit all these places."

Christina gave her an uncomfortable look, then averted her eyes and muttered, "I'm quite happy lazing in the garden."

"How long are you here for?"

"About another three weeks. The villa is taken for a month."

"Are you quite on your own?"

"Yes."

"Surely you find it very lonely? Have you no friends you could go to visit, or who could come to see you?"

"No. I don't know anyone at all down here. But . . . but I like being on my own."

"In that you are lucky," Molly commented quietly. "It is a great blessing to be content with one's own company and not be driven constantly to seek some new distraction from one's own thoughts. But all the same I should have thought you would have sometimes liked a change of scene. Don't you ever go out at all?"

Christina shook her head.

"An exciting book kept me reading very late last night, and when I got out of bed to get one of my sleeping pills I thought I saw you coming in through the garden."

For a moment the girl's face remained closed and secretive, then she replied, "Yes. I had been for a walk. I sleep most of the afternoon and go for a walk every night. I don't know why, but I've always felt listless after mid-day; then, as darkness falls, I seem to wake up and want to do things."

"Some people are like that. The astrologers say that we are influenced all our lives by the hour of our birth, and that people born in the evening are always at their best at night."

"Really! That seems to fit my case. I was born at nine forty-five in the evening." After a second Christina volunteered the additional information, "My birthday is March the sixth, and I'll be twenty-one next month."

"You will be here for it, then. It seems an awful shame that you should be deprived of the chance to celebrate. But perhaps you have relatives or friends who will be joining you before that?"

"No; I expect still to be quite alone."

There fell a pause while Molly considered this new evidence of the girl's complete isolation. A twenty-first birthday is such a landmark in any young person's life that it seemed quite extraordinary that she had not a single person in the world who wished to make it a happy day for her. Then, after a moment, Molly realized that so far she had got nowhere; she had not succeeded in getting the faintest clue to this mystery.

Swiftly she began to consider what line the favourite hero of her own creation, Colonel Crackenthorp, would take on having reached such an impasse. She knew this fiction character of hers as well as she knew herself; so the answer came automatically. The debonair and resourceful 'Crack' would employ shock tactics. Shock tactics it should be then. Looking the girl straight in the eye, she said suddenly:

"Christina Mordant is not your real name, is it?"

Caught off her guard, the girl winced as if she had been struck, and gasped, "How . . . how did you know?"

Then she recovered herself. Her face had gone white, but she slowly rose to her feet. As she did so her big brown eyes narrowed and filled with an angry light. Her whole body was trembling as she burst out:

"What has it to do with you? I didn't ask you to come here! What right have you to pry into my affairs? How dare you spy upon me and come here to catechize me? Get out! D'you hear me? Get out at once!"

This was not at all the sort of response that the shock tactics of the gallant 'Crack' would have met with in one of Molly's books. The girl would have broken down, wept upon his broad shoulder and confessed all. But then 'Crack' was a handsome fellow who had the devil of a way with women, whereas his creator was only a middle-aged lady novelist. No doubt, thought Molly, that explained why his technique had failed so lamentably in this real-life try-out. Anyhow, it was clear that she had botched the whole business beyond repair; so she stood up and said:

"I *do* apologize. My inquisitiveness was quite unjustified and I'm afraid I was very rude. I'm not either usually, and in the ordinary way I'd never dream of forcing myself on anyone. My work keeps me far too busy to waste time calling on strangers. But I couldn't help being worried by seeing you sitting on your terrace hour after hour doing absolutely nothing. And you looked so terribly unhappy that I felt sure you must be in some sort of trouble. Had other people come to see you I would never have come here; but you're very young and seemed to have no one you could turn to. I'm old enough to be your mother, and I was hoping that you might care to confide in me, because I would willingly have helped you if I could. As it is I can only ask you to forgive my unwarranted intrusion."

Mustering the remnants of her shattered dignity, Molly squared her shoulders then, with a brief inclination of her head, walked past the tall, now stony-faced, girl, through the french windows and out on to the lawn. She was only half-way across it when she was halted by a despairing cry behind her.

"Oh, Mrs. Fountain! Come back! Come back! I didn't mean what I said. You're nice! You're kind: I'm sure I can trust you. I can't tell you why I'm here, because I don't know myself. But I'm worried out of my wits. Oh, please let me talk to you."

Molly turned, and next moment the slim girlish figure was weeping in her arms. Without elation, but in faint surprise, she was conscious of the thought that good old 'Crack's' technique had worked after all.

CHAPTER III

THE MYSTERIOUS RECLUSE

A GOOD ten minutes elapsed before Christina—as she called herself—became fully coherent. During that time the only concrete fact that Molly had got out of her was that the purposeful-looking middle-aged man who had arrived in the taxi with her four days before was her father.

They were now back in the house and sitting together on the cheap, velvet-covered settee. Molly had one arm round the girl's shoulders and was gently wiping the tears from her cheeks with a totally inadequate handkerchief. When her sobbing at last began to ease, Molly said:

"My dear, do you really mean to tell me that your father brought you here and left you without giving any reason at all for doing so?"

"The . . . the only reason he gave was that I . . . I have enemies who are hunting for me."

"What sort of enemies?"

The girl gave a loud sniff, then fished out her own handkerchief and blew her snub nose. When she had done, she said in a firmer voice, "I don't know. I haven't an idea. That's just what makes the whole thing so puzzling."

Molly poured some more of the fruit-juice into a glass and handed it to her. She drank a little, said "Thanks," and went on, "He simply said that I was threatened by a very great danger, but that I had nothing at all to worry about providing I obeyed his instructions implicitly. When I pressed him to tell me what the danger was, he said it was far better that I should know nothing about it, because if I knew I might start imagining things and do something silly. All I had to do was to lie low here for a few weeks and I should be quite safe."

"You poor child! I don't wonder now that you've been unable to give your thoughts to any form of amusement, with a thing like this on your mind. But have you no idea at all what this threat might be, or who these enemies are from whom your father is hiding you?"

"No. I've cudgelled my wits for hours about it, but I haven't a clue. I've never done any grave harm to anyone. Honestly I haven't. And I can't think why anyone should want to harm me."

After considering the matter for a moment, Molly asked, "Are you by chance a very rich girl?"

"Oh no. Father left me ample money to pay for my stay here, and he gives me a generous dress allowance; but that's all I've got."

"I really meant, are you an heiress? Has anyone left you a big sum of money into which you come when you are twenty-one?"

"No: no one has ever left me anything. I don't think any of my relatives ever had much to leave, anyway."

"How about your father? Is he very well off?"

"I suppose so. Yes, he must be. We live very quietly at home, but all the same he must make a lot of money out of the factory, and all the other businesses in which he is mixed up. But why do you ask?"

"I was wondering if there could be a plot to kidnap you and hold you to ransom."

The big brown eyes showed a mild scepticism. "Surely that sort of thing happens only in America? Besides, my father is no richer than scores of other British industrialists; so I can't see any reason why kidnappers should single him out for their attention."

"What does he make at his factory?"

"Motor engines."

The reply instantly aroused Molly's instinct for good thriller plots, and she exclaimed, "Then he may be one of the key men in the rearmament drive. Perhaps he holds the secret of some new type of aircraft. It may be the Russians who are after you, in the hope that he will betray the secret as the price of getting you back."

With a shake of the head, the girl swiftly damped Molly's

ardour. "No, Mrs. Fountain, it can't be that. He only makes dull things like agricultural tractors."

Again Molly pondered the problem, then she asked a little diffidently, "Before you left England, did you go into a private nursing home to have a minor operation?"

"Yes." The brown eyes grew round with surprise. "However did you guess?"

"I didn't. It was just a shot in the dark. But since you admit it, that may explain everything. The probability is that your father brought you out here to hide you from the police."

"I can't think what you're talking about. Having an operation isn't a crime."

"It can be, in certain circumstances," Molly replied drily.

"Well, I'm sure they don't apply to me."

"They might. Is your mother still alive?"

"No; she died when I was six."

"Have you any elder sisters?"

"No, I am an only child."

Molly nodded and said gently, "That makes what I have in mind all the more likely. Even in these days quite a number of girls, particularly motherless ones, reach the age of nineteen or twenty without knowing enough about life to take care of themselves. When you found you were going to have a baby and your father put you in the nursing home to have it removed, he evidently decided that you had quite enough to worry about already without his telling you that such operations are illegal. But they are, and if the police have got on to that nursing home they are probably investigating all the operations that took place in it. Everyone concerned would be liable to be sent to prison. As you were an innocent party I don't think you need fear that for yourself; but, for having authorized the operation, your father might get quite a heavy sentence. So it's hardly to be wondered at that he wants to keep you out of the way until the police have got their evidence from other cases and the danger of your being drawn into it is past."

The girl had listened in silence, but as Molly ceased speaking she began to titter; then, with her white teeth flashing, she burst into a loud laugh. But, catching sight of Molly's rather aggrieved expression, she checked her laughter and said quickly:

"I'm so sorry, Mrs. Fountain, I didn't mean to be rude, and I'm awfully grateful for the way you are trying to help me get my bearings. But I couldn't prevent myself from seeing the funny side of your last theory; and you would, too, if you knew the way I had been brought up. I learnt all about sex from other girls, ages ago, but up to last December I've spent nearly the whole of my life in schools—including the holidays. And in all the schools I've been to we were as carefully guarded from everything in trousers as if we had been nuns; so I haven't even ever had a boy friend yet, let alone an illegal."

Molly felt slightly foolish; but, hiding her discomfiture, she smiled. "I'm glad to hear that, but what sort of operation did you have?"

"I had my tonsils out. During January I had rather a nasty sore throat, and although the local doctor said he didn't think it really necessary, Father insisted that it should be done. He put me in a private nursing home at Brighton for the job and made me stay there for three weeks afterwards to convalesce. He collected me from there to bring me straight out here."

"It rather looks, then, as if he has been attempting to hide you for some time, and used the excuse of your tonsils to get you out of the way as early as the end of January."

"Perhaps. At the time I was rather touched, as I thought he was showing an unusual solicitude about me. You see, to tell the truth, although it sounds rather beastly to say so, he has never before seemed to care very much what happened to me; and I am quite certain that he would not risk going to prison on my account, as you suggested just now. In view of what has happened since, I think you must be right; but the thing that absolutely stumps me is why he should be taking so much trouble to keep me away from everyone I've ever known."

Her heart going out more warmly than ever to this mother-less and friendless girl, Molly said, "Don't worry, my dear. We'll get to the bottom of it somehow; but I'll have to know more about you before I can suggest any further possibilities.

As you have had such a secluded life, there can't be much to tell me about that. Still, it's possible that I might hit on a pointer if you cared to give me particulars of your family and your home. To start with, what is your real name?"

"I'm sorry. I'll tell you anything else you wish, but that is the one thing I can't tell you. Father made me swear that I wouldn't divulge my name to anyone while I was down here. I chose Christina for myself, because I like it. Would you very much mind calling me that?"

"Of course not, my dear. Start by telling me about your father, then, and his reasons for always keeping you at school. We might get some clue to his present treatment of you from the past."

Christina fetched a packet of cigarettes from the hideous mock-Empire sideboard, offered them to Molly and took one herself. When they had lit up, she began:

"I can't say for certain, but I think the reason that Father has never shown me much affection is because he didn't want me when I arrived. He was then only a working-class man—a chauffeur who had married the housemaid—but he was always very ambitious, and I think he regarded me as another burden that would prevent him from getting on.

"I was born in Essex, in the chauffeur's flat over the garage of a house owned by a rich old lady. You must forgive me for not giving you the name of the house and the village. It's not that I don't trust you, but we live in the house now ourselves, and everybody in those parts knows my father; so it would practically amount to breaking my promise about not telling anyone down here my real name. Anyhow, the house had no bearing on my childhood, because when I was only a few weeks old my father chucked up his job and bought a share in a small business in a nearby town.

"We lived in a little house in a back street, and it was not a happy household. I don't remember it very clearly, but enough to know that poor Mother had a rotten time. It wasn't that Father was actively unkind to her—at least not until towards the end—but he cared for nothing except his work. He never took her for an outing or to the pictures, and he was just as hard on himself. When he wasn't in his office or the warehouse he was always tinkering in a little workshop that he had knocked up in the backyard of the house, even on Sundays and often far into the night.

"Within a year or two of his going into business one of his partners died and he bought the other out. But that did not content him. As soon as he had the business to himself he started a small factory to make a little motor, many of the parts of which he had invented, and it sold like hot cakes. When I was five we moved to a bigger house in a somewhat better neighbourhood, but that did not make things any better for Mother. He had less time to give her than ever, and he would never buy her any pretty clothes because he said he needed every penny he was making for expansion.

"There doesn't seem any reason to believe that Mother was particularly religious as a young girl, and she was only twenty-eight when she died; so I suppose it was being debarred from participating in all normal amusements that led her to seek distraction in the social life of the chapel. My memory about it is a little vague, but I know that she spent more and more of her time there during the last two years of her life, and that for some reason it annoyed Father intensely that she should do so. I was too young to understand their arguments, but I have an idea that she got religion and used to preach at him. Naturally, he would have resented that, as he is an agnostic himself, and does not believe in any of the Christian teachings.

"Eventually he became so angry that he forbade her to go to chapel any more. But she did, and on my sixth birthday she took me with her. That proved an unhappy experience for both of us, as I was sick before I even got inside the place, and had to be taken home again. She made a second attempt a few Sundays later, when Father was out of the way seeing some friend of his on business, but again I was sick in the porch. Undaunted, she seized on the next occasion that he was absent from home on a Sunday morning, and for the third time I let her down by being as sick as a puppy that has eaten bad fish, up against the chapel doorway.

"Why chapels and churches have that effect on me I have

no idea. I think it must be something to do with the smell that is peculiar to them; a sort of mixture of old unwashed bodies, disinfectant and stale cabbages. No doctor at any of the schools I've been to has ever been able to explain it, or produce a cure; so I've always had to be let off attending services. I suppose it has become a case of association now, but I am still unable to look inside a church without wanting to vomit.

"Anyway, after my mother's third attempt to take me to chapel, the connection between chapel-going and being sick must have been quite firmly established in my mind. No child could be expected to like what must have appeared to be a series of outings undertaken with the deliberate intention of making it sick; and, of course, I was still too young to realize what I was doing when I spilled the beans to Father.

"I let the cat out of the bag at tea-time, and he went absolutely berserk. He threw his plate at Mother, then jumped up and chased her round the table. I fled screaming to my room upstairs, but for what seemed an age I could hear him bashing her about and cursing her. She was in bed for a week, and afterwards she was never the same woman again; so I think he may have done her some serious injury. It is too long ago for me to recall the details of her illness, but I seem to remember her complaining of pains in her inside, and finding the housework heavier and heavier, although it is probable that her decline was due to acute melancholia as much as to any physical cause. By mid-summer she could no longer raise the energy to go out, and became a semi-invalid. Naturally her chapel friends were very distressed and used to come in from time to time to try to cheer her up. The pastor used to visit us too, once or twice a week, when it was certain that Father was well out of the way, and sit with her reading the Bible.

"It was one of his visits that precipitated her death. Father came home unexpectedly one afternoon and found him there. I was out at kindergarten, so I only heard about it afterwards. By all accounts Father took the pastor by the shoulders and kicked him from the front door into the gutter.

"Most people take a pretty dim view about anyone laying violent hands on a man of God, and the episode might have resulted in a great deal of unpleasantness for Father, but on balance he got off very lightly. For one thing he was popular, at any rate with his work-people and their families, whereas the pastor was not. For another, a story went round that the pastor had been Mother's lover, or that, anyway, Father had caught him making a pass at her. I don't believe that for one moment. I haven't a doubt that it was put about by Father himself in an attempt to justify his act, and that the real truth was that finding the pastor there had sent him into another of his blind rages against the chapel and everything connected with it.

"The affair cost him the goodwill of a certain number of his more staid acquaintances, and it stymied his standing for the town council, as he had planned to do, that winter. But it didn't prove as serious a set-back to his upward progress as it might have done; and although the pastor had talked of starting an action for assault, he didn't, because in view of what happened afterwards he decided that it would have been un-Christian to do so. He was thinking, of course, of the fact that when Father woke up next morning he found Mother dead in bed beside him.

"It was generally accepted that she had died as the result of delayed shock. There can be no doubt that such a scene must have struck at the very roots of her being. When I was older, friends who had known her told me that she had regarded her pastor as inspired by God; so for her to have seen him set upon must have been like witnessing the most appalling sacrilege. At that moment, in her morbid state of mind, I dare say my father must have appeared to her to be the Devil in person, and the thought that she was married to him may have proved too much for her. She fainted and was put to bed by a neighbour. It was she who told me most of what I know about it, some years later. The doctor was called in and he was a bit worried because Mother would not answer his questions or speak to anybody; but he thought she would be all right when she got over the shock.

"It may be true that she didn't get over it, and her heart suddenly failed, or something; but she had been taking pills to make her sleep for some time, and when our neighbour came in next morning she found the bottle empty. She said nothing about it, but it was her opinion that Mother had taken an overdose to escape having to go on living with Father. Perhaps he knows the truth about what happened, but if so he is the only person who does."

Christina paused to light another cigarette, then she went on, "For a time our neighbour looked after me. Then, in the autumn, Father brought a woman named Annie to the house. She was a big blonde creature, lazy but kind-hearted, and he gave out that he had been married to her in London; but of course that wasn't true, and I am sure now that she was just a tart that he had picked up somewhere. Mother had been much too weepy and religious to inspire a passionate devotion in any child; so I had soon got over her loss, and I grew to love Annie. She said she had always wanted a little daughter just like me, and my life with her was one long succession of lovely surprises and jolly treats. No doubt she was common, rather silly and the sort who is too lazy to earn her own living except by haunting dance-halls and shady clubs; but the nine months she was with us were far and away the happiest of my childhood, in fact the only really happy ones I ever had, and I was inconsolable for weeks after she went away.

"The affair broke up because Father was getting on so fast. He felt it was bad for business for him to continue living in the sort of house more suited to one of his own foremen; so he bought another out in the town's best residential district. To me, at the time, it seemed huge, but actually it was just an eight-roomed house with a garage and an acre or so of garden. Still, as far as we were concerned it was a great step up in the world; and although Father may not have been quite as keen on Annie as he had been at first, it was mainly because she did not fit into the new picture that he ditched her.

"It was a few days before we were due to move that I found her in tears. She told me then that they had never been married and that he didn't consider her good enough for him any longer. But she didn't make a scene. She had more natural dignity than many better-bred women whom I've met, and I'll always remember her walking out, dry-eyed and smiling, to the taxi that was to take her to the station. I never saw her again.

"For me, her going robbed the new house of all its glamour, and very soon I came to hate the place. Father never again made the mistake of getting married, or pretending that he had divorced Annie and acquired a new wife. Instead, he replaced Annie with a girl who had been one of his secretaries. They never bothered to conceal the fact from me that they slept together, but to preserve the proprieties she was given the status of governess-housekeeper. Her name was Delia Weddel, and she had been brought up in quite a good home, but if ever there was a bitch she was one.

"She was another blonde, but the thin kind, and strikingly good-looking, until one came to realize the hardness of her eyes and the meanness of her mouth. Why she should have taken a hate against me I have no idea, but she made my life hell, and she was so cunning and deceitful that neither Father nor the daily woman we used to have in to do the housework guessed what was going on.

"As a child I was subject to sleep-walking. That meant if sounds were heard in the night someone had to get up and put me to bed again. Annie used to do that so gently that I hardly realized it had happened, but Delia used to put me outside the back door until the cold woke me up. While I was there she would go upstairs, strip my bed and throw the clothes on the floor; so that when she let me in, shivering with cold, I had to make it again myself before I could get to sleep. Next day, too, she always gave me some punishment for having disturbed her, and, of course, that only made me worse.

"Then there was the agony of lessons. As she was officially my governess she had at least to make a pretence of teaching me. But all she ever did was to point out a passage in a history or geography book and order me to learn it by heart, while she read a novel or went shopping. It was torture, because I wasn't old enough to master things like that. I had got to the stage of reading only fairy stories and books about animals; yet if I couldn't say my piece at the end of the hour I knew that I was

34

going to get my knuckles rapped. I would have given anything in the world to be back at kindergarten with the common little children, singing songs and playing games with bricks. But at that age a child is absolutely at the mercy of grown-ups; so there was nothing I could do about it.

"A breakdown in my health saved me from Delia. Perhaps the doctor suspected what had led up to it. Anyhow, he advised that I needed sea air to build me up, and that as I was getting on for eight I should be sent to a boarding-school at the seaside after Christmas. Delia was only too glad to be rid of me; so in January 1939 I was packed off to a school at Felixstowe.

"It wasn't a very good school. They fed us shockingly and cheesepared on the central heating, although it was quite an expensive place and supposed to be rather smart. I had a thin time to start with, too, because most of the other girls were awful snobs. When they found out that I had been at a National Kindergarten and spent my childhood in a back street, they christened me 'the little alley cat' and were generally pretty beastly. Still, anything was better than Delia, and from then on going back to her for the holidays was the only thing I really had to dread.

"Soon after war broke out the school was moved to Wales, and when I came home the following Christmas I found to my joy that Delia had gone the way of Annie. The house was being run for Father by a middle-aged couple named Jutson. Their status was simply that of servants: she was cook-housekeeper and he did the odd jobs and the garden. They have been with us ever since. Later I learned by chance that from 1940 Father was well off enough to have a flat in London. Or, rather, that he kept a succession of popsies in flats that were nominally theirs and used to stay with them whenever he went up; so I know very little about his later mistresses.

"The Jutsons are a respectable, hard-working couple, but she is rather a sour woman. During the holidays and the Easter ones that followed she did what she had to do for me, but no more. I was fed at regular hours and seen to bed at night, otherwise I was left to amuse myself as well as I could.

I think Father has always paid them well to keep their mouths shut about his affairs, because when I asked either of them why he was often absent from home, or where he had gone to and when he was coming back, they always used to say 'Ask no questions and you get no lies!' And that has been their attitude ever since.

"That April the real war began and Father decided it would be best for me to remain at school for the summer holidays. Many of the other parents felt the same way about their daughters, so more than half of us stayed on in Wales, and while the Battle of Britain was being fought we had quite a jolly time. We couldn't foresee it then, but for most of us that was only the first of many holidays spent at school. In my case I didn't see my home again for the next five years.

"As part of the drill at school I wrote to Father every week, and occasionally he sent me a typed letter in reply. It was always to the effect that producing war supplies kept him desperately busy, but he hoped to find time to come down to see me soon. He did, about two or three times a year, but I would just as soon that he hadn't, as we had absolutely nothing to say to one another, and I could almost hear his sigh of relief when the time came for him to catch his train back to London. I must say, though, he always treated me very generously. He allowed me to take any extras that I wished, and I had only to ask for anything I wanted in one of my letters and his secretary would have it sent down.

"The summer that the war ended I was fifteen and I came home at last, but not for long. Apart from a few of Mother's old friends I didn't know a soul, and I hope I haven't become a snob myself, but I seemed to have moved right out of their class. I no longer talked the same language as their children, and although I tried to get over that, Father said he did not wish me to have those sort of people in the house. Within a fortnight I was at a dead end and hopelessly bored.

"One day Father suddenly realized how isolated I was and took the matter in hand with his usual efficiency. He explained that his own social life was in London, but for various reasons he could not have me with him there; so some other step must be taken to provide me with suitable companions of my own age. He had found a place in Somerset that ran courses in domestic science and was open all the year round. His suggestion was that I should go there for the rest of the summer holidays.

"Anything seemed better than staying at home doing nothing; so I agreed. And I was glad I had. It was a lovely old house and most of the pupils were older than myself; so we were treated much more like grown-ups than are the girls at an ordinary school. I liked it so much that I asked Father to let me go back there for good after one last term in Wales. That suited him; so I spent nearly the whole of the next two and a half years in Somerset. Occasionally, just for a change, I spent a week at home, and seven or eight times I was invited to stay at the homes of girls with whom I had become friends. My best friend lived in Bath; another one lived in Kensington, and with her I saw something of London; but such visits were only short ones and at fairly long intervals.

"I was perfectly content for things to go on that way indefinitely, but just before my eighteenth birthday the principal wrote to Father to say that as I had taken all the courses they ran and passed all the exams it did not seem right to keep me on there any longer. Faced with the same old problem of what to do with me, he decided to send me to a finishing school in Paris, and I was there until last December."

Christina lit another cigarette, and added, "I forgot to tell you that in 1949 old Mrs. Durnsford died and Father bought The Grange. . . ."

She paused and a look of consternation came over her face. "Oh damn, now I've given away the one thing I didn't mean to tell you."

Molly smiled. "Don't worry, my dear. I won't try to ferret out your name from that, and a little slip of that kind can't really be considered as breaking your promise to your father."

"No, I suppose not," Christina agreed. "Anyhow, the fact of his going back there made very little difference as far as I was concerned. The Jutsons now live in the flat over the garage

37

where I was born; but we have no other servants living in, and Father never does any entertaining. On balance, I prefer it out there in the country to living in a suburb of the town, although there are no shops and cinemas handy. When I get back I hope to interest myself in the village, but until this winter I've never lived there for more than a few days at a time; so I've had no chance yet to get to know any of our neighbours—except old Canon Copely-Syle, and I've known him as long as I can remember."

Again Christina paused, before ending a little lamely, "Well, there it is. I really don't think there is anything more to tell you."

"You poor child." Molly took her hand and pressed it. "I think your father has been terribly selfish in not providing you with a proper home life. You seem to have missed all the jolly times that most young people have on seaside holidays and at Christmas parties."

"Oh, I don't know. People never miss what they haven't been used to, do they? Except when I first went to school, I've always got on well with the other girls, and most of the mistresses were awfully kind to me."

"Perhaps; but that isn't quite the same thing. What about your grandparents? And had you no aunts and uncles to take an interest in you?"

"I know nothing about Father's family. I have an idea that he was illegitimate; but if he ever had one he must have broken with it as soon as he began to get on, so that it should not prove a drag upon him. Mother was an only child and her parents both died when I was quite young; so I have no relatives on that side either."

"Tell me about your father's friends. Although you have been at home so little, you must have met some of them. Recalling the sort of people they were might give you a line on what this present trouble is about."

Christina shook her head. "For the past ten years Father has spent a great deal of his time in London, and the only social life he has is there. He subscribes quite generously to local charities, but after he had to withdraw his candidature for the town council he would never mix himself up with public activities in the district. The only people he has ever asked home as far as I know were senior members of his office staff, and then it would only be to discuss confidential business with them over a drink in the evening."

"Just now you mentioned a Canon somebody?"

"Oh, old Copely-Syle is an exception. He lives only a mile or so from us, on the way to the village, at the Priory. Although, even when we lived in . . . in the town, he used to drop in occasionally."

"In view of your father's bias against religion it seems rather strange that he should have made a life-long friend of a canon."

"He is not a practising clergyman, and I think he helped Father to make his first start in business. Anyhow, they knew one another when Father was chauffeur to Mrs. Durnsford, and it may be partly on my account that the Canon has always called whenever I've spent a few days at home. You see, he is my godfather."

"Have you any idea what your father's plans for you are when your month's tenancy of this villa is up?"

"Yes and no. That is one of the things that worries me so much. He said that if everything went all right he would come back and collect me. If he didn't, I was to return to England and go to the head office of the National Provincial Bank in London. If I made myself known at the Trustee Department and asked for a Mr. Smithson he would give me a packet of papers. When I had read them I could make up my own mind about my future; and I need have no anxiety about money, as he had made ample provision for me to receive an income which would enable me to live quite comfortably without taking a job."

"Good gracious!" Molly exclaimed. "From that one can only infer that the danger threatens both of you, and that it is something much more serious than blackmail, or even being sent to prison."

Christina nodded. "Yes, it's pretty frightful, isn't it, to think that he may already be dead, and that if they find me I may be dead too before the month is up?"

"My dear child!" Molly quickly sought to reassure her. "You mustn't think such things. He may only have meant that he might have to leave you for a much longer period, and that during it you would have to make arrangements for yourself. I must confess, though, that in spite of all you've told me, I haven't yet got an inkling who this mysterious 'They' can be."

For a further quarter of an hour they speculated on the problem in vain; then, as Molly stood up to leave, Christina said, "You have been terribly kind, Mrs. Fountain; and just being able to talk about this wretched business has made me feel much less miserable already."

Molly went on tip-toe to give her a quick kiss. "I'm so glad; and you do understand, don't you, that you can come in to me at any time. If I don't see you before, I shall expect you to-morrow for lunch; but if you have the least reason to be frightened by anything don't hesitate to come over at once."

Together they walked out into the sunshine and began the descent of the steep garden path. They were about half-way down it when there came a rustling in the undergrowth and a joyful barking.

"That's Fido, my cocker spaniel," Molly remarked. "The wicked fellow must have seen me and broken through the pittosporum hedge."

Skilfully avoiding the prickly cactus, the dog came bounding towards his mistress. On reaching her he barked louder than ever and jumped up affectionately.

"Down, Fido! Down!" she cried in mock severity. "How dare you invade someone else's garden without being invited to call. You are as bad as I am."

Like the well-trained animal he was, he ceased his transports, but ran towards Christina, expecting to find in her a new friend.

Suddenly he halted in his tracks. His body seemed to become rigid; the hackles rose on his neck, his jaws began to drool saliva, and through them came a low whimper of fear.

"Whatever can be the matter with him?" Molly exclaimed in astonishment. "I've never known him behave like that before."

Christina's face had become half sullen and half miserable as she said in a low voice, "It's not my fault! I can't help it. But animals always take a dislike to me on sight."

CHAPTER IV

ENTER THE WICKED MARQUIS

IT WAS March 1st and John Fountain had arrived that morning. He and his mother had just finished lunch, and with a sigh of satisfaction he smiled across at her.

"What a meal! How good it is to eat in France again. I bet there were six eggs in the omelette. And that fillet of beef—as tender as *foie gras* and as big as a month's ration! Real butter instead of National grease, and the pineapple *au Kirsch* topped with lashings of cream. Most of our wretched people at home have forgotten that such food still exists."

Molly nodded. "It is years now since there has been a shortage of anything down here. Food is expensive, of course, but the markets are always overflowing with it. The rich alone could not consume one-twentieth of the perishable stuff that is offered for sale every day, and even the poorest classes show no signs of being hungry. It's simply that the French people always have spent most of their earnings on food and they still insist on the right to do so. I can't think why our people continue to allow themselves to be half starved by their Government. I'm sure it isn't necessary."

"I can answer that one." John's voice was bitter. "It's due to the Socialists and their insistence on continued bulk buying by the nation. That may have been necessary during the war, but by forcing it on us for six years afterwards they destroyed the whole organization that had been built up over centuries of private firms importing our food from the best markets at the best prices. It will be years before the incredible muddle they made can be unsorted. But tell me more about this girl next door."

"I don't think there's much more to tell, Johnny. During the past three days I've seen quite a bit of her. She is still nervous of going out in the day-time but, quite illogically, she doesn't seem to mind at night. On Sunday I always dine out for a change, so yesterday afternoon I suggested that she should come with me to the Reserve at St. Raphael. She said she would rather not, but about half-past six she turned up here and asked if she might change her mind. Of course I said 'Yes', and I'm sure she thoroughly enjoyed herself."

"Do you really believe her story?"

"Yes. She has the naturally frank expression and well-spaced eyes that can nearly always be taken as a sign of honesty; and I don't see what she could possibly hope to gain by deceiving me. After all, it wasn't a case of her approaching me and attempting to win my sympathy, perhaps in the hope of a loan; but I who invited her confidence. Then the way she inadvertently let out the name of her home and its previous occupant shows that she is not an accomplished enough liar to have made the whole thing up."

"With a pre-1949 telephone directory of Essex those two items of information should be sufficient for us to trace the village she comes from, and the initials on the manicure-set make it pretty certain that her real name begins with B; so it shouldn't be very difficult to find out who she is."

"I don't think it would be quite playing the game for us to do that."

"It may be necessary if these people who are after her suddenly appear on the scene."

"Let's not meet trouble half-way, Johnny. I'm hoping, though, that while you are here you'll give some of your time to her. With a man she would probably be less scared of going out during the day, and it would do her a world of good to be taken about a bit."

His rather thin face broke into a slightly cynical grin. "No doubt. But what about me? I'm on holiday remember. Do you think she is my cup of tea?"

Mrs. Fountain did not reply immediately, but smiled a little dubiously at her attractive son. He was of medium height, well-made, although not powerful. His principal charm lay in his lively, intelligent eyes and humorous mouth. He had dark hair and his nose was slightly aquiline. Although only twenty-three the responsible position he had secured in a good firm had matured him early; so he was very much a man now, and she was wise enough to seek no longer to control him.

She was thinking of his previous holidays. Last year he had run around with that little Italian countess, who was certainly no better than she should be. The previous year he had given her even more serious cause for secret alarm by attaching himself to an American widow of glamorous appearance, but uncertain age and most dubious antecedents. Johnny's taste certainly did not run in the direction of *jeunes filles*. That was natural enough for a young man in his early twenties, and it would do him no harm as long as he did not get himself seriously entangled. Knowing that the Riviera swarmed with harpies, she dreaded the sort of designing female that he might so easily pick up, and during the past few days she had been rather hoping that this year Christina might prove a sufficient attraction to keep him out of mischief. She thought the chances of that very slender, but she was clever enough not to spoil the market by boosting the goods, and after a moment she said:

"To be honest, Johnny, this girl is not up to your weight. She is practically a new-born lamb, and after a couple of days you may find yourself hopelessly bored with her. But she seems to have had so little fun in her life and she is so desperately lonely, it really would be a generous act to spare her an hour or two now and then."

He smiled at her. "You horrible woman! I can scent the maternal match-making instinct a mile away in this."

"Good gracious, no!" she protested. "We don't really know anything about her, and her father sounds a most undesirable type."

"One doesn't marry their fathers, dearest—except in the tale of the chap who killed the dragon, who when offered his choice said he'd rather marry the king than any of the three princesses."

"What *are* you talking about?"

Putting his head on one side, he wriggled his shoulders, smirked, and replied in an effeminate voice, "It's a fairy story."

"Johnny, you are awful," she laughed.

"On the contrary, I am nobly defending myself against a conspiracy to make me break my plighted word, given freely long ago, that when I grew up I would marry you."

"Idiot! I tell you, the idea of your entering on a serious affair with this young woman never entered my mind. It is simply that she has been starved of youthful companionship and——"

"I know. That she could be a sweet little sister to me. Really, Mumsie! How you can sit there looking so innocent while you tell such tarradiddles, I cannot think."

"But you will do as I ask?"

"Knowing that you will starve and probably beat me if I refuse, it seems I have no option."

"Splendid. I expect you would like to sleep off your lunch now; then I thought that about tea-time I would take you over and introduce you."

"O.K., honoured parent." John stood up, but before turning away he screwed his face into a leery expression and gave a slow, sardonic wink. "Before retiring to my slumbers I'd like to know just where I stand. I take it that there will be no kick coming from you if I seduce her?"

Molly knew perfectly well that he was only pulling her leg, but all the same she replied with a hint of seriousness, "I've already told you, she's as inexperienced as if she had just come out of a convent; so you'll jolly well behave yourself."

"Oh, I'll be as good as gold," he assured her blandly. "But I know these innocent types. The odds are that she'll seduce *me*. Then what? I'll get the blame, of course, and have to pay the seven-and-six maintenance for the baby. Or has it gone up to a quid now? I think that the least you can do is to guarantee me against that."

"You're a horrid boy, with a horrid, low mind, and I dislike you intensely," said mother, giving him a light kiss on the cheek. "Now, run along and get your nap. It's past three al . . ."

Her last words trailed away into silence as she caught a quick step on the gravel outside the french window of the dining-room. Next moment a tall shadow was thrown by the sunlight on the parquet, and turning she saw Christina standing on the threshold.

"Oh, Mrs. Fountain," the girl began rather breathlessly, "I hope I'm not interrupting you. I knew your son was arriving to-day, and I waited until I thought you would have finished lunch; but I wanted to talk to you rather . . . rather urgently."

"Of course not, my dear. Come in." Molly waved a vague hand. "This is John—Johnny, our new neighbour, Christina Mordant."

The two young people nodded and smiled politely at one another. Neither made any move to shake hands. John was thinking, 'God, what a nose! But her eyes really are remarkable'; while Christina thought, 'He's really quite nice-looking: what a pity he has such a prominent Adam's apple."

"Do sit down." Molly offered the cigarettes and Christina took one. As she lit it, John hurried forward. "What about a liqueur? A Béné, or a spot of Sticky Green?"

"No thanks," Christina replied quickly. "I only go in for soft drinks, and I don't want anything now."

"I expect you would rather John left us," Molly said after a moment. "He has so gorged himself with food that he can hardly keep awake, anyhow."

John sighed. "See how my own mother derides and dismisses me. But take no notice. I am hardened now to the feminist streak in her, which has ever thwarted my ambition to emulate St. George."

"What! And marry the king like your friend in the fairy story?" Molly said with a twinkle.

"That's one up to you, Mumsie," he replied with a grin.

After a puzzled look from one to the other of them, Christina's glance came to rest on Molly. "Over dinner last night you suggested telling John about me, because, if the sort of thing I have to fear happened, a man's help might prove invaluable; and I agreed. If you have told him, and he cares to stay, it would be just as well for him to hear about this new development."

"Yes. Mother has given me an account of the extraordinary situation in which you find yourself," John said, his voice now low and serious. "You must forgive our fooling; and please believe that I am just as anxious as she is to help you in any way I can."

She gave him a faint smile. "Thanks; you're both most awfully kind. Well, just before lunch I had a visitor."

Molly's face showed her dismay. "Then the enemy has run you to earth already?"

"No; this was a friend—or, at least, an old acquaintance. But I was so surprised to see him coming through the gate that for a moment I thought I must have got a touch of the sun, and be imagining things. It was Canon Copely-Syle."

"As he is an intimate friend of your father's, your father might quite well have confided to him the place where he had hidden you."

"No. That's the strange part about it. His finding me here was pure chance. He hasn't seen my father for some weeks and had no idea I was in the South of France. He has been staying at Cannes for a few days, and this morning he was motoring in to St. Raphael for lunch. He just happened to catch sight of me sitting on the terrace; so he made his friend who was driving the car stop, and came in to see me."

"There doesn't seem to be anything particularly perturbing about that," John remarked.

"Oh, but there is!" Christina protested. "His first words to me were, 'My dear child, whatever are you doing here? Why aren't you in England with your father?' I replied, 'Why should I be?' At that he looked quite staggered, and said, 'But surely you've heard the bad news about him? Has no one informed you that he was seriously injured in a car smash? I had it yesterday in a letter from a mutual friend. I would never dream of upsetting you without good reason, but I gather there are grave fears for his life.' "

"Perhaps this is just the sort of thing your father feared might happen to him," Molly said, her thriller-writer's mind having gone swiftly into action. "I mean, it wouldn't be the first time that unscrupulous people had deliberately engineered a car smash, in order to get out of the way somebody against whom they had a grudge."

"Yes; I suppose such things do happen. Anyhow, the Canon said that he is returning to England to-morrow, and he offered to take me with him."

"You will be leaving us then?"

Christina shook her head. "No. Father told me that no matter what messages I might receive, even if they were said to come from him, in no circumstances was I to leave the villa until he returned to fetch me; or, failing that, before the twentieth of next month."

"It is quite natural that he should have said something of the kind as a reasonable precaution against your falling into a trap set by your enemies; but when he said it he cannot possibly have had the Canon in mind. Didn't you tell me at our first talk that the Canon is your godfather?"

"Yes; but the fact that he is my godfather doesn't mean very much. He has always sent me a small present on my birthday, and I've written to thank him; but we have never got any closer than that. I have seen him perhaps thirty or forty times in my life, but never for any length of time, and father has always been present, except at two accidental meetings; so I've never got beyond exchanging polite platitudes with him."

"Still, he is a life-long friend of your father's; so I'm afraid, my dear, there cannot be very much doubt about this shocking news he has brought you. It is hardly credible that he would cause you such anxiety had he not been certain of his facts."

"Yes, I suppose so." Christina sighed. "I think, though, I may have unconsciously misled you a little about his relationship to Father. I have always had the impression that their association is based more on some common interest than on genuine friendship. One of the occasions when I ran into him by chance was soon after we had moved into our present home, and when I told Father about it he said that should the Canon ever ask me to the Priory I was to make some excuse for not accepting. At the time I put that down to a revival of his anti-Christian bias, and a fear that I might get religion, like Mother.

But quite apart from that I'm pretty certain that Father does not really like him, and for some reason that I can't explain I don't either."

"Apart from this personal prejudice, do you know anything against him?"

"No, nothing at all. In the village he is highly respected."

"Then it doesn't seem as if he is the sort of person who would be mixed up in anything shady, or lend himself to practising such a brutal deception on you."

"It doesn't, does it? Yet, all the same, I feel I ought to stick to Father's orders and remain where I am."

"What did the Canon say when you refused his offer to take you back to England to-morrow?" John enquired.

"He spent quite a time trying to persuade me to change my mind, and, when I wouldn't, seemed to think me very callous."

"What excuse did you make for digging your toes in?"

"I said I thought the friend who had written to him must have exaggerated Father's danger, and that his office would have been certain to let me know if my presence was really required in England; so I meant to remain here until I heard something more definite. I took the precaution, too, of telling him that I was living under the assumed name of Christina Mordant, and asking him not to divulge my real identity to anyone down here. Naturally he looked very surprised, but he did not ask me for a reason, and gave me his promise."

"Clever girl," John smiled. "There is one way you could find out about your father for certain though. Why not telephone your home or his works?"

"No, I can't do that. He said that whatever happened I was not to attempt to get him on the telephone; because, if the call was traced back, it would give away my hiding-place."

For a while longer they discussed matters without getting any further, then Molly said, "Johnny and I are going to dine in Cannes to-night, and we'd like you to come with us. We thought of going to the Carlton, but if you haven't got an evening dress with you we could go to some quieter place."

"It's terribly kind of you," Christina hesitated a second,

"but I don't think I ought to. It doesn't seem right somehow, as there is a possibility that Father may be dying."

"Just as you like, my dear; but I think it is a great mistake ever to anticipate the worst, and that you would be much wiser to let us take you out and try to cheer you up, rather than stay at home brooding about unhappy possibilities. I won't press you, but should you change your mind, as you did last night, we shall be leaving about half-past seven."

Christina did change her mind, and returned at twenty-past seven dressed to accompany them to the Carlton. As she stepped from the half-darkness of the garden into the lighted room, both Molly and John had difficulty in hiding their astonishment. She was wearing a long frock of oyster satin. It was backless, strapless and low cut, to display her good neck and shoulders to the best advantage, but at the moment she had draped over them a short cape of dark skunk. Neither of them had seen her before in anything but very ordinary and rather girlish day clothes; so the difference in her appearance was quite striking. It made her look several years older and entirely sophisticated—a change that was further stressed by a new expression in her face and a much brisker manner.

Molly was thinking, 'I wonder where she learned to dress like this? It can only have been at her finishing school in Paris. That must be quite a place! I'll swear the scent she has got on is by Dior. Too old for her—pity she didn't choose something a little less exotic. Her father may have neglected her, but he certainly isn't mean with her about money. The little number she's got on must have cost a packet.'

John's mind was running on the lines, 'Gee whizz! Call that nothing! And after lunch I thought she looked like Skinny Lizzy, the sixth form's tallest girl. All the same she must be darn near as tall as I am. If the mind under that brown hair fits this evening's turnout she won't prove as dumb as I feared. Anyhow, if we see anyone I know I shan't be accused of cradle-snatching.'

At the moment he was shaking a cocktail, and producing a third glass he said, "Can't I tempt you?"

"Why not?" she replied lightly. "When the drinks were

offered round at our social evenings in Paris, we girls were only allowed to take sherry; but I suppose one must make a start on the hard liquor some time. You must warn me, though, if you think I am getting tight."

He laughed. "As a confirmed drunk myself I should certainly lead you astray if I got the chance, but you can rely on my Mama to provide a restraining influence."

Soon after eight they were in Cannes. As it was the height of the winter season the big restaurant at the Carlton was quite crowded. Everyone was in evening dress and at the many tables one could hear spoken every language outside the Iron Curtain. French and Americans predominated, but there were Indians and Egyptians, as well as Swiss, Belgians and Scandinavians. The only major nation ill-represented for its size was Britain, but as an acid commentary on mismanagement after victory the richer citizens of the defeated nations, Germany and Italy, were back again in force, enjoying themselves once more. The fact that champagne cost £4 a bottle did not prevent its flowing freely. The scene was glittering, the service excellent and the menu a triumph in gastronomic art. Nothing more could have been desired to ensure a gay and happy evening.

Yet, before they were half-way through dinner, Molly was conscious that her little party was a flop. Johnny and Christina seemed to have nothing in common except an unhappy inability to do full justice to the good things set before them. Neither had anything but a vague recollection of the time when food had not been rationed in England, and so many years of meagre feeding had reduced the capacity of their stomachs to a point where they were incapable of containing more than would sustain life. Johnny was the worst affected, as he had eaten an exceptionally large lunch and, although he was not particularly greedy by nature, it irritated him not to be able to enjoy all the rich dishes which would normally have been such a treat; while Christina, who had also found herself defeated after the second course, was obviously worried that she might give offence to her hostess, as she kept on apologizing for only toying with the rest of her dinner.

In addition to this unsatisfactory state of things, Molly

51

found herself quite unable to get a spark going between them. They had no mutual friends, had been brought up in totally different surroundings, and seemed to have no tastes in common. Johnny, she could see, was suffering from indigestion, and although the girl had drunk two glasses of champagne, her tongue showed no signs of being loosened by the wine.

When the time came for them to have coffee, she was commiserating with herself on the failure of this expensive evening, and thinking how much simpler it would have been to draw them out had she had either of them alone. It was only then the thought struck her that the barrier between them was almost certainly herself. All men, she knew, loved to talk about themselves, but Johnny would not do so in front of her for obvious reasons; and if they were alone the girl, no doubt, would trot out her little stock of airs and graces, but not with his mama looking on.

At a table not far off there were an American couple whom Molly had known for some years. They were elderly people, and did not dance or gamble; so it was certain they would be going home fairly early, and their villa was situated not much more than a mile from hers. Before coming out she had given Johnny ample francs to pay for their evening; so with commendable guile she concealed her disappointment and said to the young couple:

"I'm sure you two will want to dance, and I'm not feeling like sitting up very late to-night. I've been overworking a bit lately and I am paying for it now with a headache; so you must forgive me if I desert you. My friends, the Pilkingtons, are over there and they are sure to be going home soon. I can easily get a lift from them, so as to leave the car for you."

Her reward was to see Johnny's quick concern, and hear his protest that she would be ruining the first evening of his holiday, which they always spent together; but Molly Fountain was not given to changing her mind once she had made it up, and, blowing a kiss from her finger-tips to Christina, she left them to join the Americans.

When John was staying with his mother on the Riviera he

often got home at unconscionable hours, and like most young people he required a lot of sleep; so it was an accepted thing that he should never be called, but should ring when he woke for Angèle to bring him coffee and croissants.

On the following morning he did not wake till nearly eleven. Then, having breakfasted in bed, he dawdled for another hour over his bath and dressing; so it was half-past twelve before he came downstairs and joined his mother.

"Well," she asked, as soon as he had kissed her good morning, "how did things go last night after I left you? I do hope you weren't too terribly bored by my little protégé?"

"Bored!" His eyebrows shot up in a comical grimace. "Believe me, Múmsie, you're jolly lucky to get me back all in one piece."

Molly smiled and patted her grey hair. "Making due allowances for your usual exaggeration, I'm rather pleased to learn that she has something that ticks inside her."

"Something that ticks! Why, the girl's a human bomb. Honestly, this new-born lamb of yours—this little sister of Saint So-and-so straight out of a convent—is a positive danger to the public."

"Oh come, Johnny! Mix yourself a Vermouth-Cassis, and one for me too. Then put reins upon your imagination, tie it up to the fence, and tell me what happened."

He walked over to the side table and while mixing the drinks spoke over his shoulder, "Well, to start with, we danced. The fact that she seems to have had very little practical experience of dancing with a man is the one piece of evidence we have in support of your theory that she has only just come out of the egg. Otherwise, hold me up, Uncle! Her sense of timing is not at all bad, so I think she'd be pretty good if she had some practice. But that's not the point. She clung to me as if I was her favourite woolly bear. I got really scared she meant to rape me on the dance-floor. And that scent of hers! It played old Harry with my libido."

"Johnny, don't be disgusting."

"Don't you pretend to be a little innocent, Mumsie. You know as well as most people what goes on in the world, and how that sort of thing can affect a chap. Anyhow, after we had danced for a bit she said she'd like to try a liqueur brandy. In the next hour she knocked back three doubles and she didn't blink an eyelid."

"She must have a remarkably good head."

"I'll say she has." John brought the drink over to his mother, and went on, "About half an hour after midnight she suggested that I should take her to the Casino to do a spot of gambling. I hedged a bit at first; as on the one hand I would have liked an excuse not to dance with her any more for the time being, while on the other I didn't particularly want to go to the rooms, because you know how it has always been with me. I can make money if I work for it, but I never seem to have any luck at the tables."

"You had a perfectly good excuse for refusing, as they wouldn't have let you in without your passports; and as she is still under twenty-one they wouldn't have let her in anyway."

He shook his head sadly at her. "Darling, how you do under-rate the resourcefulness of your offspring. I'm ten times as good as your pet 'Crack', if you only knew it. I've known that chap Fleury, the under-manager, for years. All I had to do was to ask for him and say we'd forgotten to bring our passports. It was a safe bet that he would pass me in, and anyone else who was with me. So, on the basis that if 'Paris was worth a Mass' my chastity must be worth a couple of thousand francs, I agreed. By a quarter to one we were in the Casino. And what do you think happened then?"

"How in the world should I know, silly?"

"Well, for the next hour and a half, while I piddled around dropping six *milles*, little orphan Annie played baccarat with a poker face that could hardly have been equalled had she been born inside the Sporting Club; and at the end of it she walked off with half a million francs."

"Johnny, she didn't?"

"She did, Mumsie. If I hadn't been so well brought up, I'd have had it off her in the car on the way home. Just think of it! Five hundred quid, and free of Income Tax."

Molly nodded. "How lovely for her. One hears a lot about

beginner's luck, but I must say I've never heard a better example of it."

"It must have been mainly that; although the old Canon stood behind her chair all the time, and was tipping her off what to do now and then."

"What! Her godfather, Canon Copely-Syle?" Molly sat up in surprise. "This is the first you've said of him."

"Sorry. I'm afraid I telescoped the story a bit to give you the exciting *dénouement* about her big win. The Canon was there when we entered the rooms, and came over to us."

"What did you make of him?"

"I thought he was rather a nice old boy. He's certainly a picturesque one. All black satin front, pink face, and long silvery locks curling down behind his ears—like a parson in a Restoration play. He couldn't have made himself pleasanter."

"I'm glad he didn't spoil her evening. His attitude towards her might have been pretty frigid on meeting her in such a place, after having told her only that morning that he believed her father to be dying."

"I think he was a bit shocked at first. I happened to catch sight of his face before she saw him, and he was staring at us with a rather worried, annoyed sort of look. But as soon as we got chatting butter wouldn't melt in his mouth, and he never even mentioned her father until just before we were leaving."

"Was there anything fresh in what he said then?"

"No; he only introduced us to a friend of his who had been playing at another table, for the purpose of telling her that should she change her mind about going home, and want an air passage at short notice, this chap would be able to fix it for her. He was another distinguished-looking old boy with grey hair, only the tall and thin type. With a nice red ribbon across his shirt front he could have walked on to any stage in the rôle of the French Ambassador, and he wouldn't even have had to change his name for the part. It was the Marquis de Grasse."

Molly nearly dropped her glass, and her mouth fell open. Then she gave a cry of consternation. "Oh, Johnny! What can be at the bottom of all this? De Grasse is one of the most evil men in France."

CHAPTER V

BATTLE OF FLOWERS AND BATTLE OF WITS

JOHN knew about his mother's work in the war—at least he thought he did. All she had ever told him was that her fluent French had secured her an interesting job as a secretary, and that later she had acted as P.A. to one of the senior officers of a department of the War Office situated in Baker Street. Since the war he had run across several people who had been connected with the same office, and from odd scraps of information they had dropped he had formed a pretty shrewd idea of the activities in which they had been engaged. Those who knew his mother spoke most highly of her, and the association had led him to believe that she too had actively participated in all sorts of cloak and dagger business designed to bring alarm and despondency to the enemy.

The belief was strengthened by the fact that she still kept a private armoury, consisting of two pistols and a number of other lethal weapons. She had often assured him that her 'museum', as she called it, had been acquired only because such things had always fascinated her and, in addition, helped her to describe accurately the use to which they could be put when writing of scenes of violence in her books. In this she was speaking the entire truth. Much as she would have liked to try some of them out, she had never used any of them. Neither had she ever been in the least danger, except during air-raids, as her work had lain inside the office, helping to direct the activities of others. Nevertheless, it had given her an exceedingly wide knowledge of the French Resistance, secret agents, collaborators and the crooks who were mixed up with them.

After a moment he said, "I suppose you ran up against the

Marquis when you were doing your stuff as Molly Polloffski, the beautiful spy?"

"No, Johnny. I've told you hundreds of times that there was nothing the least glamorous about my job; and I've never met de Grasse. But I know plenty about him."

"There was a chap of that name up at Cambridge when I was there. I knew him slightly, but he went down at the end of my first year."

She nodded. "That would have been the son, Count Jules de Grasse. His father is as slippery as they make 'em. In the war he was far-sighted enough to back both sides; and his having sent his boy to school in England in 1940 went a long way towards saving him from a heavy sentence of imprisonment when the French began to catch up with collaborators after the liberation. He had been in it up to the neck with the Germans, but was able to produce that card as evidence that he had always thought and hoped that the Allies would win; then plead that he had done no more to help the Germans than thousands of other patriotic Frenchmen had been compelled to do as the only alternative to having their businesses taken from them. Of course, we knew that wasn't true, but he is immensely rich and money talks in France with a louder tongue than in most countries. His story about his son proved a good enough peg on which to hang a pardon, so he was able to bribe his way out, and he got off scot-free."

"What was his business?"

"He is ostensibly a respectable shipping magnate; but that covers a multitude of sins. We had plenty of proof on our files that he used his ships for running every sort of contraband. Before the war he used to specialize in dope and white slaving; but more recently, I understand, he has concentrated on smuggling Jews out to Palestine, and arms to anyone in the Near East who wants to make trouble for us."

"How do you know that, Mumsie?"

Molly coloured slightly. "Oh, sometimes friends who worked with me in the old firm come out here, and we talk of this and that."

He laughed. "Boys and girls who are still in it, eh? I've

always suspected that they kept you on unofficially to tip them off about anything you might tumble to in their line that was going on down here."

"Johnny, you do get the silliest ideas. The department I worked for was wound up soon after the war ended."

"Maybe; but there are others: for example, your old friend Conky Bill's outfit. I know he pretends to be only a sort of policeman whose job it is to hunt out Communists; but like this shipping racket I bet it covers his poking that big nose of his into a multitude of other dubious goings on."

"And if you don't keep *your* nose out of other people's business you may one day get it chopped off," retorted Molly aptly.

"*Touché!*" he grinned. "Let's get back to the wicked Marquis, then. What else do you know about him?"

"His headquarters used to be at St. Tropez. The choice was appropriate, as before the war it had the most evil reputation of any town west of Suez. Every vice racket flourished there. At night, down by the port, it was dangerous for decent people; and your father would not allow me to leave him to do even ten minutes' shopping on my own there in the middle of the day."

"Really! On the few occasions I've been there I've never noticed anything peculiar about it."

"You wouldn't, now. The Germans, and later the French, have cleaned it up a lot since then. But I am told that de Grasse still spends quite a lot of his time there."

"He is living there at present. He told Christina so. He and his wife have a permanent private suite at the Capricorn. You know, that big modern hotel that overlooks the bay from the high ground to the right of the road, just before you enter the town. On learning that Christina had never been to St. Tropez, he said that his wife loved entertaining young people, and offered to send a car to fetch her if she could lunch with them there to-day."

Molly set down her glass with a bang. "I hope to goodness she refused?"

"No: she accepted. It is only in the day-time that she seems to shy off any suggestion that she should go out; but of course she may have changed her mind this morning."

"I'm afraid not. I had to go into St. Raphael earlier to do some shopping, and I got back only just before you came down. I remember now noticing that she was not on her terrace when I drove past it, and she always is at that hour. If you were very late getting in she may still have been sleeping, but . . . Oh, Johnny, run round next door and make certain."

Seven or eight minutes elapsed before John returned, panting slightly. He spread out his hands. "No dice, dearest. She was called for around twelve by a chap a few years older than myself. From the rather sketchy description which was all I could get out of her old Catalan woman, it might have been Jules de Grasse. Evidently she had changed her mind about going, though, and did not mean to, as she wasn't dressed ready to go out. It seems that they had quite an argument before she went upstairs and changed her clothes. It was close on half-past when they left; so you must have passed them on your way back."

Standing up, Molly helped herself to a cigarette. When John had lit it for her she drew hard on it for a moment, before she said, "I do hope she will be all right. I don't like this new development a little bit. I wish to goodness there was something we could do to ensure her getting safely out of the clutches of those people."

John shrugged. "We certainly can't arm ourselves from your museum, give chase, and do a 'stand and deliver' on the de Grasses to get her back—if that is the sort of move your agile mind is beginning to toy with. They are not the Germans and there's no longer a war on; so snap out of it, Mumsie. She went off in broad daylight of her own free will, and judging by the form last night she is perfectly capable of taking care of herself."

"You did make a pass at her, then?"

"Well, not exactly. She made it quite clear that she expected me to say good-night to her in the orthodox manner. And, although she said afterwards that it was the first time she had been kissed by a man, she took to it like a duck to water.

If it hadn't been that she didn't seem to know the opening moves of the game I certainly wouldn't have believed her, and I still have my doubts about it. But it wasn't of that sort of thing that I was thinking. I meant in her general behaviour; and particularly at the Casino, she undoubtedly had all her wits about her."

Lunch was announced at that moment. They dealt with the *hors-d'œuvres* in thoughtful silence; then when Angèle had put the sweetbreads on the table and gone out again, Molly said, "You know, I believe she is a schizophrenic."

"What, dual personality?"

"Yes. It is the only way one can account for the quite extraordinary changes which we have both seen in her. By day she is still an affectionate, overgrown child who is scared stiff that something awful is going to happen to her, and obsessed with the thought that she must remain in hiding; while by night she becomes a rather hard-boiled, sophisticated young woman, who is perfectly prepared to take the risk of being recognized for the sake of having a good time. It goes even further than that, because I am sure that during the day-time she is both innocent in mind and instinctively modest; whereas, from what you tell me, by night she is only too eager to have a necking party with the first man she sets eyes on."

"Hi! Have a heart!" John protested, swiftly swallowing a piece of fried courgette. "That is not very complimentary to your only begotten."

"Do you seriously suggest that she would have preserved a virginal aloofness had she been out with any other personable young man than yourself?"

"Thank you, Mumsie. The word 'personable' salves my wounded pride. No, to be honest, I don't. And I think you've hit the nail on the head with this theory of yours that she is a schizo'. All the same, that does not get us any further in solving the mystery of who is after her blood, and why."

"At least we now have good reason to suppose that the Canon is not to be trusted. No clergyman who had a proper respect for his cloth would show himself in the gambling-rooms of a Casino—anyhow after midnight—and his being

60

a friend of de Grasse makes him suspect in the highest degree. I wouldn't mind betting the serial rights of my next book that the story he told Christina about an accident to her father was a pack of lies, and designed solely to lure her away from her villa. Then, this invitation of de Grasse's: he and his wife are not the sort of people to spend their time showing young girls the beauties of the Riviera. It is all Lombard Street to a china orange that the Canon put him up to asking her to St. Tropez for some nefarious purpose of his own."

John nodded; his voice was serious now. "I'm afraid you're right, dearest. But there is nothing we can do about it for the moment. We can only wait to see if she gets back all right and, if not, call in the police."

That afternoon there was to be a Battle of Flowers at St. Maxime. As they had planned to go to it, they set off there immediately after lunch. The little town was only about fifteen miles away; so by half-past two John had parked the car and they were installed in the seats for which Molly had already secured tickets. Their chairs were in the front row facing the sea, with only a temporary barrier of chestnut-pale fence railing them off from the promenade down which the procession would come; and while they waited for it they could scarcely prevent their gaze from frequently coming to rest on the white houses of St. Tropez, which lay in the shelter of the headland just across the bay. Both of them were wondering how Christina was faring there, and although John endeavoured to engage his mother's attention, he did not succeed in doing so until the sounds of the town band in the distance heralded the beginning of the fête.

The battle was not on the grand scale of those held at Nice, Cannes and Monte Carlo; but there were nearly thirty carriages, and a lovely sight they made. The wheels, body and shafts of them all were entirely hidden by massed flowers, each seeking to outdo the others in colour, variety or originality. In most cases stocks, violets and carnations of many hues provided the ground work; while towers, trumpets, sheaves and fountains, on which were wired hundreds of roses, hyacinths, arum lilies and gladioli, surmounted the backs of the carriages. In each

61

rode two or more young women, specially selected for their good looks. Some were displaying their charms in *décolletée* evening frocks, or in ballet skirts below which they wore black, large-mesh, fish-net stockings, while others were wearing light summer dresses and big floppy hats; but in every case their toilettes had been chosen to carry out the main colour motive of their floral chariots.

In every carriage the girls had big baskets of surplus flowers, with which to pelt the onlookers, and everyone in the crowd had a supply of similar ammunition bought from the gaily-dressed flower vendors. At a slow walk the colourful procession passed along between the barriers, while to and from both sides hundreds of little bunches of mimosa, stock, short-stemmed narcissi and carnation heads sailed up into the bright sunlight, thrown by the laughing girls and applauding people. To give the audience ample opportunity to enjoy the spectacle to the full, at intervals of about a quarter of an hour the procession passed and re-passed three times; so it was half-past four before the battle was finally concluded.

After it was over, remembering his mother's fondness for hot chocolate, John proposed that they should adjourn to a *pâtissière*. While they were there she again became distrait. Then, after a time, she suggested that they should go on to St. Tropez in case Christina was still with the de Grasses at the Capricorn; as if she were they could pretend to have run into her by chance and by offering her a lift ensure her returning safely with them.

John considered the idea for a moment, then pointed out that as she had been asked over only to lunch the probability was that she would have left a couple of hours ago, so be home by now; while if the de Grasses had persuaded her to remain with them for the afternoon it would pretty certainly have been on the excuse of taking her for a drive, or to see the town; so the odds were all against her still being at the hotel, and it seemed going a bit far to add twenty miles to their return journey for such a slender chance of finding her.

Molly thought his reasoning sound, so she did not press her suggestion. In consequence, having collected the car, instead of heading west, they headed east for home, arriving there just before six. Leaving John to put the car away, Molly went straight up to Christina's villa, hoping to find her there, and learn as soon as possible what had transpired at the lunch. But Christina was still absent.

More perturbed than ever for the girl's safety, Molly mounted the steep path to her own house, to be met in the hall by Angèle, who told her that at about half-past three the English mademoiselle who lived next door had telephoned, but had left no message. When John came in they discussed the situation again, but there seemed nothing they could do, as to have appealed to the police on the bare facts that a girl had gone out to lunch with friends and failed to return home by six o'clock would have been laughable.

They had fallen into an unhappy silence when, a quarter of an hour later, the telephone rang. John answered the call, and it was Christina. A little breathlessly she said, "I tried to get you earlier this afternoon. I lunched with the de Grasses and am still with them. We've just got back to the hotel, and I'm telephoning from the call-box in the ladies' cloakroom; but we shall be going up to their private suite again in a minute. They have made me promise to stay and dine with them on their yacht. But I don't want to. Can you . . . can you possibly think of some excuse to come over here and . . . and get me away from them? Please, oh please!"

"O.K.," replied John promptly. "Was it Count Jules who collected you this morning?"

"Yes; and it was he who took me round the town this afternoon."

"Right! We'll be with you in three-quarters of an hour. All you have to do is to sit tight until we turn up, and in no circumstances fall for any pretext they may trot out with the idea of getting you to leave the hotel. Keep your chin up, and don't worry that pretty head of yours. We'll have you home in time for dinner."

He had spoken with calm assurance, in order to quiet her evident fears; but as he replaced the receiver he felt far from confident about the outcome of the next few hours; and, while he repeated to his mother what she had said, it became even more clear to him that to get her away from the de Grasses was going to prove an extremely tricky business.

"If they once get her on their yacht it will be long odds against our ever seeing her again," said Molly, now giving free rein to her anxiety.

He nodded glumly. "It looks as if the Marquis is at his old white-slaving game again. Unless we can pull a fast one on him that poor kid may end up in Port Said or Buenos Aires."

"Perhaps. She might, if they simply want to get rid of her. But I'm sure the Canon is behind this, and it may be that he wants to force her into doing something for some purpose of his own."

"Anyhow, I'll be damned if I'm going to let him."

John had spoken with sudden fierceness, and his mother shot him an appraising look as she asked, "You do rather like her, then?"

He shrugged, gave a quick grin, and reverted to his usual gaily inconsequent manner. "Don't be silly, Mumsie. It is solely that my sense of chivalry has been aroused. I feel like the knight who was riding through a forest and came upon a beauteous damosel tied to a tree. She cried out to him, 'Frugal me, frugal me!' So he frugalled her."

"Stop talking nonsense," Molly admonished him, turning away. "We've got to hurry. While you get the car out, I must just run upstairs. I won't be a moment."

"You had better not," he called after her, as he ran towards the door, "otherwise I shall start without you."

Five minutes later she rejoined him in the road, carrying a crocodile-skin bag that she generally used only when travelling. As she got into the car he gave it a suspicious glance, and said, "You haven't brought the armaments, have you?"

She had never lied to him, and, after a second, she admitted, "I've brought my small automatic—but it's only a very little one."

Instead of letting in the clutch, he sat back and folded his arms. "Now look, dearest. Things may be done that way in

64

your thrillers, but they are not in real life. It's too damn' dangerous. For one thing the de Grasses would make mince-meat of us, and for another, if we survived the first five minutes they are clever enough to ensure that it is we who would find ourselves in prison afterwards. Before I drive you a yard, you have got to give me your solemn promise that you won't start anything."

"All right, I promise," she said with a sigh. "But it is a bit hard. This might have been a real chance to find out what it feels like to hold somebody up with a pistol."

"Try it sometime when I am elsewhere on my lawful occasions," he advised. "Then I'll at least remain free myself to come and bail you out."

As he spoke the car shot forward. He was feeling guilty now at having scotched his mother's suggestion that they should drive on to St. Tropez from St. Maxime, as the sun was already going down beyond the hills ahead of them, and had he not opposed her they would by this time have been with Christina. In consequence, while exercising a fair degree of caution going round the sharp bends of the Corniche, he drove much faster than was his custom.

It was a good twenty-five miles from the villa to St. Tropez; but, after St. Raphael, for about half that distance the road was nearly flat and moderately straight, as it followed the shallow curve of the great bay in the centre of which lay St. Maxime; so until they reached Beauvallon he was able to make good going. There, the road made a hairpin bend round the deep narrow gulf, then wound its way along the peninsula that had St. Tropez as its seaward end. When they pulled up in front of the great modern building of concrete and glass, that looked more like a block of flats than an hotel, it was just after seven and twilight was falling.

While on their way they had made their plan of campaign, and on entering the hotel, instead of enquiring for the Marquis at the desk, they walked straight to the lift and asked the lift-man to take them up to de Grasse's suite. The lift shot up to the top floor, and as they stepped from it the man pointed out to them a door at the end of the corridor. Their footfalls making no sound on the heavy pile carpet, they advanced towards it; then John rang the bell.

After a moment the door was opened by Count Jules. He was a shortish but athletic-looking young man in his middle twenties, with slim hips, broad shoulders and a plump round face. His eyes were very dark and his lips a trifle thick, but the corners of his mouth turned up slightly, giving him an expression of humorous good nature.

For a few seconds he stared blankly at his visitors, then recognition dawned in his eyes, and he exclaimed in English that had no more than a faint trace of accent:

"Why! Surely it is John Fountain?"

"Of course," John smiled. "I thought you were expecting us."

Count Jules looked his astonishment. "Forgive me, but I did not know, even, that you were in this part of the world."

John made a gesture of annoyance. "I'm so sorry. They must have made a muddle downstairs. I asked for you at the desk, and after telephoning the chap said we were to come up. But there was a woman beside us asking for somebody else, and in making the calls he must have got his lines crossed."

A slight narrowing of the Frenchman's eyes suggested either suspicion or that he was not used to such inefficient service and meant to give the unfortunate receptionist a sharp reprimand; but before he had time to make any comment John hurried on:

"I happened to meet your father last night in the Casino at Cannes. That's how I learned you were here. My mother and I have been visiting friends in St. Tropez this afternoon. On the spur of the moment I thought I would look you up, before we drive back to our little villa for dinner."

"But how nice! I am delighted, delighted." There was no trace now in the Count's voice of anything but genuine pleasure.

"I don't think you've ever met my mother," John said.

"*Enchanté, madame.*" Count Jules took Molly's hand as though it were a fragile piece of porcelain, and went through the motion of kissing the back of it, although he did not

66

actually touch it with his lips. Then he murmured, "Forgive me for keeping you standing like this in the hall. Please to come in. We are so happy to see you."

The small hallway of the suite had four doors leading from it. That on the immediate right stood partly open. Issuing from it John had heard the murmur of voices, and he guessed that Christina was with someone there. He had spoken to Jules rather loudly in the hope that she might hear what he said, and so not sabotage his story by giving any indication that they had really come to collect her. As their host pushed the door back and bowed Molly through it, John saw over her shoulder that Christina was looking in their direction with anxious expectation. But Molly forestalled any gaffe she might have made by exclaiming:

"Why, Christina! John told me you were lunching with these friends of his, but I never expected to find you still here."

Jules' glance switched swiftly from the girl to the new-comers, and he said in a surprised voice, "You know one another, then?"

"Oh yes," Molly replied lightly. "We are next-door neigh-bours and quite old friends."

When they entered the room a woman, who at first sight looked quite young, had been curled up in one corner of a big settee. As she uncurled herself and sat up Jules turned and addressed her in rapid French:

"*Belle mère*, may I present Mrs. Fountain and her son John, who was up with me during my last year at Cambridge." Then he added in English, "My stepmother, the Marquise de Grasse."

The sitting-room of this luxury suite was unusually spacious for an hotel, and from floor to ceiling one of its sides was composed entirely of sliding glass windows. But as the light was already fading and the Marquise was sitting with her back to them, it was difficult to tell her age. She was slim, extremely *soignée*, and, in the latest fashion, she had had several curls of her elaborately-dressed dark hair dyed gold. Her eyes were round and blue, her mouth a little sulky-looking. She was wearing a silk blouse, grey slacks with knife-like creases, and over her shoulders a chinchilla fur. Extending a limp hand she said:

"I am ver pleas to meet you. But my English, et ess not much good. You forgive? Perhaps you spik French?"

Molly's French being excellent, and that of both John and Christina adequate, most of the conversation which followed was carried on in that language. But the Marquise took little part in it; except to inform Molly a little later, while John and Jules were talking over old times, that although her husband owned houses in several parts of France, she much preferred to live for most of the year in hotels, as it was far less trouble.

They were already drinking cocktails, and while Jules made a fresh mix for the new arrivals, Christina said, "Madame la Marquise and Count Jules have been most kind. They insisted on my spending the afternoon here. He took me up to the old fort, then all round the harbour; and now they want me to stay and dine with them on their yacht."

"I wish I were as young as you are and could still keep such hours," Molly replied with a smile. "If I had been up till near dawn this morning I should be dropping asleep by now."

Christina took the ball quickly. "That's just the trouble. I'm not used to late nights, and I really don't feel up to it."

"Nonsense!" said Jules. "After a few glasses of champagne you will forget there is such a place as bed."

"Unfortunately champagne does not agree with me. And as I told you some time ago, I already have quite a headache. Please don't think me rude, but I'd really rather go home."

"If you are feeling like that it's lucky we turned up," John put in casually. "We can give you a lift back, and save Jules from being late for his dinner."

"No, no!" Jules protested. "A couple of aspirins will soon put your headache right, and we are not dining till nine; so if you wish you can lie down for an hour before we start. How about lying down for a while now? Belle mère will make you comfortable in our spare room."

"No thank you. I'd rather not."

He shrugged. "Well, our friends will not be going yet. See how you feel a little later on." Turning to John, he added,

68

"There are fireworks at Le Lavendou to-night and we are taking the yacht round the cape to witness them. It would be a pity for her to miss that. I wish that I could ask you and your mother to accompany us, but unfortunately the dining space on the yacht is limited, and my father has already made up his party."

Dismissing the matter, he then went on to talk about mutual friends they had known at Cambridge.

Outside darkness was falling rapidly, and during the quarter of an hour that followed Molly noticed a perceptible change in Christina. She had become much more lively as she described with enthusiasm the things she had seen with Count Jules that afternoon. When he switched on the lights and drew the curtains, she was laughing gaily about her big win at the tables the previous night, and saying that she could hardly wait to get back to them to try her luck again.

Scenting danger in her change of mood, Molly said to her, "John was going to suggest taking you in to Cannes again to-morrow night. But you won't feel much like it if you don't get a good sleep to-night; so from that point of view your decision to come home with us is a wise one. It is a great pity that you are feeling so rotten this evening and have to disappoint Count Jules, but I'm sure he will forgive you and ask you to go out on the yacht again some other time. And, talking of time, I really think it's time that we were going."

"Oh, not yet!" cried Jules. "You have been here hardly twenty minutes, and Christina is looking better already. I feel sure she will keep her promise and come with us after all."

"How late should we be?" Christina asked.

"We need not be late at all. We shall sit down to dinner as the yacht leaves harbour. The fireworks start at ten. They last only half an hour. The yacht will be back in her berth again by half-past eleven. Normally we should then dance for a while; but if you wish I could run you straight home, and you would be in bed not long after midnight."

"In that case . . ." Christina hesitated, then said with, for her, unusual brazenness, "Give me another cocktail, and while I am drinking it I will make up my mind."

"But certainly!" As Jules jumped to his feet, to John's surprise his mother called out, "And me, too, if you please." Then, with sudden apprehension, he saw her pick up and open her crocodile-skin bag. But, to his considerable relief, she only took out her compact and powdered her nose.

When Jules had replenished their glasses, Molly drew John's attention to a rather novel arrangement of bookcases at the far end of the room, and suggested that they might be a good idea for incorporation in some of his designs. He had not previously mentioned the fact to the de Grasses that he had taken up interior decorating as a profession, but did so now, while they were all looking at the bookcases.

The Marquise showed a sudden interest, and asked his opinion of the room, which she had had redecorated to her own specification. It displayed considerable taste, so he was able truthfully to compliment her upon it, before making a few tactful suggestions on quite minor points.

For a few minutes they discussed them. Then John happened to glance at Christina. Her face had gone deadly white. With quick concern he asked:

"I say; you're looking awfully pale. Are you feeling all right?"

She shook her head. "No . . . I . . . I feel awfully queer."

The Marquise uncoiled her long legs in the beautifully tailored grey slacks, and said, "Poor little one. Would you like to go to the bathroom? Come with me. I will take you there."

"No," murmured Christina. "I don't want to be sick. I . . . just feel muzzy." She pointed to her glass, which was nearly empty, and added, "That . . . that last cocktail must have been too much for me."

"Drinking a spot too much when one is overtired often has that effect," John remarked. "But this settles it. She must come home with us; and the sooner the better."

"No!" A sharp note had crept into Jules' voice. "She shall stay here until she recovers. *Belle mère*, oblige me, please, by taking her to your room and looking after her."

"I'm afraid that is not a very good idea," John countered smoothly. "She'll only fall asleep, and wake up in a few hours'

70

time feeling like hell. Then you would have the unenviable task of driving her home."

John's contention was amply supported by the fact that, although Christina was trying to keep her head up, it now kept falling forward on to her chest. But Jules replied coldly:

"I should not in the least mind putting myself out a little for a young guest of mine who has been taken ill."

"Perhaps; but has it occurred to you that someone will have to stay with her, and that if your stepmother does so it would mean depriving her of the party and your father's other guests of their hostess?"

"That can be overcome. My stepmother's maid is most competent."

"But," Molly put in, "it would be bad for the girl when she wakes, to be taken for a twenty-five-mile drive."

Jules' black eyes had gone as hard as pebbles as he turned them on her. "She can stay here for the night. What is to prevent her?"

"I am," replied Molly firmly. "As an older woman I know better than you how to deal with a case like this. She will feel miserable and ashamed if, after having allowed herself to drink too much, she wakes up among comparative strangers and in a strange bed. I intend to take her back to her own villa."

Jules could barely conceal his anger any longer. "Madame!" he snapped, "I will not be dictated to in this manner. She is in no condition to be driven anywhere. A doctor should see her, and I mean to send for one. I insist that she stays here."

"Sorry, old chap!" John's voice was still quite good-humoured and level. "But my mother has known her for some time and is more or less responsible for her. So what she says goes."

As he spoke he advanced towards Christina, took her firmly by the arm, and pulled her to her feet. Then he added quietly, "Give me a hand to get her to the lift, will you?"

Quite suddenly Jules' determination to keep her there seemed to collapse. With a tight little smile he stepped forward, took Christina's other arm, and helped John support her to the door. The Marquise asked Molly to telephone them next

71

morning to let them know if Christina was all right, then the two older women exchanged polite adieus, and Molly followed the others out into the corridor.

There, at Jules' suggestion, she went down ahead of them in the lift, to bring the car round to a side door of the hotel, so that they should not have to take the half-conscious girl right across the big lounge. By making a great effort, Christina could manage to walk a few steps at a time, as long as she was supported on both sides. Ten minutes later, with few people having seen them, they had her safely in the back seat of the car. Just as it was about to drive off, Jules leaned forward and said smoothly through the window to John:

"My father will be so sorry to have missed you; but you must come over and see us again."

"Thanks," John replied, with the appearance of equal cordiality, "I should love to."

Molly had overheard the exchange, and as the car ran down the drive she murmured, "I thought at one moment he was going to prove really troublesome. I wonder what caused him suddenly to change his mind."

"I've no idea." John shrugged. "Anyhow, we pulled it off. But what a bit of luck that she asked for that last cocktail. God alone knows how we should have got her away if it hadn't been for that."

"Yes. That, and what I put in it."

"Mumsie!" He turned to stare at her for a second. "What the devil do you mean?"

"I gave her a Micky Finn, darling."

"You didn't!"

"Well, to be accurate, only about a quarter of one, because I didn't want to knock her right out." Molly's voice was just a trifle smug. "I'm really rather pleased with myself. I've had some of those little tablets in my museum for years. I souvenired them during the war, and I've always wanted to try them on someone, but a suitable opportunity has never arisen before. The way it worked was most gratifying."

"How on earth did you manage to put it in her drink without anyone seeing you?"

Molly tittered with pleasure at the thought of her skilful coup. "I didn't. I put it in my own, and used the cherry-stick to help dissolve it quickly. Then, when I had made you all look away from the table to the bookcases, I exchanged her glass for mine."

"Well played, Mumsie!" John spoke with genuine admiration. "But you've let the cat out of the bag, you know. This night's work dispels my last lingering doubts about your having been Molly Polloffski, the beautiful spy."

"No, Johnny. Really, I assure you I never did anything but work in an office."

"Tell that one to the Marines!" he replied, closing the conversation.

As Christina had been given only a small dose of the powerful drug, she recovered fairly quickly from its worst effects, and when they got back to Molly's villa she was able to walk up the path to it unassisted. As soon as they reached the sitting-room Molly sat her down in an armchair, then went upstairs and fetched her a bromo-seltzer.

She was now fully conscious again, but in a curious mood, half tearful and half defiant. Several times she apologized for having made a fool of herself, and for having given them so much trouble. But she did not seem to realize that they had saved her from some very grave danger. Every now and then she harped back to the de Grasses' party and said how sorry she was to have missed it. In fact it soon became clear that she now resented their having prevented her remaining at the Capricorn until she recovered, so that there might still have been a chance of her being able to go on the yacht.

At length Molly said, "I'm afraid, my dear, that this business has been getting on your nerves, and that you are no longer in quite normal state. If you were, you would recall that it was at your own request, made earlier this evening, that we got you out of the clutches of the de Grasses." Pausing for a moment she fished something out of her bag and concealed it in her hand; then she went on, "Our only wish is to get to the root of your trouble, and see you out of it. Here is something which may help us to do that, and help you, too."

As she finished speaking she threw the thing she was
holding towards Christina's lap, and cried, "Catch!"

Christina cupped her hands and caught the spinning object.
It was a small gold crucifix. The second it fell into her palms she
gave a scream of pain. Then, as though seared by white-hot
metal, she thrust it from her.

"I feared as much!" Molly said grimly. "And now we know
the worst! Every night when darkness falls, you become
possessed by the Devil."

CHAPTER VI

THE CHRISTINA OF THE DARK HOURS

WITH her eyes glaring, Christina sprang up from the armchair. Then, as though suddenly stricken by a fit, her long limbs grew rigid, she fell back into it, and little flecks of froth began to appear at the corners of her mouth.

Molly went quickly over to the side-table on which stood the drinks, filled a tumbler half full of Perrier water and, turning about, sloshed its contents into the girl's face. She whimpered, the rigor passed, and she sat up, the water dripping from her brown hair and running down her pale cheeks. Laying a hand on her shoulder, Molly said kindly:

"God help you, child; but I am right, aren't I? You are only your real self in the day-time, and at night you become possessed."

With a moan, Christina buried her face in her hands, and burst into a flood of tears.

Turning to John, Molly said, "She had better stay here to-night. Before we left I told Angèle that we might be late for dinner, so we would have something cold. Slip out to the kitchen and tell her that we shan't be ready for it for another half-hour, and that she is to go up at once and make the spare room ready."

John was standing with his mouth a little open, staring at Christina. He could still hardly believe that he had not been the victim of a sudden amnesia and imagined the happenings of the last few moments. But he pulled himself together, nodded, and left the room.

For a few minutes Molly remained silently beside Christina, then when the girl's weeping ceased she said, "My dear, you must be quite exhausted, and are in no state to talk further about this to-night. I'm going to put you to bed here, and to-morrow when you are feeling better we will decide what it is best for us to do."

"There is nothing that you can do," murmured Christina a little sullenly.

"Oh yes, there is," countered Molly, in her most determined voice "And we're going to do it; but it is not the time to go into that now."

At that moment John returned; so his mother said to him, "You had better stay with her, while I go over to her villa and get her a few things for the night."

Christina was now sitting staring at the floor. After another swift glance at her, John mixed himself a drink and, feeling extremely awkward, sat down some way from her on the edge of the sofa. For once he was completely out of his depth. The very idea of anyone in this modern world being possessed by the Devil struck him as utterly fantastic. Yet Christina had reacted to the touch of the crucifix as though she had been stung by a hornet, and there seemed no normal explanation for that. Moreover, she had made no attempt to explain it herself, or deny his mother's diagnosis of her case. In such extraordinary circumstances he could think of nothing whatever to say to her; but fortunately she did not seem to expect him to start a conversation; so they both remained sitting there in silence until Molly returned.

Much to his relief, no further scene ensued. Molly's attitude to the girl was now the same as she would have adopted to any young guest who had suddenly been taken ill in her house. With brisk efficiency, she hurried her off to bed; and Christina went without a word of protest.

Shortly afterwards Angèle came in to say that she had laid supper, and when Molly came down she found John in the dining-room pulling the cork of a bottle of *vin rosé*. As she took her seat at the table she said:

"For a moment I feared that poor child was going to run screaming from the house. It was a great relief that after her fit she became so docile, and allowed me to put her to bed, where I can keep an eye on her. She is fairly comfortable now, but as a result of that Mickey Finn she naturally does not feel like eating any dinner. I have told Angèle to take her up a cup of *bouillon*, and later I shall give her a good dose of some stuff I have."

"I suppose," John remarked, "that if we made her drink a noggin of Holy water she would start to fizz, then blow up; so no doubt you're right to play for safety and stick to your panacea for all childish ills—a grey powder disguised in a spoonful of raspberry jam."

His rather poor attempt at humour brought the quick reproof, "I was referring to some stuff which will make her sleep. And, Johnny, this is nothing to joke about."

"Sorry; but I haven't yet got my bearings. What was the big idea in putting a fast one over on Christina while she was still too doped to fully understand what was going on?"

"If you mean my throwing her that little crucifix, I should have thought my reason for doing so immediately became obvious."

"No, I didn't mean that. While she was in that state, throwing anything at her might have made her scream. I meant putting the idea that she was possessed into the poor girl's head at a time when she was too goofy to repudiate it?"

"She didn't repudiate it because she knows—or at least suspects—that it is true."

"Oh come, Mumsie! You can't really believe that people become possessed. That is now just a form of speech for a particular kind of religious lunacy."

"It is not, and *she is*," Molly announced with decision. "I have been wondering all day if that could be at the bottom of her extraordinary behaviour, and now I am certain of it. The acid test is to touch anyone who is suspected of possession with a crucifix. If they react as though they have been burnt, that is a sure sign that they have a devil inside them."

John helped himself to another chunk of *paté maison*, spread it lavishly on a *brioche*, and asked sceptically, "How do you know? Is it just that you have read about it in some old book, or have you actually seen it happen on a previous occasion?"

"I was told about it by a Roman Catholic priest whom I knew

77

years ago. He specialized in exorcism, and had witnessed many strange happenings. One experience that he told me of I shall never forget. It was in Ireland and he was endeavouring to drive a devil out of a poor cottager. The place was deep in the country, so the wife had prepared a meal. In honour of the priest she had bought a leg of mutton, but as the time when he could get out there was uncertain she cooked it in advance and placed it cold on the table of the living-room, all ready for when he had fulfilled his mission. The case proved a very stubborn one. The possessed man became violent, struggling and blaspheming, and had to be tied down. For over two hours the priest wrestled with the fiend, conjuring him to come forth without success; but at last he triumphed. A wisp of evil-smelling black smoke issued from the cottager's foaming mouth, sped across the room, apparently passing through the leg of mutton, then disappeared through the wall. When the exhausted victim had been put to bed the priest and the rest of the family sat down to supper. But they were unable to eat the mutton. When it was touched it fell from the bones, absolutely rotten and alive with maggots."

"Did the chap who told you this story produce any supporting evidence to substantiate that he was telling the truth?"

"No, and I did not need it. He was a most saintly old man. I am sure he would have allowed himself to be torn in pieces rather than lie about any matter connected with his faith."

"Have you any other sources for believing that such things still happen?"

"Not direct ones, but occasionally one sees cases reported in the French papers."

"Why the French papers, particularly?"

"Cases are probably also reported in the Spanish and Italian press, and those of other Catholic countries; but I don't see them."

"The inference is, then, that these occurrences are confined to Catholic countries?"

"No, I don't think that is so. I think that the profound

knowledge of demonology that has been handed down by the Roman Catholic Church enables certain of her priests to recognize possession and deal with it; whereas when a case occurs in a Protestant country hardly anyone is capable of distinguishing it from ordinary lunacy, so the sufferer is simply certified and put in an asylum."

John could not help being impressed, and after remaining silent for a moment he said, "If you are really right about all this, Mumsie, it looks as if we ought to call a Catholic priest in to cope with Christina."

"That is easier said than done, darling. You see, although all Roman Catholic priests are qualified by their office to perform ceremonies of exorcism, very few of them ever do so. Experience has shown it to be a job for experts who have made a special study of that sort of thing; much in the same way as only a very limited number of doctors are capable of prescribing the most efficient treatment for a rare disease. As we are not Catholics ourselves and Christina isn't one either, I'm afraid it would prove difficult to interest the local man in her case sufficiently to induce him to send for a first-class exorcist, perhaps from some distant part of France."

"How do you propose to handle this extraordinary business, then? She is quite sane most of the time, and we can't let her be popped into a loony bin."

Molly looked down at her plate. "When we've finished supper I thought I would ring up London, and try to get hold of Colonel Verney."

"What, Conky Bill!" John exclaimed in astonishment.

"Yes. He usually dines at his club in the middle of the week and never goes home much before eleven, so there is quite a good chance of my catching him. If he is not too desperately busy I might be able to persuade him to fly down to-morrow and stay with us for a few days."

"But hang it all, Mumsie, what's the idea? Of course, I know you've always had a bit of a yen for C. B., so one can't blame you for seizing on any excuse . . ."

"Johnny, I've told you often enough that I had to act as liaison between my chief and C. B. during the war, and that

79

after your father died he was extremely kind to me. That's all there is to it."

"Dearest, you know jolly well that the two of you flirt like mad whenever you are together. I think he's a grand chap, and nothing would please me better than to get tight at your wedding: but that is beside the point at the moment. The thing I don't get is why you should regard him as a suitable substitute for a Catholic priest who has trained as an expert exorcist."

"If I tell you, you must promise never to repeat it."

"Go ahead. I can give as good an imitation of a bearded oyster as you can about things that really matter."

"Well, you are quite right in assuming that for the past few years C. B. has given most of his time to checking up on the activities of Communists and fellow travellers. But that is only because they have now become the principal source of danger to our right to choose whom we want to rule us at free elections. Before the war he spent just as much of his time keeping his eye on the Fascists. Actually he is responsible for keeping his chief informed about all groups that may be engaged in subversive activities. That, of course, covers every type of secret society, including circles that practise Black Magic."

John raised his dark eyebrows. "Such circles do really exist, then? I remember reading an article some months ago in the *Sunday Empire News* by ex-Superintendent Robert Fabian, giving a most lurid account of how young girls were lured into lending themselves to all sorts of obscene rites in secret Satanic Temples. He even went so far as to state that he knew there to be such places in Kensington, Paddington and Bloomsbury. But I thought it was all poppycock, and that now Fabian is retired he was just making himself a bit of easy money."

"No; Fabian was telling the truth. And when he was an officer of the Special Branch he worked in close collaboration with C. B. You have no idea of the horrors they uncovered."

"Why are there never any prosecutions, then?"

"Because the Satanists who run these circles are too clever. They recruit their disciples from among the people who attend quite respectable spiritualist and theosophical societies, many of whom can easily be intrigued by a promise of revealing to them the real secrets of the occult at some small private gathering. The obtaining of power is, of course, the lure, and they start them off with Yoga exercises; then prescribe a special diet for them, including a course of pills which are actually aphrodisiacs to increase their sexual appetite. After that there is usually not much difficulty in involving them with some more advanced Satanist of the opposite sex. For them that starts as just a rather intriguing affair, but it is the thin end of the wedge. Their instructor promises the revelation of higher mysteries if they will consent to be hypnotized, and they nearly always do. Once they have been fully dominated they no longer have a mind of their own and become willing subjects for every kind of abomination. A few of the stronger-minded ones survive to achieve the rank of real Satanists themselves, but most of them are used only for obscenities and soon degenerate into physical and moral wrecks. Many of them end up as suicides, and those who are rescued by their friends always prove useless from the police point of view. Either they have not gone far enough to be able to give evidence of any actually criminal activities, or, if they have, they have been hypnotized into a state in which their minds are blank about the Satanists they have been mixed up with and the places where the rituals in which they participated took place. That is why there are never any prosecutions."

"It sounds a ghastly business," John said, pushing his plate away; "but I don't quite see where Conky Bill comes into it. From Fabian's article and what you say, it seems that the Satanists' only interest is to get hold of young people upon whom to practise sexual perversions at their orgies. Beastly as that may be, it is a form of private fun and has no connection with subversive activities against the State."

"You are quite wrong about that, Johnny. The people who direct these circles really are the henchmen of the Devil. The sexual excesses that take place under their auspices are only a means to an end—a focus for concentrating evil forces which they can use for the furtherance of their own wicked designs. You must have read at some time that in the old days the Devil was often referred to as the Lord of Misrule. The object of these high-up Satanists is to deliver the world up to him, and the only way they can do that is to cause the breakdown of good rule so that misrule may take its place. With that as their goal they do everything they can to foment wars, class-hatred, strikes and famine; and to foster perversions, moral laxity and the taking of drugs. There is even reason to believe that they have been behind many of the political assassinations that have robbed the world of good rulers and honest statesmen, and naturally Communism has now become their most potent weapon. So you can see that breaking up these Black Magic circles, wherever they can be found, is very much in C. B.'s province."

"Oh come, Mumsie! I agree that they may exert their influence for political evil, but by suggesting that they are working to a plan and have supernatural backing, aren't you letting your imagination run away with you a bit? After all, no one really believes in the Devil any more."

"My dear, he was part of the original creation, and no amount of popular education can destroy that. It is simply that in modern times he has gone underground, and judging by the amount of havoc and misery there has been in the world during the present century he must be very pleased with the success of his latest stratagem. It was his own apparent abolition, resulting from the decay of religion, that gave him his big chance, and he is using it with a greater skill than he has ever displayed before in his attempts to ensnare mankind."

"You honestly believe that?"

"I do. Now that more than half the people in the world have become godless, they have also become rudderless. Once they have put away from themselves the idea of a hereafter they think only of their own selfish ends of the moment. That leaves them an easy prey to unscrupulous politicians. Before they know where they are, they find themselves robbed of all personal freedom; their family life, which is their last tie with their better instincts, is broken up, and their children are taken from them, to be educated into robots lacking all individuality. That is what nearly happened in Nazi Germany and what has happened in Russia; and if that is not the state of things that Satan would like to see everywhere, tell me what is?"

John did not reply. Instead, after a moment's thought, he asked, "Have you any idea where Christina fits into all this?"

"No. I have heard that now and then one of those Paris finishing places is discovered to be no better than a high-class brothel. When girls who are just becoming women are cooped up together they corrupt one another very easily, you know; and in the type of place that caters for those whose parents want to be rid of them for two or three years at a stretch, an unscrupulous principal with a clever man behind her might get away with a vice racket of that kind for quite a long time without being found out. As sexual promiscuity is the first step towards greater evils, if Christina was at such a place she may have got herself involved in something there. But somehow I don't think so. She does not give me the impression of a girl who has gone very far down the slope of her own free will. I am more inclined to think that she is the victim of a spell, and has been bewitched."

"If we can get hold of C. B., do you think he will be able to free her from the . . . er . . . sort of trouble you have in mind?"

"I don't know, Johnny. We can only hope so. All I do know is that in the course of his job he must have picked up a lot about the principles on which Satanists work, and he is the only person I know of who may be able to advise us what to do. Even if he is busy I feel sure he will come if he possibly can, as, quite apart from any wish to help the girl, there is the de Grasse angle, and that should prove an additional justification for him to leave his office."

Three-quarters of an hour later Molly succeeded in getting Lieutenant-Colonel William Verney on the telephone. They then talked for a few minutes in the curious jargon that such people had used in the war, even when their conversations were protected from listeners-in by a scrambler. It consisted of short phrases, interspersed with apparently irrelevant allusions to mutual friends, places, books and past happenings, which could mean little to any third person, but rang bells in the minds of both. She proved right in her belief that he would respond to her appeal; and it was agreed that, unless he telegraphed her that he had been unable to get a seat on the plane, she should meet him at Nice airport on the following day.

In consequence, in spite of the concern she was feeling about Christina, Molly went to bed in a happy frame of mind; while the girl fell into a heavy slumber as a result of the draught she had been given. But John lay long awake, turning over and over all that his mother had said about Satanism, veering between belief and disbelief, and quite unable to decide whether it was only her vivid imagination that caused her to credit the Devil with being active in the modern world, or if in sober truth the unfortunate Christina was, during certain hours, possessed by some evil force that had been conjured up from the traditional Pit, said to be inhabited by Satan's legions.

At length he dropped off, but only to become the victim of a nightmare, in which he was chained to a rock and an angel and a devil were fighting over him. Both of them had Christina's face, and while that of the angel glowed with beauty, that of the devil was rendered peculiarly horrifying by the fact that luminous smoke was curling up from its flared nostrils.

In the morning, contrary to custom, his mother had him called and his breakfast brought to him at eight-thirty; so he was dressed and downstairs well before ten. From her he learned that Christina had had a good night, was none the worse for her experiences of the previous evening, and had gone over to her own villa to change her clothes, but had promised to return as soon as she had done so.

A quarter of an hour later she came in through the sitting-room window, looking a little subdued but otherwise perfectly normal, and very pretty in a square-necked frock made gay with broad bands of red and yellow peasant embroidery. In the morning sunshine it seemed difficult to believe that she was the same girl whose eyes had glared hatred during a fit as a result of having a crucifix pitched to her, in that very room, little more than twelve hours before. But all three of them were uncomfortably aware that no good purpose could be served by refraining from going into the matter, and Molly set about it with commendable briskness.

"Tell me, my dear," she said as they sat down, "how much do you remember about what happened last night?"

Christina turned her big, frank brown eyes upon her questioner. "A certain amount, but not everything. There are some quite big gaps. I remember your arrival at the Capricorn and how relieved I was, because I felt sure you would get me away from those people. Then I have a vague recollection of your disputing with them about me, and that I became increasingly annoyed with you for wanting to take me home. What occurred after that is completely gone, until I woke up feeling dreadfully ill and found myself in the back of your car. We came in here and I was trying to figure out a way of getting back to the Capricorn without your knowing. Then . . . then I had a sort of fit, and from that point on my mind is a blank again until I woke up in bed here this morning."

"Is it usual for you to have those sort of lapses of memory about much of what has been happening to you the night before?"

"Yes. Somehow at night I seem to be quite a different person. I often get up and roam about, and at such times I get all sorts of nasty impulses of a kind that I rarely have during the day. As far as I know I don't often give way to them, but I can't be quite certain of that, because afterwards I nearly always get these blackouts. The thought of what I may have done during them distresses and frightens me next morning. But to the best of my belief I do remember if I have actually done anything wicked, because I have had numerous instances of that. Any really definite action seems to register permanently in my mind."

"Can you give us any examples?"

"Well, for one thing, I'm afraid I'm a thief." Christina lowered her eyes and went on unhappily, "Honestly, I don't mean to be; but several times in Paris I stole trinkets and scent and money from the other girls at night. When I remembered what I had done the following morning I was terribly ashamed. Fortunately I was able to put the things back before my thefts were noticed; and no others were reported. It is that which makes me believe that when I do give way to these awful impulses I know what I have done when I wake up."

"Was the impulse to steal the only one that came to you?"

"No. I seem to become horribly malicious. My best friend was engaged to be married. One night I stole the love-letters that her fiancé had written to her, and burnt them down in the furnace. Several times I used a steel crochet hook to make ladders in other girls' stockings and spilt ink on their clothes, but I was so cunning that they never found out who had done it. Then I became subject to a special feeling about anything connected with religion. It is a sort of mixture of hatred and fear. I can't bring myself to touch any sacred object, but . . . but I've defiled them. Three times I did that with little lockets containing holy symbols belonging to different girls. There was a frightful row afterwards, but no one had the least suspicion that I was the culprit."

"Is there anything else you can tell us about your state during these midnight forays?" Molly asked after a moment.

Christina flushed, and her voice was very low. "Yes. I realize that if you are going to help me I ought not to keep anything back. Sometimes I feel the most awful urge towards immorality—but I'd rather not talk about that."

"Let's go back to last night," said Molly, promptly changing the line of the conversation. "Do you remember my throwing a crucifix to you, and what happened then?"

"Yes," Christina replied in a whisper. "As it touched me it felt like a live coal. I sprang up and screamed. Then you said that I was possessed by the Devil."

"I know it was a terrible thing to say, my dear; but do you think you are?"

"I don't know. At times I've wondered if I am, myself. But why should I be? What can I possibly have done to deserve such an awful fate?"

So far John had not spoken; but seeing that the girl was now very near to tears, he stretched out his hand, took one of hers, and pressed it. "We are sure it's not your fault. Even if it's true—even if you have done something to bring it on yourself—Mother and I wouldn't stop wanting to help you. And we wouldn't like you any the less."

"Thanks." She gave him a faint smile and let her hand remain in his, as Molly added, "John is quite right about that; and my own belief is that it is nothing you have done, but that somebody has bewitched you. Have you ever known anybody who was interested in witchcraft, magic or sorcery?"

"I don't think so. In Paris one of the girls used to tell fortunes with a pack of cards; but one couldn't really call that witchcraft, could one? And she wasn't very good at it. As a matter of fact I could do it far better myself, but I didn't; not when I was there. I gave it up several years ago, because it frightened me. Twice when I was at that school in Somerset I predicted serious accidents; and in one case I saw death in the cards, although I didn't say so, and the person died a month later."

Molly nodded. "Such an uncanny gift is additional proof that you have some special link with occult powers; and evidently it is not a recent one. How long is it since you took to prowling about at night, and feeling these distressing impulses?"

"Ever since I can remember; but, as I told you the other day, when I was young it took the form of sleep-walking. It may have been because I did naughty things at such times that Delia was so unkind to me. I didn't even begin to be aware of what I was doing until I was thirteen, and even then it came as a gradual transition. I must have been over seventeen before I was fully conscious when I got out of bed at nights. But the occasions on which I did so were fairly few and far between, and the impulses I felt were neither as strong nor as wicked. It is only during the past year that I have been getting so much worse. That is what frightens me so much."

"Have you ever been to a séance, or gone in for table-turning and just for a lark called on the Devil to aid your enquiries?"

"No, never."

"And there is no special episode in your childhood, or anything else you can remember, that might have a bearing on your present state?"

"No. I have already told you everything about my life that I can think of."

There fell a pause, then John asked, "How about Canon Copely-Syle? I wouldn't mind betting that he didn't turn up here by chance, and that the story he told you about your father having had a serious accident was a fake, designed to get you away from your villa. I didn't know it when we met the Marquis de Grasse at Cannes, but Mother has since told me that he is a crook. The fact that the Canon introduced you to him, and his son afterwards tried to get you on to their yacht, makes the case against the Canon pretty black. In fact, it is ten to one that he is at the bottom of the whole business."

"Yes. I came to that conclusion yesterday; although I then had little more than my instinct to go on. It was that which made me refuse to go on the yacht yesterday afternoon, when Count Jules took me down to the harbour and pressed me to. It was only after I had made an excuse not to, and dug my toes in, that he invited me to dine on board instead; and as he had first made certain that I had no engagement for the evening, I could think of no way to wriggle out of accepting. But I'm afraid I can't help much about the Canon. I told you all I know about him on the morning of his visit."

"There are two things you can tell us," Molly said, "although I hesitate to ask you, and I wouldn't if I didn't think it important that we should know them. They are your real name, and your father's address."

Christina shook her head. "I'd rather not break my promise to him."

"Just as you like, my dear. But when he asked you for it, neither of you could possibly foresee the sort of thing that has happened since; and if he knew how you were situated at present I feel sure he would release you from it. You see, now that the Canon has discovered your hiding-place, and it looks as if he is employing crooks to get hold of you, we have to face the fact that however carefully John and I endeavour to guard against it, you might be taken from us. If that happened our best hope of getting you back would be to call in the police; and it might be a great help to them in tracing you if we could give them your proper name and enable them to communicate with your father."

For a moment Christina considered the matter, then she said with sudden decision, "All right. My name is Ellen Beddows, and we live at The Grange, Little Bentford, near Colchester. My father is Henry Beddows of Beddows Agricultural Tractors."

"Thank you, my dear. Of course we shall continue to call you Christina, and you may be sure we will not abuse your confidence. Now, there is just one other thing. Your father must hold the key to both your own peculiar state and the mystery of why the Canon is so anxious to get hold of you. Don't you really think the time has come when we should try to get in touch with him?"

"No!" Christina's voice was firm. "He told me that it was unlikely that his office would know where to find him, and even if they did I must not ring him up. I have already broken one promise that I gave him, and there is some reason to believe that he may be in danger himself; so I will do nothing which might bring him here and perhaps place him in greater danger still."

"Very well then." Molly stood up. "I must leave you now, because I have to drive to Nice to meet a friend of mine at the airport. He is coming to stay for a few days, and I do hope you will like him, as it is really you who he is flying out from England to see."

"Me!" exclaimed Christina with a surprised look.

"Yes. He is not a psycho-analyst or anything of that kind; so you have no cause to be frightened that he will try to delve into your sub-conscious and drag out the sort of little personal secrets we all prefer to keep to ourselves. But he has had considerable experience of the way in which occultists get young people into their clutches; so I am hoping very much that he may know of a method of countering the evil influence that is being exerted on you. The plane doesn't get in till one;

so I shan't be back much before tea-time. But John will look after you while I am away, and I thought you might like to take a picnic lunch out together."

John and Christina agreed that a picnic was a good idea; so as soon as they had seen Molly off they set about their preparations. An inspection of the larder revealed a fine choice of good things. Angèle prepared a salad for them, while Christina stuffed some crisp rolls with ham and gruyère cheese, and John collected fruit, a bottle of wine and glasses. When they had finished packing the things into a basket, Christina said:

"As we are going to walk, I think I will put on a pair of thicker shoes. You don't mind waiting while I slip over to my villa, do you?"

"Of course not," John replied. "It has not yet gone half-past eleven; so we have tons of time. In fact it might not be a bad idea if we didn't start till twelve. That would give you a chance to pack a suitcase with some other things you may want, as Mother was saying this morning that she thought it would be best if you stayed on with us here—for the time being anyhow. I'll come across and collect it later."

"Will there . . . ?" she hesitated. "Are you quite sure there will be room for me, now that this friend of your mother's is coming?"

"Oh yes. You needn't worry about that. This villa is slightly larger than yours, I think. Anyhow, I'm giving up my room to Conky Bill—Colonel Verney, that is—and Angèle will move my things into the little slip-room at the back, next to the one you occupied last night."

"All right, then. It really means that you'll be giving up your room for me, though. I'll never be able to repay you and your mother for all your kindness."

As she turned away, he called after her, "You had better put in a frock for this evening. Not a 'knock 'em in the Old Kent Road' effect like you wore the other night; but something simple. Conky Bill is an old-fashioned type and likes changing for dinner; so black tie and sea-boots will be the order of the day."

When she had disappeared he went upstairs and carried

most of _____ ller belongings through to the slip-room, then came do_____ _____ ked Angèle to move the rest while he was out. Picking _____ e basket with the lunch in it, he walked through the s_____ room to the french windows, but halted there with a sligh_____ _____ own on his face. Count Jules de Grasse was coming up th_____ _____ ath.

The Count saw hi_____ _____ e same moment and called out gaily, "Good morning! _____ _____ _____ e how prompt I am to repay your call."

Putting down the basket, John advanced to meet him, a smile now disguising the faint uneasiness he felt. "How nice of you. I am so sorry we had to drag Christina away from you last night; but she really was not fit to stay."

"Oh, we quite understood. How is she this morning?"

"I'm glad to say she is fully recovered," John replied, as they turned back towards the house. Then, to forestall any further invitation Count Jules might have brought for her, he added, "As a matter of fact you only just caught me. I am about to take her out for the day."

"Dear me! Then I fear I have timed my visit badly."

Feeling that it would be wisest to continue this pretence of friendship, and at least hear what the Count had come to say, John waved a hand towards the french windows. "No. Do come in. We shan't be starting for a little while yet. Can I offer you a drink?"

"Thanks. If you happen to have any *pastis* I should like one."

"I expect there is some here. There is usually." Having found the bottle among the drinks on the side-table, John poured from it two good portions of the clear spirit into tumblers, added the water that turned it a cloudy opal, and handed one to his stocky, round-faced visitor.

The Frenchman raised his glass, and, having drunk, gestured with it towards the view. "You have a charming place here; and I envy you having a mimosa tree just outside your windows. Now that it is in blossom the smell is heavenly."

"My father bought this villa some years before the war, and my mother has lived here almost continuously since."

"Indeed! Then you must have been here many times yourself. I wish I had known before this that we were neighbours. There is little I do not know about the towns of the Riviera, so I could have provided you with a lot of fun."

"It's a kind thought," John smiled, "but I have managed pretty well on my own."

Jules took another swig of the absinthe and remarked, "This is really excellent. Where did you find it?"

"It is a private brew made by the barman at the Negresco. I think my father was rather a favourite customer of his. Anyhow, when my mother goes in to Nice, he still lets her have a bottle now and then."

"My congratulations on it. Also, since madame, your mother, is not here, be kind enough to give her my compliments, please."

"Thanks. I will."

A short silence fell, then Jules passed a hand over his dark, slightly crinkly hair, and said:

"I would like to have a word with you strictly in private, *mon ami*. Might we, perhaps, take our drinks down to your little terrace?"

"By all means, if you wish," John replied, much intrigued by the implication of this request.

Side by side, they walked in silence down the path between the clementine and lemon trees. When they had settled themselves on two of the white-painted, comfortably-sprung iron chairs that are peculiar to French gardens, Jules asked:

"How do you find life in England these days? I mean this decorating business of yours, and making from it a decent income?"

John shrugged. "I've no complaints about business, but money is quite another matter. The trouble is to keep a little when you've made it. We are almost taxed out of existence."

"So I gather; and it is getting to be the same way here. The illusion still persists that French people do not pay their taxes; but that is no longer true. The Government now assesses us arbitrarily and forces us to meet its demands in anticipation of our incomes. Since in both our countries the Government has become only another name for the People, it really amounts to the idle and stupid stealing from those who work hard and show initiative. But now, alas, they have come to consider it as a right; and I see little prospect of any change in this iniquitous system."

Wondering what all this could be leading up to, John nodded, and replied, "I fear you are right; and the great danger is that before any change is likely to occur they will have killed off all the geese that lay the golden eggs."

"In France that has happened already—at least, as far as those families who were the mainstay of the country up to the early years of this century are concerned. In 1914 the franc had stood for many generations at 25 to the £. It has since been devalued again and again so that it now stands at round 1,000 to the £. In one half a normal life-time it has been reduced to one-fortieth of its former value. Think what that has meant to the great property owners and others who depend mainly on fixed incomes."

Again John nodded. "Its effect must have been devastating; in fact, as destructive as a series of capital levies."

Jules lit a Gitane cigarette and let it remain dangling from his full lips. "You have said it, *mon ami*; and it is just that point I wished to make with you. Less than half a century ago my family owned great estates. They administered them well and took from them what they wanted, but in reason. Now, my father and I have only our intelligence left; so even to live in reasonable comfort we must take what we can get anywhere we can get it."

"I thought your father was a wealthy ship-owner," John remarked.

Shrugging his shoulders, Jules crossed one leg over the other, sat back and stuffed his hands in his trouser pockets. "It is true that we own a few ships, but these thieves of tax collectors always have their noses in our books and steal most of the profits. Therefore we have been compelled to develop as a side-line the acceptance of commissions for cash, which is not taxable."

"Really? I suppose you mean carrying certain cargoes without declaring them?"

"Exactly. And there is one commission we accepted recently, of which, as an old friend, I feel it is only fair to inform you." Jules paused for a moment, then went on, "It is to transport the young woman you know as Christina Mordant to England before March the 6th. On the completion of that transaction we are to receive the sum of one thousand pounds."

"I see," said John quietly.

"Now!" Jules' smile broadened. "It appears that you are interested in Christina. Why, is a question that I am still asking myself; for she is as yet no more than a hoydenish young girl, and still lacking in all the attributes which go to make women intriguing to men of our intelligence. Should you care to stand aside entirely, and not seek to prevent my collecting Christina from her villa at any time I may choose, I will willingly give you introductions to a dozen ladies, all more charming and sophisticated than she is, who live within easy reach; and you can take your pick of them to console you for your loss. Do you agree?"

"No," said John firmly. "I do not."

Jules shrugged. "I feared that might prove the case. Therefore I will put up to you an alternative proposition. As I took some pains to point out to you just now, the age of chivalry is past, and most regrettably its passing has compelled my father and me to become business men. We cannot afford to forgo a thousand pounds, but as no contract has been signed we are not strictly bound to carry out our undertaking. In view of your evident desire to continue enjoying Christina's innocent prattle, how would it appeal to you to pay us twelve hundred pounds to leave her alone?"

Such a bare-faced attempt at blackmail caused John's eyes to open wide with astonishment. For a second he felt inclined to laugh, but he knew that it was no laughing matter, and, getting to his feet, he said angrily:

"What the hell do you take me for?"

"Should you refuse both my offers, I shall take you for a

fool " Jules also had come to his feet, but his voice remained level. "If, as your attitude now leads me to suppose, you wish to marry the girl, why not approach your mother? She must make a great deal from her books, so could easily find the money."

"That is beside the point," John snapped. "I will neither let you take Christina away, nor pay you one brass farthing to refrain from attempting to. And now, get out!"

Jules' eyes had gone very dark, but his tone was still mild. "I am sorry that you should prove so unreasonable. I came here hoping that we might arrange matters on a friendly basis, and I am still sufficiently well-disposed towards you to give you a warning. Do not think that because you came out on top last night you will be lucky enough to do so a second time. I let you get away with it only because my father and I will never permit any situation to arise which might cause trouble in the hotel at which we live. If you attempt to interfere in my business again you must not blame me if you get seriously hurt."

CHAPTER VII

NIGHT MUST FALL

JOHN watched Count Jules drive off in a big blue Citröen, then he turned about and looked up at Christina's villa. It was now about a quarter-past twelve, but there was no sign of her in the garden or at those windows of the house that he could glimpse between the umbrella-pines; so it looked as if she had not yet finished her packing. Picking up the empty glasses, he stumped up the path with them, and collected the lunch basket. Then, as he left the house, he saw that she had come out just ahead of him and was now half-way down to her terrace; so they met in the road.

Assuming that she had not seen Count Jules, John decided that to make any mention of his visit would be to give her needless cause for anxiety; so he greeted her with a smile and said, "I think we'll go towards Agay, then turn inland. If you don't mind an hour's trudge uphill, there is a lovely view from the lowest spur of the ridge."

She nodded. "We will go wherever you like. But tell me about your visitor. I was ready to start at twelve o'clock, as we arranged, but I saw him with you on the terrace; so I thought it wiser to remain under cover till he had gone. What did he want?"

"He said it was just a friendly call; and he enquired most tenderly about your health."

"I bet he didn't come all the way from St. Tropez only for that. Please be honest with me, John. Now that I have told you everything I can about myself, it wouldn't be fair of you to keep me in the dark. I would much rather know about it if you have reason to believe that they are plotting anything fresh against me."

On reconsideration, he decided that she was right, and, if warned, would be additionally careful in watching her every step. So, as they walked at an easy pace along the broad, curving road, flanked with occasional stone balustrades surmounted by urns gay with geraniums and small yellow-striped cactus, he gave her the full story of his recent interview. When he had done she said with a shrug:

"He really must be crazy to have thought that you might pay him twelve hundred pounds to leave me alone."

"Oh, I don't know. Most people have the idea that popular authors make enormous sums. It isn't true, of course: few of them earn as much as most Harley Street specialists—let alone a leading barrister. Still, he probably believes that my Mama could lay her hand on a thousand or so without batting an eyelid."

"But even if she could, what can possibly lead him to suppose that she would be willing to part with a sum like that on my account?"

"You must remember that although Jules was educated in England he is very much a Frenchman, and has the typical Frenchman's outlook on women," John told her. "Custom and lack of inclination combine to prevent them from developing the sort of friendships that English people like ourselves enjoy in the normal course of events. They regard women solely from the point of view of sex, and divide them into two categories—those whose circumstances readily invite an amusing love-affair, and those who are in no position to offer such an attraction. To anyone of Jules' nationality and class it is unthinkable that a chap like myself might have an affair with a young unmarried girl; because she falls into category number two. It is not entirely a matter of principle that restrains them from entering on such affairs, but also because they would be bored to tears. They regard it as essential that their mistresses should be sexually experienced and take the matter as lightly as they do themselves, so that they run no danger of becoming permanently entangled. Therefore, Jules would argue that, since I should get little fun out of seducing you, and landing myself with a packet of trouble afterwards, the only reason for my interest in you must be that I want to marry you."

"Surely he can't think that? We . . . of course it seems much longer, but we have known one another only a few days."

"He is probably not aware that I arrived here only on Monday; and for all he knows we might have already met before you left England."

"But even if you were keen on me, it is unlikely that your mother would be willing to fork out twelve hundred pounds. Anyhow, until something had been definitely settled and we had become engaged."

"I don't know so much about that. From the French point of view such a payment might be regarded as a lever to clinch the deal, and more or less part of a contract by which you agreed to marry me."

"I have always thought that in France it was the other way about, and that in a marriage contract it was the girl's parents who had to put up the money."

"Ah, but you've forgotten that you are an heiress. If your old man owns a controlling interest in Beddows Agricultural Tractors he must be worth a packet; and you are an only child. As Jules would see it, for my mother to put up twelve hundred to get you for me as a wife would be a jolly good bet."

Christina laughed. "It is one I wouldn't care to make. As I've told you, I really know awfully little about my father's private life. I don't think he has married again, but he might have. Anyhow, by his mistresses he may have had children of whom he is much fonder than he is of me. It is quite on the cards that when he dies the bulk of his money will go to people I have never heard of, and that he will leave me only a few hundreds a year to keep me from actual want."

While they were talking they had reached the little village of Dramont, and after walking over to look at the memorial, which commemorated the landing of the Americans there on August the 15th, 1944, they took the by-road that led up into the Esterel.

Their way now lay through the pine forest, which here and there had clearings in it of a few acres devoted to intensive cultivation. In most of them stood a lemon-washed farmhouse, and the land was occupied by crops of fruit, vegetables and flowers, all growing on series of terraces which had been laboriously constructed out of the hillside and were kept in place by walls of rough-hewn stone. On some there were rows of orange, lemon and tangerine trees, or short bare-stalked vines, on others globe artichokes, young beans and *primeurs* of all sorts for the Paris markets; while many were small fields of carnations, grown in a four-feet-high wooden trellis-work which enabled long mats of split canes to be rolled over them at night to protect them from the frost.

The going was stiff; so they did not talk very much, and then only of trivial things, such as the thrifty care with which the peasants cultivated every available inch of their soil, and of how utterly different the scene was from any that could be found in England at that time of year. In an hour they had covered barely three miles, but they then came out on the summit of the lowest foothill of the range, and paused there to admire the view. Dramont was now hidden from them by the tops of the trees, but beyond it, no great distance from the shore, they could see the little Golden Isle with its pseudo-feudal tower, and to either side of the twin capes of Agay the Mediterranean stretched away in an infinity of blue.

To one side of the road lay an orchard of ancient olive-trees, their gnarled trunks and grey-green leaves standing out in charming contrast to the yellower green of the short grass in which they had been planted a century or more ago. In the hush of mid-day, with sunlight dappling the grass through leaves unstirred by a breath of wind, it was a truly sylvan spot, having that spell-like quality which made them almost expect that a nymph or faun would peep out at them from behind one of the trees at any moment. Instinctively feeling that they could find no more delightful place in which to picnic, they turned into the orchard without exchanging a word, and, sitting down under one of the trees a little way from the road, unpacked their lunch.

When they had satisfied their first hunger, John asked Christina what sort of a time she had had at her finishing school in Paris, and after describing the life there she summed it up as more interesting but not so much fun as that she had

had in Somerset. In Paris the only lessons had been French grammar and the study of the Arts; the girls had been taken to the opera, the *Salon*, concerts, classical plays, the best films, special dress shows for *jeunes filles*, the museums and all the places of historical interest. She had enjoyed all that; but the mistresses had been much stricter and the girls less friendly than at the school of domestic science, and she had greatly missed the fine old mansion that housed it, with its park, swimming-pool and lovely garden; the paper-chases and cricket in the summer, and in winter the bicycle rides on Saturdays into the local town for tea and shopping.

John had never been in Somerset, but he knew Paris well, particularly the intellectual side of life there; so they talked for a while of painting, ballet and books. The extent of her knowledge, and especially the wideness of her reading, rather surprised him; but she explained that never having been home for the holidays she had had much more time than most girls in which to devour her favourite authors and dip into all sorts of unusual subjects.

In turn she asked him about his work, and he told her that on the whole he thoroughly enjoyed it; but that like every other business it had its irritating moments. As was natural, he lamented the passing of the great house, which had given such marvellous scope to the interior decorators of the Georgian age and been so hideously abused by those working a hundred years later. In the previous year his directors had given him a real plum—a Canadian millionaire who wanted a permanent home in London, fully equipped regardless of expense, but did not wish to be bothered with any of the details, or even be informed of the colours of the rooms, until he walked into it; but that sort of thing did not happen often. Most of his clients were people compelled by taxation to move from country houses that their families had occupied for generations into medium-sized West End flats. The majority of them had taste; so they were usually not difficult to deal with, and the major trouble in such cases was generally that the furniture they wished to retain was much too big for the rooms; so it often spoiled the final *décor*. The real headaches were the black marketeers and other *nouveaux riches*, who went round on their own, buying ghastly suites or fake antiques, guaranteed to make any interior look garish or pretentious. Yet he declared that he would not for the world be in any other business, as every day brought its new problem that kept his mind alert, and now and then an achievement which gave him real artistic satisfaction.

"Do you ever have to do kitchens?" Christina enquired.

"Yes, sometimes."

"How many sinks do you put in a new scullery?"

"Why, one, of course," he replied promptly. "In these days of small staffs no one would want more."

"Then if I ever need a kitchen designed I shan't employ you," she laughed. "It makes the work infinitely lighter if one has two sinks side by side; and they should both be on a much higher level than most architects place them, to save backache from bending unnecessarily far over."

"It is certainly a thought," he admitted in a slightly chastened tone. "I suppose you got the idea from that domestic place you were at?"

"Yes: our kitchen expert had learned her stuff in America, where most wives have to do their own housework. It is scandalous how far behind we are in Britain; and in France things are even worse, in spite of the good cooking. For years past all housework has continued to be far more laborious than it need be. If I ever have a home of my own I shall install all the new labour-saving devices. I'll have toe hollows instead of protruding bases along the floor level of the cupboards, so that the paint is not knocked off, compo-rubber sinks and draining-boards to save breakage, laundry chutes, a mix-and-whip, an electric dish-washer, and one of those lovely things to throw the garbage into that chews up even bones."

"And the Queen Anne teaspoons too, when some careless woman-in fails to notice them among the debris," John added with a smile, pleased at this opportunity to get in a return shot for hers about the sinks. All the same, he was impressed with her grasp of the subject, and went on jokingly, "We had better go into partnership. You could do all the expensive gadgets on the domestic side, while I crib ideas like the arrangement of those bookcases we saw at the de Grasses last night."

Her expression immediately became serious, and she asked, "Do you think there is any risk that they may try to get hold of me by force?"

"I doubt it," he replied with a confidence he was far from feeling. "In any case, you may be sure that we shall do our utmost to protect you. Still, it is a possibility that they might lure you away by some trick, and, as a matter of fact, while we were trudging up the hill, an hour back, I had an idea about that."

"Did you? Tell me what it was."

He hesitated a second. "Well, if by chance they did manage to entice you away, we shouldn't be on a very good wicket. I mean, if we had to go to the police and ask them to trace you, they would naturally want to know what authority we had for making such a request, particularly if things pointed to your having gone off of your own free will. They would get down to the job quickly enough if we were relatives of yours, but they might refuse to act at all if they took the view that, as we were only acquaintances, we had no right to stick our noses into your business."

"I see what you mean; but I don't see how that can be got over."

"It can be. I think the germ of the idea came into my mind when we were nattering about marriage. Mama and I could raise Cain, and get them running round in circles, if I could say that you were my fiancée."

Christina's big brown eyes were round with astonishment as she turned them on him. "You . . . you aren't making me a proposal of marriage, are you?"

He had been lying full length on the grass, but now he sat up and looked at her with a grin. "Sorry, but I'm afraid I'm not. Although I suppose it is presumptuous of me even to infer that I might have raised false hopes in your maidenly breast. I only had in mind that stupid old saying 'marriages are made in heaven and engagements to be broken'. Ours, if you thought the idea worth pursuing, would be only for the 'duration of the conflict', and afterwards we should go our own separate ways, seeking more suitable partners to dig our hooks into in earnest. What do you say?"

"It is a bit shattering to have all one's girlish dreams about first proposals rendered farcical like this," she said, half seriously. "But I do see your point about an engagement giving you the right to get a hue and cry going, should I disappear. I'd feel bound to make it a condition, though, that we should tell your mother that there is nothing serious between us."

"Of course. And Conky Bill, too. I wouldn't like either of them to think later that I had bilked you. But we ought to put up a bit of a show to establish our state of bliss in the minds of the retainers."

She gave him a rather dubious look. "What exactly do you mean by that?"

"Why, the usual concrete evidence that you are about to be made into an honest woman." As he spoke, he drew a gold signet ring from the little finger of his left hand and held it up. "Here! Let me slip this on your engagement finger. It was my father's, and I regard it as one of my few treasures. So for God's sake don't lose it. You can flash it in front of that old Catalan woman of yours and Angèle. Tell them that I mean to buy you something more spectacular when we get home, but that in the meantime it is the symbol of my undying love."

"All right then," she laughed, and held out her left hand. It was shapely, but large, and he had considerable difficulty in working the ring over her knuckle. At length he succeeded, and as it slipped down to the waist of the finger he muttered:

"That's done it; but you have got big hands for a girl, haven't you?"

She flushed to the roots of her hair and retorted angrily, "Yes! And large feet, and a snub nose; so you're jolly lucky not to have got me for keeps."

His eyes showed surprise and immediate contrition. "Damn it all, Christina!" he exclaimed. Then, putting out both hands, he took her by the shoulders and looked straight in her face. "I didn't mean to be rude. I swear I didn't! You've got the loveliest eyes I've ever seen, and if you only knew it, that funny nose of yours is one of your best features. It gives you an individuality that awfully few girls have got."

"You don't mean that. You are just trying to be nice to me now, to make up for having been unintentionally nasty."

"I do mean it. And your lips are as soft as any I have ever kissed." He smiled suddenly. "You know, when one gets engaged to a girl it is usual to kiss her. That's always done, even in boy-and-girl affairs that are not intended to come to anything." Next second, before she had a chance to resist, he slipped his arms round her, pulled her to him, and kissed her firmly on the mouth.

For a long moment she lay passive in his embrace, then he withdrew his lips, smiled down at her and said, "You are not doing your best, darling. That's not a patch on the kisses you gave me the other night."

Instantly she pulled away from him. Tears sprang to her eyes, and she cried, "How horrid of you to remind me of that!"

"Why?" he asked, momentarily at a loss. "You are the same girl, and there is nothing to be ashamed of in what you did."

"I was not myself then, and you know it."

He gave a little shrug. "If you take my advice, then, should a chap ever make love to you seriously and you want him for a husband, you will let him kiss you only when you are, as you put it, not yourself."

Christina's cheeks were scarlet as she murmured unhappily, "But it isn't normal. It's not decent. No girl could do that sort of thing and not be ashamed of it afterwards—at least not until she was married."

Smiling slightly, John shook his head. "My dear, I'm sure you really believe that, but you are talking the most utter rot. I give you my word of honour that grown-up people who are going places together nearly always kiss that way—even when they haven't the faintest intention of getting married. There is no harm in it, and it's part of the fun of life. You might just as well say that, because as children we have no urge to smoke or drink, it is wicked of us to take to it when we get older. Learning to kiss properly, and enjoying it, is just one of the normal processes of becoming a man or woman. You did enjoy being kissed by me the other night, didn't you?"

"Yes," Christina whispered. "I . . . I . . . of course I did."

"Then stop being a baby, and let me kiss you again." As he spoke, he drew her gently into his arms and this time kissed her parted lips.

From the distance came the faint clink of metal against small stones as a peasant hoed one of his terrace plots, and once a seagull circled overhead; but no one came to disturb them. John sat with his back against the bole of the tree, his right arm round Christina, and her head lay on his shoulder. Few places could have been nearer the ideal for a first lesson in kissing, and once Christina let herself go she proved an apt pupil; but John was careful to keep matters on the level of a game not to be taken seriously. He had set out to take the girl's mind off the grim anxieties which he knew must lie at the back of it. That he had succeeded was clear, and he was thoroughly enjoying the process, but he said nothing which she could take as an indication that he was falling in love with her, as he feared that being so inexperienced she might think him in earnest and later, perhaps, suffer from disappointment.

As the sunny afternoon wore on they became drowsy and, still embraced, fell asleep. John was the first to wake and, glancing at his watch, saw that it was after five o'clock. With a gentle kiss he aroused Christina, and said:

"Wake up, my pretty. It's time for us to be going. We ought to have started before, really."

As she disentangled herself and began to tidy her hair she shivered and replied, "Yes, I suppose we ought. Although the sun is still shining, it has turned quite cold."

"At this time of the year it always does at this hour. The sun loses its power and the wind changes, bringing the icy currents down from the snow on top of the mountains. More elderly people die of pneumonia on this coast than anywhere else in the world. They only have to once forget to take an overcoat with them if they are going to be out after five o'clock, and they've had it. I don't wonder you're chilly in that light frock. Come on now! We'll step out and get your circulation going."

She stood up and brushed down her skirt, while he crammed the empty bottle and glasses back into the basket. Two minutes later they were on their way down the hill, but its steepness prevented their pace from being much faster than that at which they had come up; so it was well past six when they arrived back at Christina's villa to collect the things she had packed that morning.

John carried the suitcase across, and in Molly's sitting-room they found her with Colonel Verney. He was a tall, rather thin, man, and, as he stood up to be introduced to Christina, would have appeared even taller but for a slight stoop that was habitual to him. His hair was going grey, parted in the centre, and brushed smoothly back. His face was longish, with a firm mouth and determined chin; but the other features were dominated by the big aggressive nose that had earned him the nickname of Conky Bill—or, as most of his friends called him for short, C. B. His eyebrows were thick and prawn-like. Below them his grey eyes had the curious quality of seeming to look right through one. He usually spoke very quietly, in an almost confidential tone, and gave the pleasing impression that there were very few things out of which he did not derive a certain amount of amusement.

To Christina he said, "Well, young lady, I hear you are being pursued by bad men, but I usually eat a couple for breakfast; so you must lead me to them. Perhaps we can have a little talk after dinner, then I'll have a better idea how to set my traps."

Christina smiled in reply. "I don't think there is much I can tell you that I haven't already told Mrs. Fountain, but I'll answer any questions you like."

Taking her by the arm, Molly said, "Come along, my dear. Last night we had to pop you into bed just anyhow; so I'll come up with you to your room and see that you have everything you want."

C. B. and John had already smiled a greeting at one

another; so the latter followed the two women out of the room with Christina's bag. When he returned two minutes later, the tall Colonel said:

"Well, young feller! How's the world been treating you?"

"I've no complaints, sir, thanks," John replied cheerfully. "And it's very nice to have you with us again."

"To tell the truth, I was delighted when your mother rang up. I was due to spend the next few days getting out a lot of tiresome statistics, and it gave me just the excuse I needed to unload the job on to one of my stooges."

"I'm very glad you could come, sir. This seems a most extraordinary business, and I can't make head or tail of it."

"You mean the Black Magic slant to it, eh? Well, I don't suppose you would. Those boys are experts at keeping their lights under bushels; so the general public rarely hears anything about them—except from an occasional article appearing in the press, and they generally write that off as nonsense."

"May I give you another drink, sir? Then perhaps you would tell me something about it."

"Do, John." C. B. began to refill a very clean, long-stemmed pipe. "Mine's a gin-and-French. But why so much of the 'sir' all of a sudden? I know I'm an old fogey, but you've known me long enough to call me C. B. You always used to when you were a little chap."

John grinned. "Ah! But I've done my military service since then, and we were taught that we should always call the Colonel 'sir' at least three times before slapping him on the back."

"Not a bad precept either. Come and sit down, and tell me what you make of this girl Christina, and the set-up next door."

"I don't think there is much to tell about her villa." John handed the Colonel his drink, then perched himself on the sofa. "The old gardener who looks after the place and caretakes when it is empty has been there for years. Maria, the Catalan *bonne*, is a rather surly type, but as she was engaged by Christina's father there doesn't seem any reason to suppose that there is anything fishy about her. We know definitely now that the de Grasses are simply acting as the Canon's agents, but——"

"How do you know?" put in C. B. quietly.

"Because Jules de Grasse told me so himself," John replied, and went on to give an account of the visit he had received that morning.

"Sounds good enough—on the face of it," commented the Colonel. "All right. Carry on."

"I was only going to add that, while we haven't the ghost of an idea why the Canon wants to get hold of Christina, I believe we would be more than half-way to solving the whole problem if we could find out what is wrong with the girl herself."

"Good reasoning, John. Your mother is convinced that it is a case of possession: but what do you think?"

"I'm damned if I know. There can be no question about these changes in her personality. I've seen them for myself. During the day-time she is a nice kid—straightforward, good-natured, and as far as worldliness goes you wouldn't put her age as much over seventeen. But at night she becomes utterly different—bold, sensual as a cat and, according to her own account, evil-minded and malicious. If we were still living in mediaeval times I suppose one would regard possession by the Devil as a perfectly reasonable explanation; but it is a bit much to swallow in these days, isn't it?"

"For you, perhaps; but not for me. I've seen scores of such cases, John; and at this very moment there are hundreds of people in our asylums whose apparent lunacy is really due to an evil spirit—or, to call it by its right name, which I prefer, a demon—having got into their bodies."

"Well," John gave a faint smile, "as you and Mother are both so positive that such things still happen I suppose I must accept it that they do. But if what you say about the asylums is correct, why is no attempt ever made to get the devils out of all these poor wretches?"

"Because the modern medicos refuse to recognize the facts. Even if they did they wouldn't know how to set about it; and for that matter very few other people would either."

"When Mother and I were talking about it last night, she seemed to think you would."

"Lord bless you, no! I'm no exorcist. I've never dabbled in Magic—Black or White—in my life. I regard it as much too dangerous."

"Does that mean you won't be able to do anything for Christina?"

"That depends." Conky Bill's voice became low and slightly conspiratorial. "If I can get a half-Nelson on the Black who has bewitched her, I could. Even a few facts about minor breaches of the law might enable me to pull a fast one. There is nothing that these birds dislike so much as the police taking an interest in their affairs, and given something to go on there would be a good chance for me to exert enough pressure on them to get the spell taken off."

"You think Mother's right, then, about her having been bewitched?"

"I am accepting that theory for the moment."

"But why in the world should they pick on a girl like Christina? She has never been mixed up in spiritualism, or anything of that kind."

"Ask me another, young feller. But I expect we shall find that there is a tie-up of some sort. On the other hand, any girl who has so few intimate relationships is always particularly vulnerable. Nine times out of ten they are the ones who disappear; because they have no friends and relatives to start a hue and cry about them. If those people at the place where she was at in Paris had been crooks, she might have been shipped off to Buenos Aires, and her father would have been none the wiser for months afterwards."

"It looks to me as if he got in first; and it is the very fact that he got wise to it that something pretty nasty was being planned against her that accounts for her present situation."

C. B. nodded. "Yes, you've got something there."

"Do you think their object is to White Slave her?"

"No; although if they did get hold of her she would be a darn' sight better off in a brothel."

"What exactly is their game, then?"

"They are always on the hunt for neophytes. Satan is a greedy master, and to retain his favour they need a constant supply of new bodies to defile and souls to corrupt. The more victims they can offer up, the greater becomes their power."

"Apart from that, is Mother right in what she told me last night, about their being a menace to all established Governments that stand for freedom and decency?"

"Yes, if she was speaking of the high-direction of the show, she was. Of course, there are lots of little outer circles, or covens, as they are called. They are generally run by ordinary crooks who have muscled-in on the game. Most of the time their object is blackmail. They get hold of paederasts, lesbians and over-sexed people of all ages, and provide them with the chance to indulge their secret vices. Then in due course they put on the squeeze and make quite a bit of money by it. Pedalling dope is another of their activities and generally proves a pretty useful side-line."

C. B. paused to fiddle with his pipe, then went on, "But the big shots are right up and away above that sort of thing. In most cases I doubt if they even know the chiefs of the little covens. Anyhow, they leave it to their subordinates to supervise them and pick likely lads to form new ones. Their job is to use occult forces to destroy good influences. Their usual line is to cause the illness or death at a time of crisis of the key man who might be able to tide it over; or, alternatively, to produce conditions which will favour some unscrupulous individual getting control of the situation. The best example I can give you of an ace-high Black Magician in modern times is the monk Rasputin. He did more than all the Bolsheviks put together to bring about the Russian revolution; and I don't need to tell you the extent of the evil that has brought to Russia, and may yet bring to the rest of the world."

Molly rejoined them at that moment, and as John got up to get her a drink she enquired how he had enjoyed his day.

"Oh, all right," he replied casually. "We found a nice place to picnic, but as a matter of fact we slept for most of the afternoon."

"Dear me, you must have been bored then." With a smile she turned to C. B. "This business really is rather hard luck on Johnny. Three days of his holiday have gone already, and he hasn't had a moment yet to look up his old friends or hit any of the high spots along the coast. I think he is being very sweet to devote all his time to this poor girl."

"Perhaps he doesn't find her as boring as you think," C. B. smiled back; and, standing up, he carefully removed a long brown hair from the open collar of John's pale blue sweat shirt.

"Well played, Sherlock," John laughed. "But don't let that little souvenir give either of you any wrong ideas. It signifies only the sealing of the sort of deal that Hitler used to call 'A Pact of Eternal Friendship' when it suited his book to enter into a political understanding with someone for a few weeks." He told them then about his phony engagement to Christina, and the reason that had prompted him to suggest it.

"Now I'm here, I'll be able to get the French police moving, should we need them," C. B. commented, "but all the same it was quite a sound idea."

Then Molly added, "Christina showed me your father's ring and explained why she was wearing it directly we got upstairs. She told me, too, about Count Jules' visit after I left this morning."

"John has just given me particulars of that." C. B. stretched out his long legs, and went on thoughtfully, "In view of young de Grasse's threat, I think we ought to set a watch to-night, just in case they attempt a snatch. We could put an armchair on the landing outside her room. I need very little sleep, so I can easily sit up reading until two. Then if John relieved me until five, I'd come on again then. By seven your *bonne* will be about, so I could get another couple of hours shut-eye before breakfast. How about it, John; are you game to do the three hours before dawn?"

"Sure. Longer if you like. After all, now she is my fiancée I don't have to stay outside her door, do I?"

"Any nonsense of that kind, and I'll pack you off back to England," his mother said severely.

He gave a mock sigh and shot an injured look at the Colonel. "You see, sir, how old-fashioned she is in her ideas about the latitude that should be allowed to engaged couples.

I do wish you would try your hand at educating her up a bit for me."

Both of them picked up the innuendo. C. B. let his gaze fall to his big feet. Molly flushed and said quickly, "I really came down to say that if you want to change to-night, it is time we went up."

The Colonel levered himself out of his chair. "It is just as you like, my dear. As I always have a tub before dinner, I find it no more trouble, and considerably more enlivening to the mind, to get into *le smoking*, as they call it out here."

"I know you do," she smiled, "so while you are with us I have put dinner back to eight-thirty. But you and John will have to share the guests' bathroom, and it is nearly half-past seven now."

Finishing up their drinks, they followed her out. An hour later they reassembled.

John was first down, and having switched on the lights he mixed another round of cocktails. When his mother joined him he noted with secret amusement that she was considerably more made-up than usual, and was wearing a very pretty frock that he had not seen before. C. B. came in a moment later, gave her one appraising glance, and said:

"Molly, my dear, you're looking positively stunning. If it wasn't for John, here, I'd stake my oath that you couldn't be a day over thirty."

She gave a happy laugh. "Well, they say a woman is as old as she looks and a man is as old as he feels, so perhaps we had better leave it at that. But you're not looking so bad yourself. I don't wonder you like to change in the evenings. Dark, well-cut clothes instead of those baggy things you wear in the day-time take at least ten years off you."

"You sweet children," purred John, as he handed them their cocktails. "How I wish I were your age; then I should have so many new experiences to look forward to."

"You insolent pup!" C. B. made a pretence of cuffing him; and they continued laughing together until the gong went.

"Christina has been an awfully long time dressing," Molly remarked, "but we will give her a few minutes' grace."

They shared out the remaining contents of the shaker, but still Christina had not appeared; so Molly said to John, "I think you had better slip up and find out how much longer your fiancée is going to spend titivating herself for your benefit."

"Right-oh!" he nodded, and, leaving the room, ran upstairs. A minute later he came pounding down again, shouting as he came, "She isn't there! Her room's empty! She's gone!"

CHAPTER VIII

KIDNAPPED?

As JOHN burst into the room, C. B. gave him a rueful smile. "Seems we've been caught on the hop. Any sign of a struggle?"

"I don't think so: I didn't notice any."

"We should have heard it if there had been," said Molly.

"I doubt if we would have taken any notice, while we were up there dressing, unless she had let out a shout; and we might not even have heard that during the past ten minutes while we've been joking together down here."

"She must have been gone longer than that. Her evening frock is still on the bed. Come up and see." Turning, John hurried from the room.

"After you, my dear." C. B. politely stood aside for Molly. He had not so far raised his voice, and his movements, although actually as quick as those of the others, appeared quite leisurely.

Upstairs they halted together in the doorway of the big room at the back of the house that Christina had been given. At first glance there was nothing to suggest that she had been forcibly removed; neither was there any paper prominently displayed, which might have been a note left by her, giving a reason for her having left of her own accord.

"I suppose she *has* gone?" C. B. murmured. "Better look in the bathroom, though. I've known young women faint in hot baths before now."

Swinging round, Molly ran to a door on the opposite side of the passage and thrust it open. The bathroom was empty. Hastily she tried the W.C. next door, but that was empty too. Her face showed her distress as she cried:

"This is entirely my fault! It has been dark for well over an hour. It was criminal of me to forget the way her personality changes at nightfall, and that she might take it into her head to go off somewhere. I should never have left her on her own.

I could so easily have arranged for her to have changed in my room with me."

"I'm just as much to blame, Mumsie," John said miserably. "I promised her this afternoon that I'd take care of her; and now I've let her down the very first time that I ought to have been on the look-out for Jules."

"If anyone is to blame, it is the old professional," C. B. put in quietly.

"Nonsense!" Molly protested. "You had only just come on the scene."

"For God's sake don't let's stand here arguing." John's voice was sharp with anxiety. "We must get after her. Come on! Hurry!"

"Half a mo', young feller. So far there is nothing to point to the de Grasses having snatched her, and it doesn't always pay to jump to conclusions. Your mother may be right. Knowing we are on the side of the angels she may have taken a sudden dislike to us after sundown, and gone back to her own villa. Just step over and see, will you?"

"Right-oh!" John ran down the stairs and the others followed more slowly.

When they reached the hall, C. B. said:

"Got a telephone directory, Molly? There is a number I want to look up. John may find her at her villa, but I doubt it. My own bet is that the de Grasses have got her. Young Count Jules told John this morning that they had undertaken to get her to England before the 6th and to-day is the 3rd; so they haven't much of a time margin."

Molly found him the directory and he began to flick through it, but went on talking: "That is why I felt pretty certain they would try something to-night, and suggested keeping watch. It was stupid of me, though, not to anticipate that they might get to work immediately darkness made the girl vulnerable to suggestion."

"No, Bill; you are being unfair to yourself. No one would expect kidnappers to stage a raid while all of us were moving about the house. They would wait till we were asleep."

"You are wrong there, Molly my love. The changing hour

is a very favourite one with cat burglars. They shin up a drain-pipe, cling on there, and take an occasional peep through the window of the room which they intend to burgle. Then, when its occupant goes along to the bathroom, or has finished dressing and goes downstairs, they nip in and do their stuff. If they have to make a certain amount of noise, it doesn't matter, because if the servants hear it they think it is being made by their employers, or one of the guests who is still upstairs changing."

"Do you think, then, that they got Christina out by way of the window?"

"No. The dressing-table had not been pushed back out of place, and the blind was still down. It isn't easy to pull a blind down from outside; and, anyway, why should they bother?"

"Perhaps they got her out by the window in the passage. Surely we should have heard them if they had carried her downstairs?"

"Not necessarily, provided they were fairly careful about it. As I've just said, with a servant getting dinner, and people bathing and banging cupboards all over the place, no one takes any notice of noises at that hour. Besides, it is possible that she went because she wanted to, and walked quietly out on her own."

C. B. broke off for a second. "Ah, here we are—Malouet, Alphonse. Do you remember him?"

"By name, yes. Wasn't he the Inspector of Police who put up such a good show in Nice during the Resistance?"

"That's him. The old boy retired a couple of years ago. Apparently he is now living out at Cimiez. The address looks like that of a flat in one of the big hotels there that they have converted into apartments since the war. Although he is no longer on the active list, he will be able to pull more guns for me than some bird I don't know, if we have to call in the police."

Flicking over the leaves again, he added, "In case we can't get hold of him to-night, I had better look up the number of the Prefecture at Nice. That is the top police H.Q. in this part of the world, and in a case like this it is a waste of time going to the small fry." He had just found the second number when John came rushing in. Still breathless from having run up the steep garden path, he panted:

"I was right! The de Grasses have got her. Jules carried her off from her own villa about an hour ago. Come on! I'll get out the car!"

"Steady on!" C. B. admonished him. "Let's have such details as you can give us first."

Between gasps to get his breath back, John reported, "Old Maria says Christina came in at about a quarter to eight. She ran upstairs and came down again two minutes later. She was carrying a small suitcase and immediately went out with it. But she returned almost at once. Maria didn't see her come back, but saw the lights go on in the sitting-room. From her kitchen she can see the glow they throw from . . . from the side window of the sitting-room on to the trees in the garden; so . . . so she looked in to see who was there. It was Christina and a chap who answers the description of Jules. They were arguing about something. She must have given him a drink and had one with him. Their glasses are still on the table. Maria didn't hear them leave. But she doesn't think they could have remained there much more than ten minutes. She happened to glance at her clock just before the sitting-room lights were switched off again, and it had not yet gone eight."

"Good! Now we at least have a line of enquiry we can pursue." C. B. picked up the telephone.

"What are you going to do?" John asked impatiently.

"Ring up the police—or rather an old friend of mine who is an ex-police officer of exceptional ability."

"Then for God's sake hurry! They must be nearly at St. Tropez by now. If we don't start at once we may not arrive in time to prevent him from putting off to sea with her in that damn' yacht."

C. B. gave the number of Inspector Malouet's apartment, then covered the receiver with his hand. "Listen, partner. I'm not going to let you run your head into a hornet's nest, or land up in a cell at a French police station either, if I can prevent it.

We are by no means certain yet that Jules is taking her to the yacht, and——"

"Where the hell else would he take her?"

"Maybe to some hide-out anywhere between Nice and Toulon. There must be plenty of places along the coast where he has pals who would keep her locked up for the night. Remember, he has got to get her back to England by the 6th, and he couldn't possibly do that by sea. Getting her on to the yacht could be only a temporary measure anyhow. He probably means to drug her, then have her flown home."

"Still, the fact that he tried to get her on the yacht last night is the only line we have to go on."

"Agreed; and we'll draw that covert as soon as I've made this call."

"Can't you telephone your police friend later—if we fail to find her on the yacht?"

"No, we must get this chap moving as soon as we possibly can. You don't seem to realize what we are up against. That yacht is private property, just as much as if it were a house. You can't go busting your way aboard like a bandit. If you did, de Grasse's boys would be fully entitled to slog you on the head, then hand you over to the police. You have to be able to show justification for any act of that sort."

"C. B., you make me tired! What better justification could we have than knowing that poor kid has been carried off by thugs?"

Molly had never known her son display such rudeness to an older man. It crossed her mind that, *blasé* about girls as he liked to think himself, Christina, by striking an entirely new note, might have bowled him over. That could explain both the extreme agitation he was showing and his lapse of manners. Nevertheless, she spoke with unusual sharpness:

"That will do, John. Colonel Verney has not wasted an unnecessary moment; and he is the best judge of what should be done."

"Sorry!" he muttered. "But I'm damned if I'll let Jules get away with this. I'm damned if I will."

At that moment the telephone began to make shrill whistling sounds. C. B. jangled the receiver, said, "'Allo! 'Allo!"

and repeated the number, but nothing happened the other end; so he turned his smiling grey eyes on John.

"What I meant was some legal, or at least moral, justification. Strictly speaking, we are not entitled to take any action ourselves, and should turn the whole job over to the police. If there had been signs of a struggle in her bedroom, or old Maria had seen her hauled from her villa by a couple of woolly-headed negroes, we'd have some excuse for taking a hand ourselves; but as it is . . ."

Again the telephone made odd noises, but again no satisfactory result followed; so he went on, "As it is, she walked out of this house of her own accord, and left her own villa a quarter of an hour later with Jules. He is, for all practical purposes, a respectable citizen, and as far as we know she went with him perfectly willingly; so if you butted in, from the legal point of view you wouldn't have a leg to stand on."

"I'm her fiancé, aren't I?" John demanded truculently.

"Yes. And I give you full marks now for your foresight in thinking up that bright idea. In France, as marriage is so mixed up with cash and property, people take a much more serious view of a fiancé's rights than they do in England. But even that would not condone your breaking into what amounts to a private dwelling, without obvious cause. It will be a help, though, in getting a search warrant if we can bring evidence to the effect that she was definitely taken on to the yacht."

Once more noises came from the telephone, and this time it proved to be the number that C. B. had called. With a nod to the others, he said, "Our luck is in. It is Malouet himself." Then he spoke for several moments in his own particular brand of French. It was good French from the point of view of fluency, but it did not sound good, as he spoke very quietly, and without using any of the ejaculations or inflections of the voice which are such a feature of that language.

When he hung up, he said, "As you may have noticed, I had to be a bit obscure; but the old boy tumbled to my meaning. He confirms my own view of the matter. In the remote chance of our happening on somebody prepared to vouch for it that they saw Christina either taken aboard by force, or carried aboard unconscious, the authorities will not hold it against us if we force our way on to the yacht and insist on being taken to her. But if such evidence as we can get is to the effect that she went aboard of her own free will, the only way in which we can insure against a nasty come-back is for John, as her fiancé, to swear an affidavit, stating that he believes her to have been lured aboard for an illegal purpose; then we will be granted a search warrant."

"So *that* is all we have been wasting a precious ten minutes to be told," said John sarcastically. "Why didn't you get on to your office in Whitehall and ask them to send us a couple of hundred forms to fill up?"

"Johnny!" his mother exclaimed. "You will apologize at once!"

"Sorry, C. B.," he murmured a trifle sullenly. "But for goodness' sake, let's get going and *do* something."

C. B. gave him a good-natured pat on the shoulder. "That's all right, John. Now you can run and get the car out."

"I'll just slip upstairs," said Molly.

John gave her a quick look. "Going to collect the armaments, Mumsie? Good! I'll come with you."

"What's that?" exclaimed C. B., as they ran across the hall. Then he called after them, "If you are thinking of taking any of those museum pieces of yours, Molly, scrap the idea. Otherwise you can count me out."

Both of them ignored him, and as John ran up the stairs close on his mother's heels he muttered, "Funny he should say that, isn't it? Just the line I took with you last night; but now things are very different."

With a sigh C. B. decided he had better check up on them. His long legs moving effortlessly, he took the stairs three at a time, and entered Molly's work-room just as they went down on their knees in front of a cupboard. She pulled it open, revealing on the bottom shelf an array of highly-dangerous objects. Among them were pistols, bowie-knives, grenades, a garotter's cord, several stilettos and coshes, a knuckle-duster and a stick of gelignite. Looking down between their shoulders, he asked:

"Has that Mills bomb still got its detonator In?"

"Of course!" Molly replied with an air of pride. "Otherwise it would not be a perfect specimen."

"You crazy woman! Some day a maid will have the bright idea of cleaning it, and when she pulls the pin out it will go off."

"Oh no. I'm much too fond of my little collection to let anyone clean it except myself," she replied lightly.

John was quickly cramming 9-mm. bullets into the spare magazine of the larger of the two automatics. C. B. stooped and with a swift, unexpected grab picked up the weapon. "Nothing doing, partner," he said firmly, pushing it into his own pocket. "If you insist on risking a spell in a French prison, that is your look-out; but I dig my toes in at your taking a running jump to land on the guillotine."

Turning an angry face up to him, John protested, "You said yourself that if anyone saw her shanghaied we could bust the yacht open without waiting for the police. It's only common sense to take a weapon of *some* kind."

Stooping again, C. B. selected a light cosh. It was a beautiful thing, about twelve inches long, its head egg-shaped and filled with lead, its stock a thin nine-inch steel spring, the whole being covered with dull black leather. "Here, take this then. But don't lam anyone on the head with it; a blow on the shoulder would be quite enough to land most people in hospital for a week."

"Thanks," John murmured a little ungraciously; and he began to stuff it first in one pocket, then in another, in an endeavour to find a suitable place for it.

"Ram it down the front of your trousers," C. B. advised. "Provided you don't push it too far, the top end will keep it from slipping, and it won't prevent you from sitting down in comfort. It is easy to draw from there, and if anyone frisks you for a weapon, in that position there is quite a good chance of it being overlooked."

As John tucked away the cosh, C. B. turned to Molly. Relieving her of the smaller automatic, which she had been just about to slip in her bag, he said in a tone of mild reproof,

"Now, ducks, I really can't allow you to go around shooting people." But slipping out the magazine he handed it back to her and added, "Lord forbid that I should rob you of all your fun. You can point it at anyone you like now, and it's a small beer to a magnum of champagne that it will prove every bit as effective."

"Oh, really, Bill!" she pleaded. "Can't I have just one bullet in the chamber, in case I get a chance to fire it? I do so want to see how much light the flash gives."

"No. I'd rather you took a pot-shot at me in the garden to-morrow night, if you must have a human target to aim at."

"You *are* rude! You infer that I couldn't hit a haystack."

"Come *on!*" cried John angrily, from the doorway. "By nattering like this you two are chucking away our only chance of saving Christina."

C. B. glanced at his watch. "It is just twenty-two minutes since we discovered her disappearance. Not bad, considering I had to make a telephone-call to Nice. But we would have saved four minutes if you had gone to get the car out when I asked you to, instead of abetting your mother in her whimsies about weapons. Get cracking now."

John dashed downstairs. The others followed him and collected their coats from the hall. As they walked down the garden path, C. B. said to Molly, "I'm taking you only as a spare driver, if we have to leave the car. I'll have my hands quite full enough preventing that boy of yours from sticking out his neck. You are under orders again. Is that clear?"

"Yes, sir," said Molly, out of ancient habit and quite meekly.

Once they were in the car John lost not a second, and the moment they were under way he jammed his foot down on the accelerator. As they rounded the second corner they met one of the big auto-buses returning from the St. Raphael direction to Cannes and had to swerve violently to avoid it. Molly was thrown sideways on the back seat; C. B. stiffened his long legs and cried:

"Go easy, young feller, or you'll break all our necks!" Then he went on in his normal voice. "Don't get the idea that I am sitting down on the job, but the fact is that five minutes either way is unlikely to make much difference now. Try to consider our prospects dispassionately. Jules has the best part of an hour's start of us. If he meant to take her to the yacht and the crew were only waiting till he got her on board to put to sea, they will have sailed long before we get there. We couldn't have caught them, even if we had set off the moment we discovered her disappearance. On the other hand, he could not have been certain that he would succeed in getting hold of her, or if he did at what hour he would be able to pull it off; so the odds are that he would not have ordered his crew to stand by from half-past eight till dawn, and will have to collect them."

"That shouldn't take him long."

"It all depends how many of them there are and whereabouts they live when they are on shore. But that is not my main point: it is his mental attitude of which I am thinking. Once he has got her on board I see no reason at all why he should burst a blood vessel in getting the yacht out of harbour."

"He would hardly be such a fool as to gamble on our not learning of Christina's disappearance until to-morrow morning. She may even have told him that we were expecting her to dine with us."

"True, but what has he to fear if we do turn up? If we go on board he can have us thrown off again—that is unless we are accompanied by the police with a search warrant."

"How long do you reckon it would take us to get one?"

"As we have not got the ghost of a case, we should have one hell of a job in persuading the police that we had real cause for alarm. We should have to show great persistence and tell our story four or five times before we got high enough up to secure action. With waits between interviewing a series of unenthusiastic officials, that might take us anything up to three hours. Jules must know all about the slowness of police procedure when the applicant for help can produce no definite evidence that any crime has been committed; so up till about eleven o'clock he can afford to snap his fingers at us. Anyhow, that is my appreciation of the situation. Either the yacht has sailed already or we'll find when we get to St. Tropez that, like Drake, we'll have plenty of time for a game of bowls before we go into action."

"I suppose you are right," John admitted grudgingly. "I wish that I could take matters so calmly." But he moderated his pace a little, and did not let the car out full again until they were through St. Raphael and had entered the long flat stretch round the curve of the great bay. It was ten to ten when he jammed on the brakes and brought the car to a halt on the cobbles of St. Tropez harbour.

In summer, at that hour, it would still have been thronged with people, drinking both at the scores of tables outside the cafés on the waterfront and in the cabins of dozens of craft in the port itself. But it was too early in the year to sit outside at night, and the season for the small yacht owners had not yet begun.

Like most of the ports on that coast, the harbour formed a rectangle with tall, ancient houses on three sides of it. The basin was partially filled by several groups of shipping moored beam to beam. Most of them were fishing-boats, or sailing yachts that had been dismantled for the winter; a few were larger, fully-powered craft, although not of the size that millionaires had kept for luxury cruises in those waters before the war. Apart from riding lights, it was from the cabins of these bigger vessels that the only lights showing in the harbour came, but the landward end of it was lit by the windows of several cafés, which were still open and occupied by a sprinkling of people.

Scrambling out of the car, John glanced quickly up and down. Outside the cafés the broad quay was deserted, except for a group of three loungers standing some distance away on the edge of the pavement. In the uncertain light they looked like seamen, and he began to run towards them.

"Hi!" C. B. called after him. "Where are you off to?"

Slowing his pace, he called back over his shoulder, "I'm going to ask those chaps which the yacht is—if she's still in the harbour."

"No, you're not." In a few long strides C. B. caught up with him and added in his conspiratorial voice, "We don't want to let the whole town know our business. You go back to the car and leave this to me."

After giving the crestfallen John's arm a friendly squeeze, he walked on to the end of the block and entered a café on the corner. He was absent for about six minutes. When he returned, he said:

"She hasn't sailed yet; but you can't see her very well from here. Her berth is up near the entry to the port on the right-hand side; and from the description I was given we can't mistake her. I'm told there is a good little fish restaurant up there that will still be open, and I'm beginning to miss my dinner; so while we are waiting for developments I think we'll have a snack at it."

"Damn it, C. B.!" John exploded. "How can you be so heartless while that poor girl——"

"I know! While that poor girl is at the mercy of a double-dyed villain. Try to be your age, John. Count Jules' only interest in Christina is to get her to England and collect a nice wad of banknotes. The odds are that he is feeding her on asparagus and pêche Melba at the moment and that, in her present state of mind, she is thoroughly enjoying herself."

"But you spoke of 'waiting for developments'. Since the yacht's still here we mustn't waste a moment in finding out if she is on board. Why should we wait for anything?"

"Drive me to my chosen grazing ground, sonny, and I'll tell you on the way."

With an ill grace John got the car moving, and C. B. went on in a lower tone, "I didn't telephone old Malouet only to ask after his health. The police always have several narks on tap in all these ports. I wanted the name of the best one here. He told me to ask for Henri at that café on the corner. It is the favourite *bistrot* of the yacht stewards, and as barman there Henri picks up from them most of the dirt about what goes on. He pointed out de Grasse's yacht to me and he is going to slip out for a quarter of an hour to get us a little info'. By the time we have fortified the inner man with oysters and a glass of wine, I shall be very surprised if he is not able to let us know definitely whether Christina is on that yacht."

In the back of the car Molly burbled her admiration for his efficiency with the same delight that a mother will display at seeing her offspring do its parlour trick, but John only asked: "What happens if the yacht puts off in the meantime?"

"Then you've had it, chum. There is nothing you can do to stop her sailing, anyway."

They pulled up at the fish restaurant and went inside. Two of its tables only were occupied, by people lingering over the last stages of their dinners. C. B. chose one in a corner, which was well away from the other diners, and ordered *marennes* with a bottle of Pouilly. While they ate he talked in a low monologue about butterflies, the collection of which was his hobby; but his companions appeared singularly disinterested. When they had finished the oysters, he invited them to join him in attacking a dish of sea-urchins, but they declined; so, still discoursing on the habits of the *Papilio machaon*, he set about a plate of the spiky crustaceans himself.

He was only half-way through them when the outer door opened and a short, tubby figure came in. C. B. glanced casually in the direction of the newcomer, then as though suddenly recognizing an old acquaintance cried, "Hello, Henri! How is the world using you?"

The plump man had been advancing towards a buffet on which were displayed a selection of sea-foods, fruit and cheeses. At the greeting he turned his head, smiled, swerved from his course and, coming up to the table, bowed politely. "Thank you, Monsieur; I cannot complain. It is a pleasure to see you here; but unexpected so early in the year. Do you stay long?"

"No, I am only down here on business for a few days this time." C. B. added something about Henri mixing the best Angel's Kiss on the coast and introduced him to Molly and John in a mumble that made their names unintelligible. Meanwhile the patron of the place had come out from behind the buffet.

At his approach, Henri said, "Excuse me, please," turned,

shook hands with him and asked, "Can you let me have two dozen *rosés*? I have an American in my bar. He is a little drunk and he demands *rosés* to eat while he goes on drinking; so I said I would slip out and get him some."

"Certainly." The patron smiled. "A pleasure to oblige you, Monsieur Auer."

As he went off to get a paper bag in which to put the prawns, Henri said to C. B., in a voice hardly above a whisper, "The crew were warned for to-night, but given no hour of sailing. The girl is on the yacht. She arrived in the car of Count Jules at about nine. His chauffeur and the boatswain, Chopin, were with them. Chopin went off on foot—I expect to let his crew know the hour at which they will be wanted. Count Jules took the girl on board. There was no suggestion of violence. They were laughing together."

"Any idea when the yacht will sail?" murmured C. B.

"Not for a while yet, I think; otherwise the crew would have reported by now. It is possible that Count Jules is expecting a second passenger to arrive at a later hour. I fear there is no more that I can tell you."

"Thanks; you have been most helpful." C. B. slipped a five-*mille* note into Henri's hand, and when the patron returned with the bag of prawns they were talking of the prospects for the summer season. Having shaken hands all round, Henri bowed himself out, and C. B. looked across at John.

"Now we know where we stand, anyway; and the situation might be worse. It would be if Jules had taken her to some dive along the coast, and we hadn't the faintest idea where to look for her. But her having gone on board willingly rules out your doing the irate fiancé stuff except at the risk of being arrested if you offer him or any of his people violence."

"I could go to the yacht and demand to see her."

"You could, but I doubt if it would get you much further. The odds are they would let you go below, then beat you up and afterwards hand you over to the police with a cut-and-dried story about your having started it."

"To do that they would have to call the police in. Once they came on the scene I could bring a counter charge of assault against Jules and demand a full enquiry. There would be a good hope then of the authorities preventing the yacht from sailing. To-morrow morning Christina will be herself again, and whatever may happen to me, you and Mother would be able to get her away from them."

C. B. shook his head. "I'm afraid it wouldn't work out like that. They are much too leery to call in the police before the yacht sails. They would probably put you ashore in a boat just as she is leaving harbour. Or they might take you along to keep you out of mischief; then swear afterwards that the row had started only after she had sailed!"

"What do you suggest then?" John asked impatiently. "I flatly refuse to just sit here and let things take their course."

"Since you feel that way about it," replied C. B. thought-fully, "I can put up to you two alternatives. Malouet should be here round about midnight and——"

"Will he?"

"Yes. At the end of our talk on the telephone the old boy agreed to get out his car and start at once. But it is the best part of a two-and-a-half-hours' drive from Nice. He will go straight to Henri's café and I am to meet him there. The police will take his word for anything that may happen while he is with us; so when he does turn up he could accompany you on board for a show-down. In his presence they would not dare to touch you."

John nodded. "I must say you have done everything you possibly could in the circumstances, C. B., and I'm jolly grate-ful to you. But the devil of it is that the yacht may have sailed by midnight."

"I know. The period during which Jules can reasonably count on immunity is getting short now; so my bet is that she will sail within the next half-hour."

"Then what is your alternative to waiting for Malouet, and probably missing the boat?"

C. B. put a finger alongside his big nose, winked and whispered, "To go with her."

CHAPTER IX

ILLEGAL ENTRY

JOHN regarded C. B. with a puzzled frown. "I don't get the idea. How could we manage to do that?"

C. B. shook his head. "This would not be a case of 'we', I'm afraid; and I'd better make my own position clear. I am a Civil Servant and have very definite responsibilities; so I have to think twice before I risk blotting my copy-book. If I had been put on this job officially I might consider it worth while to take that risk. If Jules were just off to Russia with our latest H-bomb secrets in his pocket, I certainly would. But if I got myself arrested and was unable to convince my Chief that it had happened while I was engaged on some matter of real importance to British interests, there would be the hell of a stink. Still worse, it might seriously prejudice the outcome of other work on which I am engaged."

"I quite understand that. It seems, though, that you have changed your mind about me, and are about to suggest that I should do something illegal."

"I am. Mind, I wouldn't, but for the fact that you've just said that you refuse to sit here and let things take their course. What I am about to propose may land you in for the very things I have been trying to keep you out of—namely, a beating-up and finding yourself in the cells to-morrow. I don't like it a bit, but——"

"Since there seems to be no legal means of intervening on the yacht, I mean to take that risk anyhow."

"It will be a certainty, instead of a risk, if you simply go on board and demand that Christina should be restored to you. My idea is that you should attempt to slip on board unobserved."

"What then?"

"Lie doggo. If the yacht has not sailed by midnight we

will come aboard with Malouet. Then you can come out of hiding and stake your claim to Christina. If the yacht sails earlier, you will sail with her as a stowaway."

"I don't see how that would improve my chance of getting Christina out of their clutches."

"It won't if they find you; and I've already warned you that by going on board at all, without the police, you are asking for a packet of trouble. But if you can remain hidden for eight or ten hours there is quite a good chance that you may succeed in pulling the chestnuts out of the fire."

"How?" asked Molly, now considerably concerned for John's safety.

C. B. leaned across the table and his voice sank still lower. "They have got to get her to England by the 6th; so they can't be taking her far. Toulon or Marseilles, perhaps. But at present we have no idea of their destination. If she sails in the yacht as things are, we lose track of her; but we won't if John is in the yacht too and has succeeded in keeping himself under cover. At the first opportunity to-morrow morning he could get ashore and let us know where the yacht has docked. By that time Christina will have, as one might say, come out from under the influence. Now, she would probably tell us all to mind our own damn' business, but by then she will be ready to scream 'murder'. As soon as John informs us where the yacht has got to, we'll come down with Malouet like wolves on the fold, and young Jules will be darn' lucky if he doesn't find himself in quod for kidnapping. See the idea?"

Molly nodded rather ruefully. "As a plan, it is as good as anything we can hope for; but I'll never forgive you if they do John a serious injury."

"At least it gives a sporting chance for him to keep out of trouble." C. B. shrugged. "I put this up only to prevent his butting his head right into it."

"That's true enough, Mumsie," John declared. "Don't you dare blame C. B. if anything goes wrong. But it is nearly half-past ten; so if I'm to get on that yacht without being spotted we had better be moving."

C. B. paid the bill and they went out into the darkness. The yacht lay only two hundred yards or so further seaward along the quay. Keeping in the shadow of the buildings, they walked along until they were opposite to her.

At a steep angle her fo'c'sle sloped up from the base of her single mast and bridge-structure, which were placed well forward. The two-thirds of her abaft the bridge lay much lower in the water. No trail of smoke came from her one large squat funnel, as she was diesel-engined. Her design gave the impression of rakishness and power; and C. B. judged her to be of about eight hundred tons burthen.

Some of her main cabins were lit, but as their portholes lay just under the level of the wharf edge the light from them came only as a diffused glow amidships. Except for a pool of brightness below her mast light and another on her bridge, her upper structure was plunged in deep shadow. A gangway, the slope of which was scarcely noticeable, led up from the quay to her main deck, just astern of her bridge. She might have been completely deserted, had it not been for an occasional movement in her bridge-house, which showed that someone was keeping watch up there.

After they had studied her for some moments, C. B. said to John, "I thought you might have to borrow a small boat, approach her from the seaward side, and shin up on deck as best you could; but I don't think that is necessary. Her deck is so near level with the wharf, and she is made fast so close against it that you should be able to jump to the rail near her stern and scramble over. All that is needed to give you a good chance of getting aboard unseen is for us to occupy the watchman's attention while you approach as quietly as possible."

"Johnny," Molly whispered anxiously, "you are not used to this sort of thing. Do be careful, won't you?"

He gave her a swift kiss on the cheek. "Don't worry, Mumsie; of course I will."

Ignoring the interruption, C. B. went on, "Let's all go back to the car now. Molly and I will get in it, and we will give you a bit of a lead before we start. Walk right on the edge of the quayside, so that you will have only to swerve and jump at the critical moment. Don't walk too fast, because I want to pass you in the car about fifty yards before you come level with her stern; but for God's sake don't give the impression of stealth, in case anyone notices you. The noise of the car engine will drown any noise you make, and when I pull up opposite the bridge of the yacht our lights will be pointing away from you; so you will have the extra benefit of the contrasting darkness behind us. Whatever you do, don't jump before we have pulled up and you have heard me hail the chap in the bridge-house; otherwise he may be looking in your direction. I shall pretend that we are trying to find another yacht that was supposed to have docked this evening, and will hold his attention for about three minutes. That should be ample for you to do your stuff."

Still keeping in the shadow of the buildings, they walked back to the fish restaurant. While they did so C. B. made Johnny repeat their programme, to make certain there should be no slip-up. He had only just finished when they reached the car.

Knowing that C. B. disliked driving, and never did so if he could get anyone else to do it for him, Molly gave John's hand a quick squeeze, then slipped into the driver's seat.

C. B. said to him in a low voice, "Should anything go wrong, and you have to make a bolt for it, go round a few back streets then come to Henri's café. Your mother and I will be waiting there until Malouet turns up. Off you go, now. Good luck!"

With a nod and smile, barely glimpsed in the semi-darkness, John turned away, while C. B. got in beside Molly. He did not at all like the idea of letting the boy tackle such a dangerous business on his own, but had seen no way to prevent it. In the past he had on many occasions risked worse things than were likely to happen to John, but he was not his own master, and knew it to be unfair to his department to embroil himself in matters that had no definite connection with his job. He could only console himself with the thought that, as from the first John had shown a determination to stick his neck out, he had at least now been manœuvred into doing it in a way that might, perhaps, prove well worth while.

Molly, meanwhile, was torn by conflicting emotions—her confidence in C. B., which gave her assurance that any plan of his would combine the maximum amount of caution possible with a fair prospect of success, and her distress that her beloved Johnny must inevitably run considerable risks in carrying it out. For a few moments she watched him walking away, until he had disappeared beyond the beams thrown by the car lamps; then she started the engine and slipped in the clutch.

The timing was good, as when the car passed John, and he was momentarily thrown up in the glare of its headlights, he was still too far from the yacht to be noticed by anyone in her. He had just about halved the remaining distance when the car pulled up, and by the time he drew level with the yacht's stern C. B. already had the watchman engaged in conversation.

John's glance switched to the gulf that gaped between the quayside and the yacht's rail. For a second his heart contracted. It was much wider than he had expected. Poised there on the edge, he stared down at the oily water gurgling sinisterly ten feet below him. If he bungled his jump and fell into that dark crevasse it could easily prove a death-trap. Wide as the gap appeared on the wharf level, it looked much narrower further down, and the horrid thought flickered through his mind that he might find himself jammed between the ship and the wharf with his head under water. Yet he knew that every second was now precious; so, striving to suppress his qualms, he launched himself into space.

Those nervous fears lent extra strength to his muscles; so his leap would have carried him double the distance. His outstretched hands overshot the mark, and instead it was his stomach that came into violent contact with the top of the rail. The wind was driven from his body; his arms and legs flailed wildly. For a moment he was in acute danger of slipping backwards into the gulf before he could get a foot- or hand-hold. A desperate wriggle saved him. His head went down, his legs up, and he fell inboard on to the deck.

Alarmed at the noise he had made, he scrambled hastily for the nearest cover. It was a hooded wooden hatchway leading down to the deck below. Crouching behind it he wondered what he had better do next. The obvious course seemed to creep down and look for a good place in which to hide; but while leaping on to the rail he had glimpsed a thing which was inconspicuous from the level of the wharf. On either side of the long after-deck there were three large sloping skylights, and the four nearest were all aglow, suggesting that the saloons below them were occupied. If he went down this after-companionway it seemed highly likely that he would run straight into somebody.

Peering round the side of the hatch, he saw that all was still quiet forward. It was darker up by the bridge; so it seemed probable that there were fewer people below decks there. Feeling certain that if he could reach the waist of the ship unobserved he would find another companionway, he left his cover, but at a crawl, so that he could instantly flatten himself out beside one of the skylights if he heard anyone approaching.

He took the starboard side of the deck, and on reaching the first skylight paused to peer down through it. Below lay the galley, bright with steel and copper fitments. In it two men were eating at a small square table. From their dress, one was obviously the chef and the other the steward. A bottle of wine stood between them, and it looked as if they were making a hearty supper from the planned surplus of a meal that had been served earlier in the dining saloon.

Wriggling on again, John peered through the next skylight. Below him now was the dining saloon. Although the light there was still on, the table had been cleared and the room was empty. He was just about to move towards the skylight further forward, from which no light showed, when he heard, faint but unmistakable, a laugh that he felt certain was Christina's. It had come from the skylight opposite, on the port side of the deck, which was open a little for ventilation.

Regardless of the fact that three minutes had already gone, so it was not to be expected that C. B. would be able to keep the watchman in conversation much longer, John could not resist the temptation to slither swiftly across the deck and peep through the skylight from which the laugh had come. It gave on to the saloon, which occupied as much space on the port side as did the dining saloon and galley together on the starboard side. By holding his head at an awkward angle, John could see both Jules and Christina.

She was sitting in a corner with her legs up on the *banquette* that ran along the ship's side. Jules was ensconced opposite her in an armchair. Between them on a small table stood two squat, tulip-shaped glasses and a bottle of Grand Marnier. No one else was present, and they were talking and laughing together like old friends.

Looking at them had a curious effect on John. He knew that he should have been pleased to find Christina safe, well and apparently happy, but he was not. Even making allowances for her change of personality after dark, it annoyed him to see her enjoying Jules' company. He now admitted to himself that, in spite of the additional danger in which it would have placed him, he would rather have come upon her in some difficult situation, from which there could have been no excuse for his not attempting her immediate rescue.

Even as it was, he began to play with the thought of endeavouring to get her away before the yacht sailed. The lights glowing through the four skylights had suggested that quite a number of people were down there in the compartments below the after-deck. But that had not proved the case. There were only the chef and steward in the galley and Jules and Christina in the saloon.

John felt that if he could surprise Jules he would have quite a good chance of overcoming him. But what then? Even if Jules were swiftly rendered incapable of giving a general alarm, the sounds of the struggle might bring the two servants from across the passage. And what of Christina? If she came willingly and at once they might gain the deck, race down it and across the gangway on to the wharf, before they could be stopped. But if she at first refused to budge—if he had to waste precious moments trying to persuade her to come with him— the steward and the chef would be upon them before they could even get up the companionway.

Reluctantly, John decided that he dare not chance it. He

must stick to C. B.'s plan and stow away until the morning, when he would be certain of Christina's co-operation. Stealthily he moved again towards the darker area of deck amidships.

Suddenly a horn sounded, the arcs thrown by headlights swept across the buildings on the far side of the wharf, and a car ran past moving in the direction of the town. John knew that it must be C. B. and his mother. They had done their job, and he was supposed by this time to be under cover; but he was not, and now the watchman was again free to keep a general look-out.

It was the first time that John had ever done anything of this kind. He was not at all frightened, but felt terribly excited. His worst handicap was that, owing to lack of experience, he did not realize the importance of making swift decisions. While he was still hesitating whether to risk going forward towards the bridge, another horn sounded, lights flashed again on the quay, and a *camion* drew up opposite the gangway. Out of it piled seven or eight men, who came aboard laughing and joking.

Crouching behind the nearest skylight, John watched them vanish down the companionway in the middle of the bridge-structure that he had hoped to use himself. He reckoned that the crew of such a yacht would number somewhere around a dozen. With one on the bridge and two in the galley, the newcomers nearly made up that complement.

As they had all disappeared, the long stretch of deck to the gangway was now clear again, but he no longer dare risk going below by the midship companionway, even if he could reach it unseen from the bridge. The arrival of the crew had left him no choice but to retreat down the after-hatchway in the hope of finding a good hiding-place somewhere in the stern of the vessel.

Cautiously, he made his way back to the hatch behind which he had first hidden. After listening for a moment, he tip-toed down the stairs beneath its hood. The first flight brought him opposite a long passage, in which he knew that the galley and dining saloon were on the right and the saloon on the left; a second flight, immediately under the first, led down to a lower deck.

Feeling that the further he could get from the major activities on board the yacht the safer he would be, he crept down the second flight. Again he found himself faced by a long corridor, but in it there were double the number of doors. On each side there were six, and evidently they were those of the cabins for the passengers. Beyond them a bulkhead, with a door in it, presumably cut the after part of the ship off from the engine-room and crews' quarters.

Advancing stealthily, John peered through the partly-open door of one of the cabins. It was empty, and showed no sign of occupation; so he wondered if he dare doss down there for the night, but decided against it as too risky. Moving on, he reached the bulkhead, cautiously opened the door in it and looked through.

As he did so the hum of engines struck his ears, and only then did he realize that they had been almost imperceptibly reverberating through the ship for several minutes past. Evidently she was very shortly about to put to sea.

For a moment he stood where he was, wondering whether to step through the door in the hope of finding a good hiding-place further forward, or to return aft and look for a cubby hole right in the stern. He was still trying to decide which course offered the better possibilities when all chance of making a choice was suddenly snatched from him.

Without any sound of warning, a cabin door some ten feet beyond the bulkhead was pulled open. Through it stepped a big, ginger-haired man. His uniform, and the single band of gold braid round its cuffs, showed that he was a junior officer. His glance instantly fell upon John. Surprise dawned in his blue eyes; then, striding towards him, he exclaimed:

"Who are *you*? What do you want down here?"

CHAPTER X

'ONCE ABOARD THE LUGGER . . .?'

THE unexpected encounter had taken John as much b
surprise as it had the ginger-haired officer. For a moment the
stared at one another. John's first impulse was to turn and run
but he knew that would be fatal. This was obviously a case fo
bluff—if he could only think of one. He wondered what lin
C. B. would have taken in these circumstances, but could no
for the life of him, imagine. The big man spoke again, mor
sharply:

"What are you doing down here? Answer me!"

"I am looking for Count Jules," John blurted, that bein,
the first plausible lie that had come into his head.

"How did you get aboard?"

"By the gangway, of course."

"And the watchman did not give you directions where t‹
find Monsieur le Comte?"

"No, he was busy talking to someone else at the time."

"Why did you not wait and ask?"

"I was in a hurry, and I thought that in a small yacht lik
this I would have no difficulty in finding him."

John's voice gained in confidence as he developed his bluf
but his heavily-built questioner continued to stare at hir
suspiciously, and muttered with a scowl, "You are a foreigner
are you not?"

There being no point in denying it, and his accent makin,
it futile to do so, John nodded. Then, in an attempt to escap
from this dangerous interrogation, he said, "I'm sorry to hav
invaded the private quarters of the ship, but I must have com
down a deck too far by mistake. I'll go up again and——"

Before he could finish his sentence and turn away, the ma
interrupted aggressively, "What do you want with Monsieu
le Comte?"

"I am an old friend of his."

"Is he expecting you?"

For a second John hesitated, and in that second he was lost. His 'Yes' came too late to carry conviction. The blue eyes staring into his showed frank disbelief. In two strides the officer was upon him. Seizing John by the arm, he rapped out:

"Very well! I will take you to him."

John's brain worked quickly enough now. He realized that if he once allowed himself to be taken up to Jules his goose would be cooked. He might have tackled Jules alone, had he followed his impulse of a few minutes back to take him by surprise in the saloon, but he could not hope to overcome both Jules and this strapping young man. It seemed certain now that he had let himself in for just the sort of thing C. B. had feared might happen to him if he took the law into his own hands by coming aboard the yacht. They would first beat him up, then hand him over to the police. Such a prospect was bad enough, but the thought which infuriated him beyond all else was that his attempt to protect Christina should be foiled almost before it had started. It was barely ten minutes since he had come on board, and he was now to be lugged before her as a captive. It was revolt at such a swift and ignominious end to his venture that spurred him to action.

The officer had him firmly by the left arm, but his right was free. Thrusting his hand under his coat, he whipped out the cosh, raised it, and struck sharply at his captor. He did not need to deliver a second blow. The leather-covered egg-shaped piece of lead came down on the man's uniform cap with hardly a sound; but his blue eyes suddenly bulged, his grip on John's arm relaxed, and he slumped in a heap on the deck.

For a second John held his breath; then he felt himself beginning to tremble. He had belatedly remembered what C. B. had said about using the cosh with caution. If he had killed the officer it would be a clear case of murder. Thrusting the weapon back into his trouser top, he stooped, and with frantic hands pulled the limp body towards him, so that he could thrust off the cap and examine the man's head.

The passage was lit only dimly by the small blue ceiling lights that are usually kept on permanently in ships' corridors. Anxiously John peered down at his victim's mat of short, ginger curls for signs of blood. He could see none, and his searching fingers found only a little wetness. With intense relief he realized that the man's cap and the thickness of his hair must have saved him from serious injury. Even if his skull was slightly cracked the absence of any mushy depression or copious bleeding seemed clear indications that there was no risk of his dying.

Relief at being freed from the awful thought that he might have killed a man was swiftly succeeded by a lesser, but still pressing, anxiety. If he had not got a corpse on his hands, he had something like it. The limp body at his feet showed no signs of returning animation; so he was not faced with the unhappy choice of either humanely rendering it assistance at his own peril or giving it another biff on the head to prevent its calling on anyone else to do so; but if he left it lying where it was some other member of the crew might come upon it at any moment. Should that happen, and a general alarm be raised, unless he had first found himself a safe hiding-place, he would again be caught before the yacht left harbour.

The obvious course was to carry the unconscious officer back into the cabin from which he had emerged. John knew that good old 'Crack' and others of his mother's fiction characters performed such feats without the least difficulty; but, being of slight build himself and having already felt the dead-weight of the powerfully built body, he had serious misgivings about his ability to get it there. Nonetheless, feeling that to be the only step by which he could prevent the discovery within a very short time that an act of violence had been committed aboard, he set about the job with feverish energy.

Getting his hands under his victim's arm-pits, he endeavoured to half-lift, half-drag him towards the cabin; but the best he could manage was to pull him a few inches at a time along the floor. At every tug his head jerked and rolled ludicrously on his shoulders, his arms flapped like mechanical fins, and the heels of his boots scraped noisily on the boards.

140

While John heaved, strained, and panted from his exertions, he expected every moment that someone would appear at one or other end of the corridor and catch him red-handed; but after three minutes' gruelling struggle he had the body over the door sill. For him to have got it up on to the bunk unaided would have required further precious moments of exhausting effort; so, instead, he pushed a pillow under the injured man's head before stepping out of the cabin and closing its door behind him.

Breathless, and still trembling a little, he again considered whether his best prospects of coming upon a good hiding-place lay forward or, through the bulkhead, astern. As he hesitated a sudden thought struck him with fresh dismay. Getting the unconscious officer back into his cabin had only put off the evil hour of discovery. In a crew of only a dozen or so he would soon be missed. Someone was certain to come down to his cabin to look for him. Had John been able to lock it, there would have been a chance of them assuming that the officer had been detained ashore and missed his ship. But there was no key in the door, so whoever came to look for him would walk straight in on his body.

That would mean an immediate enquiry. Perhaps by then he would have come round sufficiently to describe how he had been attacked. In any case he would do so before many hours had passed. The yacht would then be searched from stem to stern as a precaution against the foreigner who had attacked him still being on board. An 800-ton yacht was very different from a liner, or even a tramp; it had no great air-ducts, baggage holds or mountains of cargo, which would help a stowaway to elude a search.

As these disconcerting thoughts ran through John's mind he was quick to see that wherever he concealed himself the chances were now at least ten to one on his being dragged from his hiding-place within the next hour or two. By knocking out the ginger-haired man he had burnt his boats, and could now only save himself by getting ashore again before the yacht sailed. If he failed to do so he was not only liable to be rough-handled by the crew, but would later find himself faced with a charge of having assaulted a ship's officer in the execution of his duty.

Visions of a French prison spurred him to fresh action. A few swift steps took him back through the bulkhead. Pausing only to close the door in it behind him, he hurried along the semi-dark corridor to the foot of the after-companionway. In going up it he proceeded with more caution, and, before exposing himself to view in the better-lighted corridor above, peered along it at deck level, to assure himself that it was still empty.

It was, and as his glance swept it the sight of a key, protruding from the lock of a door which he knew must be that of the galley, stirred in him a sudden impulse to rail against fate. He felt that it was ill-luck alone that had brought his venture to nought, and compelled him to abandon it so quickly; for he might have been safely hidden by now, had he not had the misfortune to run into the officer; and, even then, had that key been in the door of the man's cabin, instead of in that of the galley, the simple act of turning it would at least have spared him the mortification of having to make a bolt for it from fear that a hue and cry might start after him at any moment.

On tip-toe he ascended the upper ladder of the companionway, and from behind its curved hatch peeped out along the deck. It was still in semi-darkness, and the members of the crew whom he had seen come aboard were still below decks. He glanced towards the rail, but decided against again leaping the gulf between the ship and the quay, as the rail would make it so awkward to get a good take-off from this direction. Not much more than sixty feet of clear deck lay between him and the gangway. He had only to cross it at a run and before anyone had a chance to stop him he would be ashore. The watchman might shout after him, but that was very different from being challenged when coming aboard. Even if he were pursued he should have no great difficulty in getting away down one of the dark alleys that intersected the buildings facing the quay.

Swiftly now his thoughts flowed on. Why should he risk pursuit at all? There was still no sign of any intention shortly to take the yacht to sea. If he walked calmly along the deck and down the gangway the watchman would probably think that he was one of the crew going ashore for ten minutes on some small errand, and would not even challenge him.

Standing up, he moved out from behind the hatchway, his eyes fixed on the bridge. It was dully lit, but he could see no one up there; so it looked as if the watchman was either in the wheel-house, which faced forward, or behind the canvas screen at its starboard side, where, leaning on the rail, he could look down on the wharf. With firm, light steps John walked forward along the starboard side of the deck.

As he reached the first skylight he gave a swift glance through it. Below in the galley the steward and the chef were still at table: the latter was busily mixing a large bowl of salad. A few paces further on John came level with the skylight through which he had seen Jules and Christina. It lay on the port side, and ten feet away, but he could not resist the temptation to cross over for a quick peep. On his way he glanced up at the bridge to assure himself that nothing had altered there; then he peered down between the brass protecting rods of the skylight into the saloon. Jules and Christina were still sitting on either side of a small table and, apparently, had hardly altered their positions since he had last seen them.

In the interval he had been subject to so many emotions that it was difficult for him to realize that not much over ten minutes could have passed; and that during them events had entirely re-orientated the impulses that governed his actions. Then they had been inspired by a determination to protect Christina; now, they were the outcome of a craven fear to get out of danger as quickly as he could.

It was looking down on them again that made him aware of the change in mentality he had undergone, and no sooner was he conscious of it than he began to feel terribly ashamed. It had been bad luck to run into that officer, but he had handled the situation promptly and, as yet, had no reason at all to suppose that anyone else suspected his presence on board. As a result of the encounter he might find himself in very hot water unless he got off the yacht before she sailed; but that was no reason why he should not attempt to take Christina with him.

His prospects of succeeding in such an attempt were considerably better than they had been when he had contemplated making it ten minutes earlier. The major part of the crew could not turn up unexpectedly just as he was hoping to get Christina away, as they had arrived and gone below already. Having now had experience in using his cosh effectively, he felt far more confident of his chances of rendering Jules *hors de combat* before he could give the alarm. The way was clear from the after-hatch to the gangway. Above all, he knew now that he had but to turn the key in the galley door to ensure that the only two people within Jules' call would be unable to come to his assistance if they heard him give a shout.

With a fresh wave of shame, it was borne in on John that he had been granted as near perfect conditions for a rescue as anyone could hope for, yet had very nearly thrown the opportunity away during a brief period of unjustifiable panic. He quailed at the thought of what C. B.'s opinion of him would have been afterwards had he done so, and that imperturbable secret agent had ever learned the facts. It needed only this last goad to his *amour-propre* to confirm John in his new resolution. Turning away from the skylight, he walked swiftly back to the after-hatch.

Losing not a second now, he ran lightly down the ladder, turned the key in the galley door, crossed the passage, opened that of the saloon, stepped inside, and closed it behind him.

Lack of experience in resorting to violence robbed him of an advantage he might otherwise have taken. Jules was sitting with his back to the door. A gangster or professional agent would have had the cosh ready in his grasp as he entered the saloon; so could have run forward and laid Jules out with it before he had time to get up and swing round. John took a couple of strides, then had to pause while he pulled the cosh out from his trouser top. Short as the delay was, it was long enough for Jules to spring to his feet, half turn, and kick the chair in which he had been sitting against John's legs.

John had the cosh only shoulder high as the chair caught

him. He stumbled and fell half across it, his arms shooting forward. Instantly Jules leapt at him. With his right he struck John a glancing blow on the side of the face, with his left he seized the wrist that held the cosh and gave it a violent twist. The attack was so sudden that, still off his balance as he was, John had no chance to defend himself. A second blow from Jules landed on his left eye. Again his wrist was wrenched down and backward. With an "Ouch" of pain, he dropped the cosh.

For a moment more they struggled with the chair between them, then Jules let go John's wrist, gave him a swift push, and stepped back. John was panting and uneasily aware that so far he had had the worst of the encounter. He too stepped back, and his glance swiftly swept the floor, seeking the cosh, in the hope that he might recover it; but it had rolled away under a settee. Jules had seen where it had gone and, now that he had disarmed his attacker, appeared fully confident of his ability to deal with the situation. He was not even breathing quickly, and an amused smile twitched his full lips as he said:

"I thought you might put in an appearance in spite of the warning I gave you. I told my father so, but he said it would not matter if you did; and, of course, he was quite right, as you cannot possibly bring any charge against us."

"Don't you be too certain of that," John snapped, and his eyes switched to Christina.

As he burst in she had removed her long silk-stockinged legs from the *banquette* and, with a newly-lit cigarette between her fingers, half risen; but had then sat down again. Now, she had both elbows planted on the table and was smoking calmly, while watching the two men with the detached air of one looking on at a scene in a play.

Jules laughed. "If you are expecting my charming guest to go ashore with you and tell the police that I brought her here by force, you are much mistaken. We have been having a very pleasant time together. You, on the other hand, have come aboard clandestinely, and assaulted me. We are waiting only for my father to join us before putting to sea. I will leave it for him, when he arrives, to decide if we shall have you thrown into the harbour, or hand you over to the police."

John had recovered his breath and, now that he had landed himself in real trouble, found his brain working with unexpected clarity. It seemed obvious that he could expect no help from Christina; but if he could get round the chair there was a chance that by hurling himself on Jules he might yet put him out of action.

Without taking his eyes from John, Jules spoke again. "Christina! Just behind you there is a bell-push. Please ring for the steward. He is quite a gorilla; so we'll let him take charge of our uninvited guest. Then we can resume our conversation."

"No," replied Christina composedly. "I am enjoying this. You can fight it out between you."

Shaken out of his complacency, Jules shot her a surprised glance. It gave John just the opportunity for which he had been hoping. The second that Jules' eyes left his, he thrust the chair aside and sailed in.

John was much the slighter of the two, and at both school and university he had tended to despise athletics; but during his military service he had been made to take up boxing and had not done at all badly for his weight. Now, these bouts under the exacting eyes of tough Army instructors stood him in good stead. Jules put up his fists, and awkwardly fended off the first few blows, but was driven against the after-partition of the saloon. John slammed a left to his chin and his head banged back against the wooden panelling. As it jerked forward he opened his mouth to yell for help, but John drove a right into his stomach. With a gasp he half doubled up, thrusting his head out and clutching at his belly. He was now so obviously helpless that for a second John was reluctant to strike again; but he knew that to forgo this chance of finishing him off would be crazy. Stepping back a pace, he landed a blow that had all his force behind it under Jules' left ear. The Frenchman pitched over sideways, struck his head hard on the leg of a chair as he went down, and rolled over, out cold, face upward on the carpet.

146

"Well done! Oh, well done!" The words came from Christina more as breathless gasps than exclamations.

Sucking the broken skin of his knuckles, John turned towards her. She had stubbed out her cigarette and was standing up now, her huge brown eyes round with excitement. Pushing her way out from behind the table, she ran to him, flung her arms about his neck and, opening her mouth wide, glued it on his.

It was the sort of kiss calculated to rock any man's senses, and John was no exception. She had nothing on over her thin day frock and through it he could again feel the warmth of her body; yet it seemed an entirely different body from that which he had held in his arms during the afternoon. That had been soft and hesitantly yielding with occasional tremors due to girlish diffidence. This strained against him with a fierce virility, and every few seconds was shaken by a spasmodic trembling caused by uncontrollable passion.

Momentarily overcome as he was, his brain instantly protested that this was no time or place for love-making. Then instinct rowed in and told him that love played no part in this monstrous embrace, or even natural passion. It was night and Christina was not her true self. She was the victim of a primitive emotion which had been aroused in her by witnessing a scene of violence. She was the female who had just seen two males fighting over which of them should possess her. With shock, and almost a feeling of nausea, it suddenly came to him that had he been the senseless body on the floor and Jules the victor, it was Jules whom she would now be seeking to devour with her luscious, breathless kisses.

Lifting his arms from about her, he grasped her wrists, broke her grip round his neck, thrust her away from him, and cried:

"Christina! Pull yourself together! We've got to get out of here; and at once."

She seemed to sober, and murmured, "All right," but gave him a slightly sullen look as she turned to pick up from the back of a chair a heavy Shetland tweed coat, and added, "Now you have settled matters with Jules, what's the hurry?"

147

"I'll give you all the reasons later," he said, endeavouring to humour rather than bully her, as he helped her into the coat.

"Anyhow, there is time for you to get this off me." As she spoke she turned. He had noticed with vague surprise that she was wearing gloves, and drawing off the left one she thrust her hand out towards him.

"D'you mean my ring?" he asked in a puzzled voice. "But why?"

"Of course, stupid!" she exclaimed, turning away her head. "It has been hurting me all the evening. It's like a hot band round my finger, and I can't look at it. Every time I do it dazzles me."

He stared at the signet ring and wondered if he could possibly be imagining things. To him it was not dazzling, but its gold seemed to be shining with a brighter, purer light than it had ever done during the years he had worn it himself. His father, to whom it had originally belonged, had not been a pious man, but upright and fearless, and the thought flashed into John's mind that perhaps the precious metal had mysteriously absorbed some of his father's qualities; so was now having on Christina, in a minor degree, a similar effect to that of the crucifix his mother had thrown to her the previous night. Seeing that the knuckle above the ring was red, angry and swollen, he said:

"You have been trying to get it off yourself, and failed; so I don't suppose I can."

"That was Jules," she replied with an impatient shrug. "I asked him to try, and offered to kiss him if he could; but he couldn't; so I wouldn't. But you put it on; so you must get it off."

Suddenly it occurred to him that the ring might, perhaps, be acting to some extent as a charm against evil and, as long as she wore it, would reduce the strength of her nocturnal inclinations to play into the hands of her own enemies; so he shook his head.

"No. I'll take it off to-morrow morning for you if you like; but there is no time now. We've lost a couple of minutes as it

148

is. And Jules isn't the only person I've had to lay out in order to get hold of you. Ten minutes ago I slogged an officer. Any moment——"

"Did you?" she broke in, her eyes glowing again. "Oh, John, I think you're wonderful! Let's get away then. I'll go anywhere you wish."

"Right; come on!" He grabbed her by the arm and hurried her to the door. "It's not Jules I'm worried about, but the other chap. The Captain may send someone to look for him. The moment they find him the hunt will be up. Alarm bells, lights all over the ship, and God knows what else. If that starts before we can get ashore our number will be up."

The passage was empty. No one was battering on the door of the galley; evidently the steward and the chef had not heard the struggle in the saloon, or yet discovered that they were locked in. Still holding Christina by the arm, John drew her up the companionway after him. As his head emerged above deck level he glimpsed through the stern rail a man standing on the quay, some thirty feet away, by a bollard round which was looped the yacht's stern hawser. It looked as if he was awaiting orders to cast off, but the deck of the yacht was still in darkness.

Feeling certain that if they ran the length of the deck they would be bound to attract the watchman's attention and that, with his suspicions aroused, he would dash down the ladder from the bridge in an attempt to stop them before they reached the gangway, John whispered:

"Steady, now. We must walk off just as if we had dined aboard and I was now going to see you home. With luck the watchman may take me for Jules, as he and I are about the same height. If we could be laughing over something, that would be all to the good. My mind is a blank about funny stories at the moment, but perhaps you can think of one."

"Yes," replied Christina promptly, as they set off along the deck. "Do you know the one about the five brides describing to one another what had happened on the first night of their honeymoon? The first said, 'My husband was just like Roosevelt, he . . .'"

The rest of her sentence was drowned by the siren of a car. Next moment its headlights rolled back the darkness from the quay. As it ran past them it was slowing down and its driver brought it smoothly to a halt opposite the gangway.

"Hell!" exclaimed John, pulling Christina up. "That will be the Marquis! Quick! We must hide!"

But it was too late. He had scarcely got the words out when there was movement on the bridge, a whistle shrilled, and all the lights were switched on. Momentarily dazzled by the glare, they were caught in it, standing between two of the skylights right in the middle of the deck.

The passengers were getting out of the car; two tall men and one short one. A bearded officer, who looked as if he might be the Captain, was leaning over the after-bridge rail looking down at them. Another man stood beside him. Two more sailors ran out from the bridge-house and took up positions on either side of the gangway.

Suddenly it dawned on John that of all these people not one was looking in the direction of Christina and himself. If they could get below again and find some place in which to conceal themselves Jules would believe that they had succeeded in getting ashore before his father's arrival. With luck they might remain as stowaways, undiscovered, until the yacht reached its port of destination, then slip ashore there. Swiftly he turned Christina about and pushed her towards the afterhatch at a quick walk.

They still had ten feet to go when they caught a muffled shouting from the galley; then, as they reached the hatch, a loud banging on its door. The steward and the chef had just discovered that they were locked in, and were endeavouring to draw attention to their plight.

Before John was half-way down the companionway, the banging abruptly ceased. As he neared its bottom he saw the reason, and consternation seized him. Jules had come round from being knocked out and striking his head on the chair leg much more quickly than might have been expected. Perhaps he had pushed the buzzer for help, and it was that which had led to the steward, on going to answer it, finding that the galley door was locked on the outside. In any case, Jules had staggered out into the passage and, only a moment earlier, unlocked the door. He now stood swaying, a little drunkenly, as the steward and the chef tumbled out through it.

Once more John's lack of experience in affairs of violence had let him down; but it was vain now for him to curse himself for not having had the forethought to tie Jules up and gag him while he had the chance.

A trickle of blood was running down from a cut on Jules' forehead into his left eye. With a shaky hand he brushed it away and focused his unsteady glance on John's legs as they appeared down the companionway. The second he saw his face, he flung out a pointing arm and shouted to his men: "There he is! Get him! Get him!"

The chef was a small plump man with a mild expression, and did not look at all a type who would willingly get himself mixed up in a rough house; but the steward was a brawny specimen with a low forehead, flattened nose and bull-dog jaw. Jules' description of him earlier as 'quite a gorilla' had been an apt one.

John gave the group one glance, swung about, yelled to Christina to get back up the ladder, and scampered after her. Quick as he was, they would have been on him before he was half-way up had it not been that the chef, who was nearest, hesitated a second and the steward had to push past him.

Christina stubbed her toe and tripped over the top step. Hopping out on to the deck she let go a spate of foul language that sounded peculiarly shocking coming from her young, innocent-looking mouth; but John registered the fact only sub-consciously. In tripping she had held him up for a moment. The gorilla-like steward was right on his heels and grabbing at them. He cleared the top step only just in time, but, swinging round, managed to kick his pursuer in the face.

With a howl of rage and pain, the man swayed backward. His eyes goggling and his hands clutching frantically at the empty air, he hovered for a second, then overbalanced. More yells came from below as his heavy body went crashing down on the little chef and Jules, who had been mounting the ladder behind him. Seizing the advantage this débâcle had given him, John stepped back, swung to the double doors of the hooded hatch cover, and flicked over into its staple the stout iron hook that secured them.

But his victorious retreat from below gained him no more than a breathing space. The shouting and sounds of strife had been heard up on deck. The group from the car were now half-way along it. In the lead was the tall, hatchet-faced Marquis, and beside him a man of about forty, with a large, fair, fluffed-out moustache of the style favoured by some R.A.F. pilots. Close behind them were the little man, who looked like a valet, and the two sailors who had stood by the gangway. Others were running up from amidships, and the officers on the bridge were now staring aft to see what the commotion was about.

John gave a hurried glance over his shoulder. The stern rail was only a few feet behind him. In three paces he could reach the spot where it curved in towards the wharf. To balance on it for a jump would be almost impossible; but he could scramble over, cling to the rail with one hand, then leap. The ease with which he had cleared the gap when coming aboard proved that it was nothing like as formidable as it looked.

Now, though, his situation was very different. Someone on the yacht had only to call 'Stop Thief' to the wharf-hand, who was waiting to cast the hawser off from the bollard, for the man to run forward and grab him as he landed on the quay. Then there was Christina: her legs were long enough to make the jump, but might easily become entangled in her heavy coat. To urge her to attempt it would be asking her to take an appalling risk.

These thoughts flashed through his mind within a moment of his fastening the doors to the companionway; but even in that brief span of time the dispositions of the other protagonists in the scene had changed. The approaching group and Christina had both taken a few quick steps towards one another. Barely fifteen feet now separated them. With a swift contraction of the heart John accepted it as certain that in another minute he would be attacked, and that against such odds he had no possible chance. Then all his preconceived ideas of what was about to happen were suddenly altered by the totally unexpected attitude of the Marquis.

Sweeping off his hat he made a smiling bow to Christina. "My apologies, Mademoiselle, that a tiresome appointment should have prevented me from joining you earlier. And Mr. Fountain, is it not? This is an unexpected pleasure. When we met the other night in Cannes, I did not know that you were an old friend of Jules. I trust that he has been giving you both a pleasant time?"

John was so nonplussed that he could think of no immediate reply. Then it occurred to him to take the Marquis's words at their face value, in the wild hope that he meant them. Hastily he blurted out, "Thank you, sir. Yes, it's been grand. I'm sorry you should arrive to find us on the point of leaving."

By then the Marquis had taken Christina's hand and was going through the gallant motion of kissing it. By then, too, Jules, the chef and the steward had had time to sort themselves out at the foot of the companionway, and one of them had run up it. There came a loud hammering on the doors of the covered hatch, accompanied by muffled shouts and curses.

The Marquis glanced in that direction, shrugged, and said suavely, "I fear some of my new crew are ill-disciplined fellows. No doubt the reason why Jules is not with you is that he remained below, endeavouring to quell a brawl among them. I am desolated that your visit should have been terminated so unpleasantly. Permit me to escort you to the gangway."

He was still holding Christina's hand. Drawing it through his arm in a paternal manner, he turned and led her forward. John could hardly believe his ears and eyes, but followed automatically and found himself in the middle of the little group that had come aft.

As they walked forward the Marquis conveyed kind messages to Christina from his wife. It seemed that the Marquise had also intended to dine aboard, but had been prevented from doing so by a slight indisposition. Had she not been aware that young English ladies were quite accustomed to dispensing with the presence of a chaperon she would naturally have made a special effort, but as things were she felt sure Christina would forgive her.

No one said a word to John. The sailors and the little man had deferentially stepped aside, so were now behind him; the tall R.A.F. type with the fluffy moustache was walking at his side, but in silence.

The sixty feet of after-deck was soon covered. They passed round the big squat funnel. Just beyond it, to starboard, lay the gangway. Six feet further on the bridge-structure rose up across the whole breadth of the yacht. Between it and the funnel lay a band of deep shadow. It was broken only in the middle by the glow of light coming up from the main companionway, which lay under the centre of the bridge.

The Marquis turned towards the gangway, and said to Christina, "I see there is no car here to fetch you. But no matter; you must allow me to send you home in mine."

Suddenly into John's brain there flashed an explanation for the Marquis's strange behaviour. The reason why he had pretended not to grasp the fact that he had come upon them endeavouring to escape, and continued to ignore the shouts and banging that still came faintly from the stern, must be because it had never been intended to take Christina to sea in the yacht. As C. B. had pointed out, their contract was to get her to England by the 6th, and they now had barely two days in which to do the job. It must be that Jules had got hold of her much earlier than he had expected; so brought her to the yacht as a temporary measure until his father had completed their other arrangements. The Marquis had arrived only to collect her, and was now in the act of doing so.

In an instant John forecast the next move. The Marquis would put Christina in the car, get in himself, then give a swift order to his men. They would seize him, so that he could not attempt to follow, while the Marquis drove off, carrying Christina to some dive where she would be doped, then put on a plane for England. There were only a matter of seconds to go and John raked his mind frantically for a means to sabotage this plan at the last moment.

There were four men round him and others within close call; so he knew that any attempt to stop the car or rescue Christina was far beyond his powers. The only thing he could do was to anticipate the order to seize him. If, the second his foot was on the wharf, he dodged between the men about him and ran for it, he might get away. Should he succeed, he could be with C. B. at Henri's bar in ten minutes; and although he would temporarily have lost Christina, they could at once set about tracing the car in which she had been kidnapped.

These swift thoughts had barely coursed through John's mind when the Marquis reached the head of the gangway. Still keeping hold of Christina's arm, he halted and looked back. Suddenly he shot out his free hand, pointed it at John and cried:

"Throw him down the hatch!"

CHAPTER XI

THE MARQUIS CALLS THE TUNE

BEFORE John could raise a finger, the man with the moustache and one of the sailors were upon him. His assumptions had been only partially correct. The Marquis had, in fact, assessed the true situation at a glance as soon as he had come on board; but his subtle tactics had had a different aim from the one that John had guessed. He had been quick to realize that a fight on the open, brightly-lit deck could be seen from the buildings on the quay, and that later police enquiries might elicit the fact that a woman answering Christina's description had been involved in it; so he had led his visitors into the shadow cast by the bridge and funnel before resorting to violence to prevent their escape.

The *mêlée* in front of the companionway was brief. John saw the Marquis pull Christina back from the gangway and push her towards a dark doorway that stood open in the bridge-structure. After that he had only a confused impression of a violent struggle with himself as its centre. Both his arms were seized and he was forced forward. Next moment he was hurtling down the companionway ladder. He struck the middle steps, which slightly broke his fall, and slithered head-foremost to the bottom. Following him came the sound of pounding feet, and before he could rise his attackers were on him again. One kicked him in the ribs; two more grabbed him by the shoulders and lugged him to his feet. As he stood swaying there, half-dazed between them, the man with the moustache hit him hard beneath the chin. Stars and circles in vivid array danced on a background of dense blackness before his eyes: he felt his knees sag, and he passed out.

When he came-to, his first sensations were the throbbing of his head, a horrid ache in his ribs, another in his right forearm, and several minor pains in various parts of his face and body. After a moment he remembered how he had come by them and realized that he was still on board the yacht.

For a while he lay unmoving, wondering vaguely how long he had been unconscious. The yacht was pitching slightly, so obviously she was now at sea, and he had the impression that it was days ago that he had been flung down the companionway, although he knew that it could not really be so.

Gradually he began to take stock of his surroundings. He was lying on a hard bunk in a narrow, dimly-lit cabin. It had no porthole, so must be below the water-level. Such light as there was filtered in through an iron grille in the door, which suggested that this was not the first time the place had been used as a prison. That, he concluded, was why his captors had not bothered to tie his feet and hands.

Getting painfully off the bunk, he verified the impression. The door was of steel and had no bolts, handle, or even a key-hole on its inner side; so even had he had some implement available he could not have attempted to pick the lock. The cabin had no furniture other than a single chair and a small, dirty wash-basin with a cracked mirror above it. There was no bulb in the solitary electric fitting in the ceiling, so he could not switch on a light. But his eyes were now getting accustomed to the little light there was, and peering at his face in the mirror he turned it first one way, then the other, in an endeavour to assess the damage it had suffered.

His dark hair was rumpled and his face streaked with dirt. The left side of his chin was swollen and very tender, where the man with the moustache had hit him. It gave his face a slightly lop-sided appearance, which was accentuated by the fact that his left eye was half closed and colouring up, as evidence that Jules had had the best of their first encounter.

Pressing the single button-tap, he ran some water into the basin and, as there was no towel, used his handkerchief to bathe his hurts. The cold water refreshed him and helped to clear his head a little; but there was nothing he could do about the injuries to his body. His forearm was scraped raw where he had slithered on it down the last few stairs of the companionway, and his side pained him every time he took anything approaching a deep breath, although on gingerly feeling his ribs he did not think that any of them were broken.

While examining himself he found that his pockets had not been rifled and, rather belatedly, it occurred to him to look at his watch. On holding it up to the light from the grille he saw that its glass had not been broken and that it was still going. To his surprise it was only twenty-five minutes past eleven, and as a single blow on the chin could hardly have rendered him unconscious for over twelve hours it now seemed clear that he must have come round quite soon after the yacht had left harbour. Seeing that it was not yet midnight made him realize that, wherever she was bound, there was small likelihood of her reaching port for some hours to come; so he lay down again on the bunk.

A little grimly he began to wonder what they would do with him when she did reach port. C. B. had warned him that if he went aboard without an authority to do so he would risk a beating-up, and he had been beaten-up; but he did not now think it very likely that they would hand him over to the police, as C. B. had forecast they would should he find himself in his present circumstances. Any police doctor would attest that injuries such as he had sustained could not normally have been received simply while being prevented from attacking someone. It would be clear that it was he who had been attacked, and handled much more brutally than even being caught while committing a theft could warrant. Moreover, he could now justify his having come on board to look for Christina. Whatever might have happened earlier, he could swear that when he, as her fiancé, had been escorting her ashore, he had been set on himself and had seen the Marquis forcibly prevent her from walking down the gangway. The de Grasses would surely not willingly give him the opportunity to make a sworn deposition of that kind.

On the contrary, it was to their interest to keep him silent. But how would they do that? His close acquaintance with his mother's professional efforts immediately suggested the now unnerving phrase, 'Dead men tell no tales.' Yet he could not believe that the de Grasses would run the risk of committing murder in order to cover up the much lesser crime of kidnapping. It seemed far more probable that they would keep him a prisoner until they had got Christina safely to England and had had a chance to manufacture ample evidence that she had gone willingly. They would then have very little to fear if they released him, particularly if they first gave him a crack on the head, followed it when he came round with a shot of something to keep him muzzy, and then took him to a hospital with a story that they had found him wandering. There would not be much point in his mother and C. B. swearing that they had seen him board the yacht illegally; and any evidence he might give of recent events would be most dubiously regarded owing to his condition.

Such a prospect was very far from pleasant; but he felt that Christina's prospects were infinitely worse. He had good reason to suppose that she was still on board, but if she had been taken off after he had been thrown down the companionway, that made no difference. She was now in the clutches of these people and there was not a soul who could do anything to aid her.

At the moment, under the strange influence that night had upon her, it was probable that she was not at all apprehensive about her future; but she would wake to-morrow a young and frightened girl, knowing herself to be at the mercy of men she knew to be her enemies. It seemed unlikely that the de Grasses would do her any injury; but what would happen to her when they had delivered her in England? If C. B. was to be believed —and his word must be accepted as authoritative on all criminal matters—she would be drugged, hypnotized, bedevilled and given over to the lusts of evil men, until such time as the evil had entered into her to the exclusion of all else and, debauched in mind and body, she willingly lent herself to every filthiness that imagination could suggest.

The thought of what she would suffer during periods of lucidity, and the awful fate that must finally overtake her, made the perspiration break out on John's forehead. For a long time he sought desperately for possible ways of saving her, but each grew more far-fetched and hopelessly impractical, until at last he drifted off to sleep.

He was woken by the steel door of the cabin being swung back with a clang. Starting up, he saw two seamen standing in the doorway. Both were brawny, tough-looking fellows with hard eyes. The elder, whose hair showed grey at the sides under a rakishly-worn peaked cap, beckoned to him to come out, and said:

"Get between us; and keep your hands at your sides, or it will be the worse for you."

The yacht's diesels had been stopped and her only movement now was a gentle rise and fall; so it seemed that she must have entered a port or have anchored in some sheltered bay. John gave a quick glance at his watch. It was a quarter-past three. That told him that she might have run between forty to fifty miles along the coast, but in which direction he had no means of guessing. Obviously this was no time to argue; so he slid off the bunk, placed himself between the two sailors, so that the three of them formed an Indian file, and in this manner allowed himself to be escorted up on deck.

He saw then that he had been right in believing the yacht might be anchored in a bay. The moon was almost down, but the stars were bright and there was sufficient light for him to make out a headland on either side, from which the land dropped away. Between them rose an outline of dark hillside, with low down on it several lighted windows which appeared to be in one large, solitary house.

A rigged gangway, slung from davits on the yacht's portside, had been lowered. John was marched on to it, and saw that a motor-launch was rocking gently beside the square grating which formed the lowest stage of the ladder. As he walked down to it he began to play with the thought of taking a swift dive; but he was not much good at swimming under water; so he was very doubtful of his ability to get out of sight before he could be spotted and recaptured. The idea was definitely rendered stillborn when they reached the launch by the grey-haired sailor producing an ugly sheath-knife, showing it to him and saying:

"Should Monsieur show any desire to go for a swim, he will enter the water with this in his liver. Those are my orders."

Evidently the man felt that it was not for a member of the crew to enter the launch's cabin, as he prodded John towards the bow and made him sit down on the fore-deck with his back against the cabin's forward end, then sat down beside him. A moment later John heard voices, and among them Christina's, confirming his belief that the Marquis had not taken her off in his car, but detained her on the yacht. By turning his head he caught a glimpse over the low top of the cabin of several people coming down the gangway, and she was among them. The party scrambled on to the launch and, as soon as they had settled themselves in the cabin, it cast off.

John's spirits were now on the upgrade. As long as he had been in his cabin prison he had thought it certain that he would be kept there, perhaps for several days, or anyway until Christina had been got safely away, and that it was even possible that he might never see her again. But now it looked as if they were both to be taken to the house with the lights, and that the place was to be used as a staging point in the arrangements for getting her to England. If so, it was at least conceivable that a chance might occur for him to rescue her, or to escape himself and let C. B. know where she was before she was moved on again.

Two-thirds of the way to the shore these new hopes were sadly dashed. The launch passed close to a small seaplane that lay rocking gently at its moorings. The sight of it instantly brought into John's mind the tall man with the fair fluffy moustache. He looked a typical pilot and probably this was his aircraft. If so, here were the means by which Christina was to be transported to England, and the odds were that they meant to fly her off at dawn. With so short a time to go, all chance of rescue, or bringing C. B. and Inspector Malouet on the scene, would be ruled out.

John had barely assimilated this new cause for depression when the launch pulled in at the shoreward end of a long curved mole that formed a small private harbour. The party in the cabin landed first, and he could now see that it consisted of Christina, the Marquis, Jules, the pilot-type and the little man who looked like a valet. John's escort again showed his knife, then signed to him to follow them.

With the Marquis and Christina leading, they crossed the hard, went through a gate in a low wall and entered a garden. The trees there made it darker than it had been on the water, but there was still enough light to see by. The ground sloped up, but not sufficiently to require a path with hairpin bends, and as soon as they were within a hundred yards of the house John could make out its main features.

Unlike most large properties on the Riviera, it was a flat-faced, pedimented eighteenth-century château with tall windows. It had two floors only of residential accommodation and from the first jutted out a broad terrace. Below the terrace the façade was broken only by a low central door and on either side of it a row of small, square windows protected by iron grilles. As John was aware, it was usual for the ground floor of such buildings to be used solely as cellarage, store-rooms and offices; and as no lights showed from any of the small windows it seemed that this château was no exception.

The central door opened on to a small, stone-flagged hall with a low vaulted ceiling, and a curved stairway having a wrought-iron balustrade, which led up to another much loftier hall on the main floor. When they reached it the Marquis opened one of a pair of tall, white, heavily-gilded double doors and bowed Christina through into a brightly lit *salon*. With its panelled walls, tapestries, Aubusson carpet and delicate furniture, it had all the elegance of a genuine *Louis Seize* apartment. The others followed, but as John stepped inside Jules said to the sailor who had brought up the rear of the party:

"You may go now, Chopin. Monsieur Upson and I will take care of your prisoner."

The Marquis meanwhile was addressing the little man who on closer inspection was obviously a servant, and John heard him say:

"Frederick, see that all is in order in the du Barry room. Mademoiselle may like to rest there for a while before she sets

162

out on her journey. Then prepare our special accommodation downstairs for Monsieur Fountain. He will be our guest for some days."

These orders confirmed John's belief that within a few hours they intended to fly Christina off in the seaplane. It was the first chance he had had to get a proper look at her since they had been separated on the yacht, and as Jules closed the door behind him he shot a glance at her.

She was half-turned away from him, so he could not catch her eye; but he was given a swift indication of her mood. As the valet left the room by a further door, she asked the Marquis angrily:

"Where are you sending me?"

"To England, Mademoiselle." He waved a hand towards the pilot-type, who was now leaning negligently against a large marble-topped table. "I have already presented Mr. Reg Upson to you. He was an ace airman in the last war, so you need have no fears for your safety while he flies you home."

Jules and John were still standing within a few feet of the door to the hall. Seeing that everyone's attention was concentrated on Christina, this seemed to John as good an opportunity as he might ever get to make a bolt for it. Taking a swift step back, he seized the door handle.

Quick as his movement had been, Upson's was quicker. Out of the corner of his eye he had seen John brace himself and guessed his intention. Whipping a small automatic from a shoulder holster, he cried in English:

"Halt; or I fire!"

John had not even got the door open. Under the menace of the pointing pistol there was nothing he could do but let go of the handle and give a resigned shrug. Jules then grabbed him by the arm, pulled him into the middle of the room and pushed him into an armchair.

The airman laid his automatic down on the top of the table and said in a lazy drawl, "It's just as well you stopped when you did, or I'd have put one through the calf of your leg."

Riled by Jules' rough handling of him, but knowing it to be no time to start another fight, John turned and snapped at

163

Upson, "If you are an ex-R.A.F. officer you ought to be ashamed of yourself."

"Got to earn a living somehow," Upson replied indifferently. "And I'm paid darn' well for taking care of troublesome types like you."

Christina was still staring at the Marquis, and she suddenly burst out, "I will not be sent home! I wish to remain out here!"

"We are not concerned with your wishes, Mademoiselle; and you will do exactly as you are told," said the Marquis coldly.

She was standing within a few feet of Upson. Turning towards her, he said, "And while you are with me, little lady, don't try any funny business. Can't afford to do gentle restraining acts in a small aircraft like mine. If you start anything, you'll get a backhander, hard, right on your snub-nose. Understand?"

With glaring eyes she spat at him, "I am not coming with you! I'll scratch your eyes out if you try to make me."

Upson shrugged, and looking across at his employer broke into French. "Monsieur le Marquis will agree that it would be dangerous to take her up in her present state, as she might easily bring about an accident. May I suggest that she should be given a shot of dope?"

The Marquis nodded, and Jules commented, "We thought that might be necessary. Obviously it is, and we'll see about it in good time before you start."

Christina's lips drew back in a snarl. "I will not let you! I will tear the face off the first one of you who touches me!" Then, after a moment, she added in a different tone, "I will go only if you will let John Fountain come with me."

"That," said the Marquis firmly, "is impossible."

Jules turned to John and said, "I may as well tell you now what we intend to do with you. I warned you that you would get hurt if you tried to interfere with us, and you have. I got hurt, too, although not as much, and that's all in the day's work; so I bear no malice. But that is beside the point. By butting in you have seen enough to bring a case against us for kidnapping; therefore we cannot afford to let you go. In fact, you have made it necessary for us to keep you out of the way for a considerable time. You will remain here for a few days, then you will be picked up by one of our cargo steamers on its way from Marseilles to North Africa."

"Africa!" John exclaimed, aghast.

"Yes. You will be put ashore without money or papers in some small Libyan port, and by the time you have made your way home all this will be ancient history. Should you still bring a case, we shall be able to show that you went at your own wish, and had been suffering from mental trouble."

John had come to his feet, but he endeavoured to keep the anger and apprehension out of his voice as he asked, "How would you show that?"

"Because you are going to write a letter to me, saying that, owing to overwork, you have recently caught yourself imagining things and fear a nervous breakdown; so feel that a long sea trip is just what you need to put you right, and are very glad to accept my offer to send you round the Mediterranean in one of our vessels. Incidentally, should it come to a case, our Captain will swear to it that you left the ship without warning him of your intention to do so; and to land without money or papers will be further evidence that you have been off your nut."

"And what if I refuse to write such a letter?"

Jules sighed. "I fear that we shall be unable to provide you with food or drink until you do."

To everyone's surprise Christina cried, "Send me to North Africa with him!"

"You are going to England," declared the Marquis, his lean face for the first time showing irritation.

"I am not! I refuse!" cried Christina furiously. Then she pulled off her left glove and, looking away from it herself, displayed the glistening ring on her swollen finger. "Do you not see! I am tied to him by this. I must go wherever he goes."

Jules stared at her in astonishment. "But . . . but you told me this evening that your engagement to him was only a phoney one."

She shuddered and violently shook her head. "That was

before the two of you had a fight. When he overcame you I knew I was his. Now I am bound to him . . . bound to him."

Flecks of foam had appeared at the corners of her mouth, and they all thought that at any moment she was going to have a fit. The Marquis moved quickly over to a side-table on which there was an array of drinks. A siphon was among them, and squirting some soda-water into a glass he carried it over to her.

"Mademoiselle, calm yourself, I beg," he said. "Drink this, and sit down for a moment."

Christina took the glass and drank most of its contents. She gasped and set it down on the marble-topped table, but she did not sit down. No one spoke for a moment, then Jules said to John:

"There is another letter which it would be advisable for you to write. This one would be just as much in your interest as in ours. It would be to your mother, to allay her anxiety about your disappearance. You could simply say that you have accepted an invitation from me to go for a cruise round the Mediterranean and expect to be back in about six weeks."

"You want me to do that in the hope that it will stop her putting the police on to you?"

"Exactly. She will realize, of course, that the 'invitation' was one which you were not allowed to refuse; but if she knows what has happened to you and believes you to be safe, there will be no point in her asking the police to trace you."

"Again, what happens if I refuse?"

"Nothing!" Jules smiled. "We shall have to have you kept on board the ship a few weeks longer, to counteract the possibility of a French Consul having you flown back, should your case have been put on his list by the police if your mother asked them to conduct a search for you; but that is all. The point is that once you are on board it will be quite impossible for the police to trace you until you land. And no one else will inform your mother what has become of you, unless you agree to do so yourself. Therefore, if you refuse this offer, she may be caused great distress for some time to come, believing you to be dead. It was to suggest to you that you should write this letter now, for delivery to-morrow, that we had you brought up here instead of putting you straight into a cell. Come, what do you say?"

John found himself caught in a cleft stick. The last thing he wanted to do was to protect the de Grasses from police enquiries, and by giving a reason for his disappearance he might hamper his mother in getting them to take the case further than a routine questioning of Jules—who, of course, would have a plausible story all ready for them. On the other hand, he knew how desperately worried his mother would become if she had no news of him. To allow her to remain in a state of terrible anxiety for several weeks, when he could easily reassure her, was unthinkable. So he said:

"Very well. I will write to my mother on the lines you suggest."

It was at that instant that Christina shot the Marquis.

CHAPTER XII

THE FIGHT IN THE CHÂTEAU

JOHN did not see Christina grab the gun up from the table, or fire it. He was looking at Jules; and Jules, the Marquis and Upson were all looking at him, waiting to hear whether he would decide to write the letter to his mother. Christina had taken advantage of that moment. She had stretched out her hand as though to pick up the glass she had set down a few moments before and finish the drink the Marquis had given her; instead, she snatched the automatic that Upson had left lying within a few inches of his own hand, aimed it, and pressed the trigger.

Simultaneously with the crash of the pistol, the Marquis clasped his right shoulder. Reeling back, he collapsed on a *Louis Seize* settee. It was as well for him that he did, as Christina sent a second shot at him. It thudded into the Gobelin tapestry behind his head.

Upson was the first to move. The Marquis had hardly staggered under the impact of the bullet before the airman swung a blow at Christina's head. She ducked it as she fired her second shot, sprang away and turned the pistol on him. There was murder in her eyes. Seeing it, his face blanched and he made a futile gesture, throwing out his hands as though to ward off the bullet.

There was barely four feet between them; so had it not been for John he would certainly have been shot. But, as he had struck out at Christina, John had swung round on his other side, run in, and struck at him. The blow landed squarely on the side of his face. He was already slightly off balance and it sent him spinning. Christina's third shot sang harmlessly over his shoulder.

Jules was standing near the table on which was the tray of drinks. Snatching up a bottle of Dubonnet by the neck, he flung it at Christina. The cork came out as it flew through the air, and the sticky liquid splashed all over her face and neck, but the bottle missed her.

Letting out a scream of rage, she ran towards him, firing as she went. With extraordinary agility he flung himself aside, pirouetted like a ballet dancer and kicked her on the thigh. She went over with a crash and the pistol exploded for the fifth time. Her fourth shot had missed Jules, but the fifth paid an unexpected dividend. At that moment the door by which the valet had left the room opened, and he poked his head in. The bullet fired at random splintered the woodwork within an inch of his chin. His eyes popping with fright, he jerked back his head and slammed the door shut again.

As Christina measured her length on the floor Jules ran at her, but John was in the act of rushing at him. They collided. John's rush had carried him half across the room, so there was more force behind it. Jules went over backward, striking his head hard on the parquet floor. He rolled away, then struggled to his knees, but remained there grasping a chair with one hand and swaying from side to side, temporarily incapable of further action.

Christina was up again, the automatic still clutched in her hand. The Marquis had also staggered to his feet, and with his sound arm was clutching a silken bell-rope. As he jerked it up and down a bell could be heard clanging in the distance. Christina had pitched forward to within a few feet of him. No sooner was she up than she pointed her gun at his heart. Only just in time to stop her from committing murder, John knocked it aside. The bullet shattered the centre panel of a cabinet displaying a beautiful Sèvres dinner service.

The tinkle of glass and china merged into the thunder of feet charging across the parquet. As John and Christina stood together Upson was coming at them from behind with a chair raised above his head. They swung round to face him. For a second it seemed certain that it must fell one, or both, of them.

There was no time to step aside; no time even for Christina to bring up her pistol. John gave her a push that sent her reeling back on to a chaise longue. Lowering his head he went

right in under the chair and butted the airman in the stomach
Upson lost his grip on the chair; it crashed to the floor behind
John's back. He managed to keep his feet, but Upson went
over backwards, the breath driven from his body, and lay
writhing in agony.

From the time Christina had fired her first shot, not one of
these violent, kaleidoscopic actions had occupied more than
ten seconds; yet in this bare minute or two the crack of the
shots and the clanging of the bell had roused the house. The
sound of running feet could be heard pounding along a corridor
somewhere beyond the door through which the valet had
poked his head.

As Christina pushed herself up from the chaise longue on
to which John had thrust her, he grasped her arm, turned her
towards the double doors by which they had been brought in
and cried:

"Quick! The servants are coming! This way, or they'll
catch us!"

Still clutching the pistol, she ran through into the hall. He
darted after her, but as he slammed the door behind him he had
the presence of mind to swing round and turn the big ornate
key that protruded from the lock. In three strides he reached
the head of the short flight of stone stairs. Christina was half
way down them. Suddenly she lurched sideways, let out a yell
and fell, sprawling the last few steps to bring-up against the
terminal post at the bottom of their curved wrought-iron
balustrade.

"You hurt?" he panted, helping her to her feet.

She took a couple of steps and screwed up her face with
pain. "It's my ankle. It twisted under me."

The little automatic had been dashed from her hand, but
had not exploded. John stooped, grabbed it up, put on the
safety-catch and slipped it into his pocket as he cried anxiously
"Will it bear you? Can you possibly manage to run?"

"It has got to," she gasped, her eyes flashing with determination.

"Well done! Here, lean on my shoulder."

She flung an arm round his neck, and together they trotted

across the stone flags to the outer door. On emerging from it they could hear loud banging on the doors of the *salon*, and excited shouts. Jules was yelling for the servants—"Marcel! Henri! Frederick! Where the devil are you?"

As the fugitives ran out into the garden, by contrast with the brightly lit interior of the château it seemed pitch black. The moon had now set and the stars gave only a pale light in the open spaces between the trees. Their instinct was to take the way they had come and head down the broad central walk for the harbour. But no help was to be expected there, and, after a second, John realized that they would stand a better chance of getting away if they could find a side entrance to the grounds. Swerving to the right, he ran Christina along under the terrace till they got to the end of the building. A wall continued from it, in which there was a tall arch with a wrought-iron gate leading to a stable-yard.

By the time they reached the arch, the windows of the *salon* had been flung open and several people had run out on to the terrace. Jules was shouting to the servants, "Get out into the garden. Quick now! Quick!"

John pushed open the iron gate. As he did so a furious barking started and a big wolfhound came bounding from a kennel towards him. Christina screamed and he swiftly pulled the gate shut. At that instant two men ran out from the main door of the house. Hearing the barking and the scream, they swerved to the right and came racing towards the stables.

The second John had the gate shut, he and Christina made a dash for a path that led down the side wall of the garden. It was screened from the château by a belt of trees and thick shrubs which hid it in almost total darkness. Fifty feet along it he came upon the thing he had been hoping so desperately to find—a postern gate. As his hand grasped the latch he prayed frantically that it would not be locked. His prayer was answered: at the first pull it flew open. With Christina still leaning on him, he stepped through it.

One glance in each direction, and his heart sank with dismay. It gave on to the road leading up from the harbour to the carriage entrance of the château, and on, inland. On its

far side was a steep bank topped by another wall, which ran
unbroken both ways as far as he could see. Behind them they
could hear the flying feet of their pursuers nearing the stables.
Christina was moaning with pain, and the tears were running
down her face. The road between the two walls was like a
long, curved corridor, and in it there was no scrap of cover.
Once out on it, the stars would give enough light for them to
be seen. However game Christina's effort, within two hundred
yards they must be run down and caught.

Pulling her back, John whispered, "We must hide: it's our
only chance."

Leaving the postern door wide open, he drew her swiftly
with him down the path. Fifty feet farther on he pushed her in
among the bushes and they stood there with their hearts
pounding, trying to still the rasping of their breath.

It was none too soon. Jules' men had found the iron gate
to the stable-yard still shut and the hound baying on its far
side. Realizing that the fugitives could not have gone that way,
they darted towards the dark path. Fifty feet along it they came
upon the open postern. As John had hoped, they ran through
it. He gave them a minute, fearing that, seeing no one up or
down the road, they might come back. Then, after a mutter of
voices, he heard their running steps again as they headed
towards the nearest bend, which lay up the slope.

Coming out from their cover, John and Christina continued
to follow the path, but now at a quick walk and making as
little noise as possible. Temporarily they had escaped from the
likelihood of immediate capture; but people calling to one
another from the centre of the garden told them that Jules,
Upson, and perhaps some of the other servants had come out
to join in the hunt; and where the shrubbery was thinnest John
twice caught the flash of torches.

He knew that now there was little chance of slipping
unseen out of the gate down by the port, and was desperately
casting about for some place where they might hope to lie
concealed when the hunt moved in their direction. By this time
they were nearly at the bottom of the garden and could see
part of the wall that ran parallel with the shore. Above it

showed the starry sky, but at the corner where the two walls met a patch of blackness reared up to double their height, its faint outline having the appearance of a square, topped by a triangle. After a second John realized what it was, and whispered:

"That's a gazebo just ahead of us. With luck they will think we got away along the road. They may not look in there. Anyhow, it's our best bet. We must chance it."

"A what?" murmured Christina.

"A gazebo—a raised summer-house built on the corner of the wall, to give a view of the bay."

Swiftly but cautiously, they covered the short distance to the end of the path and made their way up the curving wooden stair they found there. The door of the gazebo was not locked, but it squeaked a little and, fearful of being heard, when they had crept inside they closed it gently behind them. For a moment they could see nothing, then panels of greyness showed the position of the windows and they realized that the place was sexagonal with a window in each of its sides except that occupied by the door. By groping about they found that it held basket chairs with cushions in them, a table and a low cupboard. Lowering themselves into two of the chairs, they subconsciously stilled their breathing while listening anxiously for sounds outside.

Muffled now by the wooden walls of the garden house, they could still hear the calls of the searchers. Once they caught the quick tread of heavy feet nearby, and the reflected glow from a torch lighted one of the windows on the garden side; but after a quarter of an hour of agonizing apprehension no sound had reached them for several minutes, so it seemed that the search had been abandoned.

Till then neither of them had dared to speak from fear that one of Jules' people might be hunting about in the shrubbery beneath them; but now John thought it safe to ask in a whisper:

"How is your ankle?"

"Not too bad," Christina whispered back. "It gave me hell while we were running; but since I've had it up on a chair the pain has eased a lot. I don't think it's sprained—only twisted."

"It ought to have a cold compress on, but there's no hope of that. Still, I could bind it up tightly, and that may help when we have to move again. Shall I try what I can do?"

By this time their eyes had become a little accustomed to the darkness; so he could just make out her nod. "I wish you would; but do you think you can see enough?"

"We could use my cigarette-lighter, but I don't like to risk it. This place may be visible from the house." As he spoke he knelt down and groped about till he found her foot. Having taken off her shoe, he felt the ankle gently with his finger-tips. It was swollen, but not very much. Getting out his silk handkerchief, he folded it on the seat of a nearby chair, as well as he could by touch, cornerwise into a long strip. Then he said:

"You had better take off your stocking."

She undid the suspender and rolled it down for him. He peeled it off and for a moment held her bare foot in his palm. It was cool, firm and delightfully smooth. His hand closed round it easily, and on an impulse he remarked:

"You were grumbling this afternoon about the size of your feet. I can't think why. This is a lovely little foot." The words were scarcely out when he regretted them from the sudden fear that she might take the compliment as an amorous overture. He had experienced how swiftly she could be aroused to uncontrollable passion during the dark hours, and the last thing he wished for was to have to repel advances of which she would be ashamed in the morning light.

His fears were not altogether unfounded. After a second's hesitation, she said very softly, "If you like to kiss the place, that might make it well."

Instead, he laid on the bandage. It was the handkerchief he had used to bathe his face in the cabin, so it was still damp and cold. As it touched her she gave a little gasp, and, to distract her mind from the thoughts on which he felt sure it was running, he told her about the use to which he had put it; then, as he drew the bandage tight and tied the pointed ends in a knot a few inches above her heel, went on to describe the hurts he had received on the yacht.

The ruse served to some extent, as she immediately became

all concern. Then leaning forward she found and stroked his face, as she murmured, "Poor John! You've had a frightful time. And all for my sake. But I'll do anything I can to make it up to you."

He got her stocking on over the bandage, then told her to pull it up; but she gave a low laugh.

"No; you do it for me, darling. I'm glad you like my feet; although you'd find them much bigger than you think if you saw them. Of my legs, though, I have real reason to be proud. They are a lovely shape and above the knees as soft as satin. Just feel, here by my suspenders."

Suddenly taking his hand, she pulled it forward till it touched the inner side of her thigh on a line with the top of her other stocking. The flesh there was like a cushion of swans-down under a taut-stretched skin of tissue-thin rubber; it had that indefinable quality of being cool at first touch, then instantly radiating heat. The back of his fingers were pressed for only a second against it. Jerking them away, he tore his hand from hers, and snapped:

"That's quite enough of that! Do it up yourself."

For a moment she was silent, then she said in a voice near to tears, "Oh, John, you are unkind. Have you been playing with me? Don't you love me at all?"

His mouth had suddenly become dry. He swallowed, but his words came huskily in the darkness. "If you want to be seduced, ask me to fix your stockings for you to-morrow afternoon. But I'm damned if I'll make love to you now, while you are under some accursed influence."

She sighed. "But it's now I want you to. I'd make you if I wasn't so tired."

He laughed a little grimly. "You would probably succeed if I wasn't so tired myself. My ribs are still giving me gyp, and I'm one big ache all over. It must be past four o'clock, too; so it is over twenty hours since we had any sleep, except for our nap in the olive grove."

"That was nice." Her tone was warm at the memory. "But I'm such a stupid little fool in the daytime. I was nervous of you then."

"I like you better when you are like that, because you are your real self."

"What is my real self?" she asked cynically. "My feelings are as real by night as they are by day. I shall be the way you like me best again soon, though. The change always comes an hour or so before dawn, and I can feel it coming on. But you can't have it both ways. If they find us here and we have to try to escape again I'll probably behave like an hysterical schoolgirl, and I'll never have the pluck to fire that gun."

"Don't worry. I have it, and I felt it over soon after we got in here. There are still two bullets left in it. They should be enough to give us a sporting chance of a break-out if we are found here, but it looks as if they have made up their minds that we got away along the road. The thing that troubles me is your ankle. I should like to give them another half-hour, then go out and reconnoitre. If no one is about it would be the perfect opportunity to slip away inland behind the château. No one would ever find us up there in the *maquis*. But there is always the chance that we might be spotted leaving the garden and have to run for it again; and, anyway, I'm sure your ankle would never stand up to a long tramp over broken ground up into the hills."

"No, John. I'm afraid I should let you down if we tried that. Still, if they don't look for us here soon, it is very unlikely that they will to-morrow; so we could stay here in hiding all day. By the evening my ankle will be much stronger and we could slip away soon after dark."

"We'll be jolly hungry and thirsty by then; but it would certainly be our safest plan."

"A day's fasting won't do either of us any great harm. If you agree, let's try to get some sleep now."

"All right," he said, standing up. "There is a bigger chair here with a pull-out for the legs. I'll pile some cushions on it and you had better have that."

When he had arranged the chair, she rested one hand on his shoulder and pulled herself up beside him. Quietly, with no hint of seduction in her voice, she asked, "Do you care about me at all, John? Tell me honestly. I want to know."

"I can only say that in a very short time I have grown very fond of you," he hedged. "I've already told you that I refuse to make love to you except in the daytime."

"You are still afraid of me," she whispered, "but you needn't be. The windows are lighter already, with that pale light that comes before dawn. But I still have enough shamelessness left to tell you something. I love you. You may think that is just because I've never been kissed by any other man. It's not. It's something deep inside me. I know that at night my wanton thoughts might make me easy game for anybody; but during the day, although I am shy and awkward, I long every bit as much to feel your lips on mine. I love you. I love you terribly. I'd die for you, John, if I had the chance."

He could find no words with which to reply, and after a moment she went on, "Even if you are only a little fond of me, do something for me, please. Let's lie down in the chair together. I want to feel your arms round me. You have been so gallant in the way you have protected me; but at any time my enemies may prove too much for you. We may never have this chance again. Although you can't tell me that you love me, let me go to sleep making believe that you do."

Gently he lowered her on to the pile of cushions, then lay down beside her and took her in his arms. She put her cheek against his, but made no attempt to kiss him. Her limbs relaxed and she gave a sigh of contentment. On a sudden impulse that overbore all his scruples, he murmured, "I love you, Christina. I love you," and drew her more closely to him.

For making love the pile of cushions on the long basket chair was quite adequate, but not for a prolonged sleep. It was too narrow, and beneath the cushions its arms dug into their backs. Dozing was all that either of them could manage, and some three hours later John kissed Christina lightly on the forehead, then got up.

He did so cautiously, as it was now full daylight; and if he showed himself above the level of the window-sills of the gazebo there was a risk that he might be seen. First he peeped out on the garden side. He could see no one in it, and the iron roller blinds of the château windows were all down. A glance at his watch showed him that it was just after half-past seven, so the lack of activity was not surprising in view of the fact that its occupants could not have got to bed much before half-past four.

Still crouching, he crossed to one of the windows overlooking the shore. That, too, presented a peaceful early morning scene, but a disappointing one. John had hoped to see there at least a few fisherfolk who in an emergency—such as Jules suddenly thinking of the gazebo later in the day and ordering it to be searched—could be called on for help. There was not a soul to be seen and it was quite clear now that the little harbour was a strictly private one. The only craft in it were a twenty-foot sailing yacht, a sailing dinghy, a speed-boat and Upson's seaplane. The big yacht in which they had been brought there was still lying at anchor about a quarter of a mile beyond the point of the mole. Made fast to it were the launch in which they had come ashore and another more powerful vessel that looked like a converted submarine-chaser.

He was just wondering if they could get out of the garden unobserved, swim out to the speed-boat and make off in it, when the submarine-chaser cast off from the yacht and turned her nose in towards the harbour. In a graceful curve she rounded the point of the mole, reversed her engines, and manœuvred a little until her pilot had brought her skilfully alongside its outer end. Two sailors with lines jumped ashore and she was swiftly made fast. A moment later a gangway was put out and a group of people landed from her.

Suddenly John jerked himself erect and gave a shout. "Christina! We're saved! There's Mumsie! I'd know that absurd hat of hers anywhere. And there's C. B.! They've got the police with them. Hurrah! They must have found out where the yacht had gone, and come to rescue us."

Christina had still been dozing. She scrambled to her feet and joined him at the window. Both of them could make out the group clearly now, as it advanced along the mole. In addition to Molly Fountain and C. B. it consisted of a very tall old man with a drooping grey moustache, and three men in uniform.

178

"Come on!" cried John. "Let's go down and meet them. But how is your ankle? Is it up to walking?"

She tried her weight on it. "Yes, it's much better. I'll be all right if you give me your arm. Oh, John, what wonderful luck their coming and finding us here."

As she spoke they turned to look at one another. It was the first time they had done so in daylight since the evening before. Neither realized what a sight they themselves presented, and grinned at the marks of battle on the other.

"You *are* in a mess," Christina laughed. "Your chin's all swollen and you have a glorious black eye."

"You look as if you had been dragged through a hedge backwards, yourself," he retorted cheerfully. "The sticky liquor from that bottle Jules shied at you has collected so much dirt that you'll have to scrape it off your neck with a knife; and your hair is a veritable bird's-nest."

As he spoke he took the little automatic out of his pocket, and added, "I'll keep this handy, just in case anyone tries to stop us between here and the gate. Come along now! Let's go!"

When he opened the door of the gazebo the garden still appeared to be deserted; so they went down the steps to the path. On their way to the gate he said, "Now that the police have been brought into this we ought to be careful what we say. If I had had the wit and the chance to snatch this gun last night I have no doubt I should have shot someone with it myself; but such acts usually have repercussions. Mind, I don't think there is the least likelihood of the Marquis bringing an action against you. He would find it much too difficult to explain away his part in the affair. I'm only a bit worried that wounding with firearms may be what is termed a crime against the state. If so, and the French police are told about it, they would have no option but to arrest you; so I think we had better skip your grand performance with the heavy armaments."

"Tell them what you like," she shrugged. "I was mad as a hatter at the time; so I suppose it's lucky I didn't kill someone; but I'm not feeling a bit like Two-gun Annie now."

"May be," he answered with a smile. "But it would be

pretty mean of me to let them infer that I rescued you, when it was really you who rescued me. I think I'll say——"

"Oh, don't be silly, John! I could never have got away without you. The less you say about my part in it, the better. They are much more likely to believe that you slew all the dragons and carried me away across your shoulder. Anyhow, I'll leave all the talking to you."

On reaching the gate they found that it was not locked, so they walked straight out on to the hard; and there, now only fifty feet away, were the group from the submarine-chaser.

With exclamations of surprise, followed by shouts of delight, the rescuers joined the rescued. Molly was so overcome at seeing her boy safe and sound that she dared not kiss him from fear of bursting into tears; so, much to his surprise, she shook him vigorously by the hand. With a laugh, he picked her up and hugged her. Then, in turn, she hugged Christina. C. B. introduced the tall old man as ex-Inspector Malouet, and the senior police officer as Sergeant Bouvet. The next ten minutes passed in a gabble of questions and explanations.

It emerged that they were on the island of Port Cros, the smallest of the three main islands known as the Iles d'Hyères. The de Grasses had long owned the château and a fine estate there, but otherwise it was almost uninhabited. On arriving at St. Tropez, Malouet had suggested it as the most likely place for the yacht to have taken Christina, as in any public harbour along the coast the arrival of a vessel of her size would at once have been reported. After a lengthy discussion with the local police, he had persuaded them to co-operate by getting the customs temporarily to place at his disposal one of the fast craft they used for the prevention of smuggling. On reaching the Ile de Port Cros they had boarded the yacht with a search warrant. Her Captain had refused all information, so they had spent an hour going through her; then, having drawn blank, they had just come ashore to pursue their enquiries at the château.

John gave an abbreviated version of what had happened to him and Christina, concluding with their escape to the gazebo. When he had done, Sergeant Bouvet said:

"It appears that Mademoiselle accepted an invitation to go aboard the yacht, and that Monsieur joined her there in an irregular manner. However, that could not excuse the treatment to which you allege that you were later subjected. Does either of you wish to make a charge? If so, I must take down your deposition in detail."

"Hold yourself, my son, hold yourself," said the elderly Malouet, patting him kindly on the shoulder. "Your enthusiasm does you credit, but there is more in this matter than appears on the surface. If you will permit me, I should like to talk privately with these young people before they commit themselves to any legal action."

"But of a certainty, Monsieur," replied the sergeant, and from his tone it was clear that he regarded the ex-inspector with a sentiment akin to veneration. "It is a privilege to have your guidance in such an affair, and you have only to make your wishes known to me."

Malouet favoured him with a courteous little bow. "Since you are so kind, I suggest that we should all return to our ship. For the time being I think it would be as well if we made it as difficult as possible for anyone to trace Mademoiselle's movements. I am, therefore, loath to take her back to St. Tropez. Perhaps on your way there you could land us at some little-frequented place. Later, should it be decided that a charge is to be preferred, you may be sure that I shall lose no time in getting in touch with you."

"As you will, Monsieur. Let us go back on board, then. Have you as yet decided whereabouts you would like us to land you?"

For a minute or two the old man did not reply; but when they had covered about fifty paces towards the submarine-chaser he said, "If we take the route between the islands and the coast we must pass a little place called Cavalaire. The village is on a shallow, sandy bay, facing eastward; but it is not that I have in mind. To the south of it there is a headland, and on the headland is a small hotel called the Sur Mer. In the old days it was owned by a man named Gandini and was famous for its good food, as he was once a *maître d'hôtel* at the Negresco.

He has long since sold it, but it has a private bay on which we could be landed from a boat."

"I know it!" The sergeant waved an airy hand. "You are as good as there already, Monsieur. A perfect spot to go ashore discreetly, observed only by a handful of people. So early in the year I doubt if even the hotel itself will be open."

"I had rather hoped it would," Malouet confessed, "as I am beginning to feel the need for my *petit déjeuner*. But if it is not, we can walk down to the village, hire a car there, and drive to some other small place for a meal, before progressing further."

Ten minutes later they were on board and the vessel had cast off. Having installed Molly, Christina, Monsieur Malouet, C. B., and John in the after-cabin, Sergeant Bouvet tactfully withdrew; so they were able to talk more freely.

Rounding the western point of the Île de Port Cros, they left the much larger Île de Porquerolles on their left, and headed in towards Cap Benat on the mainland. Meanwhile, John and Christina gave the old walrus-moustached ex-inspector a more detailed account of what had happened to them during the night, suppressing only Christina's hectic performance with the gun. Then Malouet asked her to tell him of her earlier meetings with the de Grasses, and anything else she could remember having a possible bearing on her case that had occurred since she had come to the South of France, and she did so while the low-throbbing craft carried them swiftly across the bay towards Le Lavendou.

Although it was still only the first week in March, no cold or boisterous wind disturbed the serenity of their short voyage. The sun was shining in an almost cloudless sky of pale blue, and its rays could already be felt, promising another day of pleasant warmth. The sea still held the greeny-blueness of early morning, but its surface was unruffled by white horses and the wave crests were hardly perceptible except where they creamed upon the rocks along the shore. Behind them lay the Iles d'Hyères, now holding the suggestion of romance that always attaches to green islands set at a distance in a sparkling sea. Ahead rose up the indented coast of the mainland, with its rocky foreshore, verdant slopes and background of snow-topped mountains.

The twenty miles was soon covered and by half-past eight the ex-submarine-chaser was nosing her way into a small bay with rugged cliffs on either hand. A dinghy was lowered, Sergeant Bouvet and the captain of the vessel were taken leave of with warm thanks for their help, and the shore party were landed on a flat shelf of rock at the foot of the right-hand promontory, from which visitors to the hotel bathed in summer.

Slowly they made their way up the rough, steep path to the hotel. It was a small two-storey building, having only a dozen bedrooms and a single *salon*, the whole length of its ground floor on the seaward side being devoted to a covered terrace which served as its restaurant. It had not yet been opened for the season, but the proprietor and his wife readily agreed to provide breakfast for their unexpected visitors. A small boy was despatched on a bicycle to buy *croissants* in the village, 'Monsieur' set about his preparations for making a big ham omelette, and 'Madame' showed her guests up to five bedrooms that had fixed basins, so that they could freshen themselves up after their night out.

John was still in his shirt-sleeves, putting the finishing touches to his hair with a borrowed comb, when there came a gentle knock on the door of the room he had been given. On his calling, "Come in," Christina limped in and closed the door behind her.

She held out her left hand. The middle of the engagement finger was covered with a thick lather, and she said, "I've come for you to get your ring off. The knuckle is still a bit swollen, but I think you will be able to wriggle it over now I've made it slippery with soap."

"Why do you want to take it off?" he asked in surprise.

"You said you would this morning. You promised to just after you had had your fight with Jules in the cabin of the yacht."

"I wasn't speaking seriously. I said that only to pacify you at the time. You know how different you become from your real self at night."

She coloured, looked quickly away from him, and stammered, "I . . . I'd rather not talk about last night. I mean about . . . about what occurred between us. Although my memory of it is a bit blurred now, I know that I behaved abominably. I feel terribly ashamed."

"You needn't be." He smiled, cutting her short. "You were really very sweet once we had settled down in the summer-house."

"It was you who were sweet to me. You said you loved me, and I shall never forget that." Her words came out in a rush now. "I know you don't really, and that you probably said it only to comfort me, but please don't admit it, or protest that you do, out of kindness. You see, you may have really meant it just for that brief time. Anyhow, I'd like to believe so, because it will be a lovely memory to take away with me."

"Take away!" he echoed. "What on earth are you talking about?"

She extended her hand again. "That is why I want you to have back your ring. I'll have no more use for it now, even for make-believe. I thought it all out while we were dozing early this morning. I have repaid your mother's kindness by causing her a night of desperate anxiety about you, and I brought you into a situation where you might have lost your life, or anyhow have been seriously injured. That isn't right. This horrible affair is a matter for myself and my father. If anyone is responsible for me, it is he; so I have decided that the time has come when I must disobey his orders. I am going back to join him in England."

CHAPTER XIII

PRISON FOR ONE

"You can't do that," John said quickly. "He brought you out here to keep you out of danger."

Christina nodded. "I know that was his idea; but it has failed. The danger has caught up with me just the same. As soon as our secret enemies discovered my hiding-place his plan broke down; so there is no point in my staying here any longer."

"Oh, yes there is. For some reason we can't yet guess at, they want to get you back to England. To go there would be to play into their hands."

"You may be right about that, but there is a chance that when Father knows what has happened he may be able to think of a new plan to foil them. Anyhow, I have caused your mother and you more than enough trouble already. You've both been wonderful to me; but I can't let things go on like this. If Father is in no position to help me I'll go into hiding somewhere and face what is coming on my own."

"No you won't! I won't let you."

"John, I've made up my mind about this, and I am in my right senses now. Please take off your ring."

He shook his head. "Nothing doing, my dear. While you were distraught last night you declared that it bound you to me. As far as you are concerned I am on the side of the angels, and if you felt that so strongly even in the dark hours, it is a symbol that you cannot yet afford to do without. So you are going to stay bound to me until we have seen this business through. Afterwards you can give it back to me if you like."

"All right then," she sighed. "I'll keep your ring. But that doesn't alter what I said about going back to England."

"We'll talk about that over breakfast," he hedged. Then with a sudden grin he held out his arms. "In the meantime you continue to be my fiancée; so come and give me a kiss."

Her big brown eyes were full of tears as she put up her hands, took his face between them, and said, "Very well then; but this is good-bye."

"No it isn't, silly," he smiled. "It is only good-morning."

As they kissed another knock came on the door, and 'Madame's' voice called, "Breakfast will be ready in about five minutes, Monsieur."

"*Merci, Madame,*" he called back, and they broke their embrace; but, seeing that her left hand had made the right side of his face soapy, Christina picked up a towel and began gently to wipe it. As she did so, she murmured:

"What a good thing that I didn't mess up the other side. Your poor eye still looks awfully tender."

"If it is not too repulsive a sight, a kiss on it might help to make it well," he suggested.

As soon as he had spoken he regretted his words. Christina went scarlet, exclaimed, "How horrid of you to make me remember!" and throwing down the towel, ran limping from the room.

Down on the terrace he found his mother, C. B. and Malouet already assembled; but it was some time before Christina joined them, and when she did he saw that she had been crying. During the first part of the meal she was very silent; then gradually she seemed to forget the episode that had caused her such distress, and responded more readily to the questions Malouet put to her.

Although the previous afternoon now seemed days away to all of them, it was not yet twenty-four hours since C. B. had left London, and so far he had had no opportunity to hear Christina's own version of her story; so when the meal was finished he asked her, for his own benefit as well as Malouet's, to tell them all she could about her life from the beginning.

It took her the best part of an hour, and while there was nothing new to Molly and John in her account, when she had done both the old Frenchman and C. B. agreed with their view, that she was suffering from possession. As John had expected, none of the others would listen to her when she announced that she had decided to return to England; so he felt that he could leave it to their united firmness to dissuade her. They all pointed out in turn that the worst that was likely to happen to her while she remained in France was that the de Grasses might yet succeed in kidnapping her; whereas a far graver danger would threaten her once she had crossed the channel; so it would be absurd for her to go to meet it voluntarily, when they might be able to save her from it altogether.

As she proved very stubborn, a prolonged wrangle ensued, but eventually their various arguments based on the same theme took effect and she agreed to stay on, at least until after the 6th, which appeared to be the target date for whatever was being hatched against her.

However, out of her wish not to expose her friends to further trouble and danger, one new factor of considerable importance had arisen. Previously she had been adamant in her determination that her father should not be informed of what was happening to her, in case any communication by her should jeopardize his own plans; whereas now she had conceded that he was ultimately responsible for her safety as well as his own, and had proposed to go home and tell him what had happened herself. From this it followed that she no longer had any real grounds for objecting to anyone else doing so.

At first she protested, but both Malouet and C. B. pointed out that her father alone held the key to the mystery that surrounded her, and that it was not only unreasonable, but now also illogical, for her to insist on their fighting her battle for her in the dark. C. B. proposed that he should return to England that afternoon, and on his promising to use the utmost discretion in getting in touch with her father, she was persuaded to agree.

The next question was how best to protect her from further attempts by the de Grasses to get hold of her until C. B. returned and, having found out what they were really up against, some new plan could be made.

"Couldn't we stymie the de Grasses by bringing an action against them for kidnapping and assault?" Molly asked.

Malouet shook his head. "I would not advise it, Madame. That is why, having made use of our good friend Sergeant

Bouvet, I temporized with, and got rid of, him. Mademoiselle went on board the yacht willingly and your son clandestinely. Although they were both forcibly detained later, you may be sure that none of the crew would give evidence to that effect. There is the fact, too, that your son knocked out one of the officers who was quite rightly asking what business he had on board. That renders his position most precarious, and would certainly lead to a counter prosecution if we started anything. They are very averse to having the police enquire into their affairs; so I think it most unlikely they will bring an action against him. On the other hand, I am equally strongly of the opinion that he may get into serious trouble unless we let sleeping dogs lie."

Thinking of the Marquis with a bullet in his shoulder, John remarked, "In view of the rough handling we managed to give them before we escaped from the château, I should have thought there was quite a good chance that they may feel they have had enough of this affair. After all, they are only acting as agents; so they may quite well decide that the game is no longer worth the candle, and throw their hand in."

"Perhaps." Malouet pulled thoughtfully at his long moustache. "The sum they were offered was a thousand pounds, was it not? That would not mean very much to M. le Marquis, and you will note that he has hardly appeared in this matter himself. That the sailing of the yacht was delayed for him last night suggests that his reason for going to the Ile de Port Cros had no connection with Mademoiselle. It seems probable that from the beginning he regarded the matter as small game, and so handed it over to Count Jules. M. le Comte may, as you suggest, now feel that it has become too trouble-some a way of earning the amount concerned; but I think we should be most unwise to assume that."

"Besides," C. B. glanced at John, "no one likes being made a monkey of; and, the money apart, your having got the best of Jules may now have made him hopping-mad to get his own back on you. In any case it is up to us to take all the precautions we would if we were certain that he meant to have another crack."

John admitted that his idea had been prompted by unreasoning optimism, and said that he did not mean to suggest for one moment that they should relax their vigilance in guarding Christina. They then reverted to their discussion about what to do with her.

It was obvious that her own villa and Molly's were no longer safe; and Malouet thought that if they took her to any hotel upon the Riviera there was a strong probability that the de Grasses' grape-vine would soon locate her; so there would then be an immediate renewal of the risk that they would again succeed in luring her away. To form a more accurate estimate of that risk, he asked her to tell them again in more detail how Jules had managed to do so the previous night, and exactly what her feelings had been while she was with him.

Looking at Molly, she said, "You will remember that when John and I came in I spent only a few minutes downstairs being introduced to Colonel Verney; then I went up to my room to arrange my things. Darkness had fallen some time before I had finished and began to think of changing for dinner. It wasn't until I had had my bath that the thought of the frock I was going to wear came into my mind. I had brought over rather a quiet little thing, and I decided that I should look much nicer in a red and silver affair that I bought just before I left Paris; so I slipped on my day dress again and went over to my villa to fetch it.

"I put it with its etceteras into a small suitcase, and had just left the house when I met Jules coming up the garden path. He told me that he was on his way back from Cannes to St. Tropez with a friend, and felt that he must just look in to see if I had quite recovered from my attack on the previous night. By then we had walked back to the sitting-room, and although I had only fruit-juices I felt that I ought to offer him a drink. Rather to my surprise, he accepted, and naturally I had one with him.

"Perhaps he slipped something into mine when I was not looking. I couldn't say for certain. All I know is that after I had finished my drink I felt a little muzzy; and I don't remember anything more very clearly until I found myself sitting

189

with him in the back of a big car. A chauffeur was driving it, and with him in front there was a grey-haired man wearing a yachting cap, whom I later heard them call Chopin.

"By that time we were half-way to St. Tropez; and, although no mention was actually made of it, I was subconsciously aware that I had already agreed to dine with Jules in the yacht. I had the sort of light-headed, irresponsible feeling that I get at such times, and was rather amused at the thought that you and John would wonder what had happened to me. In fact, far from having any sense of guilt at my rudeness in going off without a word, I felt that I had played quite a clever trick in slipping away; and when the car drew up alongside the yacht I went on board without any suspicion that I was running into danger.

"Temporarily, the memory of my resistance to Jules' previous attempts to get me on to the yacht was entirely obliterated. To dine on board was a novel experience for me, and I thoroughly enjoyed it—apart from one petty annoyance. That was the discomfort caused me by John's ring. It was not only physical discomfort, owing to a queer heat that it seemed to be generating, but that tied up in some way with a growing mental uneasiness, vaguely suggesting that, although I was enjoying myself, I was playing with fire.

"But it was not till John actually appeared on the scene that I was seriously disturbed. Then I suddenly found myself a prey to violently conflicting emotions. One half of me intensely resented his intrusion; the other demanded that I should do whatever he told me to. I felt like that all the time he was fighting Jules, but the moment he knocked Jules out the tension disappeared. I knew then without a shadow of doubt that John had come to save me from something terrible, and that at all costs I must get away with him."

For a moment they were silent, then C. B. said, "That is interesting about the ring. Don't take it off whatever you do."

Malouet shrugged. "It is a strange phenomenon and one of which I have never previously heard; but clearly it is not sufficient to protect her. I wonder if M. le Comte did slip anything into the fruit drink? I think he must have, as how else can we account for her sudden muzziness followed by a lapse of memory lasting some twenty minutes?"

"I don't think the point of much importance," C. B. rejoined, giving his big nose a quick rub. "In my view the crux of the matter lies in Christina's sudden impulse to wear a more striking frock. It was that which got her out of the house, and it was followed by another—to ask Jules into her villa, instead of threatening to shout for help unless he cleared off. Those two mental processes taken in conjunction show that she was being influenced by some occult force to her own detriment before Jules even had a chance to open his mouth, let alone dope her drink."

"I am sure you are right," Molly agreed, "and it is that which sets us such a problem in devising means for her protection. All I can suggest is that we should go to some small hotel, and that she should share a room with me. I should be on hand then to counter these dangerous impulses, and at least that would make it much more difficult for anyone to get at her."

"It would certainly be a big help," C. B. conceded. "But I'm afraid even an arrangement of that kind would be far from watertight. You see, I consider it certain that the Satanists who are interested in Christina are having her overlooked from time to time by means of a crystal. That is how they know the right moment to send out a thought wave which gives her a certain impulse—such as that which led to her going across to her own villa last night just as Jules was due to come up the garden path. If you come into the picture they will try to work on you too."

"Then they won't have much luck," declared Molly truculently.

"Don't you be too certain of that. They are much too clever to try to make you do anything abnormal, but they might get at you in ways you would never suspect. You have got to sleep sometime; so they would send waves of sleep at you in the hope that you would drop off and leave them a free field with her. Even if you managed to keep awake all night, I am sure you would find it difficult to remain with Christina for every moment between dusk and dawn; and if they could succeed in separating you from her for only a few minutes that might prove enough for them to get her away altogether. Then, occult forces apart, if Jules has his dander up he may try a snatch. Remember, he came with a pal and a driver last night, which shows he was prepared to use violence if he did not find Christina open to suggestion."

"Well, can you think of any better plan?"

"Not for the moment. I feel sure that it was Christina being overlooked that enabled the Canon to discover her first hiding-place so quickly. For that reason I don't think it would help if you took her off to Lyons or Genoa. He would soon locate her and offer some local gang the thousand quid to do a snatch. Better the devil you know than the devil you don't, and we do know the de Grasses; so I think it would be wiser to keep her down here. I was only pointing out the sort of thing you and John may find yourselves up against while acting as her guardians."

"How about pretending she has had a nervous breakdown and putting her temporarily into a private mental home?" John suggested. "The nurses and porters in such places would never allow a patient to walk out in the middle of the night."

C. B. shook his head. "You are wrong there, John. We could not tell them that we had put her there to prevent her being kidnapped; so it would be easy to distract their attention. Our unknown enemy would have her out of a place like that in no time."

"I could have solved the problem for you had the war still been on," smiled Malouet. "At times, when the pace was getting too hot for some key man in the Resistance, we used to pretend to mistake him for an habitual criminal, pick him up under the criminal's name, fake a charge against him and pop him inside. The Boches never got wise to our using the prisons as hiding-places, and as soon as the hue and cry died down we let our friend escape. If only we could put Mademoiselle behind bars for a few days, neither the de Grasses nor a score of Satanists would be able to get her out. But unfortunately for our present business, it is no longer possible to commit a person on a false charge."

John was sitting beside Christina. He gave her a swift glance, then took Upson's pistol from his pocket and showed it to her under the table. She nodded; so he said to Malouet:

"What would happen, Monsieur, if I had shot somebody through the shoulder last night, and now surrendered myself at a police station, confessing what I had done?"

"They would take you into custody pending an enquiry."

"And then?"

"Presumably the person you had shot would come forward and charge you with having caused him grievous bodily harm."

"Say that for his own reasons he preferred not to bring a charge and denied that anything of the kind had happened?"

"Then you would be discharged as a harmless lunatic."

"Say he did bring a charge? I take it that in spite of my confession I should still be entitled to plead that I shot my man in self-defence?"

"Certainly; and if you could bring a reliable witness to swear to that, or even sound circumstantial evidence in support of your plea, the probability is that a verdict would be given in your favour. That, too, would be rendered all the more likely through your having surrendered yourself in the first place."

Again John looked at Christina, and again she nodded. He laid the pistol on the table, and said, "Then Christina and I propose that she should give herself up for having shot the Marquis de Grasse with that soon after half-past three this morning."

His announcement created quite a stir. At first the others would not believe that it was Christina who had used the weapon; but John gave them the true version of the fight in the château, and Christina filled in some of its more lurid details herself. Their account was so vivid that it carried conviction, and when they had done Molly exclaimed, with an envious glance at Christina:

"Oh, you lucky girl! What wouldn't I give to have had such an experience."

"Her luck is that she didn't kill him," commented C. B.

grimly. "If she had, she could not possibly escape being tried for murder; and as she went on the yacht willingly, even a plea of self-defence might not have saved her from a nasty sentence for manslaughter."

"Nevertheless, I congratulate Mademoiselle on her courage." Old Malouet made her a courtly little bow. "And I am sure this will enable me to arrange matters. We will not, I think, make use of our friend Sergeant Bouvet at St. Tropez. It will be better if I take you in to Nice, as I am more intimate with many of the officials there; so can make certain that you have every comfort that is allowed during your stay in prison."

"Thank you," said Christina. "You are very kind. Going to prison is a far from pleasant prospect, but it certainly seems the best idea for my protection, and I am sure you will do your utmost to make it as little disagreeable for me as possible. How long do you think they will keep me there?"

"To-day is Thursday, the 4th. Should M. le Marquis decide to charge you, the case could not come up for a first hearing before Monday. You would then be remanded while the lawyer we should find for you prepared your defence, and we could get you out on bail—if that was thought desirable—until you had to come up for trial. But, as I have already said, I think it very unlikely that the de Grasses will wish to have their affairs gone into in open court. Should M. le Marquis say that you shot him by accident and fled in panic afterwards, as he probably will, you will be released; but again, not before Monday, as once having been taken into custody you must be formally discharged by a magistrate. So in either case you will remain in prison over the week-end. And that is the important thing, for Saturday the 6th appears to be the critical date by which your enemies wish to get you to England."

Christina gave a rueful smile. "My birthdays have never meant very much to me, but all the same it seems a bit hard that I should have to spend my twenty-first in prison."

"What's that?" exclaimed C. B. "D'you mean that you will be twenty-one on the 6th? If so, that may be very important. Why didn't you tell us so before?"

"I'm sorry," Molly put in. "Christina did tell me the first time I talked to her. I ought to have told you, but there has been no mention of it since, and it entirely slipped my memory when I was telling you her history last night."

"Why may it be important?" Christina asked.

"Because it is the principal landmark in anyone's life. In addition the three sevens have a special magical property. As it is Satanists who are after you, that would explain why they are so anxious to get hold of you by that particular date. It looks now as if they are planning some special ritual at which the presence of an unmarried girl of twenty-one is required. To make use of her on her actual birthday would, of course, enormously increase the potency of the conjuration. In fact, that is probably essential to the success of the whole business."

"If that is so, and we can protect her over Saturday, she will be out of the wood then?" John put in eagerly.

C. B. nodded. "Yes, if we can do that I think the worst danger to her will have been averted. But we should still have to get her freed from this spell, or whatever it is, that causes her personality to become evil at night. Her father must hold the key to that; so putting her in prison will not affect my decision to go and demand his help."

John looked at his mother. "If Christina is to be put behind bars there will be nothing that I can do here; so, if you don't mind, Mumsie, I think I'll go with C. B. to England. Should Christina's father resent C. B.'s interference, I could justify it by telling him that I am her fiancé. That might make him more willing to co-operate."

"Yes, that's true. Then go by all means, dear."

"If you do, and her old man thinks you would make a good husband for her, this fake engagement of yours may land you in for a breach of promise case," C. B. grinned.

"Not a bit of it." John laughed. "If she jilts me, it is I who will bring the action. You've forgotten that she is an heiress."

Christina coloured slightly, but joined in the general laughter.

After a glance at his watch, C. B. said, "It is half-past ten; so if John and I are to get to England to-day, we ought to be moving. I wonder which is the best bet for an aircraft, Nice or Marseilles?"

"Nice is some thirty kilometres nearer," replied Malouet, "and there is a plane that leaves at one o'clock for London. Even if you cannot get places on it, a lot of air traffic passes through Nice now; so you should be able to get an Air France or some other line by which you could go *via* Paris."

"Going by Nice has the additional advantage that you could collect your things at the villa on the way," Molly added.

"Come on, then." C. B. stood up. "I'll pay the bill while one of you telephone the local garage for a car."

Malouet did the telephoning, and ten minutes later an ancient but comfortable car arrived from the village to pick them up. The sun was hot now and as they skidded down the rough track they could smell the scent of the pines and wild thyme growing in the *maquis* through which it ran. At the village they turned on to the main coast road and three-quarters of an hour's drive brought them to Molly's villa. There, Christina, John and C. B. hastily packed suitcases and said good-bye to her. Another three-quarters of an hour, with the driver urged on by the promise of a handsome *pourboire*, and the others were set down at the Nice airport.

It was twenty-five to one when they got there, and they were lucky enough to pick up two seats that had been returned that morning on the B.E.A. plane. C. B. sent a telegram to his office, asking that his car should be sent to meet him at Northolt; then, as there was still a quarter of an hour to spare, they had drinks and some delicious snacks at the airport bar.

When the time came to say good-bye, John and Christina both tried to make light of the matter; and he jokingly told her that when he met her at the prison gates on Monday he would have his pockets sewn up, as it was certain that by then she would have become a real old lag. Since they were in public he made no attempt to kiss her, but their eyes held one another's in a long glance as they parted. Malouet watched with her until the plane had taken off, then they returned to the car and did the last four miles in to the centre of Nice. By two o'clock Christina's name had been entered on the prison register, and, now a number, she was being escorted by a fat, garlic-breathing wardress to a cell.

The journey in the aircraft proved uneventful; and, having been up most of the night, John and C. B. slept through the greater part of it. The Côte d'Azur, with its sun and palms, was soon left behind. Over Avignon they ran into cloud and only occasional patches of land or sea were visible for the rest of the way. When they came down at Northolt it was raining. Everyone at the airport was polite and helpful, so the formalities of landing were over in a few minutes, and a pretty air hostess led them out to the place where C. B.'s car was waiting. He took it over from the junior who had brought it out, made John get into the driver's seat, and soon after four o'clock they set out for Essex.

North of London the earliest daffodils and almond-trees were not yet out, so there was no colour in the gardens, and the branches of the trees still displayed their winter bareness. The skies were grey, a chill wind was blowing and the rain lashed against the windows of the car; so their sixty-mile drive was a depressing contrast to the one through a smiling land of summer they had taken only that morning. It was already dark when at six o'clock they entered Colchester.

There, they engaged rooms at the Red Lion for the night, dropped their bags, and, having enquired the way to Beddows Agricultural Tractor plant, drove straight out to it.

As the factory was working night shifts, it was brilliantly lit and still a hive of activity. On asking for Mr. Beddows they were told that he was not there, and had not been to his office for a week or more. They then asked to see his secretary. She had gone home for the night, but after stating that their business was personal they were shown into a garish modern waiting-room. Presently a Mr. Hicks came down to see them, and he proved to be a senior member of the staff. In spite of all their pressing that they must see Mr. Beddows on a matter of the utmost urgency, he assured them that his chief had gone abroad ten days before, leaving no address, and orders that all correspondence was to be dealt with in his absence as he could give no certain date for his return.

Their failure to learn Beddows' whereabouts was a bitter disappointment; so they returned to the Red Lion, had a wash, and sat there very despondently drinking Gimlets until dinner was served. The meal, and even a bottle of claret, followed by half a bottle of port, to wash it down, did little to cheer them.

There was, however, still a chance that something might be learned at Beddows' home, so at half-past eight they got out the car again and took the road leading east out of Colchester to Walton-on-the-Naze.

The country they were now entering was that north-eastern segment of Essex which has its curve upon the sea and its two sides formed by the Rivers Stour and Colne. Its only towns of any size are the pleasure resort of Clacton in the south and the naval base of Harwich in the extreme north. For many centuries the two rivers almost enclosing it shut it off from easy communication with neighbouring districts; so no great highway passes through it, and to this day it remains almost as unindustrialized as it was when Cromwell raised a company of his Roundheads from its scattered hamlets.

When they had covered a few miles the road forked, and they ran on through a series of narrow, winding lanes. Twice they took wrong turnings and had to ask their way—once at an old thatched cottage and once of a benighted cyclist from whose mackintosh-cape the rain was streaming: but at length they came to a triangular village green with half-a-dozen buildings dotted round it. One was a pub called the Weaver's Arms. On C. B. enquiring at it, they found that this was Little Bentford and that The Grange lay about two miles beyond it on the road to Tendring.

After following a sharp bend for half a mile, they passed an ancient stone church with a squat, square tower, and a little further on a moderate-sized private house of hideous Victorian-Gothic design; they then ran through a wood and out again into the open country.

From the description C. B. had been given, they had no difficulty in finding The Grange. It stood some way from the road in a slight hollow and a curved drive led down to it. As the car approached and the headlights threw it up, they saw it was one of those inelegant, nondescript houses, not uncommon in the English countryside, which have resulted from two or more generations adding bits in the style of their own day to an original building. No light showed in any of its windows; in spite of the rain a suggestion of mist lurked round it up to the first-floor level, and it had a chill, forbidding air.

C. B. got out and rang the front door-bell. He could hear it ringing, but no one came to answer it; so, after waiting a few minutes, he rang again. Still there was no reply and there was no sound of movement within the house.

John left the car, went over to join him and said, "I remember Christina telling us that the only servants were a couple named the Jutsons, and that they lived over the garage, in the flat where she was born. Let's go round there and see if they are about."

At the back of the house they saw lights in two first-floor windows of the outbuildings and, locating a narrow door next to the big ones of the garage, C. B. rang the bell beside it. Footsteps sounded on the stairs and the door was opened by a thin-faced, rather sour-looking middle-aged woman. To C. B.'s enquiry she replied:

"No: Mr. Beddows is away. I'm afraid I can't help you."

C. B. clinked some silver in his pocket. "We're very anxious to get in touch with him; perhaps you could suggest some way . . ."

A man's voice cut him short by calling, "Who's that, Mary?"

There came more clumping of feet, then Jutson appeared and pushed past his wife. He was a small man with grey hair close-cropped at the sides; his face was careworn and tight-lipped. He was in his shirt-sleeves and wearing an unbuttoned waistcoat, but no collar. A wireless was reeling off sporting news upstairs, and evidently he was annoyed at being disturbed, as he gave his callers a most unfriendly stare while C. B. repeated his request.

"No." He shook his bullet head. "The guv'ner's from

home. Has been for near a fortnight, an' we dunno when 'e'll be back."

"Can't you possibly think of someone who might be able to help us?" John asked persuasively. "We are friends of Miss Chris . . . Miss Ellen Beddows."

"That don't make no difference. I tell you 'e ain't 'ere, an' we dunno where 'e is neither. 'Tain't none of our business; an' it's no good you fiddlin' with your note-case neither. G'night."

With that Jutson slammed the door and they were left standing in the rain. As they walked back to the car John said miserably, "What appalling luck! Everything depends on our getting hold of him. How else can we hope to free Christina from this beastly thing that gets into her at night? There must be some way we can trace him."

"I'll get on to a pal of mine at Scotland Yard to-morrow. They will do more for me than for most people without asking any questions." C. B. made the promise in the hope of cheering John up, but he was by no means optimistic of getting results, as it now seemed certain that Beddows was still abroad.

Climbing into the car again, they took the road back to Little Bentford. Half a mile before they reached it, on the corner of a lane opposite the church, there was a pillar-box, and the car lights showed a man just posting a letter in it. His back was turned to them, but they could see that he was elderly, as a rim of silvery hair caught the light between the collar of a dark cloak and the clerical hat he was wearing. As they passed him John said in an excited whisper:

"I'll swear that was Canon Copely-Syle. Christina said that he lives in the village at a house called The Priory; so it must have been."

C. B. turned quickly in his seat and looked back. He saw that the elderly clergyman was now crossing the road diagonally towards the pseudo-Gothic house. "Pull up, John," he called, as they entered the long bend that led to the village green. "I think I've got the germ of an idea."

John brought the car to a standstill, and they sat in it for some minutes in silence, while C. B. smoked a cigarette. As he stubbed the end out he said, "Turn round and drive back a little way, so that you can park in the shadow of that belt of trees. I'm going to pay the old boy a visit. Maybe it will come to nothing, but with a little luck I might find out a lot."

When John had driven the car in under the trees, C. B. murmured in his most conspiratorial voice, "Now listen, partner. This bird may be dangerous. If he catches me out all sorts of unpleasant things might happen to yours truly. I don't want you to start anything prematurely, because if matters go well I may be with him for a considerable time. But if I am not out of his house by midnight you are to go along to the village, telephone the police, then come in to get me."

CHAPTER XIV

THE BLACK ART

THE rain was still falling in a steady downpour, and now that the light was failing the little turrets surmounting the steep gables roofing the house presented only a blurred outline. As C. B. squelched his way up the garden path the coppice twenty yards away on his right was already pitch-dark, but to his left the tall, ancient yews of the churchyard still stood out, like sombre sentinels guarding the dead, against the heavy grey sky that presaged a night of inky blackness.

Under the Gothic porch there lingered enough light for him to make out a scrolled iron bell-pull beside an arched front door of solid oak and studded with massive nail heads making a curious pattern. He jerked it vigorously and heard the bell clang hollowly in a distant part of the house. No approaching foot-steps told him that anyone was on the way to answer it, but after a moment the door swung silently open on well-oiled hinges.

Framed against the dim light from a Moorish lantern that hung in the centre of a small square hall stood a manservant of a type that one would hardly have expected to find in an Essex village. He wore a red fez and was robed in a white burnous. His skin was very dark, but only his thick lips suggested negro blood; and C. B. put him down at once as an Egyptian. Crossing his black hands on his chest he made a deep bow, then waited silently until C. B. asked:

"Is Canon Copely-Syle in?"

The man salaamed again and replied in excellent English, a slight lisp alone betraying his foreign origin, "My master has just settled down to his writing, and at such times he is averse to being disturbed. But if you will give me your name, sir, I will enquire if he is willing to receive you."

"My name is Verney; but that won't convey anything to him. Just say that I arrived from Nice this afternoon."

As C. B. spoke he stepped into the hall and the Egyptian closed the door. His felt slippers making no sound on the tiled floor and his white robe billowing out behind him, he seemed almost to float away down the corridor. Two minutes later he returned; his white teeth flashed in a smile, he bowed and murmured, "Allow me, sir, to take your things. Then if you will follow me . . ."

Having divested himself of his wet coat, C. B. was led to the back of the house and shown into a room that, unlike the appearance of the house itself and the Egyptian servant, had nothing even suggestive of the sinister about it. In fact it might well have been the workroom of a wealthy but unimaginative clergyman. Wealthy, because of the great array of valuable books that covered all its walls from floor to ceiling: unimaginative, because its owner was evidently content to have left unchanged its Victorian *décor* and hideous furnishings of elaborately-carved light oak. Nevertheless, it had an air of solid comfort. It was a large room, but the fact that it was not very lofty made it cosier than it would otherwise have been. The light from three standard lamps shone warmly on the gilding of the books and a big log fire blazed on an open hearth. In front of it stood the Canon.

C. B. thought John's description of him good. He was shortish and plump both in face and figure. His cheeks were rosy but tended to sag a little; the rest of his skin had such a childlike pinkness that it was difficult to visualize him ever having the need to shave. His forehead was broad and smooth; his long silver hair swept back from it to fall in curls on the nape of his neck, but gave no impression of untidiness, suggesting rather the elegance of a Georgian parson. His eyes were hazel, but very pale, and his expression benign. His features were well cut, the only thing unpleasant about them being an exceptionally thick and out-jutting lower lip. He was dressed in a black frock-coat, ribbed satin vest, clerical collar, breeches, gaiters and black shoes with silver buckles; all of which added to the impression that he was a divine of a past generation.

Stepping forward, he smiled and extended a plump hand

as he said, "I take it you have news for me, Mr.—er,—Verney. It was good of you to come here in such shocking weather."

His smile detracted from the pleasantness of his expression, as it revealed a lower row of blackened, uneven teeth. His hand was slightly damp and so soft as to seem almost boneless. C. B. found its touch so repulsive that he had to restrain himself from withdrawing his own unduly quickly, as he replied:

"Yes, it's a horrid night, isn't it? But our mutual friend, de Grasse, had an urgent message for you, and knowing that I was returning to England to-day he asked me to come here this evening."

The Canon pushed a big horsehair-covered armchair a little nearer to the fire and murmured, "Sit down, Mr. Verney. Sit down and warm yourself." Then he bustled over to a table on which stood an array of drinks, and added, "A whisky-and-soda now? You must need it after your chilly journey."

C. B. would have preferred to accept neither food nor drink while in that house, but as his object was to win Copely-Syle's confidence he accepted, and, producing his pipe, said, "D'you mind if I smoke?"

"No, no. Please do." The Canon carried over two whiskies, handed one to his caller; and went on, "I trust you have not come to tell me that de Grasse has bungled this affair. It is to me of the utmost importance."

"I gathered that." C. B. began to fill his pipe. "So I'm afraid you won't be very pleased to hear what I have to say. Mind, it's through no fault of de Grasse that things have gone wrong, but on account of the interference of that infernal young man, John Fountain."

The Canon made an impatient gesture. "Then de Grasse *has* bungled the affair! How utterly infuriating. With his resources he should never have allowed a boy like Fountain to get the best of him. That is no excuse. No excuse whatever! But tell me what happened."

In his usual leisurely manner C. B. then related all that had taken place, from Jules de Grasse luring Ellen—as he now called her—away the previous evening, to her escape that morning; except that he refrained from making any mention of his own participation in these events. When he had done, the Canon said petulantly:

"Really! To think that a man like de Grasse should allow two children to set him at defiance. But he is not the type to lie down under such treatment. No doubt he means to teach that young man a lesson; and even if he has to use force will get the girl back again from Mrs. Fountain to-night."

"I don't somehow think he'll be able to get her to-night," said C. B. slowly.

"Why not? His wound may incapacitate him personally, but it should not prevent his sending Jules and some of his people to carry her off."

C. B. felt confident that next morning's post would bring the Canon an airmail letter from de Grasse with full particulars of the latest situation; so, there being no point in concealing it overnight, he replied, "It's not quite as simple as that. The girl is no longer with Mrs. Fountain. She is in prison."

"What!" Copely-Syle's drink slopped over, and he jumped to his feet. "What's that you say? In prison! Surely de Grasse has not been idiot enough to bring a charge against her for shooting him?"

"No, it's not that."

"What then?"

"We don't know ourselves. At least de Grasse didn't know when I left him. All we know is that soon after she landed this morning she was taken into custody. Perhaps she thinks she killed de Grasse, so gave herself up pending enquiries. Or, as she has been living under a false name, it may be something to do with her passport."

"But this is calamitous!" The Canon's heavy underlip trembled and his babyish face screwed up, so that for a moment C. B. thought he was about to burst into tears. An instant later it became apparent that the contortion of his features was due to rage. Abandoning all control, he began to stamp up and down the room, flinging wide his arms and reviling de Grasse in the most filthy language for his incompetence. Then, turning about, he screamed curses at C. B. for having brought him such unwelcome tidings.

C. B. watched the performance with detached interest, pulled on his pipe, and said with a suggestion of a smile, "It's no good swearing at me; and cursing de Grasse can do your case nothing but harm."

At his quiet words the Canon's fury subsided as swiftly as it had arisen. He took a gulp of his drink and muttered, "You are right. This is no fault of yours, and curses should be used only with solemn intent."

"Exactly; so if you are hoping that de Grasse may yet pull the chestnuts out of the fire for you, it's silly to hamper his efforts with even the most casual vibrations of ill-wishing."

Copely-Syle gave him a half-furtive glance, and asked, "What do you know of such matters?"

"Oh, quite a bit." C. B. shrugged the question aside. Having sown the seed, and feel ng that enough had now passed between them for him to begin his probe without arousing suspicion, he said, "I can understand your being annoyed at young Fountain having thrown a spanner in the works; but surely the girl being temporarily in prison scarcely justifies your getting into such a tizzy? The odds are that she'll be out before the end of the week; then de Grasse's boys should have little trouble in collecting her for you."

"The end of the week!" Copely-Syle threw up his plump hands and the little veins in the whites of his eyes became suffused with blood from the intensity of his annoyance. "That's no good! No earthly good! This matter is one of the utmost urgency. Surely I cannot have failed to make that plain to de Grasse?"

C. B. felt that he was getting warm, and nodded with becoming solemnness. "Yes, I feel sure you did. That must be why he was so upset this morning. Of course, I'm not in on this thing, except as an old friend whom he knew he could trust to bring you an account of what has happened to date. I know only the bare outline of the affair—merely that you are anxious to get this young woman back to England. But why the frantic haste?"

206

"Because to-day is the 4th. I must have her here by the 6th."

"Can't you possibly rearrange your plans so that a few days' delay won't make any difference?"

"You might as well suggest that I should attempt to stop the stars in their courses," snapped the Canon. "The 6th of March is her birthday. At nine forty-five that evening she comes of age. If she is not under my control by then the hopes that I have cherished for years will be dashed."

"Oh, I see; this is a family affair and a case of a young woman having kicked over the traces," remarked C. B., deliberately misunderstanding. "Naturally, then, you are anxious to have her back in time to bury the hatchet on her twenty-first birthday. May I ask what relationship she bears you?"

"None; but I have known her since her birth, and am, in a sense, her guardian."

"Has she given you this sort of trouble before, or behaved like a flighty type generally?"

"On the contrary. She has lived a very retired life, and shown no inclination to do otherwise."

The quiet indifference of C. B.'s tone when he made his next remark did much to lessen its impertinence. "Then, as she didn't run away with a man, there's some hope of her still being a virgin?"

The Canon's pale eyes narrowed a trifle and he said quickly, "What leads you to speculate on that?"

"The thought automatically came into my mind that a combination of three times seven years and virginity have immense mystical significance. In fact, there is no state which even approaches its tremendous potence for good or evil; and that if . . . But no, this is your affair and nothing to do with me."

"If what?" the Canon insisted.

"Why, that if the hesitant manner in which you admit your guardianship of this young woman is due to your status being unofficial; er—like, shall we say, one who prefers to remain in shadow . . ."

Copely-Syle had slowly risen to his feet. As he did so he

seemed to increase in stature. His plump face lost all trace of babyishness. It looked old now, but extraordinarily strong and menacing. Suddenly he burst out harshly:

"You have said either too much or too little. Explain yourself, or it will be the worse for you."

C.B.'s work brought him into touch with all types of tough customers; so, although he knew that he was on exceptionally dangerous ground, he remained outwardly imperturbable, and even smiled slightly as he replied:

"Hold your horses, Canon. There's nothing to get excited about. I thought I had made it clear that I'm not one of de Grasse's thugs, and that our association is simply that of two people who have been of use to one another from time to time. You have no need to fear that he suspects the reason for your interest in the girl and may start trying to blackmail you. I shouldn't have suspected it myself but for what you've just told me—and the fact that, although you may not remember it, we've met before."

"Have we? Where?"

"I can't remember exactly, but I know it was with Aleister Crowley."

"That charlatan! I hardly knew him."

With the object of passing himself off as a brother initiate in the Black Art, C. B. had risked a shot in the dark. He had felt confident that anyone of Copely-Syle's age and interests must have come into contact with the infamous Crowley at one time or another, and, although the Canon's reactions were disappointing, he could not now go back on his statement. To get on firmer ground, he began to reminisce about the dead magician.

"If you had known Aleister as well as I did, you certainly wouldn't dub him a charlatan. Of course in his later years he couldn't have harmed a rabbit; everyone knew that. The poor old boy degenerated into a rather pathetic figure, and was reduced to sponging on all and sundry in order to keep body and soul together. But when he was a young man it was a very different story. He unquestionably had power, and there were very few things of this world that he could not get with it.

Even as an undergraduate he showed how far advanced he was along the Left Hand Path. You must have heard about the Master of John's refusing to let him put on a bawdy Greek play, and how he revenged himself. He made a wax image of the Master and took it out to a meadow one night with some friends when the moon was at the full. They formed the usual circle and Crowley recited the incantation. He was holding the needle and meant to jab it into the place that was the equivalent of the image's liver, but at the critical moment one of his pals got the wind up and broke the circle. Crowley's hand was deflected and the needle pierced the image's left ankle. That was a bit of luck for the Master of John's. Instead of dying of a tumour on the liver, he only slipped and broke his left ankle when coming down the college steps next day. Up to then Crowley's friends had regarded the whole business as a joke spiced with a vague sort of wickedness; but afterwards they were scared stiff of him, and naturally they were much too impressed to keep their mouths shut; so the facts are known beyond any shadow of doubt."

Copely-Syle shrugged slightly. "Of course, it's perfectly possible, and I do remember hearing about it now. But the story can be no more than hearsay as far as you are concerned. You are much too young to have been up at Cambridge with Crowley."

"Oh yes. I didn't meet him till years later, when he was in middle life and at the height of his powers." After pausing for a moment C. B. added the glib lie, "I was initiated by him at the Abbaye de Thelema."

"Really? I was under the impression that Crowley did no more than use his reputation as a mystic to lure young neurotics there, and kept the place going as a private brothel for his own enjoyment."

"Most of its inmates were young people, and as the whole of his teaching was summed up in '*Do what thou wilt shall be the whole of the Law*' a state of general promiscuity naturally followed from it. New brothers and sisters soon lost their shyness, and after that he had little difficulty in persuading them to participate in sexual orgies when the stars were propitious for the performance of special rites. But you can take it from me that he knew his stuff, and that the perversions practised under his auspices were only a means to an end. You must know as well as I do that certain types of Satanic entity feed upon the emanations given out by humans while engaged in the baser forms of eroticism. As far as Crowley was concerned the orgies were simply the bait that lured such entities to the Abbaye and enabled him to gain power over them."

The Canon had sat down again. He now appeared deeply interested as he said, "You are really convinced that he conducted Satanic rituals with intent, and not merely performed some mumbo-jumbo as an excuse to possess a series of young women?"

"Each of his rituals was performed with a definite intention. Of that I am certain, and I know that many of them produced the desired result. He always insisted on everyone present behaving with the greatest solemnity, and when celebrating pagan rites he was most impressive. He could even render the receiving of the *osculam infame* a gesture of some dignity, and his memory was prodigious; so he experienced no difficulty at all in reciting the lines of the Roman communion backwards."

"In Christian countries there are few ceremonies more potent than the Black Mass; but from my memory of him I am much surprised to learn from you that he ever proved capable of celebrating that mystery."

"I have never seen it better done," C. B. averred seriously. "Although, of course, he was not able to fulfil the technical requirements in their entirety."

"You mean that among the women neophytes there was never a virgin who could be used as an altar?"

"No, I didn't mean that. It's true that on most occasions he had to make do with young women who had already been seduced, but twice while I was there he managed to get hold of a virgin. And naturally there was no difficulty about holy wafers for desecration and that sort of thing. I was simply referring to the fact that to be one hundred per cent potent the celebrant should have been a Roman Catholic priest, and Crowley had never been ordained."

"Quite, quite. That was a pity, but would be overlooked if suitable propitiation were made to the Prince by way of blood offerings. Did Crowley—er—ever achieve the apotheosis in that direction?"

"I can't say for certain. In mediaeval times life was held so cheap that adepts such as Gilles de Rais could decimate a dozen parishes for the furtherance of their magical operations, and no one powerful enough to interfere felt sufficiently strongly about it to do so. But in these days matters are very different. The Italian police must have had a pretty shrewd idea of the sort of thing that went on at the Abbaye; but they were a tolerant lot and were well bribed to keep their ideas to themselves, so they never gave us any trouble. I'm sure they would have, though, had they had the least grounds to suppose that we were offering up human sacrifices. Usually Crowley used cats or goats, and once I was present when a monkey was crucified upside down. After I had left I heard rumours that one or two children had disappeared from villages round about; but I'm inclined to suppose that was simply malicious gossip put about by Crowley's enemies."

The pale eyes of Copely-Syle had a faraway look as he murmured thoughtfully, "Ah, for the culminating act in such rituals there is nothing so efficacious as the warm blood of an unweaned child."

C. B. had to bite hard on the stem of his pipe to repress a shudder; but he felt that he was now well on the way to achieving his object in going there, which was to establish such an apparent community of interests with the Canon that the latter would voluntarily give himself away. For a few moments they both sat staring silently into the fire, then the Canon said:

"From all you say, Crowley must have reached at least the degree of Magus, if not Ipsissimus. What I cannot understand is how by the middle nineteen-thirties, when I met him, he should have degenerated into an impotent windbag, incapable of impressing anyone except a handful of credulous old women."

"That is easily explained. It was that unfortunate affair in

Paris towards the end of the nineteen-twenties. You are right in supposing that before that he ranked as an Ipsissimus, but that night he was cast right back across the Abyss. In fact, he was stripped of all his powers and afterwards the most callow neophyte could have bested him in an astral conflict."

"What an awful thing to happen to an adept," said the Canon a shade uneasily. "Did he then recant and offer to make a full confession in exchange for being accepted back into the Church? I can imagine no other act deserving of such terrible punishment."

"Oh no, it was nothing like that. It was simply that his ambition was so great that he over-reached himself. If he could have bent Pan to his will he would have been the most powerful being on earth. With Pan's pipes playing as he directed he could have made even governments dance to his tune. He attempted to master Pan, but he wasn't quite strong enough; so he paid the price of failure: that's all."

"I find this most interesting," said Copely-Syle in a low voice. "Do you happen to know any details of what took place?"

"Yes. As a matter of fact I was still one of his disciples, so with him at the time." C. B. was on safer ground now, as he had actually had a first-hand account of this grim affair from one of Crowley's young men, and he went on:

"The attempt took place in Paris. Crowley made up a coven, so including himself there were thirteen of us; and in this instance we were naturally all males. We were staying at an hotel on the Left Bank. The proprietor was an initiate, and it was quite a small place; so we took the whole premises for the night, and all the servants were got rid of from mid-day to mid-day. There was a big room at the top of the house which seemed just the thing for the purpose. In the afternoon we moved out every scrap of furniture and cleaned it with the utmost thoroughness. Then in the evening all of us assisted at the purificatory rites; but fortunately as it turned out, Crowley had decided that only his senior disciple, a chap who had taken the name of McAleister, should assist him at the actual evocation.

212

"At ten o'clock the rest of us robed them, then left them there, and Crowley locked the door behind us. He had already issued strict injunctions that whatever sounds we might hear coming from the room, even if they were cries for help, we were in no circumstances to attempt to enter it; as such cries might be a trick of Pan's made in an endeavour to evade him, and any interruption of the ritual would render the spell abortive. We had fasted all day, so our associate, the landlord, had prepared an excellent cold buffet for us downstairs in the dining-room. It wasn't a very gay meal, as all of us were aware of the magnitude of the task the Master Therion had set himself. We had great confidence in his powers, but it was probably several centuries since any adept had had the audacity to attempt to summon the Horned God in person, so we were naturally a bit nervy.

"It was just on midnight when we heard the first noises upstairs. There were thumpings and shouts, then all Hell seemed to break loose. Piercing screams were mingled with what sounded like sacks of potatoes being flung about. We had the impression that the whole building was rocking. In fact it was, as the chandelier above us began to swing, the glasses jingled on the sideboard and a picture fell from the wall with a loud crash. It was like being in the middle of an earthquake, and the room in which we were sitting had suddenly become icy cold.

"We had all been inmates of the Abbaye at one time or another and had passed pretty severe tests in standing up to Satanic manifestations, so we were by no means a chicken-hearted lot. But on this occasion we were seized by abject terror, and none of us made the least effort to hide it. We just sat there, white to the gills and paralysed by the thought that at any second the terrible Being up above might descend on us.

"After a few moments the pandemonium subsided, and we tried to pull ourselves together. With our teeth chattering from the cold, we debated whether we had not better ignore Crowley's orders and go up to find out what had happened. But the room began to get warm again and that, together with the continued silence, led us to hope that Crowley had won his battle and succeeded in binding Pan. If so, for us to have gone in then might still have ruined everything, and Crowley's rage would have been beyond all reckoning. Knowing his powers, none of us felt inclined to risk the sort of punishment he might have inflicted on us for disobeying him; so we decided to let matters be, and I for one was not sorry about that.

"We were all too scared to face the solitude of going to bed, and started to drink in an attempt to keep our spirits up; but that didn't work. Somehow we couldn't even get tight, and we sat on hour after hour, hardly speaking.

"At last that miserable night ended. Dawn came and we began to hope that Crowley would soon come down, his fat face beaming with triumph, to make our fears seem ridiculous; but he didn't. We waited till seven o'clock. There was still not a sound from the top of the house, so by then we felt that we were no longer justified in evading the issue. All the same, we didn't exactly run upstairs, as by that time we were feeling pretty apprehensive about what we might find when we got there. For a moment or two all eleven of us stood huddled on the top of the landing, listening; but with the early morning noises coming up from the street we could not definitely make out any sound coming from the room. Someone suggested that after their exhausting ordeal Crowley and McAleister might still be sleeping, and the idea gave us fresh hope for the moment; but another fellow knocked hard on the door, and there was no reply. That left us with no alternative but to break down the door."

CHAPTER XV

CHAMBER OF HORRORS

Like the good *raconteur* that he was, C. B. paused to knock out his pipe. Copely-Syle jerked his head forward and exclaimed in a breathless whisper, "Go on, man! Go on! What did you find?"

C. B. looked him straight in the eyes, and, certain of his facts on this final point, said quietly, "McAleister was dead. He was stretched out on his back with his arms flung wide, absolutely rigid, just as though he had been electrocuted, and with an appalling look of stark horror on his face such as I never wish to see again. Crowley's pontifical robes were scattered in ribbons about the floor. It looked as if they had been ripped from his body by some ferocious animal. He was crouching in a corner naked. He didn't know any of us. He had become a gibbering idiot."

The Canon took a quick gulp at his drink and muttered, "Horrible, horrible! Have you any idea what went wrong?"

"No; none of us had. We could only suppose that McAleister had been unable to take it, and cracked at the critical moment. Crowley was in a private asylum outside Paris for six months. He was very lucky to recover his sanity, and afterwards he would never speak of the affair. In fact, I doubt very much if he had any definite memory of what had happened. But you'll understand now why from that time on he seemed like a washed-out rag, and why when you met him he entirely failed to impress you."

"Yes," the Canon nodded. "I was not introduced to him until the early 'thirties, and what you have told me explains the disappointment I felt at the time. But we have not yet recalled where it was that I met you."

Again C. B. was on dangerous ground, but he knew that Crowley had spent much of the 'thirties in London, and that the better-off mystics preferred the privacy of houses to living in flats; so he punted for that area of the capital which then had a greater number of moderate-sized private houses than any other, and said, "For the life of me I can't recall the occasion definitely, but I have the impression that it was at a party held out Regent's Park way, or in St. John's Wood."

"Ah!" said the Canon. "Then it must have been at Mocata's house: at least at a house just behind Lord's that he made his headquarters for a while; although I believe it was actually owned by a wealthy young Jew who had become a disciple of his."

This was the acid test. C. B. was acutely aware that, if Copely-Syle entertained any suspicions of his *bona fides*, in the question of where they might have met before lay the perfect opportunity to set a trap. He had only to suggest a place in which he had never been and, if his visitor accepted it, unmask him as a fraud. But C. B. felt it reasonable to hope that their talk of Aleister Crowley had gone a long way to still any early doubts about himself that the Canon might have held, and that his suggestion was free from guile. Gambling boldly on that, and using his excellent knowledge of London even to gild the lily a little, he replied:

"Of course that must have been it. And unless my memory's failing me again the house was in Medina Place."

"That is so," the Canon nodded. "I went there on a number of occasions and on none of them were there less than twenty people present. That is why I failed to recall you at first sight. There was an observatory at the top of the house, and it proved most useful for the performance of certain rituals."

"It was Crowley who took me there, but only once." C. B. hedged cautiously to avoid being questioned on how well he knew this Mr. Mocata; but his host went on reminiscently:

"Poor Mocata; he too fell by the wayside through attempting too much. That must have been shortly after we met, as the house at St. John's Wood was his last address. He was engaged in a search for the Talisman of Set, but he came into conflict with a White Magician of greater power than himself, and was

216

found dead one morning outside a house called Cardinal's Folly, in Worcestershire. The coroner's jury brought it in as heart, of course; but I've no doubt at all that it was the rebound of an unsuccessful curse sent out by himself that killed him."

"I trust," said C. B., "that the work you are engaged upon is not of such a dangerous nature."

Copely-Syle's light hazel eyes lit up again, and now held a fanatical gleam. "There is always danger in great magical operations; but I should have no fear whatever of the outcome if only this accursed girl had not eluded me. Whatever it costs, whatever risks are run, she must be in my hands by the evening of the 6th."

"You have less than forty-eight hours left to work in; and as long as the French authorities keep her in prison I don't see how de Grasse can get hold of her for you."

Standing up, the Canon began to walk agitatedly up and down. "You are right. De Grasse can do nothing now except under my direction. I must handle this myself."

"How do you propose to set about it?"

"I shall fly out to France to-morrow. Some of de Grasse's thugs will at least be able to help from their knowledge of the prisons and the warders."

"In so short a time it is not going to be easy to plan an escape—or rather, the even more difficult job of an abduction —as it is unlikely now that she would be willing to leave prison with any of de Grasse's people. It may take days of cautious enquiry before one or more jailers who are susceptible to bribery can be seduced, and then one would have to wait until it was their turn to go on night duty."

"No, no!" The Canon's voice was sharp with impatience. "This is a case for the use of occult weapons; only so can the time factor be overcome. I shall telephone de Grasse to find out the names of the jailers who will be on duty to-morrow night. Then he must get me some things belonging to them. Nail clippings or hair are too much to hope for at such short notice, but it should not be difficult to steal some of their soiled linen; unwashed pants or pyjamas would serve quite well. With those to work on I could easily bemuse their minds and make them temporarily my servants. As for the girl, after sunset she is ruled by Asmodeus, so will do as she is directed."

Having let the Canon know that Christina was in prison, a few hours before he would otherwise have learned it, had enabled C. B. to fish very skilfully for the steps her pursuer would take in consequence. Now that he knew them he was able to make a bid to counter them in advance; and, being no mean psychologist, he put a price on the bait in the trap he was laying so that the Canon would be less likely to suspect it to be one. With a thoughtful air, he remarked:

"I came back from the South this morning only on account of some urgent personal business I had to attend to in London. I tackled that before coming down here, and I am flying out again to-morrow. I have quite enough experience to perform the minor magics you have in mind, so could save you the trip —if you cared to make it worth my while."

The fat little Canon halted in front of him. "That certainly is an idea, as de Grasse would give you the same co-operation as he would me. But are you absolutely certain you could do that which is necessary? Remember, should you fail there will be no second chance; for if we do not get her out of prison by to-morrow night there will be no time left to transport her to England before her birthday is over. No! I dare not risk it. Much as I dislike air travel, I must fly down to-morrow and cast these spells myself."

"Just as you like." C. B. shrugged with apparent in-difference. "But I performed just the type of operation you have in mind successfully several times during the war. During the latter part of it I was working in France for the Gestapo, and I managed to get several of their agents out of the clutches of the de Gaullists by such means."

"What grade do you hold?" asked the Canon uncertainly.

"I have eight circles and three squares."

"Really! Then you are past the Abyss."

"Yes. I passed it on Walpurgis Night, 1946."

"As a Magister Templi you could hardly fail. But what did you mean by 'making it worth your while' to act for me? With such powers you surely cannot be short of money?"

C. B. shook his head. "It is not that, and it will cost you nothing. What I had in mind was this. Virgins of three times seven years are never particularly easy to come by, and to procure one for use on the night of her twenty-first birthday, when nearly every girl is given a party of some sort, makes the success of such a quest a matter of extreme difficulty. That such a combination is essential to the completion of your work tells me that you must be engaged on a magical operation of quite exceptional importance. As an initiate of twenty-five years' standing I am naturally interested now only in the most advanced types of conjuration; but in those I am very interested indeed. Would it be too much to ask you to tell me the end towards which you are working and, perhaps, when we have got the girl, allow me to act as your assistant in the final transubstantiation?"

Copely-Syle thought for a moment, then he replied, "Were you still below the Abyss I would not consider it fitting to disclose to you such formula as I must use; neither would I risk allowing you to make one in a coven for such a ceremony were I not an Ipsissimus, and free to choose my associates within certain limits. But since you are an Adept of the S.S. with only two circles to gain and two squares to lose before reaching the highest plane of the Order, I see nothing against acceding to your request. I should warn you, though, that this is a matter which it would be sheer madness for anyone of a lesser degree than Ipsissimus to attempt, for it is the greatest of all the Great Works."

"You must refer to the achieving of Oneness with God," said C. B., stroking back his grey hair.

"Yes. No one would deny that the transmutation of base metals into gold, or the distillation of the Elixir that will renew youth and prolong life indefinitely, are Great Works; but for many years I have devoted myself to a greater. I have now reached a point where only one thing is necessary for me to become the equal of God. On the 6th of March I, Augustus Copely-Syle, will also create Life."

"Homunculi?" murmured C. B., suppressing a start.

The Canon bared his ugly, blackened teeth in a smile. "Yes,

homunculi; and one of them at least shall be a creature capable of thought and speech."

C. B. was swiftly recalling all he could remember about this strange and awe-inspiring subject. There were many legends of minor deities having transformed inanimate objects into human beings, and the experts on folklore now recognized that such legends were usually race memories of priest-kings and witch-doctors who had actually lived in pre-historic times. No doubt during many generations of repetition the story-teller's art had embellished these legends to such a degree that in their final form they bore little resemblance to the original happenings; but the possibility remained that some of them at least had been based on more than entirely factless imagination.

From the earliest historical times, through all the great civilizations of antiquity, and in the classic Graeco-Roman era, the practice of magic had been not merely widespread, but accepted as the proper occupation for every priesthood, and a natural subject for study by everyone with any pretence to education. In consequence, among the clay tablets of Babylonia, the papyrus of Egypt and the esoteric writings of the great nations of the Mediterranean, ample evidence could be found of attempts to create spontaneous generation, often with claims to varying degrees of success.

The spread of Christianity had driven the old religions underground; but it had never quite succeeded in smothering the knowledge gained by countless generations of Pagan priests, who had based their teachings on their observations of natural laws rather than on blind faith. Much was lost until, after a thousand years, there came the revolt against the Church's power to fetter men's minds, and the age of reason ushered in that of scientific investigation. Even then, many secrets known to the ancients had not been recovered; yet through the centuries others had been handed down and, not infrequently, put to the test by bold men and women who were prepared to risk being burnt at the stake as the price of acquiring power, riches or wisdom.

Among those who had trafficked in these forbidden

mysteries was a Count von Küffstein, and C. B. remembered reading in an old book of the experiments he had carried out in the year 1775 at his castle in the Tyrol. With the aid of an Italian Abbé named Geloni, the Count had succeeded in producing ten living creatures who resembled small men and women. They had, however, been more in the nature of fish than mammals, as they were incapable of living for long in anything so rarefied as air, and had to be kept in large strong glass jars that were filled with liquid. Once a week the jars were emptied and refilled with pure rain water, to which certain chemicals were added, and human blood on which the homunculi fed. That they had been capable of thought and emotion was instanced by perhaps the strangest of all love stories, for one of the males was said to have escaped from his jar and died from exhaustion while attempting to get into the jar that imprisoned the prettiest of the females.

The evidence for these extraordinary happenings was given unusual weight by the fact that they had not been recorded by the Count himself, but in a secret diary kept by his butler, which had not come to light until long after the events described; also, it was further stated that, among others, such reputable noblemen as Count Max Lemberg and Count Franz-Joseph von Thun had visited the castle and vouched for having examined the homunculi themselves.

C. B. also recalled that the great German scientist, Paracelcus von Hohenheim, who had been the first doctor to give his lectures in the vulgar tongue at the University of Basle, had expressed himself as entirely satisfied with his experiments in imbuing inanimate matter with life.

All these thoughts raced through C. B.'s mind in a few seconds as he sat with his long legs stretched out in front of him, staring at the round, excited face of the Canon. His reading told him that this fantastic thing was just remotely possible, as there was too much evidence for it to be shrugged aside as utter nonsense; yet he considered it much more likely that this evil little man was mad.

"You don't believe me, eh?" Copely-Syle's thick underlip

was thrust forth in an aggressive grin. "Well, come with me and you shall see."

Turning abruptly, he led the way out of the room and down a corridor connecting the new with an old part of the house, till they reached a heavy iron door built into a low stone archway that must have been many centuries old. Taking a small key attached to a long gold snake-chain from his pocket, he inserted it in a modern Chubb lock, gave a quick turn, pressed, and the weighty door swung silently open.

They were standing at the top of a flight of stone steps, and C. B. found himself looking down into as strange and eerie an apartment as it was possible to imagine. At first sight it appeared to be a chapel, but as its floor was a good six feet below ground-level it could, perhaps, be more accurately described as a crypt. A double row of slender pillars supported its roof. At its far end, fifty feet away, three broad shallow steps led up to an altar, now partially hidden by flanking curtains. On it a candle burned before a shadowy something that C. B. could not make out. This solitary candle apart, the place was lit only by the reddish glow coming from a large furnace to the right of the flight of steps, at the top of which they stood.

As the vaguely-seen furnishings of the chamber became clearer, C. B. felt as though he had been transported back to the Middle Ages, for before him were spread out all the paraphernalia of an alchemist's laboratory. To his right stood the open furnace with its scalloped canopy, funnel-shaped chimney, and iron pull-handle for working its bellows: to his left was a great astrolabe and a human skeleton with wired joints such as are used to teach medical students anatomy. In the centre of the chamber were four stout oak refectory tables. On them stood many strange-shaped bottles, balances and retorts, and beneath the nearest showed the outline of a mummy-case. Behind the pillars, in one side aisle, stood a line of what looked like huge round tea-cosies, and in the other, only dimly seen, what appeared to be a number of large hen-coops. The only items lacking to complete the traditional picture were a stuffed alligator and other fearsome reptiles hanging from the roof; yet even this type of adjunct to the wizard's art was not entirely lacking, as the scampering of little feet and a faint whimpering, coming from the coops and a row of cages beyond them, told of living things imprisoned there for the magician's use.

C. B. had hardly gathered a general impression of the place, and taken one step down, before the Canon first closed and locked the door behind them, then switched on a row of electric lights.

Now every detail of the interior could be seen, and it instantly became obvious that in addition to being a 'puffer's workshop' this ancient half-crypt was used as a Satanic Temple On one of the curtains which partially shut off the semi circular bay containing the altar there was embroidered in rich colours the figure of a rearing goat, on the other the figure of a woman who had seven breasts and a serpent's tail. Between them the altar could now be clearly seen. Against a beautiful backcloth showing Adam and Eve in relation to the Macrocosm, a black and broken crucifix stood out. Nailed to it, head uppermost, which in this instance was the equivalent of upside down, hung a large bat. Upon the altar lay a jewelled sword, a vellum-bound book and a gold, gem-encrusted chalice. The front of the altar was covered with cloth of gold, into which were woven semi-precious stones forming the ten signs of the Cabala; but in places the fabric showed brownish stains, suggestive of dried blood. The solitary candle that burned in front of the desecrated crucifix was black.

Feeling that some remark was called for, and knowing that in no circumstances must he show surprise or disgust, C. B. said, "You have splendid quarters here. I don't think that I've ever seen better."

"I was lucky to find them," replied the Canon. "It is extremely difficult to acquire a comfortable house which has adjacent to it an altar that was consecrated for many centuries; and, of course, the use of it enormously increases the potency of my operations. I chanced to hear of it shortly after the first world war. For many years it had been lived in only by a succession of caretakers. As it was the abode of quite a number of elementals, I got it for a song."

While he was speaking he turned to the furnace and began to make it up. It was similar to those used by old-fashioned blacksmiths—a great open bed of coke in an iron trough nearly five feet square. By a few puffs from the bellows the lower layers of fuel could soon be made white-hot, but now they gave out only a reddish glow that shone here and there through cracks in the layers of still-black fuel above them. The Canon spread a new layer of coke on top, blotting out the glow entirely, then damped it down for the night by spraying cold water on it.

As soon as he had finished, he led the way over to one of the big tables. Pinned out upon it were what amounted to a number of blue-prints, each showing in the greatest detail the structure of various portions of the human body. Beyond them were rows of glass-stoppered jars containing pieces of skins, muscles, ligaments, arteries, kidneys, livers and other viscera pickled in spirit. The sight of them told C. B. that whatever element of magic there might be in this horrible process it must be basically, at least, scientific; and a moment later Copely-Syle confirmed his thoughts by saying:

"To you, as a Magister Templi, I need hardly refer to the fact that magic is no more than the application of natural laws as yet unrecognized by all but a very limited number of people, such as ourselves. In the initial stages of my work I do nothing of which a moderately intelligent biologist is not capable, given the necessary materials and a considerable degree of patience. Even in the more advanced stages there is little that a fully trained scientist would find difficult to follow and imitate. In fact, were I prepared to give my secrets to the world and the masses could be prevented from sabotaging such work on account of their childish prejudices, there is no reason whatever why an unlimited number of homunculi should not be manufactured."

C. B. suppressed a shudder at the idea of a world in which even a limited proportion of the population were soulless robots, liable at any moment to behave like homicidal maniacs should they escape from the control of their creators. In an attempt to counteract the horror he felt, he remarked lightly:

"Wouldn't that lead to virgins of twenty-one soon becoming in short supply—that is, if the assistance of one is needed for the creation of each homunculus?"

Taking his observation quite seriously, the Canon replied, "To begin with, yes; for, like mules, the early types of homunculi would prove incapable of breeding. But that is a deficiency which science could undoubtedly find a way to make good in due course. In the meantime, a government such as that of Soviet Russia, which is not hampered by the scruples and inhibitions of its people, might consider it well worth its while to segregate for several years large numbers of female children, in order to ensure their retaining their virginity until they reached an age when they could be used for the production of homunculi. You see, for any country bent on making war the process offers a new weapon of inestimable value. As suicide troops these fabricated beings would prove enormously superior to the most patriotic humans, because they would require no food other than the blood from the bodies of their enemies, and under the hypnotic direction of their masters they would carry out their allotted tasks with the same ruthless efficiency as machines."

The hair on the back of C. B.'s neck prickled as he listened to this ghastly conception. Judged by all standards, moral or divine, he considered Copely-Syle to be a criminal lunatic, who should be shot with even less scruple than a mad dog; but that did not alter the fact that he displayed none of the symptoms which made a man certifiable. On the contrary, his conscientious research and logical reasoning showed him to be possessed of an unquestionable, if perverted, sanity. All C. B. could think of to mutter was:

"The Atlanteans did as you suggest, didn't they? And to people like ourselves it is common knowledge that it was their magicians producing large numbers of homunculi which led the White Powers to destroy the whole continent of Atlantis by fire and flood."

"True; but the human race was much younger in those

days. In the past century, working through Communism, which openly denies all manifestations of God, Prince Lucifer has secured a far firmer grip upon it than he had then. With the minds of nearly half the population of the world attuned in opposition to the so-called Light, I do not think the Brethren of the Right Hand Path would now prove strong enough to bring about another deluge.''

The plump little black-clad man paused for a second, then shrugged and went on, ''However, it is for the Lord of this World himself to decide when and how we should give battle. For us, it is sufficient that we are working towards His ends, and that our reward will be great. Come now and see my contribution to our Master's business.''

As he spoke he led the way across to the row of huge, conical tea-cosies. Each of them stood about four feet high, and as he removed one at the end of the line, C. B. saw that its thick padded material had concealed a great glass jar over two feet in diameter.

Again C. B.'s hackles rose, and, in spite of all that had gone before, he could hardly believe his eyes. In the clear liquid that filled the giant bottle was a naked female monster. She was about the height of a child of eight, yet far broader, having big breasts and thick thighs; but from the crutch downwards her legs were tied, and ended in tiny tapering feet, so that she resembled a squat and hideous mermaid. Her flesh was pink. There were no hairs on any part of her body and she was entirely bald. As he stared at her she slowly opened a pair of red-rimmed lashless eyes and blinked at him.

Fighting down his disgust, C. B. uttered the sort of exclamations of astonishment and interest that he knew were expected of him, then he asked, ''Will her legs always be tied, or can you perform some operation, magical or otherwise, to separate them?''

The Canon shook his silvery head. ''No; about that there is nothing I can do. As you will see, most of the others are also imperfect. I assemble the basic ingredients for the creation of flesh, muscle, bone, blood and glands, but it is impossible to forecast how they will develop. All I can do is to improve my blends by experience, and thus endeavour to control un-natural or extraneous growths. These I keep only in order to record changes in their development and to ascertain how long they will live." Replacing the cover, he removed those of the other jars in turn.

One male had only stumps where its arms should have been; another was much smaller than the rest, but had an enormous organ of generation. Among them were an hermaphrodite, a female with two heads and another whose head rose grotesquely straight out of her shoulders without the least trace of a neck. Only one other was bald and the males all had sparse beards. The faces of all of them were hideous and their gaze held a stony malevolence. Only the last had no obvious deformity.

Like the first, she was a squat and repulsive-looking female. Unlike several of the others, she had grown both hair and nails, but the latter, which protruded from thick, stubby fingers, looked more like talons. Her mouth was very large and she kept opening and shutting it slowly in the same manner as a fish. When the cover was first removed from her jar she appeared to be asleep, but almost instantly she woke and became imbued with horrid life, grimacing at them and clawing furiously at the glass as though she would rend and devour them if she could.

Copely-Syle stood there smiling at her, obviously immensely proud at having produced this evil travesty of a human being, and after a moment he murmured, "Behold the child of my creation, who is to be the first of our new race. Another forty-odd hours and the final mystic rite will render her capable of breathing air as easily as we do; then she will be able to come forth into the world. Although her womb will never bear fruit, she is destined to be the forerunner of many of her kind; so is the Lord Satan's answer to Eve."

"I count it a great privilege to have seen her still, as it were, in a state of gestation," replied C. B. "But if she continues in her present mood, aren't you afraid that she will give you great trouble when once she is out of her bottle?"

"No. In this stage she is still an animal, so it is quite

227

natural that she should display an animal's resentment of confinement; but when she emerges she will be a different creature. You will recall that God blew into the nostrils of Adam to give him Life, but He did not blow into the nostrils of the animals He had made; so Life in that sense was something quite other than the capacity to move in obedience to instincts. The rite that I shall perform on the 6th is analogous to that final act of creation which differentiated man from beasts, so it will bring about a fundamental change in her. Besides, in Ellen Beddows we are fortunate in having a young woman of mild and pleasant disposition."

"I see; you are, then, assuming that her personality will exert an influence on the formation of a personality in this creature?"

"I think it is bound to have some effect, as the homunculus will be infused with her spirit."

C. B. swallowed hard. He had thought it certain that the Canon intended to perform a Black Mass on Christina's body, and that probably she would be subjected to certain physical obscenities afterwards. Unless she was hypnotized and rendered unconscious first, the shock would be appalling and perhaps even result in temporarily unbalancing her mind. That would have been bad enough, but what the Black Magician actually implied was infinitely worse. It was nothing less than the drawing forth of her spirit from her body, and, while it was absent, there was the awful possibility that some elemental might take possession of her permanently, by day as well as by night, turning her into a lunatic. After a moment he asked:

"How long will the ceremony take?"

"No great while," replied the other placidly. "I shall, of course, first celebrate Mass, with the girl's body lying on the altar. After that come the recitation of the formula of the Holy Grail, and that of the Temple of Solomon the King, for the achievement of Unity with the Cosmos and as signifying the completion of the Great Work. The jar containing the homunculus will be placed on the floor on the left of the altar, close up to it, and the young woman's body will be so arranged that her head dangles down off the end of the altar over the open top of the jar. Having uttered the Gnostic Name of the Seven Vowels to evoke the Soul of Nature, and called upon Our Lady of Babylon as my witness, it will remain only for me to slit the girl's throat with the sacrificial knife and ensure that her life-blood, which will carry her spirit with it, shall flow into the jar."

Few men had such a wide knowledge of unorthodox crime as C. B. In the course of his work he had broken up secret societies, freed a Cabinet Minister from blackmail, supervised the execution of a spy in the Tower of London, unravelled plots involving a dozen political murders, and, on occasion, when convinced that it was in the best interests of his country to do so, taken life himself without legal warrant. But never had he come across anything so utterly heinous as this project for the cold-blooded murder of an innocent girl. For him it was a new experience to feel faint; yet he did so now as he visualized Christina with her head half severed from her body, and the blood pouring from her neck to feed this loathsome, fiendish montrosity that, barely a yard away, was still glaring at him with a hatred beyond any of which even the most savage animal was capable.

His tongue clove to the roof of his mouth. He could no longer think of anything to say. Yet he knew that if he allowed the Canon to sense the horror he felt it would immediately expose him as an impostor. In vain he strove to get a hold over himself so that he might cope with the situation. His brain refused to work. Suitable words of understanding and approval simply would not come. Then, at the very moment that he thought his sick repulsion of the whole frightful business must become obvious, he was given an unexpected chance to conceal it.

A heavy knocking sounded on the iron door. The Canon stepped forward and quickly replaced the cover over the homunculus, turned on his heel, and hurried across to the steps. C. B. took a deep breath and, whipping out his handkerchief, swiftly wiped away the tell-tale perspiration that had broken out on his forehead. As Copely-Syle opened the door the flutter of a white robe disclosed the presence of his Egyptian servant on the far side of it. The two of them exchanged a few low-voiced sentences in Arabic, then the Canon glanced over his shoulder and said, "Excuse me, please. I shall be back quite soon." Stepping through the door, he locked it behind him, leaving C. B. alone in that chamber of horrors.

Within a few moments he had fully regained his composure and his mind was once more working with its accustomed lucidity. A glance at his wrist-watch showed him that it was close on half-past ten, so he had been in the house for an hour and a quarter. The time, he felt, had been remarkably well spent, as he had achieved far more than he had hoped to do when he had, on the spur of the moment, decided to make this reconnaissance. He had found out not only that even prison was no certain sanctuary for Christina, but also the steps the Canon would take to get her out, and by offering himself as their instigator had now ensured that they would not be taken. By the time Copely-Syle discovered that his visitor had been an impostor it would be too late for him to make the arrangements necessary to secure Christina's release from prison during the night of the 5th, and if she remained there until the 6th it would then be too late for him to get her back to England on her birthday. More, by his skilful winning of the Black Magician's confidence, C. B. had become privy to the foul and terrible operations in which he was engaged, and had a good prospect of being able to render them abortive.

As he looked again at the row of huge tea-cosies he was tempted to do so now, by using one of the furnace irons to smash the jars, and so end the horrid, unnatural life that squirmed and grimaced within them. But to have done so would have jeopardized his chances of saving Christina, and by disclosing to their evil creator that he had been discovered, enable him to escape retribution. Feeling that he had the situation well in hand, and now had only to maintain his imposture a little longer in order to clean up the whole revolting business in a satisfactory manner, C. B. quickly decided against precipitate action, and once more began to glance about him.

Now that he was alone his attention was again caught by the shuffling, squeaks and low whining that came from the other side of the crypt. Walking round the big tables, he crossed to the aisle in which stood the row of coops and cages. Behind the pillars the light was dim, but when he got to within a few feet of them he could see that each contained an animal, bird or reptile. There were black cocks and white hens, bats, toads and doves, evidently for use as sacrifices. Then he suddenly became conscious of a new horror.

The birds and reptiles were free, but the animals were not. All of them were crouching or lying in unnatural positions with their limbs pinioned. There were dogs, cats, rabbits, a badger, a mongoose and four monkeys: all were alive, but all had had some operation performed upon them. Many had had their genitals removed, some had had legs amputated, others lacked eyes or had had their claws cut out. From the bandages of several of them small bottles and test tubes protruded, into which was draining the fluid from their wounds.

At this heart-rending and nauseating sight C. B. was filled with a furious rage. Again the impulse came to him to take immediate action and put these miserable little creatures out of their agony. But again he fought down his personal feelings from the realization of how much was at stake and must be forfeited if he disclosed his hand prematurely.

How many minutes he stood staring with a sick feeling at these small martyrs to Evil he could not have said, but a slight sound behind him caused him to swing round. Unheard and unseen by him, the Canon had re-entered the crypt and was standing in his rear beside the nearest pillar.

Still the picture of a benign and erudite prelate of another age, Copely-Syle was smiling as he said, "I see that you are interested in my pets?"

In spite of his age and silver hair, C. B. itched to pound his smooth face into a jelly; but he stuffed his hands deep into his trouser pockets, and twisted his lips into a semblance of a grin, as the Canon went on blandly:

"They are indispensable to my work. Ample quantities of

gland secretions are an essential in the production of homunculi. It is regrettable that I should have had to make do with animals, and it is that, of course, which accounts for the ill-proportioned lumpishness of my creations. Had I had human beings at my disposal I could have produced men and women fair of face and shapely in form. But the day will come. Oh yes, the day will come when having seen my prototype the people for whom it has been designed will readily supply me with more suitable materials."

Carefully controlling his voice, C. B. said, "I take it you refer to the people in the Kremlin?"

The Canon nodded. "Who else? For is it not into their hands that the Lord Satan has placed the greatest power to serve him? I have no doubt whatever that they will be most interested when I submit my masterpiece to them."

For a moment he stood there, his pale eyes glowing with a fanatic light. Then they dimmed a little and he said with a swift change of manner, "But now that I have shown you my great secret we have no more to do here for the moment. It is still pouring with rain, and I do not know what arrangements you have made. If you prefer not to face the elements, I should be happy to offer you a bed here for the night."

"Thank you." C. B. shook his head. "It is very kind of you, but I arranged to pick up a taxi in the village, and I've booked a room at the Red Lion in Colchester. I think I had better go back there, as I must catch the first train up to London in the morning."

"Just as you wish." Copely-Syle turned and took a few paces towards the door; then he halted in his tracks and exclaimed, "Ah! There is one thing I nearly forgot. Since we are to work together, and you are to do that which there is to do on my behalf down at Nice to-morrow night, it is only fitting that before you depart we should pledge one another in the cup of Brotherhood."

C. B. was most reluctant to participate in any such rite, quite apart from the fact that he expected it to entail his having to swallow at least a few sips of some horrid brew; but he saw no way in which he could evade the proposal without arousing

232

belated suspicions in his host's mind; so, comforting himself with the thought that within a few minutes now he would be out of this den of iniquity, he agreed with tactful promptness.

Leading the way to the altar, the Canon took the gold chalice from it: then he went to a cabinet nearby, produced a wicker-covered bottle and poured about a wineglassful of its contents into the chalice. Returning to the altar he genuflected three times before the crucified bat, elevated the chalice, and in a sonorous voice chanted a few sentences of Abracadabra in what C. B. took to be Hebrew. Putting the chalice to his lips, he tilted back his head, held it so for a moment, lowered it, and wiped the moisture from his mouth with the back of his free hand; then, with a courtly bow, he handed the vessel to C. B.

Having bowed in reply, C. B. lifted it in turn and took a small sip. To his surprise it was no Devil's potion distilled from frogs' testicles and newts' tails, but a rich wine highly flavoured with aromatic spices; so he took a small mouthful before lowering the chalice.

As Copely-Syle stretched out a hand for the vessel he saw that a good part of the wine remained in it. His eyes seemed to flash with suspicion, and he exclaimed angrily:

"You, a Magister Templi, should know better than to leave unconsumed wine that has been offered as a sacrament."

To cover his blunder C. B. replied swiftly, "I had not intended to leave any. I was taking my time to savour this beautiful concoction." Then he lifted the vessel again and emptied it.

As he lowered the chalice a second time the Canon began to laugh. It was not a pleasant genial laugh, but a gloating chuckle that rose to a high-pitched malicious titter.

Suddenly C. B. was filled with a terrible fear. That evil mirth confirmed an impression of which he had become conscious only a moment earlier. As the liquid he had drunk coursed through his veins he could feel his limbs becoming paralysed. With extraordinary swiftness his body assumed an intolerable weight. Turning, he took a few faltering steps in the direction of the door; but he knew that he could never reach it. His knees sagged and the Canon gave him a sudden push. Losing his balance, he slumped into a carved ebony elbow-chair that stood to one side of the altar steps. That contemptuous push destroyed his last desperate hope that he might be the victim only of some natural seizure. He had been tricked into drinking a powerful drug, and was now at the mercy of the most unscrupulous Satanist he had ever encountered.

CHAPTER XVI

DEAD MEN TELL NO TALES

THE Canon's pale face, no longer a benign mask, but displaying unconcealed the evil in his soul, leered down into C. B.'s. His thick lower lip jutted out aggressively and from between his blackened teeth he spat the words:

"You fool! You miserable fool! You would have done better to walk naked into a den of lions than to come here. That you managed to deceive me for an hour shows that you know enough to have some idea of the risk you ran. How could you hope to pit yourself against me—an Ipsissimus? In a day or less it was certain that I should have found you out and caught up with you."

C. B.'s sight, hearing and the faculties of his mind remained unimpaired, but all his limbs had become limp and useless. Concentrating his will, he strove desperately to struggle to his feet. The attempt was futile and resulted only in a slight stiffening of his spine. He could do no more than wriggle feebly where he sat, and by the greatest effort raise one hand a few inches. While he squirmed there helplessly, the Canon went on:

"When I left you just now it was because an authentic messenger sent by de Grasse had just arrived from France. From my description of you he identified you at once as Mrs. Fountain's friend who arrived from London yesterday. I know you now, Colonel Verney, for what you are. And you may be sure that I do not mean to allow you to carry away with you the secrets you have learned to-night."

"You damn' well let me go or . . . or it'll be the worse for you," muttered C. B. thickly.

"There is no way in which you can harm me."

"Not at the moment, perhaps. But . . . my friends know that I came here. If . . . if I don't rejoin them they will soon be asking you some . . . very awkward questions."

"They will ask none that I shall not be able to answer to their satisfaction. I have already decided how to deal with this situation, and what I shall tell them. You called here at a quarter-past nine and left again at about eleven o'clock. In view of the wildness of the weather we decided that you should take the short-cut through my garden to the village. My servant will say that he let you out of the back door and described the way you should go. At the bottom of the orchard there is a little gate. Beyond it lies the railway line. The last train from London passes at about eleven-five. To-morrow morning, when your dead body——"

"My body!" gasped C. B. "You can't mean——"

"To murder you?" the Canon finished for him. "Yes: why not? But no one will suspect me of having done so. As I was about to say—when your mangled body is found it will be assumed that you tripped in the dark, fell, and stunned yourself when crossing the rails."

C. B.'s mind was still perfectly clear; but he was having great difficulty in keeping his chin from falling forward on his chest, and his tongue felt swollen and clumsy. He had not often been really frightened in his life, but he was frightened now. Jerking back his head, he forced out the words:

"You're mad! You can't do this!"

"Oh, but I can!" The Canon's voice had become cruelly bantering. "It is only a little after half-past ten, so there is ample time to put you on the line before the train passes. Even should someone enquire for you during the next half-hour, if they are told that you have already left I do not believe for an instant that they would risk breaking in without some concrete reason for supposing that harm has befallen you. To do so would ruin your own success, had you managed to carry through your imposture; so before taking any action they would certainly go back to the inn to make quite sure you had not returned there. You are as much my creature now as any of the homunculi, and there is no power in the world that can prevent my doing what I like with you."

"Perhaps. All the same . . . if you do as you say you . . . you'll swing for it."

Copely-Syle shook his silvery head and smiled. "Wishful thinking, my poor friend; wishful thinking. There will not be one scrap of evidence against me. Your death will so clearly be an unfortunate accident. 'How sad,' people who know you will say. 'Colonel Verney was really no age, and such a nice man.' Naturally, although you were a stranger to me, as you met your death soon after leaving my house I shall send a wreath. Have you any preference in flowers? Since it was poking your nose into other people's business while in the South of France that has brought you to this sorry pass, I think carnations and mimosa would be rather suitable."

"You . . . you'll swing, I tell you!" C. B. croaked. "The people who knew I was coming here knew my suspicions about you. If I'm found dead they'll pull this place to pieces. They'll find what I found. Once they've nailed your motive for getting rid of me, the rope will be as good as round your neck."

His face suddenly distorted with rage, the Canon took a step forward and began to strike C. B. again and again in the face with his small flabby hands.

"Swine! Swine! Swine!" he cried. "So owing to you there is now a risk that my sanctum here may be desecrated! That clods incapable of apprehending the significance of the most elementary mystery may break in; may destroy my priceless possessions; may ruin the work of a life-time. But no! Once you, who have some understanding of these things, are out of the way, I can deal with them."

Calming down with the same suddenness as he had flown into a passion, he added, "This is England. No one will dare force their way into the house without a search warrant. If I held you prisoner they might apply for one. But your body is certain to be found soon after it is light; so there will be nothing for which to search here. You did not know about my homunculi before I told you of them; so your friends cannot suspect the work upon which I am engaged. They can know nothing more than that I planned to have Ellen kidnapped. I shall find no difficulty in fooling anyone who may call here to make enquiries."

"That will not save you!"

"Yes it will. You are my only danger. Once you are silenced for good I shall have nothing to fear."

"You are wrong." C. B.'s voice came hoarsely. It was still an effort to speak, but he knew that he was fighting for his life. "I shall still be a danger to you when I am dead. However cleverly you may lie to my friends, they will still be suspicious at my sudden death. They will insist on a post-mortem. My body will be found full of this infernal poison. They'll get you on that."

The Canon laughed again, his good humour quite restored. "No, no! As with most drugs that paralyse the body while leaving the brain unimpaired, its effects are only temporary. They soon wear off. To keep you as helpless as you are at present I shall have to give you another dose before we carry you out, and yet a third when we leave you on the line. By the time your body is found all traces of the drug will have disappeared."

This piece of information brought C. B. a glimmer of hope. Perhaps it was no more than the effect of suggestion, but he had the impression that his feet were not quite so dead to all sensation as they had been when he had first endeavoured to struggle up from the chair. If he could keep Copely-Syle talking for a while there now seemed a chance that he might recover the use of his limbs at least enough for one violent movement. The Canon obviously lacked both muscle and stamina. If suddenly sprung upon by a much weightier man, it was certain that he would go down under the impact. Once down and grasped by hands that would be growing stronger every moment, it would be long odds against his being able to free himself. C. B.'s fears eased a little. He knew that he was very far from being out of the wood, yet all the same he began to savour the thought of getting his long fingers round that plump neck.

His hopes were short-lived. Almost as though the Canon had read his victim's thoughts, he said, "With such a big man as yourself, Colonel Verney, the effects of the drug may be of unusually short duration, and such a hearty specimen of

British manhood can hardly be expected to accept calmly the fact that death is waiting for him at the bottom of the garden. There is too much at stake for me to take any chances. Just in case you should recover sufficiently to show a belated resistance to my will, it would be best if I put any temptation to do so beyond your powers."

As he spoke he went over to the cabinet from which he had taken the bottle containing the drugged wine. From a drawer in the lower part of it he got out a ball of string and a pair of scissors. With deft movements he cut off several pieces of string, each about a yard in length, and proceeded first to lash C. B.'s wrists to the arms of the chair, then his ankles to its front legs. C. B. was still too weak to put up anything but a feeble opposition, and, once the job was done, even had he been in possession of his full strength, he could not have moved without dragging the heavy chair with him like a snail's shell on his back, much less broken free from it.

Again C. B. felt fear closing down like a black cloud on his mind. Yet still a lingering hope sustained him. If his death was to be made to appear an accident, it was clear that they could not leave him bound hand and foot when they laid him on the railway line. Neither would they dare gag him. Although he could speak only with some difficulty, he might be able to cry out loud enough to attract the attention of a passer-by. At such an hour and in such weather that hope was an incredibly slender one. But there was another one slightly more substantial. They could not remain with him until the train was actually in sight, from fear of being seen in its headlamps. He would have at least a few minutes unbound and alone. As the effects of the drug wore off so quickly, he might regain just enough strength to squirm clear of the rails.

The thought had hardly come to him when it was shattered by another. Copely-Syle would not be such a fool as to give him that last chance, and risk finding himself facing a judge on a charge of attempted murder. He or the Egyptian would knock their victim on the head before they left him. To do so would not add in the least to any chance of his death being traced to them, as his fractured skull would be assumed to be one of the injuries received when the engine made mincemeat of him.

Once more it seemed as if the Canon read his thoughts; but he had other views for ensuring against any last-minute escape, for he said smoothly, "No doubt you are hoping that when we leave you on the line you will manage to wriggle off it. Do not deceive yourself. I shall take precautions against that. As you are aware, homunculi must be fed on human blood. Fortunately the modern practice of people giving their blood to hospitals saves me considerable trouble in obtaining supplies. For a sufficient recompense a man in London finds no difficulty in arranging for several bottles to be stolen from the hospitals for me every week; but your visit provides me with an opportunity to save a little money."

His meaning was clear enough, and a shudder ran through C. B. at the thought that his blood was to be used to sustain the life of those foul creatures in the jars.

"A pint is the usual quantity given by blood donors," the Canon went on thoughtfully, "but that hardly affects them; so I shall take from you at least a quart. Such a drain on your vitality will more than double the effect of the drug; so for a quarter of an hour or more you will be too weak to lift a finger. And to render you incapable of all movement for ten minutes will be ample for our purpose."

C. B.'s strength was now fast returning to him. He could move his toes, clench his fingers, and flex the muscles of his arms and legs. Temporarily giving way to the fear that was upon him, he began to shout curses at the Canon and strive violently to free himself. His struggles were in vain; the string cut into his wrists and ankles, but his efforts failed even to loosen it materially.

With a contemptuous smile, the Canon watched his abortive squirming for a few moments; then he said, "Directly I learned that you were an impostor I hurried back here, in case you took it into your head to harm the homunculi during my absence; so I have yet to hear the full report of de Grasse's messenger. It would be a great mistake to put you on the line unnecessarily early, in case someone stumbled on you. I am, therefore, about to fill in ten minutes by listening to what else the messenger has to say, and putting in a personal call to de Grasse for midnight, so that I may give him fresh instructions. When I return I shall give you your second dose of the drink you found so palatable. They say that when near death one recalls one's childhood. My having to hold your nose while you take your medicine should help you to remember similar episodes when in your nursery. We shall then perform the little operation by which you will donate your blood to such an admirable cause. That should take us up to about five minutes to eleven. In the meantime my man, Achmet, will have brought the wheelbarrow round from the gardener's shed. The margin of ten minutes I have left should be just right for me to give you your final dose, and have you transported to the scene of your execution."

Turning on his heel he walked sedately the length of the crypt with his hands clasped behind his back. As he switched out all the lights except two and left it, locking the door after him, C. B. watched him go with a feeling of sick despair. There seemed such an air of terrible finality about the Satanist's present calmness. That he was apt to fly into rages was evident from the intense anger he had shown at the suggestion that his sanctuary might be invaded; but there was something infinitely more menacing in his general behaviour since he had discovered that C. B. was an impostor. Swiftly, yet carefully, he had made his arrangements to commit a cold-blooded murder, and had discussed it in detail with such unruffled composure that it looked as if nothing short of a miracle could prevent his going through with it.

A cold perspiration broke out on C. B.'s forehead as he thought how slender were the chances of such a miracle occurring. He had already dismissed the idea that he might be rescued by John as in the highest degree unlikely. He had told John that if he was not out of the house by midnight he was to telephone the police and come in to find him. But by midnight, if the train was punctual, he would have been dead for fifty-five minutes; and John would certainly not attempt to force his way in more than an hour before the time he had been given. For all he knew, matters were going excellently and, as the Canon was certain to recognize him as Ellen's friend, his premature entry, seeking C. B., might have thrown a spanner in the works at their most promising point. Besides, there was no earthly reason why he should ignore his instructions and risk upsetting everything, unless . . .

C. B. stiffened in his chair . . . unless John had seen the messenger arrive and recognized him as one of de Grasse's people. If that had happened he would know that the odds were on C. B. being caught out. Then, if C. B. did not appear within quite a short while, there would be grounds for assuming that he was in trouble. What would John do in such circumstances? If he enquired at the front door he would be told that C. B. had already left by the back entrance and was taking the short-cut to the village. He would not believe that, but he might decide to return to the village to make certain. In any case he would do so, to telephone the police before taking further action. Then what? John would come back and endeavour to get into the house. If he succeeded, and was discovered, he would be one against three. Even if he managed to get in undetected he would not know where to look for C. B. The windows of the crypt had all been bricked up, so there was no chance of his entering it direct from outside; and he could not possibly force its iron door. Only one slender chance remained: he might come upon the Satanists when they were carrying their victim out into the garden.

With frantic anxiety C. B. began to calculate times. De Grasse's messenger had arrived just before half-past ten. John would wait at least ten minutes to see if C. B. came out of his own accord, before taking any action. To enquire at the front door would take him from three to five minutes, and it was a good ten minutes' walk to the village. There might be a public call-box on the green, but never having been in the place before John would not know where to find it, and the odds were all against his running into it in the darkness. He would have to telephone from the pub, but that would now be closed. To knock it up and get on to Colchester would take him another ten minutes; then he would require ten more minutes to walk back to the house. There was the possibility that he would take the car both ways, but on such a short distance the best to be hoped for from that was that it would reduce the total time from forty-five to thirty-five minutes. Therefore, at the earliest reasonable moment that John could be expected to begin reconnoitring the house for the easiest place to break into it, the London train would be thundering over C. B.'s body; and even that was on the assumption that he had seen de Grasse's messenger, recognized him, and decided to take prompt action.

At the conclusion of his calculations C. B. let go a gasp rather than a sigh. It was no good. He was caught without hope of rescue. His number was up, and he must face it. He had barely a quarter of an hour of life left.

Fruitlessly, he cursed himself for his foolhardiness in having walked into such danger on an impulse, and without making provision for an adequate life-line. He felt that he, of all people, had had experience enough to know better. Yet, on consideration, had he really been so very rash? At worst there had been no reason to anticipate anything more serious than that the Canon might find him out and have him beaten up, then locked up in a cellar or attic till the morning. Had he speculated for a week on the possible outcome of such a visit, it would still not have occurred to him that by making it he might lose his life. Neither would there have been the least likelihood of his doing so, had not the success of his imposture led to his being taken into the Canon's confidence so unreservedly and shown things, the existence of which he had not even remotely suspected.

It was his having learned about the homunculi that put the rope round his neck, and it was that which made it futile to hope that Copely-Syle was seeking only to frighten him. Having given away his awful secret, no oaths or pledges that the Canon could extract from his prisoner would satisfy him that he might not now be called on to account for his hideous practices. Should he once release C. B. he would lose all power to enforce his silence, whereas in this next half-hour he had the chance to close his mouth once and for all. It was this final realization that the Canon had no option but to kill him that made C. B.'s heart contract with despair and his face sweat with terror.

Yet he was not the man to give in until in the last ditch. For several moments he succeeded in almost banishing his fears, and even reducing a little the furious pace at which his heart was beating, while he cast hither and thither for some means of escape or an argument with which he could induce the Canon to postpone his execution. By the end of that time he had thought of nothing. Again there intruded on his mental vision a picture of himself lying helpless in the dark night across the railway line, and feeling it vibrate as the train hurtled towards him.

He began to pray, but the picture would not go. It became a series of pictures. Himself, half-comatose, being wheeled through the garden, his long legs dangling from the barrow. The Canon and the Egyptian arranging his limp body on the line. The train roaring down upon him at sixty miles an hour. His mangled corpse, the head severed from the body, still lying there at dawn. Its discovery by plate-layers on their way to work.

It was then an idea came to him. He could not save himself, but he could revenge himself on the Canon. Into his mind there came the vaguely-remembered story of a British sergeant who had been taken prisoner by the Japanese and mercilessly tortured by one of their camp guards. It was to the effect that the soldier, having had his tongue cut out, had, with extraordinary fortitude, carved the name of his torturer with a penknife in the flesh of his own stomach; and he had survived long enough for that to lead to the execution of the swinish Japanese.

C. B. was in no position to emulate this act, even had he had the time and courage to do so; but by dragging at his wrists and ankles with all his might he could cause the string that bound them to cut so deeply into his flesh that the marks would remain visible long after he was dead. Next day, when his body was found, it would be obvious that his hands and feet had been tightly bound, and that would immediately suggest that he had been the victim of foul play. No accusation that John could bring would lead to a prosecution, unless some direct evidence of assault could be brought to support it, but with such evidence Copely-Syle's carefully-built-up picture of an accident would be blown sky-high, and he would find himself facing a charge of murder.

Gritting his teeth, C. B. set about screwing his wrists back and forth and jerking up his knees with all his force, so that the tight string cut into his ankles. The pain made him wince, but he kept at it till he had drawn blood at both his wrists, then he allowed himself a breather.

As he sat, slumped now in the chair, panting heavily, another thought came to him. For a second he hardly dare consider it as a real possibility; then he saw that it was perfectly logical. With the wounds he had inflicted on himself he might yet save his life. When Copely-Syle returned he would show them to him, then dare him to stage his 'accident'. The Canon was no fool; and even by the aid of magic it was hardly thinkable that in the few minutes, which were all that would be at his disposal, he would be able to cause bleeding wounds to disappear so that they left no trace. He would know that to carry through his plan would now bring him into acute danger. He might be a criminal lunatic, but he was not mad in that way. He would either devise some other plan for killing and disposing of his victim or, if he could, would perform an involved magical ceremony to heal the wounds, before having him taken out and put on the line to be run over by a night goods train. Whichever course he took it meant a postponement of the execution. And even half an hour might now bring John, and after him the police, upon the scene.

It was at that moment, tense with excitement at this new-found hope, that C. B. suddenly realized that something was happening at the far end of the crypt.

He had caught the sound of a faint 'plop'. Screwing round his head he stared towards the furnace. From it there was coming a hissing noise. The only lights the Canon had left on were near the altar, so since he had gone from the crypt the whole of its bottom end had been plunged in deep shadow. The bed of the furnace, under its big scalloped canopy, now looked like a black cavern; yet it seemed to C. B. that wisps of steam were rising from it. There came another heavier 'plop', then something began to writhe upon the furnace bed among the greyish swirls of steam.

C. B. drew a sharp breath. His heart began to hammer violently. He was seized by a new fear, and one totally different from that which had afflicted him since he had drunk the poison from the chalice. That had been straight physical fear at the realization that he was in acute danger and within twenty minutes, or less, might find himself face to face with a most painful death. This was a terror of the spirit.

The walls of this ancient stone chamber had witnessed many fearsome rites. Only God and the Devil could know to what abominations Copely-Syle had resorted in order to give his homunculi life. That life at present was only fish-like, and they were powerless to leave their glass prisons. But the whole place reeked of Evil. For his hellish acts of creation the Canon would have had to compel the aid of those strange potent Spirits that govern the behaviour of Earth, Air, Fire and Water. He would also have had to call up those brutish groping foeti from the Pit; things that lived upon a lower plane, yet were always seeking means to enter this one and, given propitious circumstances, could not only appear to human eyes, but also take hideous solid form. It was even possible that to complete his devilish work he had had to invoke some chill intelligence of the Outer Circle: an entity beside which even the terror inspired by the loathsome horrors of the Pit would pale; for such Sataii could drive men mad or strike them dead, as had proved the case with Crowley and McAleister.

Fearful of what he might see, C. B. peered with straining eyes into the shadows. Within a few seconds of his having heard the second 'plop' he knew that his senses had not deceived him. The bed of the furnace was no longer flat. It seemed to have arched itself up into a hump. Among the smoke and steam some fearsome thing was materializing from it. Swiftly the hump rose, a whitish blob appeared in its middle and it assumed an irregular outline. C. B. distinctly heard the

246

coke crunch under it. Next moment it heaved itself outward from the furnace bed and landed with a thud upon the floor.

Now it was hidden from C. B. by the tables. His spine seemed to be dissolving into water. Shrinking back, he grasped the arms of the chair, while cold sweat broke out anew on his face. For an instant an intense bitterness surged through his mind at the thought that he should have devised a means of saving himself from the Canon, only to fall a victim to one of the dread Satanic forces that he had made his familiars. He could hear the monster scrabbling on the ground. Dreading intensely what he would see when it emerged from behind the tables, he closed his eyes and began to pray. Urgently, frantically, he called upon the God of Mercy, Peace and Love to help him in his dire extremity.

There came the sound of swift movement across the stone flags of the crypt; then, as a lump rose in his throat that almost choked him, his prayer was answered. Loud, clear, unmistakable, John's voice was calling him by name; and, an instant later, a human hand grasped his shoulder.

As C. B. opened his eyes, John's words came tumbling out. "Thank God I've found you. Twenty minutes ago a taxi drove up. As its passenger was paying off the driver I caught sight of his face. It was Upson, that air pilot of de Grasse's—the fellow Christina snatched the gun from. I felt certain that if he ran into you there would be trouble. I padded round the house till I found a bay window with lights showing through the chinks of the curtains. One of the windows was a few inches open. I listened at it and caught the old boy's voice. He was in a screaming passion. I gathered that you were waiting for him in the chapel, and that he was just about to pull a fast one on you. I lost ten minutes trying to find a way in here. As a last resort I climbed up on the roof to see if there was a skylight. There wasn't, but the chimney is a good three feet square inside; so I threw my mac down first, in case there was a fire going at the bottom, then let myself drop on to it."

"Well done! Well done!" breathed C. B. "If you hadn't found me the odds are I'd have been dead before morning. But we haven't a moment to lose. That fiend may be back here

247

any second. Look! There's a sword on the altar. Use it to cut me free."

Obediently John snatched up the sword, but as he clasped it he cast a scared glance over his shoulder, and muttered, "This place gives me cold shivers down my spine. What's been going on here?"

"Never mind that now," C. B. said impatiently. "For God's sake cut these strings."

The blade of the sacrificial sword was sharp as a razor. Once John set to work the strings parted under it with as little resistance as though they were threads of cotton. Yet even for so short a time C. B. could not keep his eyes on the strokes that were liberating him. A new fear impelled him to keep darting swift glances from side to side into the shadows behind the two rows of pillars. The possibility of the Canon surprising them before they could get away had now taken second place in his mind. It seemed as if some malignant unseen force, already in the crypt, was stirring into evil life with intent to prevent their leaving it.

As the last string snapped C. B. jerked himself to his feet, and John, his thin face now chalk-white, gasped:

"Come on! For Christ's sake let's get out of here!"

Side by side, they began to run down the crypt. But their feet felt as though they were weighted with lead. The strength seemed to be ebbing from their limbs as though they had received many wounds and their life-blood was draining away with every step they took. Half-way along the tables they faltered into a walk. The air ahead of them no longer had the feeling of air. It had become intensely cold and was as though they were endeavouring to force their way through water.

In a half-strangled voice, C. B. began to recite the Lord's Prayer aloud. "Our Father which art in Heaven . . ."

Almost instantly the pressure eased and they found themselves able to stagger forward to the furnace. When jumping from it John had pulled his mackintosh after him. Sooty and scorched, it lay on the ground nearby. As he snatched it up, C. B., still praying aloud, looked hastily round for something else to throw on the bed of coke that would protect their feet

248

from burning. His glance lit on the robes used by the Canon when he officiated as a minister of the Black priesthood. They were of heavy scarlet satin embroidered in black with magical insignia, and hung upon a stand on the far side of the door. While John sprayed the top layer of coke with water, C. B. fetched the vestments and flung them on to the hissing furnace bed; then he cried:

"Go on, up you go!"

John hesitated a moment, glancing at C. B.'s bleeding wrists; but the older man pushed him forward, so he scrambled up into the steam-filled cavity. His head and shoulders disappeared into the wide funnel made by the chimney, and he quickly began to feel about for hand-holds inside it. Within a few seconds his searching fingers found the iron rungs that had been used by sweeps' urchins in times gone by. As he began to haul himself up, C. B. followed. Two minutes later, grimy with soot and half choked by coke fumes, they stood side by side on the roof of the chapel.

Yet so powerful was the evil radiating from the gateway to Hell below them that they did not feel safe from pursuit. Scarcely heeding the danger of slipping on the wet roof, or tripping in the darkness, they scrambled down its slope to the nearest gutter, hung by it for a moment, then dropped the eight feet to the ground. Picking themselves up from the soaking grass, by a common impulse they ran round the side of the house, across the garden to the road, and down it for nearly a quarter of a mile before the fresh night air and the rain in their faces restored their sense of security sufficiently for them to pull up.

In their terror they had passed the car; but now they walked back to it, got in and bound up C. B.'s wrists as well as they could with their handkerchiefs. Then they lit cigarettes. After a few puffs they began to feel more like themselves, and C. B. gave John an outline of the hour and a quarter he had spent with the Canon. At the description of the homunculi John was nearly sick, but his nausea turned to fury when he learnt of the fate planned for Christina, and on hearing of the cold-blooded murder which would at that moment have been taking place had he not got C. B. away, he wanted to drive off at once to fetch the police.

C. B. laid a restraining hand on his arm. "Easy, partner! It's not quite so simple as all that. You could give evidence that you found me tied to a chair; but that's no proof of intended murder. The old warlock, his Gippy servant and the airman would probably all swear themselves blind that they had caught me breaking into the house; and it is a fact that you broke in later. If they took the line that we had gone to the police first with a cooked-up story, because we feared being caught and charged to-morrow, it would be only our word against theirs."

"Yours would be taken. Your people in London would vouch for you."

"Oh yes. A telephone call to the Department would bring someone down to-morrow to identify me and give me a good character. In fact had you fetched the police before coming in to get me, that's what I should have had to do. It would have been worth it, even as an alternative to remaining locked up in a cellar indefinitely, which was the worst I feared when I went in. All the same, I'm extremely glad that you managed to get me out without calling in the minions of the law."

"From what you tell me, if I'd spent half an hour collecting them before going in your goose would have been cooked by the time we got there."

"Yes. That's one reason; and I can never thank you enough, John, for the guts you displayed in coming in on your own when you did. Another reason is that, even when acting officially, I am no more entitled to break into people's houses without a warrant than any other citizen; and in this case I haven't got even the unofficial blessing of the Department; so if Copely-Syle had charged me with breaking and entering that would have put me in quite a nasty spot."

"I see. All the same I think it's monstrous that this criminal lunatic should be allowed to get away with attempted murder and all the other devilry he is up to."

"We won't let him. But we've got to play our cards carefully if we are to lay him by the heels without burning our own fingers. We've got to get some solid evidence against him before we can make our next move."

"What about the homunculi? Surely his having those filthy creatures in the house is against the law?"

"I rather doubt it. As far as I know there is no precedent to go on; and since such matters were removed from the jurisdiction of the old ecclesiastical courts prosecution for the practice of witchcraft has dropped into abeyance. Besides, we have not an atom of proof that he intends to harm anyone or is, in fact, engaged in anything which could not be defended as a scientific experiment. All the same, I wish we had remained there long enough to smash the jars and kill the horrible things inside them."

John shivered. "I don't think I could have done it. I mean, stay on there for a moment longer than I positively had to. I wasn't frightened about going in—at least no more than I would have been when breaking into any other place where I might have got a sock on the jaw—but once inside I felt as if I was being watched by invisible eyes all the time. It was as though there was something indescribably evil lurking in the shadows behind me: something that had the power to rend and destroy, and that at any second might leap out on to the back of my neck. Then, just before you began to pray, I felt as if I was being suffocated; and I began to fear that I'd never get out at all."

C. B. nodded. "I felt the same. The explanation is that the place has become the haunt of some very nasty elementals. As the Canon's familiars they would naturally try, in their blind, fumbling way, to prevent our escape. Perhaps if we had lingered they might have materialized. Anyhow, I had the feeling that they might, and I was scared stiff. My one thought was to get away while the going was good, and I wasn't capable of thinking of anything else till we were well down the road."

Stubbing out his cigarette, John put his foot on the self-starter. As it ceased to whirr and the engine began to fire, he said, "Since we've had the luck to get out all right, I'm glad we went in. It enabled you to find out a tremendous lot, and at least we know what we are up against now. I wish we could have made a job of it to-night, and called in the police to haul him off to jail; but since you've ruled that out, the sooner we can grab a hot toddy, get our wet things off, and hop into bed, the better."

"Not so fast, laddie," C. B. replied, as the car gathered speed. "I'll gladly dig the barman out to fix us hot toddies, whatever time we get back to Colchester, but I've no intention of returning yet. First, I mean to try to pick up a little evidence against his Satanic Reverence."

Slowing down the car, John turned and stared at him. "You . . . you don't mean that you're going back into that hellish place?"

"No. I'm not poking my head into that hornets' nest again till the hornets have had a chance to settle down. But we are up to our necks in this thing now, and we've got no time to lose. I hate to think what my Chief will have to say should matters go wrong, and you had better keep out of it; but I really do mean to risk finding myself in the dock this time. I intend to break, enter and, I hope, burgle private premises without the least excuse to justify my act if I am caught."

CHAPTER XVII

THE MYSTERY OF THE GRANGE

JOHN let out a low whistle, then said, "It's not for me to teach my grandmother to suck eggs, but d'you really think you ought to take such a risk, C. B.? I mean, of blotting your copy-book so badly that even your Department will feel that it must wash its hands of you?"

"Yes. I think so in a case like this, for which no provision is made by our ordinary laws. I don't want to sound stuffy, but there are times when every man must be guided by his own conscience, and this is one of them. We have learnt to-night that we are up against not just a dabbler in Black Magic who threatens the well-being of one young woman, but a Satanist of the first order, who is striving to perfect and launch upon the world one of the worst horrors that even his master, the Devil, can have conceived. To stop that I am prepared to go to any lengths."

"Since you put it that way, you are absolutely right; but where is this place you intend to break into?"

"I mean to pay a midnight visit to The Grange."

"What good will that do us, as Beddows isn't there?"

"Probably none. It's just a long shot; but there's a chance that we might find some useful pointers to Beddows' whereabouts and his tie-up with the Canon."

John spoke with a touch of deference. "I don't pretend to be psychic, but I didn't at all like the atmosphere of The Grange when we called there this evening. Perhaps that is because it is such a gloomy old place, but as these two beauties appear to be mixed up together I should think it is quite on the cards that The Grange, too, has got some pretty nasty spooks in it. Haven't you had enough of that sort of thing for one night?"

"To be honest, John, I have," C. B. replied quietly. "But in the late war, whenever one of the R.A.F. boys was shot down, or made a crash landing, they used to send him up again just as soon as they could. It was an excellent principle. That's the way to keep one's nerve, and if it wasn't for the fact that the Canon and his pals must be on the *qui vive* I'd make myself go back into that crypt. As such a move would mean sticking out my neck a bit too far, I'm going into the moated Grange at midnight instead."

"Well, you're the boss." John tried to make his voice sound flippant. The few minutes he had spent in the crypt had been more than enough for him. He could only guess what C. B. must have been through while bound hand and foot there and expecting to be murdered within the hour; but he knew that to show admiration for the elder man would only embarrass them both, so without further remark he took the car round the village green and drove back the way they had come.

As they were passing the church, C. B. said, "All the same, John, you mustn't get the idea I'm about to risk running into something very nasty, or having to appear in the dock, for no better reason than to test my own nerve. I'm going into The Grange because this matter has become too urgent for me to neglect any chance of getting a new line on these people. We left France with the object of interviewing Beddows, because we felt confident that he would be able to tell us what lay behind Copely-Syle's attempts to get hold of Christina. We have found that out from the Canon himself; but what we have learnt to-night makes it more important than ever that we should get hold of Beddows with the least possible delay. At the moment we have only half the picture. He must be able to give us the other half. We've got to know why it was Christina that the Canon selected as his potential victim, and why her father left her marooned in the South of France. I have an idea that Copely-Syle may be blackmailing him. If so, we'll get something on the enemy that way. If not, he may be able to provide us with some other line by which we can use the normal processes of the law to spike the Canon's guns. But we've got to trace him first, and it seems to me that our best chance of doing that is by raiding his house. With a little

luck we may find some papers there which will give us a lead
to where he has got to."

"I hadn't thought of any of those things," John admitted
ruefully, and, angry with himself for having suggested going
to bed while the night still held a chance to further elucidate
the grim mystery which surrounded Christina, he pressed his
foot down on the accelerator.

Two minutes later he drove the car a little way up a blind
turning that he had noticed earlier, barely a hundred yards
from the gates of The Grange, brought it to a standstill and
switched out its lights. C. B. produced a big torch from under
the seat and went round to the boot. From it he got out
several implements that are not usually found in a motor
repair outfit, then they walked along the road to the entrance
to the drive. As they reached it, C. B. said:

"Now this time——"

"Sorry, C. B.," John interrupted him before he had a
chance to get any further, "I'm much too cold and wet to
hang about here. I'm coming in with you."

"Then if we are caught we may both be jugged for house-
breaking."

"No. You know jolly well that doesn't follow. If we are
surprised, the odds are that one of us will have time to get
away. I couldn't go in with you before, because the Canon
would have recognized me; but this is different. Honestly,
we'll both be much safer if we stick together."

"You won't, because you will be taking a quite unnecessary risk." C. B. grinned at him in the darkness. "Still, since
you insist, I won't deny that I'll be glad to have you with me.
Come on, then."

In single file they walked along the grass verge of the
drive until they reached the sweep in front of the house; then
C. B. led the way round to its back. The rain had eased a
little and in one quarter of the dark heavens the moon was
now trying to break through between banks of swiftly drifting
cloud. The light it gave was just enough to outline dimly the
irregularities of the building, parts of which were four hundred
years old, and it glinted faintly on its windows. No light

showed in any of them, neither was there now any sound of a wireless; but as it was still only a little after eleven o'clock C. B. feared that the Jutson couple might not yet have gone to sleep; so he continued to move with great caution.

As John peered up at the flat over the stables in which they lived, he whispered:

"I wonder if they keep a watchdog."

"If they do it would be a pretty definite indication that there is nothing worse here. Dogs will always run away rather than stay in a place where there are spooks."

No growl or whine disturbed the stillness and, having been right round the house, they turned back. Drawing on a pair of rubber gloves, C. B. told John to put on his wash-leather ones; then he selected a small window in a semi-circular two-storied turret that jutted out from a main wall, and had evidently been built on at a much later date. Inserting a short jemmy opposite the catch, he pressed down on it: there was a sharp snap, and the window flew open.

Climbing inside he found, as he had expected, that the turret contained a back staircase, added no doubt when the original farm-house had been enlarged and become the property of gentry. As he turned to help John in after him he whispered:

"Never break in by a room, my lad, unless you know it to be the one room in the house you want to get into. Otherwise the odds are that you will find its door bolted and may have half-an-hour's hard work before you can get any further. On the other hand, if you come in by the hall or stairs the whole house is your oyster."

He flashed his torch for a second. It disclosed a short passage ahead of them and a baize door. Tip-toeing forward, he reached the door and pushed it gently. Yielding to his touch, it swung silently open. They listened intently for a moment, but no sound came to them. C. B. shone his torch again and kept it on while he swept its beam slowly round, then up and down. The door gave on to the main hall of the house. It was large and lofty, with heavy oak beams. A broad staircase on one side of it led up to the landing of the first

256

floor, and there was a small minstrels' gallery on the other. Opposite the intruders stood the front door, and to either side there were other doors, evidently giving on to the principal rooms of the house. The moving beam was suddenly brought to rest on a large oak chest under the stairs. On it stood a telephone.

Moving softly forward, C. B. shone the light down behind the chest till it showed a square, plastic box that was fixed to the skirting. Producing a pair of clippers from his pocket, he cut the main wire a little beyond the box. John, who had come up behind him, said in a low voice:

"In for a penny, in for a pound, eh? We won't be able to laugh off the breaking and entering business now by spinning a yarn that we found a window open and just came in out of the rain."

"Worth it," replied C. B. tersely. "On a job like this, cutting the enemy's communications as a first move quadruples one's chances of getting away safely. If it becomes necessary to run for it they can't call out the police cars to scour the roads."

"It's a great comfort to be in the hands of a professional." John's voice betrayed his amusement.

"That's quite enough from you, young feller. I have to know these things; but my own visits to strangers are nearly always by way of the front door, with a search warrant."

"I suppose that's why you carry such things as jemmies, wire-cutters and rubber gloves in your car kit, and always . . ."

John's banter was cut short by a faint noise that seemed to come from the top of the house. It sounded like the muffled clanking of some small pieces of metal. C. B.'s torch flicked out: they stood in silence for a minute; then John whispered a trifle hoarsely:

"What was that? It . . . ghosts don't really ever rattle their chains, do they?"

"Not as far as I know; but it certainly sounded like it," C. B. whispered back. "Keep dead quiet now, so that next time we'll hear it clearly."

For three minutes, that seemed like thirty to John, they

stood absolutely still in the darkness; but the only sound they could catch was that of one another's breathing. At last, switching on his torch again, C. B. shone it aloft and round about. There was no sign of movement up on the landing or in the minstrels' gallery, and nothing to be seen other than the black oak beams outlined against the white walls and ceiling. Lowering the light, he said:

"False alarm, I think. Just one of those noises there is no accounting for that one often hears in old houses at night. Come on! Let's explore."

Crossing the hall, he opened the door on the right of the entrance. It gave on to a long low-ceilinged drawing-room. The place had a slightly musty smell, as though it had been shut up and no fire lit in it for a considerable time. The furniture in it was very ordinary: some of it had faded chintz covers, the rest was black, spindly-legged stuff. On the walls there were some quite awful pictures, of the "Monarch of the Glen" and "Souls Awakening" type, in gilt frames.

As they advanced into it John caught sight of a photograph of Christina on an occasional table, which must have been taken when she was about seventeen. Picking it up, he stared at it and said:

"How fantastic that anything so sweet should be even remotely connected with such ugly surroundings as these."

C. B. had always preferred small, fair, vivacious women, so he saw nothing particularly attractive in Christina; and, being a realist, it was on the tip of his tongue to reply, 'I've known better lookers who were reared in the slums of Paris and Vienna', but it occurred to him that that might be unkind; so he forbore to comment and continued to flash his torch this way and that, until he had decided that the room contained nothing worth closer examination—at all events for the time being.

Leaving the drawing-room, they crossed the hall to the room opposite. It proved to be the dining-room. It also had an air of long disuse and chill dampness owing to lack of regular heating. John followed C. B. in and walked straight over to the bulky Victorian sideboard. At one end of it stood a tarnished silver tantalus containing the usual three square cut-glass decanters. Taking the stopper from one, he smelt it and said: "Good. This is brandy. Shine your torch here a moment, C. B., and we'll have a quick one."

"I see you are becoming quite a professional yourself." C. B. smiled as he focused the beam.

John found some glasses in one of the sideboard cupboards, poured two stiff tots, then turned and grinned back. "Oh no; I'm only carrying out my rôle of Christina's fiancé. If I were really Mr. Beddows' prospective son-in-law, I'm sure he would expect me to play host to you in his absence."

"You've certainly taken to the rôle like a duck to water," C. B. twitted him. "I believe you have become jolly keen on that girl, although you haven't yet known her a week."

"We've seen a great deal of each other in a short time, and in quite exceptional circumstances," John replied in a non-committal voice. "That makes a big difference; so naturally I've a very personal interest in helping to protect her."

"Here's to our success in that, then."

They clinked glasses and drank. The brandy was not of very good quality, but it was nonetheless welcome at the moment. John's shoes were soaked right through from standing about in the mud and wet, while C. B. had had to leave his hat and coat in the Canon's house; so he had since had a steady wetting from the drizzling rain. Both were feeling the chill of the raw night; and, although their behaviour was now light-hearted, beneath the surface the nerves of neither of them had yet fully recovered from the shaking they had had in the crypt.

Warmed in body and fortified in mind by the fiery spirit, they put the glasses back and resumed their reconnaissance. While they were drinking, C. B. had already surveyed the dining-room, and it contained no piece of furniture in which it seemed likely that papers would be kept; so they went out into the hall and tried a door under the stairs. It led only to a stone-flagged passage, which was obviously the way to the kitchen quarters. Closing it quietly, C. B. shot its bolt, so that should Jutson be roused and, entering the house by a back door, seek to come through it, he would find his way blocked. They then

259

tip-toed across to the door opposite and, opening it, found themselves in a study, three walls of which were lined shoulder-high with books.

"Ah, this looks more promising," C. B. murmured, as the torch lit up a big roll-top desk. "You stay by the door, John, and keep your ears open, just in case the Jutsons are not asleep yet and we have disturbed them. If you hear anyone trying that door across the hall that leads to the kitchen quarters, slip in and warn me. We'll have time then to get back into the drawing-room and out through one of the front windows."

While he was speaking he walked to the study window and drew its curtains as a precaution against the Jutsons seeing a light in the room, for it looked out on to the backyard. Then, producing a bunch of queer-looking keys from his pocket, he set to work on the desk. In less than a minute he had its roll-top open.

With swift, practised fingers he went systematically through one pigeon-hole after another. When he had done, the owner of the desk would never have guessed that the papers it contained had been examined; but the search had revealed nothing of interest. The pigeon-holes and shallow drawers held only Henry Beddows' household accounts, note-paper, cheque-books, pencils, rubbers and so on. None of the bills or receipts suggested any activity which could be considered unorthodox.

C. B. was just about to reclose the desk-top when John stepped back through the door and swiftly swung it nearly shut.

"What is it?" C. B. asked below his breath.

"The clanking of that chain again," John whispered.

He was still holding the door a few inches open. C. B. stepped up to him and, their heads cocked slightly sideways, they listened with straining ears for some moments. As no further sound reached them, John mumbled rather shame-facedly:

"Sorry. I could have sworn I heard a chain being dragged across the floor somewhere at the top of the house; but I must have been mistaken. Nerves, I suppose."

"The dank, unlived-in atmosphere of this place is enough to give anyone the willies," C. B. said understandingly. "It was probably a fall of soot in one of the chimneys brought down by the rain."

Returning to the desk, he closed its top, and set about opening the drawers in its two pedestals, most of which were locked. The locked ones he found to contain a number of stamp albums and the impedimenta of a philatelist.

A glance showed him that the albums covered only the British Empire. Quickly he flicked through a couple of them and saw that they were a fairly valuable collection. Then he noticed a curious thing. The pages for some of the smaller Colonies had on them the remains of a number of stamp hinges but not a single stamp of any denomination. Turning to John he said:

"This is interesting. Beddows evidently started a general collection of the British Empire; then, unless I'm right off the mark, he began to specialize in Barbados, Cyprus and perhaps a few other places. Being a rich man, he could afford to buy rarities and his special collections soon grew too valuable for him to leave them with the rest; so he removed his pet Colonies into a separate album."

"Where does that get us?" asked John, a little mystified.

"Come, come, my dear Watson. Surely you realize that a keen philatelist would never keep the best part of his collection in his office, where he couldn't look at it in the evenings. The fact that it is not here suggests that it is in a safe somewhere in the house. If Christina's papa has a safe, it is there that he would also keep the sort of highly private papers in which we are interested."

"That sounds logical; but if there is a safe surely it would be a bit beyond you to get it open?"

"Probably, but not necessarily. If it is an old type, patience and my skeleton keys might do the trick. Anyhow it would be worth trying."

Returning the stamp albums to their drawers C. B. re-locked them. He had already noticed a door between two sets of bookshelves that stood against the further wall. Walking over, he opened it and looked through. The room beyond was another sitting-room. From some fashion magazines, a bowl of *pot-pourri* and a work basket it looked as if it might be Christina's sanctum on the rare occasions when she was at home. After a quick glance round he left it and they returned to the hall.

Next to the passage leading to the kitchen they found a breakfast-room, and beyond it another room that was half-pantry, half flower-room. Neither contained anything having the remotest resemblance to a safe; so, as they had now explored all the downstairs living-rooms without success, it seemed that if there was a safe in the house at all it must be up in Beddows' bedroom.

At the foot of the main staircase they paused, while C. B. shone his torch upward. No movement was to be seen and no sound reached them. Yet the very silence of the damp, chill house seemed to have something vaguely sinister about it; so that, instead of advancing boldly, both of them half-held their breath and trod gently as they went upstairs.

They were within two steps of the main landing, and could see across it to a dark rectangle between a pair of oak uprights, through which a narrower flight of stairs led to the top floor of the house, when the clanking came again.

This time it was distinct and unmistakable; a noise of chains being dragged across a wooden floor. The sound was so eerie, so uncanny, in that dark, deserted house that it caused their hearts to leap. The blood seemed to freeze in their veins, and momentarily they were inflicted with a semi-paralysis. Yet it was the very terror that caused their throats to close and their muscles to contract that saved C. B. from a broken neck.

He was in the act of planting his right foot on the landing. Instead of coming down firmly, it was arrested in mid-air by the same nervous shock that made his scalp prickle. For a second or so it hovered; then, by no act of will but by the residue of its own momentum, it sank gently on to the carpet.

The carpet gave as though it was a feather bed. There came a faint snap, then a swift slithering noise. A large piece of carpet suddenly flopped downwards from the topmost stair.

262

Its loose end and sides had been secured to the main carpet of the landing only by threads. It now hung straight down between the newel post of the banisters and the wall, leaving a four foot square gulf of blackness. The square of carpet at the stairhead had been cunningly suspended to conceal the fact that the flooring beneath it had been removed. Anyone stepping firmly upon it must have been flung down into the hall fifteen feet below.

C. B. gasped, staggered, and recovered his balance. Then, flashing his torch through the gaping hole that the vanished carpet had left in the nearest corner of the landing, he muttered:

"My God, that was a near one! It's a modern *oubliette*. The sort of death-trap that the French Kings used to have in their castles for troublesome nobles whom they invited to stay with intent to murder. But this one must have been made quite recently. Look at the torn edges of those boards, where some tool has been used to prise up the ones that have been removed."

John nodded. "Anyhow, this isn't the work of spooks. It is good solid evidence that friend Beddows keeps something up here, and is so anxious that no one should see it that he doesn't even stick at killing as a method of keeping out intruders."

As he finished speaking there came the rattling of the chains once more.

It was a horribly unnerving sound. In spite of what had just been said the blood drained from the faces of the two men as they looked quickly at one another.

"I expect it is some mechanical gadget made to scare people," John said a little dubiously.

"Perhaps." C. B. hesitated. "On the other hand, if Copely-Syle and Beddows are buddies it may be something very different. Still, if you're game to go on, I am."

The vitality of both was now at a very low ebb, and John would have given a lot for a sound excuse to abandon their investigations there and then; but he hated the idea of losing face with C. B.; so he said in a low voice:

"All right. But as we cross the landing I think you had better recite the Lord's Prayer, as you did in the crypt, and I'll join in."

Handing the torch to John, C. B. grasped the newel post firmly and swung himself across the gap, carefully testing the firmness of the floor beyond before letting go. John passed him back the torch and followed. Together, they began to pray aloud. Shining the light downward on to the floor and taking each step cautiously, in case there was another trap, C. B. led the way across the landing. In the archway he paused, put one foot on the lowest stair of the upper flight, tested that, then swiftly raised the beam. The thing it fell upon caused them to break off their prayer. The chain clanked loudly. Simultaneously they jumped back.

For a moment the light had swept across a crouching form and lit up two reddish eyes. A dark hunched thing, with eyeballs that glowed like live coals, was squatting half-way up the narrow flight of stairs.

In a choking voice John cried, "For God's sake let's get out of here!" And turned to run.

C. B.'s flesh was creeping and his tongue seemed to cleave to the roof of his mouth. Yet, as he swung round to follow, he managed to shout a warning:

"Careful! Look out for the hole!"

John was already half-way across the landing. He pulled up so abruptly that C. B. cannoned into him. The torch was knocked from C. B.'s hand, fell to the floor with a crash, and went out.

Total darkness descended upon them like a pall. John had been thrown off his balance. He staggered sideways a few steps. Their collision had robbed him of his sense of direction. He was no longer certain if the gaping chasm in the floorboards was in front of him or to his left. A few steps either way and he might become a whirling mass of arms and legs, hurtling down into the hall.

The chain was now rattling violently. Other sounds mingled with it. There was an irregular thumping, as if a soft, heavy body was flopping about on the upper stairs; and a quick champing noise, like the repeated snapping together of strong teeth.

John felt a cold sweat break out all over him. He was terrified of the Thing behind him, yet was held where he stood from fear of breaking his neck. Meanwhile C. B., cursing furiously, was on his hands and knees, frantically searching for the lost torch.

Within a matter of seconds his right hand knocked against it. Snatching it up, he pressed the switch. To his infinite relief it lit. The bulb had not, as he had feared, been broken. Still on his knees, he swung the beam towards the opening through which lay the upper stairs.

It was barely thirty seconds since he had dropped the torch. He expected to see that hideous Thing framed in the opening and about to spring upon them. There was nothing there—nothing whatever. Yet the rattling of the chain and the other noises continued with unabated violence.

As the torch flashed on, John swung half-right and grabbed the newel post at the head of the main stairs. Only his sense of loyalty to C. B. restrained him from jumping the hole and dashing down them; but hearing no following footsteps he halted, looked over his shoulder, and shouted:

"Come on! What the hell are you waiting for?"

C. B. was still kneeling in the middle of the landing with his torch focused on the archway from which came the din of clanking, banging and champing. Without taking his eyes from it, he called:

"Half a minute! Don't go, John! I'm going to have another look."

"You're crazy!" John shouted back, but he turned towards the landing again. With tightly clenched hands he watched C. B. rise and walk forward, once more reciting the Lord's Prayer. As he reached the opening he made the sign of the Cross in front of his face, then he shone the torch upwards.

Again it fell upon the hunched form and pair of burning eyes; but this time he kept it there. Round the eyes there was dark shaggy hair; below them a huge mouth, in which two rows of yellowish, gleaming teeth were gnashing. Chattering with fury, the creature began to leap up and down, its long limbs throwing grotesque shadows against the stairs behind it. C. B.'s voice came, no longer sharp from tension, but level and unhurried:

"The fact that it didn't come down and attack us made me think that this particular bogy must be chained up; and I was right. Its chain is attached to a post in the wall of the upper landing."

John moved up beside him. For a moment they both stood staring at the creature on the stairs. It was a big ape; not as large as a baboon, but quite big enough to maul a man and do him serious injury. The chain was attached to a thick leather belt round its waist.

"The presence of this pretty pet in addition to the *oubliette* makes one thing quite certain," said C. B. softly. "There is something up at the top of the house that friend Beddows is extraordinarily anxious that no one shall see."

"Yes. But how the devil are we to get up there?"

"As you know, I've got quite a way with animals; so given an hour or two I don't doubt that I could tame this chap sufficiently for him to let us pass. But we haven't got that time to spare; so we'll have to take stronger measures."

As C. B. spoke, he turned away towards the nearest of fo doors that were ranged round the landing. It opened on to bedroom. Beside the bed hung an old-fashioned bell pul. Getting up on a chair he detached the rope from the wire spring and handed it to John, with the remark:

"This is just the thing with which to secure our furry friend. By slipping one end of the rope through the pull ring a the other you'll have a lasso that will run much more smoothly than if you knotted a loop. I want you to throw it over his head when I give the word. Get it well down to his waist, so that it pinions his arms, and tie it as tight as you can. But watch out that he doesn't claw you with his feet."

Taking the eiderdown from the bed, C. B. led the way back to the stairs and propped his torch up on the lowest one so that its beam shone full upon the angry, snarling animal Holding the eiderdown in front of him by two of its corners, he went up a few steps until he was near enough to flick its lower end as a matador does his cape. The enraged ape sprang at him, but was brought up with a jerk by the chain. C. B. darted forward up two more stairs, threw the eiderdown over the brute and grasped it firmly round the body.

"Quick, John!" he called; and next moment, squeezing past him, John had the rope round the heaving bundle. The strength and fierceness of the ape made it a far from easy matter to truss him securely, but the rope was long enough to take a second turn round his thighs, and after that had been managed the rest was easy. They rolled him up in his own chain till they had him up on the top landing, and there slipped his feet through a half-hitch in it.

To secure the creature without injury to themselves had required all their attention as well as their strength, so it was not until the job was done that either of them noticed another surprise that was in store for them. The top landing was quite small and had only two doors leading from it. From under one of them came a ribbon of light.

They would not have noticed it, had it not been almost dark up there, owing to C. B. having left his torch at the bottom of the stairs. It was faint, but quite unmistakable, as its glow was enough to show the outline of the ape's water-trough and a tin tray on which were the remains of his last meal. Their attention was caught by the narrow strip of light almost at the same second, and they looked quickly at one another, wondering what this new mystery could portend.

Why should there be a light in a room at the top of the house in the middle of the night, unless the room was occupied? If it was, even if its occupant had dropped asleep with the light still on, he must have been roused by the noise made by his guardian ape and the struggle with it that had ensued. Why, knowing that intruders were in the house, and on their way up to his well-protected sanctum, had he shown no sign of life?

Stretching out a hand, C. B. grasped the door-handle firmly and turned it. But the door did not yield to his pressure: it was locked. Not a sound came from beyond it. Except for the faint scuffling of the trussed ape, the house was again utterly silent.

John slipped down the stairs, retrieved the torch and shone it on the door. The light revealed nothing to indicate the use to which the room was put. Apart from the black oak beams in the walls and ceiling, the woodwork of this upper landing was painted cream; but it looked as if a dozen years or more had passed since it had received its last coat. About the bare boards of the floor the ape had scattered some of its food; otherwise the landing was reasonably clean, but the doors showed the slight griminess and innumerable small scratches that only time can bring. It seemed reasonable to assume that they led either to box-rooms or servants' bedrooms.

For a second it flashed into C. B.'s mind that Christina might have been wrong about the Jutson couple being her father's only servants. Perhaps he had some other private retainer; or had taken someone else on since she had left The Grange, and they had their quarters up here. But that seemed unlikely when there was such a good choice of rooms more conveniently situated at the back of the premises. Again, why should they seek to protect themselves with an *oubliette* and a ferocious ape? If they had sought refuge up in these remote attics, behind such ugly barriers, of what were they afraid? If they were huddled in terrified silence behind the door, what form of menace could it possibly be that they must be expecting to see come through it at any moment now?

C. B. knocked on the door. There was no reply. Again he rapped, louder this time. Still not a sound came from the room. Putting his shoulder to the door, he threw his weight upon it. The upper part gave slightly but the lock held. Taking a few steps back he ran at the door, lifting his right foot so that it landed flat across the key-hole with the full force of the kick behind his heel. There was a sound of tearing wood and the door flew open.

The room was much larger than they had expected, and lofty enough for the crossbeams of its roof to be only vaguely discernible by a dim blue light that radiated from the centre of its floor. It was, in fact, a huge attic which must have

268

occupied the full breadth and nearly half the length of the house. In it there was no furniture, carpet or curtains, and its three dormer windows appeared to have been pasted over with thick brown paper. The low walls were naked; the whole place was as empty as a drum but for a single human figure and a number of strange objects in its immediate vicinity.

Of these, the thing that first sprang to the eye was a great five-pointed star. It was formed of long glass tubes, all connected together in the same manner as strip-lighting designed to show the name over a shop; and through their whole length glowed electric wires that gave off the cold blue light. Five tall white candles were placed in the points of the star; but these were unlit, so evidently there only against an emergency failure of the electric current. Behind them were placed five bright, brand-new horseshoes. In the valleys of the star were five little silver cups half full of water and some bunches of herbs. More faintly seen were two thick circles that had been drawn in chalk on the floor. The inner, which was about seven feet across, connected the valleys of the star; the outer, which was very much bigger, connected its points. Between the two were chalked a number of Cabalistic formulæ and the signs of the Zodiac.

Unmoving, in the very centre of the star sat a man. He was dressed in striped pyjamas and socks, but appeared to have on several layers of underclothes beneath the pyjamas, as their coat was stretched tightly across his chest. He was short, thick-set and looked about fifty. His hair was dark, his face broad, and his square, determined jowl so blue with bristles that it looked as if he had not shaved for a week. He was sitting cross-legged upon a thick pile of blankets, his back lightly touching a large tea-chest, and he was facing the door.

Neither of his uninvited visitors had the least doubt who he was. C. B. took a step into the room and said, "We must apologize for breaking in on you like this, Mr. Beddows; but our business is extremely urgent."

The man neither moved nor spoke.

"You are Henry Beddows, aren't you?" C. B. asked.

Still the man stared through them as though they were not there.

"Come on!" exclaimed John impatiently. "We've come all the way from the South of France to see you. They told us at your office that you had gone abroad; and when we called here the Jutsons lied to us. Now we've run you to earth in spite of them, for goodness' sake stop pretending to be dumb. Your daughter Ellen is in great danger."

The man's hands began to tremble and he averted his eyes, but he did not speak.

Together John and C. B. advanced into the room. The latter said, "What my friend has told you is quite true, sir. At the moment your daughter is in prison. We are doing our best——"

"In prison!" exclaimed the man, coming swiftly to his feet. Then his expression changed from one of surprise to disbelief. Suddenly he stretched out his hand, made the sign of the Cross and cried loudly:

"Avaunt thee, Satan!"

John stared at him and muttered, "Good Lord! I believe he's mad."

C. B. shook his head. "No, he's not mad. And he is Beddows all right. His attitude explains the mystery of all we've found in this house. Somebody is after him and he is scared stiff. That is why he has gone into hiding. The *oubliette* and the ape were to prevent his enemy paying him a visit in person; but there is something which terrifies him much more than that. He is afraid that some frightful monster from one of the lower astral planes may be sent to get his spirit. That's why he has made this pentacle. He has locked himself up in what amounts to an astral fortress, and he doesn't believe that we are real people at all. He thinks we are evil entities sent to lure him from safety to destruction."

Suddenly Beddows gave a defiant laugh, then cried, "And so you are! Your cunning talk does not deceive me! Get back to him who sent you!"

"Don't talk like a fool!" John snapped at him. "Surely you can tell real people when you see them? We're real and we're friends. You're the only person who can give us the truth about this whole awful business; and we've got to have it to help us in our fight to save Christina . . . to save Ellen."

"Liar! And spawn of the Father of Lies! Get back whence you came."

"We are real flesh and blood, I tell you!" cried John angrily. "Since you won't believe me I'll prove it to you."

As he moved forward to step into the pentacle, C. B. gave a warning shout. "Stop! The shock may kill him."

But his cry came too late. In a stride John had crossed the line of blue light, and was stretching out a hand to touch Beddows.

The wretched man's face became transfixed with terror. He threw up his arms, gave a piercing scream, and fell at John's feet as though he had been pole-axed.

CHAPTER XVIII

WITHIN THE PENTACLE

BEDDOWS had fallen flat on his face. His outflung right hand had knocked over one of the small vases that stood in each of the valleys of the pentacle; but his magical fortress had suffered no other damage and the big five-pointed star still glowed without a flicker.

C. B.'s mind was racing with visions of an inquest and all sorts of awkward questions which might have to be answered; yet within a moment he had jumped forward to give John a hand. Together they turned over the limp body and got it up into a sitting position.

In the full light of C. B.'s torch the unconscious man's face looked an ugly sight. His head now lolled back over the edge of the tea-chest, his mouth hung slackly open—a dark cavern in his heavy blue jowl—and the whites of his turned-up eyes could be seen between half-closed lids. John got his victim's pyjama jacket open and tore frantically at the buttons of the three vests beneath it. As he exposed a V of hairy chest, C. B. thrust his free hand into the opening, held it there a moment, then gave a sigh of relief.

"His heart is quite strong, and it doesn't look as if he had a stroke. I think he fainted from sheer terror. He'll probably be quite all right when he comes round."

"Thank God!" John murmured. "From what you said I thought I'd killed him."

Ignoring the remark, C. B. swivelled round, set the fallen vase upright, and picking up another poured from it about half its contents into the one that had been knocked over.

"What's the point of doing that?" John asked.

"To repair the breach in this astral defence work, of course."

"Do you really think that herbs and horseshoes and candles can protect people from evil spirits?"

"Certainly I do; if they are arranged in accordance with the proper formula. There are natural laws which govern everything. These, although scorned and ignored by modern science, are just as potent in achieving their object as a radar screen, or the use of our latest inventions for dispersing fog."

John glanced round a little nervously. "After the terror I felt in that crypt to-night, I'm no longer sceptical about there being all sorts of horrors lurking in such a place as this; so it's a comfort to know you think this bag of tricks will provide an effective protection for us."

"I'm not quite so worried about ourselves, as about him," C. B. said, and he began to slap Beddows' face in an attempt to bring him round. As his slaps had no effect, he lowered the body into a more comfortable position and went on, "I don't think we've much to fear at the moment, but the danger to him will be acute as long as he remains unconscious."

"Why should that be, since he is in the pentacle with us?"

"Because his spirit is temporarily out of his body. That will give his enemies the best possible chance to capture it. If they were quick off the mark when we broke the magic circle by entering it, and the vase was upset, they may have done so already. If not, I think there is a good chance of the restored pentacle protecting him. But I don't know enough about these things to be certain. All I do know is that in his present state he is ten times more vulnerable than we are; so it's obvious that if there are any evil forces in this room it is him they will attempt to destroy."

"What . . . what will happen if they succeed?"

"When he comes round it won't be him. The personality inside him will no longer be Henry Beddows. His body will have been taken possession of by a demon."

"Just as you say occurs with Christina every night?"

"No. Far worse than that. She still makes sense. He will be permanently demented. Off his chump for good."

"You are really convinced that evil spirits can drive people mad?"

"I haven't the least doubt about it. Ignore the Bible if you will, and scoff at all the records of such happenings in mediaeval times as based upon ignorant superstition. That gets you nowhere, unless you can account in some other way for certain types of loss of mental control that have afflicted great numbers of people from the earliest times, and still continue to do so. Most cases of lunacy are obviously due to physical causes; but any doctor will tell you that he has met with forms of madness which cannot be explained by any theory so far accepted by science; and most of the honest ones will admit that the symptoms in such cases tally with those described by the priests of all nations who have studied these things, as indications that the victim is 'possessed of a devil'."

John nodded. "I suppose in these days we are far too apt to discount the Bible; and, if one believes at all, one can hardly refuse to accept the account of Christ and the Gadarene swine. Still, all that apart, it seems to me that we have good grounds for regarding this chap as a bit round the bend already. No one who wasn't would choose for a costume in which to sit up all night three suits of underclothes and pyjamas, instead of day things and an overcoat—or anyway a good warm dressing-gown."

"On the contrary, the clothes he is wearing show that he understands what he is up against." C. B. flashed his torch round the floor. "Look how thoroughly the whole place has been swept and garnished before the pentacle was laid out. That shows he was aware that elementals are helped to materialize by dirt and filth. Above all they are attracted by the impurities of the human body. When he decided to fortify himself in here he evidently took every possible precaution against bringing in with him anything that might aid the enemy. Soiled clothes of any kind, or cushions and rugs that had been in use, would do so; that is why he made do with such underclothes and bedding as he could take straight from the linen-cupboard."

"From the bristles on his chin it looks as if he has been sitting here for several days; but I suppose he must have left the pentacle now and again in the daytime."

"Why? Were you thinking about his natural functions?"

"Yes. If you are right about human impurities, his own would form a dangerous focus within the pentacle, and he could not possibly have controlled himself long enough to grow that beard."

"An Indian fakir could; so could he if he is an expert practitioner of Yoga—particularly if he has eaten very little. Each time he left the pentacle he would have to remake it to restore its maximum potency, and seeing the state he was in it is most unlikely he would leave its protection even for a few minutes, unless it was absolutely unavoidable."

"He must practise Yoga then, otherwise . . ."

"No. He got round that problem another way." C. B. was shining his torch down into the tea-chest. More than half of it was occupied by a large metal container, and he added, "Look, I'll bet that thing is a form of Elsan specially fitted with an air-tight lid."

The only other things in the chest were two tins of dry biscuits and a dozen bottles, about half of which were still full of water. "I expect you're right," John conceded. "Anyhow, you are about his not eating much."

"He wouldn't dare to bring meat, game or fish into the pentacle, and after a day or two even fruit might start to go bad."

"He must have been mighty scared to shut himself up here and go on a prison diet."

"Yes, scared stiff," C. B. agreed, switching out his torch to economize its battery. "But what luck to have found him here. If only he is all right when he comes round, and we can get him to talk freely while he is so scared, we shall have solved the riddle of where Christina stands in all this."

"We know that already. That devilish Canon is after her to feed her blood to his filthy homunculi."

"I mean we'll get to the bottom of the whole business: we'll find out how she came under Copely-Syle's influence in the first place, and what the tie-up is between him and her father. I thought it might be blackmail, but there's more to it than that. Finding him in this pentacle shows that he, too, is an occultist of no mean order. I want to know if he is another Black who has quarrelled with the Canon, or a White who has found the odds too much for him; and if either or both of them are associated with other practitioners of the Black Art. We know that the day after to-morrow is the peak point of Christina's danger; and we have every hope now of keeping her out of their clutches till it is past; but we've got to think of her future too. Having been mixed up with these people, she is highly liable to get drawn in as a witch unless we can take steps to prevent it. Only by getting at the full truth can we hope to free her from their evil influence once and for all."

John nodded. "Of course, we've got to do that somehow, or the way in which they are able to dominate her mind at night will continue to make her vulnerable at any time. But what is likely to happen if, when Beddows comes to, we find that he is possessed?"

"Then we are in for something extremely unpleasant," C. B. replied grimly. "He will probably act like a raving maniac and attempt to kill us."

"In that case we'll have no alternative but to knock him on the head."

"If he becomes violent, yes. But he may resort to cunning, and by some plausible story attempt to lead us into danger."

"What is the drill, then?"

"We'll give him his head for a bit. Fortunately the sort of elementals that get possession of humans are said to be of very low intelligence. They usually give themselves away; so we should be able to tell whether it is really Beddows who is talking to us or some horror that has got into him and is making use of his tongue. Anyhow, if we have any doubts there is one acid test we can apply."

"What is that?"

"The little vases have Holy water in them. They would be pointless otherwise. I shall take a few drops from one and sprinkle it on him. Demons can't stand Holy water. If he is possessed, he will scream as though he had been scalded."

Beddows still showed no sign of coming round, so they settled themselves beside him to await events. The glow from the blue ribbon that formed the star was sufficient to make large print readable inside the pentacle, or a few feet from it; but farther off the gloom thickened into almost complete darkness. Even now that they had been there for some minutes without the torch, so that their eyes had had a chance to become accustomed to the faint blue light, they could barely make out by it the dark beams and uprights in the white walls, while above them the great rafters were only vaguely discernible as strips of denser blackness in the black vault overhead

As soon as they stopped talking they again became conscious of the uncanny silence that gripped the old house. Out on the landing the ape had ceased its scuffling attempts to free itself. C. B. was troubled for a moment by the thought that they might have suffocated the poor brute; but, tightly as its arms were pinioned, he felt sure that enough air would get up between the folds of the eiderdown for it to breathe. The odds were that its struggles had tired it out and it had dropped into a doze.

John tried to keep his thoughts on Christina, but they would slide away from her to the fact that the motionless body at his side was that of her father, and to the fantastic situation in which they had found him. It seemed unbelievable that a twentieth-century industrialist should be mixed up with witchcraft and have shut himself up for days on biscuits and water in a pentacle as the only safe refuge from evil spirits. Yet that he had done so was beyond dispute.

From that it was only a step to imagining the sort of things he had feared to see while sitting there day after day and night after night. John closed his eyes, hoping to shut out from his mind the winged and crawling monstrosities that his memory of Breughel's paintings conjured up so vividly. The darkness of closed eyelids proved less conducive to such gruesome imagery than the pale light that hardly reached the walls. Nevertheless, he found that he could not keep his eyes closed for more than a few moments at a time. The urge to open them, to make quite certain that nothing was stirring in the shadows, proved irresistible. Each time he did so his glance wavered swiftly back and forth, probing anew the darkest

277

corners of the room, seeking reassurance that no unclean denizen from the grim world of Eternal Night was forming in any of them.

There came a moment when he could have sworn that at the far end of the room from the door, where it was darkest, a humped thing like a big turtle had taken shape, and that the curve of its back was slowly undulating as it pulsed with malevolent life. Loath as he was to risk making a fool of himself by giving a false alarm, he had just made up his mind to attract C. B.'s attention to it when Beddows gave a loud groan.

It was an eerie sound in the tense stillness that held the lofty room. John, staring into the darkness, had his back turned. His whole body jerked at the unexpectedness of it, and he swivelled round as swiftly as if a glass of cold water had been poured down his spine. C. B. switched on his torch. As he brought it round to level it on Beddows' face, the beam cut the darkness at the far end of the room with a swathe of light. Swift as its passage was, John was in time to glance over his shoulder while it swept the floor. With a gasp of relief he realized that either he must have imagined the humped thing, or the powerful light had caused it instantly to disintegrate.

As the beam came round on Beddows they saw that his eyes were open and that he was licking his dry lips. He groaned again, made a feeble gesture as though trying to push the light away from his face, then struggled into a sitting position. John helped him up and C. B. lowered the torch a little. Neither showed the acute anxiety they felt, but the thought uppermost in the minds of both was how much hung on the next few moments. If Beddows was himself and sane, their journey to England should prove a hundred times worth while, as he must know the truth about the strange relationship between his daughter and the Canon; and, with his help, the tie could be broken for good. On the other hand, he might be possessed and, instead of helpful, highly dangerous.

His opening move on regaining consciousness was by no means reassuring. Thrusting them aside, he got to his knees and cried in a harsh voice:

278

"Who are you? How the hell d'you get here?"

"My name is Verney," replied C. B. quietly, "and that of my friend is John Fountain. We mean you no harm: on the contrary——"

"Why should I believe that?" shouted Beddows.

"Anyhow, you'll admit now that we are real?" John cut in.

Beddows turned, glared at him and muttered, "I wonder! I wonder!"

"Oh come!" John put a hand on his shoulder; but he shook it off and staggered to his feet with the evident intention of jumping out of the pentacle.

C. B. caught him round the knees in a rugby tackle. Next moment he was sprawling full length on the blankets. As he attempted to rise John joined in, and between them they held him down flat on his back.

He was a powerful man and he struggled violently, but in spite of that they managed to keep him down. The very fact that they were able to do so inclined C. B. to suppose that he was not possessed, but simply a very frightened and angry man. So when Beddows stopped cursing from lack of breath, he said:

"Now listen! You have got yourself into an unholy mess, and we are here to help you out of it."

"I don't believe it!" Beddows panted. "I don't believe it! How did you get up here? Jutson or his wife must have let you in, and told you about the trap and the ape. In spite of all their promises they've sold me out to Copely-Syle."

"Oh no they haven't. We broke in."

Beddows gave a sudden snarl. "If that's true I'll have the law on you."

"No you won't. Not unless you are prepared to have a full description of how we found you to-night come out in court. How would your shareholders react to that, eh? Can't you imagine the headlines in the papers: 'Chairman of Directors found sealed in magic pentacle. Satanic rituals practised in Essex manor house,' and so on?"

"Damn you!" Beddows gave a mighty heave, and nearly succeeded in breaking away.

279

"Steady!" C. B. shifted his grip and pressed down with his full weight on him again. "Don't be a fool, Beddows. Just now you tried to hurl yourself out of the pentacle. That wouldn't be a very clever thing to do, would it? As long as you are inside it you are safe, but once you leave it all sorts of unpleasant things might succeed in getting hold of you."

Beddows relaxed. For a moment he lay silent, then he let out something between a sigh and a moan and said, "What the hell do you want of me?"

Sensing that his resistance was lessening, C. B. said firmly, "We want the truth about your association with Canon Copely-Syle."

"That has nothing to do with you."

"Yes it has. Fountain and I came all the way from the South of France specially to talk to you about it."

"It's none of your business."

"It *is* our business. It is the business of every decent person to lend a hand in scotching the sort of devilry that Copely-Syle is engaged in. And you've got to help us."

"No! No! I won't talk about him! I daren't! The danger I am in from him is bad enough as it is."

C. B. loosened his hold a little and took a more persuasive tone. "Come! Pull yourself together, man. You're not the only one in danger. How about your daughter Ellen?"

"Ellen!" Beddows repeated miserably. "I . . . I thought I had managed to keep her out of this."

"Far from it. She has been in very grave danger indeed, and is a long way from being safely out of the wood yet."

Now that Beddows was no longer actually being held down, he struggled up into a sitting position and demanded, "What has been happening to her?"

"The Canon is after her blood. I mean that literally, and I'll bet any money you know what he would do with her blood if he got it. That's why we came back to England to hunt you out. You've got to tell us everything you know about the Canon."

"No! I'm not talking!"

"Damn it, man!" John cried. "Think of your daughter!

How can you possibly refuse to help us free her from the influence that devil exerts over her?"

"No!" Beddows repeated doggedly. "I did my best for her. I can't do more. She must take her chance now. I'm not talking. It's too dangerous."

"Yes, you are going to talk," said C. B. quietly. "Do you know what I mean to do if you persist in your refusal?"

"What?" faltered Beddows uneasily. "What will you do?"

"I shall smash this pentacle to pieces; then Fountain and I will leave you here alone."

"No! No! You can't do that."

"I can and I will. Either you are going to answer any questions or I'll make hay of your astral defences."

For a moment Beddows sat there panting heavily, then he muttered, "All right. What do you want to know?"

"How long have you known Copely-Syle?"

"A bit over twenty years."

"Where did you first meet him?"

"Here."

C. B. raised his eyebrows. "I thought you bought this place only in 1949?"

"That's so." Beddows now seemed to have resigned himself to talking freely, and went on in a normal voice, "I'd been wanting to for a long time, but the stiff-necked old bitch who owned the place wouldn't sell. Even after the war had reduced her to scraping in order to stay on here she still refused my offers; so I had to wait till she died. Her name was Durnsford—the Honourable Mrs. Bertram Durnsford—and I was her chauffeur from 1927 to 1931."

"I see; so it was while you were employed here as chauffeur that you first met the Canon?"

"That's right. When I said I had known him for twenty years, it's really nearer twenty-five; but to begin with it was only as a servant knows his mistress's visitors. He was a great chum of the old girl's, and from the time I took the place he was often here."

"Was she a witch?"

"Yes. There's a lot of it still goes on in Essex. Parts of it are so isolated that modern influences are slower to penetrate than in most other places. She had been mistress here so long that she always thought of herself as one of the gentry; but she wasn't. She started life as daughter of the village witch and, so they say, put a spell on the young squire here to marry her. It's said, too, that as soon as she got tired of him she used a wax image to cause him to sicken and die. After that she acted the high-mightiness and ruled the village with a rod of iron. She was over eighty when she died and more or less bedridden for the last few years; so she had lost much of her occult power, and with it most of her money; but she still had enough power by such means to keep me from getting her out after she had refused my offers to buy."

"Why were you so keen to own The Grange?" John asked.

"Sentiment," came the unexpected reply. "I came here as a young man of twenty-three. I—er—formed an attachment soon after I took the job, and one of the few really decent things I have got out of life are the memories of it. I wanted the place on that account. I suppose, too, the idea of owning the big house in which I had once been a servant appealed to my vanity. But it was wanting to live where *she* had lived that made me determined to have it."

"Let's get back to Copely-Syle," said C. B. "How did it happen that you got to know him more intimately than as one of your mistress's visitors?"

Beddows gave a heavy sigh, then shrugged resignedly. "Well, since you insist, I suppose I had better give you the whole story from the beginning."

CHAPTER XIX

THE SAGA OF A SATANIST

AFTER a moment Beddows started to talk in a flat, low monotone, more as if he were talking to himself than to them. He began:

"It can't be news to you that I'm a self-made man. I've never sought to conceal it. I was born less than a dozen miles from here as the son of a farm labourer, and I started life myself as a farmer's boy. But for all that I was born ambitious. I soon made up my mind that two-ten a week and work in all weathers wasn't good enough. Knowing about machines seemed to me the one way out; so instead of spending my pennies on the pictures and trashy novelettes, I bought the weeklies from which I could learn about the insides of motors. That way I picked up enough to get a job in a garage.

"Later they let me drive one of their hire-cars; then one of their customers, who was a doctor, took me on as his private chauffeur. I stayed with Doc for eighteen months, and while I was with him I attended evening classes at the Colchester Technical College. You see, by then I'd made up my mind to become an engineer. I got a lot out of those classes, but nothing like as much as I should have if I'd had more time for home study; and by the nature of things, a doctor's chauffeur is far harder worked than most. That's why I left him and came here. Mrs. Durnsford was already over sixty and didn't go out very much. In fact, sometimes during the winter months a whole week would pass without her using the car at all; so the job offered just the easy hours I wanted to go in for correspondence courses and study for exams.

"For a year or so I did quite well in that way, then my thoughts were taken right off engineering. I don't propose to go into the details of what happened, but for a long time I never even opened one of my books. As I told you just now, I formed an attachment for a certain person, and afterwards . . . well, afterwards I simply hadn't the heart to start work again.

"It was while I was still in that state that I got involved with Hettie Weston. She was the parlourmaid here. Pretty young thing, and the flighty type. She asked for trouble and she got it. If it hadn't been me, it would have been the next feller who came along. I didn't give a cuss for her, but she set her cap at me, and if ever a chap needed a warm-blooded young woman to take him out of himself, I did. I bought it all right, and the next thing we knew was that the silly young bitch had let herself get in the family way.

"Well, plenty of them do that in these country parts long before there's been any talk of marriage. If the feller is willing they make a go of it and put up the banns. If he's not, there are usually a few tears, but no harm done. The girl picks on another likely lad to go hedging and ditching with on her evenings off, and lands him with the kid. Second or third time lucky, and she usually gets some mug to the altar. That's what would have happened in Hettie's case if it hadn't been for the old woman.

"Hettie spilt the beans to the mistress and I was put on the mat. I suppose I could have told her to go take a running kick at herself. If I had, the worst that could have happened was that I'd have lost my job and had a maintenance order made against me for seven and six a week. But I didn't. I was still in a state of not giving a damn what happened to me, and believing that I had no future worth making a struggle for. You must add to that several other factors, one of which I was certainly not aware of at the time.

"To start with, there was the hereditary angle. Youngsters of my class had allowed themselves to be dictated to for countless generations by old women in Mrs. Durnsford's position, especially when it seemed that moral right was on their side. Next, as a person she was pretty formidable. When those beady black eyes of hers bored into you, it wasn't easy to say 'No'. Lastly, although I didn't realize it then, she knew all

284

about me. She knew both how ambitious I had been, and what it was that had caused my ambitions temporarily to take a line that had nothing to do with engineering. It wasn't any high-falutin' motive of wanting to see the right thing done by Hettie that made her row in as she did. It was the malice that was in her. From what she knew had gone before, she got a special kick out of getting me married to a parlourmaid and saddled with the sort of liabilities that make it near impossible for a young working man to rise above his station.

"Anyhow, she bullied me into making an honest woman of Hettie and we settled down in the flat above the stables, where the Jutsons are now. It took a bit of time for me to realize what a muck I had made of my life; but in a young man ambition dies hard, and in me it started to stir again after the new experience of being married began to wear off. I somehow couldn't find the energy to take up my correspondence courses again, but I was subconsciously seeking a way out. Then, three nights before Ellen was born, it seemed as if it had been thrust right at me.

"I'd been out doing a bit of poaching, and returned late. The curtains of one of the drawing-room windows were not quite drawn, and through the chink I caught sight of a flicker that might have meant the place was on fire. I took a peep in, and what d'you think I saw? The flicker I'd seen was fire all right, as the room was lit only by a pile of logs blazing on the hearth. But all the furniture had been pushed back to the sides of the room, a lot of circles and figures had been drawn on the parquet, and in the middle of them stood my mistress and the Canon. Both of them were stark naked.

"He must have been getting on for forty then, so he was already well past his youth and had a little pot. I found him comic rather than repulsive, but there was nothing the least funny about her. She was twenty years older and the scraggy kind. Her withered shanks and flabby, hanging breasts made her a horrible caricature of what a woman should be. You can imagine how weird they looked against the firelight, and how I stared. But after a minute it was not at them I was looking; it was at the thing that stood between them. I can only describe it as a sort of blacksmith's anvil, and belly up on it they had tied a live cat.

"The cat didn't remain alive for long though. As I watched, the Canon produced a knife and slit its throat. Old Mother Durnsford caught the blood in the sort of chalice you see on the altar of a church. Of course, I know now that it must have been stolen from one; but at the time all this made no more sense than if I'd found myself at the Mad Hatter's tea-party. Still, this was clearly no tea-party, as the next thing they did was to each drink some of the cat's blood.

"The sight turned my stomach, so for a bit I missed seeing what they got up to after that. When I looked again they both had some clothes on. She was rubbing the chalk-marks off the floor and he was pushing the furniture back into place. Knowing her reputation as a witch, I suppose I ought to have put two and two together, but somehow I didn't. It was catching them naked that was uppermost in my mind. I thought then that he was a proper clergyman, and that the business with the cat was some sort of sexual perversion, or that drinking cat's blood might be a way of making old people feel young again.

"Anyhow, as far as I was concerned one thing stuck out a mile. Here was my opportunity to break out of the dead end in which I had landed myself. Setting up house with Hettie had cost me the hundred or so I had put by. Since we had been married I'd had little chance to start saving again, and I knew that once the baby arrived I'd have even less. By then I was twenty-seven. Ten years had slipped by without my getting very far—ten of the best years of my life—and I didn't want to remain a chauffeur all my natural. Here was my chance to make a brand-new start.

"We may as well call a spade a spade. My mind instantly turned to blackmail. I reckoned that the Canon and the old woman were good for five hundred smackers between them, and that they'd pay that to keep my mouth shut. For a pound a week I could park Hettie and the baby back on her parents. Then I'd go to London. Four hundred, eked out by taking night jobs in garages now and then, would see me through two years as a full-time student at a technical college. Before I was thirty I'd emerge as a qualified engineer, capable of earning good money. It didn't take me long to work that out, or how to set about it.

"They had to dispose of the body of the cat. I reckoned they wouldn't risk the stench that would fill the house if they burnt it on the drawing-room fire; so all the odds were that the Canon would take it out to the furnace. I nipped round there and hid behind the boiler. Sure enough, a few minutes later in he comes, opens the furnace door, rakes up the coke a bit and pops in the dead pussy. The moment he had gone I fished the animal out. Its fur was a little singed, which showed that an attempt had been made to burn it, and its throat was slit from ear to ear; so it provided the evidence I needed to turn the heat on him.

"Next morning I put it in an oyster-barrel filled with brine, to preserve it, and hid the barrel in the loft. Then in the evening I cycled over to The Priory to have a little talk with the Canon. But I was told that he had gone to London and was not expected back for about a week. Two days later Hettie had her baby. As it happened I didn't have to call on the Canon after all, as the day he got back he came to see the old woman. Having seen him go into the house, I lay in wait for him in the garden until he came out. As he turned a corner of the shrubbery we came face to face. Nice as pie, he congratulates me on becoming a father and asks me what I would like for the child as a christening present.

"I say, 'Five hundred pounds in pound notes to be delivered before the end of the week at a place and time chosen by me.'

"At that he gave a rather twisted grin, thinking it just a cheeky sort of joke. But when I told him what I knew, and how I meant to make the neighbourhood too hot to hold him unless he paid up, his grin became even more twisted.

"Of course he tried bluster, and said that no one would believe me. Even when I told him I had got the body of the cat, he still maintained that proved nothing, as anyone might have killed and partially burnt it. But I was ready for that one. I told him that I had taken the furnace-rake to a friend of mine

287

who was a sergeant in the Colchester police, and asked him, just as a matter of interest, to see if he could get any finger-prints from it. The prints were there all right and we had photographed them. So if I had to tell my story about the goings on at The Grange and he sued me for defamation of character, he would have to explain how his finger-prints had got on the furnace-rake in somebody else's back premises on the night in question.

"I was lying about having a friend in the police; but he couldn't know that, and it sank him. He agreed to find the money in exchange for the body of the cat, and he asked me to come to his house that night to arrange when and where the exchange was to be made. I suspected a trap, but he pointed out that as long as I had the cat and the furnace-rake, I had the whip hand of him; so I agreed to go.

"That night he received me in his study, and after giving me a drink, asked me what I meant to do with the money when I had it. I saw no reason to conceal my plans; so I told him. When he had heard me out, he said, 'You don't mind being separated from your wife and child, then?' and I replied, 'Why should I? Hettie was forced on me against my will, and the child means nothing to me.'

"He asked me, then, into what church I intended having the child baptized. The question seemed natural enough coming from a parson, as at that time I took him to be. I had been brought up C. of E. myself, but Hettie was Chapel; and in spite of her flightiness as a single girl she thought a great deal of standing well with her own Chapel folk; so we'd been married Chapel and I took it for granted she'd want her brat christened there. I told the Canon how matters stood and he went on to talk about religion for a bit. Then he said:

"'You know, Mr. Beddows, the little scene that you chanced to witness last week had nothing to do with sex. It was a religious ritual—a sacrifice to a God far older than Christ, and one who was universally worshipped when the world was a much happier place than it is to-day. He still exists, of course, since Gods cannot die; and he is still worshipped in secret by a few of us who understand his mysteries.'

"At that, the local gossip about old Mother Durnsford being the daughter of a witch, and a witch herself, came back to me. It all fitted in, so I said, 'I suppose you are talking about the Devil?'

"He nodded; and as I've a first-class memory for statements made to me, I can still recall pretty well word for word his reply, which was, 'That is a name that was bestowed upon him in fear and opprobrium by the early ascetics, when they were still striving to win the nations over to the worship of the Jewish tyrant God, Jehovah; but he is more fittingly called the Lord of this World. In any case, while the God of the Christians offers nothing to His followers but the meagre possibilities of an austere heaven in a life to come, the God whom I serve rewards those who honour him with wealth and happiness here and now. There may or may not be a hereafter; but everything in this life is his to give. Even the Christian Church admits that; and it is only superstitious fear that prevents people from returning to the old faith. You should give it a trial, Mr. Beddows, for at little cost to yourself you could make an offering to my Master which would ensure his behaving most· generously towards you.'

"Naturally I didn't get what he was driving at, *then*; neither could I make up my mind if he was really in earnest about this old religion. His saying that the cat had been a sacrifice certainly had the ring of truth, and he didn't sound as if he was goofy; but all that about getting riches in this life was a bit too much to swallow. More to see what replies he would make than anything else, I began to question him about it. His answers seemed logical enough, but even so I couldn't bring myself to believe him. Then he asked me if I would like him to reveal my future.

"Well, everyone likes having their fortune told, and I saw no harm in that. When I'd agreed, he took me through to the old part of The Priory and down into the crypt. It had evidently been used as a chapel at some time, but he had turned it into a sort of laboratory. There, he made me sit in front of a mirror. It wasn't made of glass, but of some highly polished metal, and it was pitted round the edges as though it was very old. He gave me a big brass bowl to hold in my lap and put some cones of incense in it. When he had lit them he said to me as follows:

" 'Within certain limits all men have free will; therefore their futures are not irrevocably fixed, but depend upon the decisions they take at certain major crossroads in their lives. I am about to give you an idea what your future will be, should you decide to rely upon my guidance and become the servant of Prince Lucifer. Keep your eyes fixed on the mirror and through the smoke you will see pictures form upon it.' Then he began to chant in a sing-song voice behind me, and I seemed to become a little drowsy.

"You will remember what it says in the Bible about Satan taking our . . . our . . . taking J. C. up on to the mountain and showing Him the kingdoms of the Earth. Well, me being just a chauffeur saddled with an unwanted wife and kid, it wasn't far off that. There were quite a number of pictures and afterwards they became a bit confused in my mind. The general impression was of myself, a little older, but not much, dressed in expensive clothes, wining and dining with other rich men, and having necking parties with lovely women in the luxury suites of big hotels. But a few of the scenes I saw remained clear cut. There was one of me walking through a great machine-shop where hundreds of people were working, and from the respectful way they all looked up at me as I passed it was clear that I was the boss of the whole outfit. Another confirmed that: it was the outside of my plant near Colchester pretty much as it stands to-day; and blazoned across its front in letters six feet high were the words 'BEDDOWS AGRICULTURAL TRACTORS'. The one that really got me, though, was myself in a check suit, standing in front of a long, low grey car. That car had something that no car in the time of which I am talking had got. Its rake was completely different. It was quite unlike anything that had so far been made and obviously an advance in design. It was something slap out of the future, and I knew that whatever else Copely-Syle might have faked up to gull me he couldn't have faked up that.

"When the show was over I told him at once that he had

made a convert, and asked what I must do to become the me in the pictures I had seen. He replied, 'There is nothing very difficult about it, if you are prepared to forswear the gloomy Christian God and all His works. Prepare yourself for that by reciting the Lord's Prayer backwards every night from now on, and return here at the same hour a week from to-day.'

"It wasn't until he was showing me out of the front door, a few minutes later, that I remembered the reason I had come to see him; and with a sudden feeling that somehow he had made a monkey out of me, I said pretty sharply, 'We haven't settled anything about that five hundred pounds.'

" 'No,' he said, 'and if you've any sense we shan't need to. When you come here next week you'd better bring that dead cat with you as a first offering. If you don't I will buy it off you later, as we arranged this morning. But don't imagine that the money will do you any good. By taking it you will decree a very different future for yourself from the one I showed you. The choice is yours.'

"During the week that followed I was torn first one way, then the other. After all, the five hundred smackers was as good as a bird in the hand, and I hated the idea of giving it up; yet I couldn't get the image of that car of the future out of my mind, and as a sort of token payment towards it in advance I wrestled for half an hour each night with the tricky business of getting through the Lord's Prayer said backwards. When the week ended I still hadn't made any definite decision; but, all the same, when I called again at The Priory I took the dead cat with me.

"That night Copely-Syle took me straight to the crypt, and the first thing he did was to shove the cat into the furnace there. Then he said to me, 'Now I propose to call upon Prince Lucifer in order that you may make your bargain with him.'

" 'What bargain?' I asked, rather taken aback.

" 'Why, the usual one, of course,' he replied a little sharply. 'As Lord of this World he will give you every reasonable success, pleasure and gratification in it that you may desire; but for all that he naturally asks something in return. You must sign a pact making yourself over to him body and soul.'

"I didn't much like the idea of doing that, and I said so.

"He laughed then, and gave me a pat on the back. 'Don't worry. You must sign it, and in your own blood; but you need never honour it. In your case it will merely be similar to a Life Insurance Policy lodged at a bank as security. You are lucky in having just had a little daughter. All you have to do is to have her baptized into the old faith, and undertake that should she reach the age of twenty-one you will produce her here in this crypt on her twenty-first birthday. In that way you may redeem your bond and it will be handed back to you.'"

John gave a low exclamation of horror at this frightful revelation, but C. B.—who had guessed what was coming from what had gone before—grabbed his arm and squeezed it sharply, to check him from bursting into angry words that might have put an abrupt end to Beddows' story; while Beddows, now apparently almost self-hypnotized by the recital of his confession, ignored the interruption, and went straight on:

"Although I didn't give a damn for the brat, it did not seem right somehow; but what was I to do? By letting him burn the cat I had burnt my own boats. I no longer had anything on him. It had become a choice of my going through with the business and a prospect of getting everything I'd ever wanted, or of walking out of the house worse off than I had ever been before; because in him I would have made a powerful and unscrupulous enemy, who could have got me the sack and used his influence to chivvy me out of the district.

"Well, I signed the pact, and afterwards he put me through a long ritual that I could not make head nor tail of, except that in symbolical submission to Lucifer he made me kiss his arse; but by that time I felt it was a case of in for a penny, in for a pound; so I made no bones about it. Then he gave me his instructions about the baptism of the child and sent me home.

"By that time I'd tumbled to it that the five hundred didn't mean much to him, and it wasn't either to save it or to get me as a convert that he had gone to quite a lot of trouble. It was the child he was after, and I was still in half a mind to ditch him about that. I think I would have, but for the fact that three days after I had signed the pact I learnt that I had won seven hundred and twenty-three pounds in a football pool.

"It wasn't a fortune, but it seemed to me a real earnest of Prince Lucifer's good faith. All the same, there was something a bit frightening about getting a sum like that out of the blue so soon after I had abjured the Christian God. It scared me enough to make me decide that I had better not try to wriggle out of taking the baby to be baptized.

"We had fixed on the following Saturday night for that, and I slipped some dope that he had given me into Hettie's evening cup of cocoa. No sooner was she in bed than she was sleeping like a log. I wrapped the child up well and carried her to a field about a mile away from The Grange, where the Canon had told me to meet him. There were a number of other people there, women as well as men, and among them old Mother Durnsford, although I did not know that at the time, as all of them were wearing cloaks and great animal masks that hid their identities. Later, when I was made a regular member of the coven, I got to know them all; but she would never forgive me for having tried to blackmail Copely-Syle, and nothing I could offer would persuade her to sell me this house. But to get back—I saw only the beginning of that first Sabbat I attended, as the Canon was very anxious that the child should not take a chill. The actual baptism didn't take long. It was a revolting business; but as soon as it was over he packed me off home with her.

"As you've met Ellen, you will probably have noticed that she is different from other girls. She can't go into a church without being sick, and animals won't go near her. At night, too, she seems to assume a different personality. Naturally, she has never understood why she should be affected as she is, because she knows nothing at all of what I've told you; but it is having been baptized into the Satanic faith which causes these instinctive reactions, and the fact that during the hours when the Powers of Darkness are abroad she becomes readily subject to their influences.

"For many years I had no cause to regret what I had done.

293

Once I had taken the plunge, Copely-Syle advised me that I'd be a fool to strive for success the hard way, by going to London and spending two years studying engineering; so I used my win from the football pools to buy a share as a working partner in the business of a secondhand agricultural implement dealer in Colchester. It was only a small concern, but from the day I started there it began to flourish. I found myself imbued with enormous energy, so that I could work eighteen hours a day and enjoy it.

"All sorts of ideas came to me, too. I began to design gadgets that made tractors more efficient and took out patents for them. Soon they were bringing me more money than my regular earnings. My senior partners were an old man and his son. When I'd been with them just on two years the son had a car smash one night coming home from a dance, and died as a result of his injuries. His loss caused the old man to lose all interest in the business, and he let me buy him out for a song. That was in '33, and in '34 I started a little plant of my own to make the first Beddows All-purposes Garden Motor. It was an instantaneous success. Another invention to do with de-carbonizing brought me enough capital to expand without taking in a partner. By 1936 I was employing four hundred hands. In '38 I merged all my interests as Beddows Ltd., with a capital of half a million, and in the same year work was begun on the big factory. It was completed just in time for the war. By the end of it I was rolling in money and a director of half-a-dozen big firms, in addition to being chairman of my own.

"To begin with I saw quite a lot of Copely-Syle and often assisted him in his magical rituals. That is how I learned enough to erect this pentacle myself last week: but as my own concerns began to occupy me more and more I lost interest in the higher aspects of the Great Art. Then it gradually got down to my simply paying homage to Prince Lucifer once a year, at the great Sabbat on Walpurgis Night. Apart from round about the time of those annual gatherings I never gave a thought to the real source of my money and success.

"That may sound strange, but it isn't really, because my principles were no better and no worse than those of most of the other big business men with whom I was constantly mixing, and it seemed to me that my achievements, like theirs, were the natural outcome of ability, shrewdness and hard work.

"It wasn't till after last Walpurgis Night that I began to worry a bit. Attending the great Sabbat brought it home to me with something of a shock that I had only just over ten months to go before I was due to hand over Ellen. But even then I didn't think about it much, as a hundred and one urgent business matters drove it into the back of my mind. Then, just before Christmas, Ellen came home for good, and that gave me a real jolt.

"I don't think I've mentioned it, but poor Hettie committed suicide while Ellen was still only a little girl. I've never married again, but I took several women to live with me for various periods, and that was one of the reasons why I sent Ellen away to boarding-school at the age of eight. The other was an instinctive feeling that, anyhow until she was grown-up, I ought to keep her away from Copely-Syle. Of course I could not prevent her from meeting him now and then, but she has never been at home for long enough at a time to fall under his influence. It was for that reason, too, that when she was too old to stay at boarding-schools any longer I sent her to a finishing place in Paris. Her two-and-a-half years there came to an end last December, and her return brought me face to face with the fact that my twenty-one years of having everything for nothing were darn' near up.

"Ellen has been at home so little in all this time that I hardly know her; so I'm not going to pretend that I suffered frightful pangs of remorse at having sold her to Lucifer when she was a baby. She has meant practically nothing in my life, and I imagined that all that would happen when she was twenty-one was that she would be initiated as a witch. I reckoned that by having kept her away from Copely-Syle and seeing to it that she was educated by decent people I was doing the best I could for her in the circumstances. Naturally, I disliked the idea of having to hand her over to the Canon, but that was all I had undertaken to do, and it seemed to me that at the age of twenty-one she would be perfectly capable of telling him to go to blazes if she felt that way. If she liked the idea of becoming a witch, that was her look-out. If not, they couldn't make her practise witchcraft against her will. Anyhow I'd quieted my conscience with the idea that I could honour my bond, while ensuring that when she had to take her decision she should do so with an unprejudiced mind.

"Had I been right in my belief that there was no more to it than that, I should be taking her to The Priory on the evening of her birthday; but purely by chance I found out that I had been fooling myself. Ever since I've been in business in a fairly big way I've given Copely-Syle sound financial tips from time to time, and he has quite a bit invested in my companies. A few months ago I wanted to tip him off to sell out from one of my subsidiaries. Instead of dropping him a line, as I usually did, I called in at The Priory one evening on my way home. After we had had a drink his vanity got the better of his discretion, or perhaps he thought that I know less about magical operations than I do. Anyhow, he took me to his crypt and showed me his homunculi.

"Apparently he has been working on them for years, although I was unaware of that. He has got one there now as near perfect as any magician is ever likely to produce. To enable it to leave its jar and function like a normal human being it needs only one thing—the lifeblood of a twenty-one-year-old virgin.

"Naturally he never hinted that to me; but it so happened that I knew it. In a flash I realized what he was planning to do with Ellen. It solved, too, a question that had vaguely puzzled me for a long time. He had never pressed me to give him an opportunity to get to know Ellen, and had most heartily endorsed my policy of keeping her at school until she was grown up. I saw then that he had done so to lessen the risk of her meeting some young man and being seduced, or getting married, before she was twenty-one.

"Well, I knew then that I was up against it. Although I had no special love for the girl I couldn't let that happen. After a lot of thought I decided that there was only one thing for it—both Ellen and I must go into hiding for a time and remain so till after the fateful day.

"It may sound queer to you, but it is a fact that Prince Lucifer is quite a sportsman. He has always been willing to match cunning with cunning. There are plenty of cases in which people have enjoyed his gifts and managed to cheat him in the end. Ellen was used to doing what she was told without argument; so I decided to get her out of the way. She had a nasty sore throat just after Christmas; so as a first step I fixed it for her to have her tonsils out, and whisked her off to a nursing home at Brighton. Then I made arrangements to get her quietly out of the country and park her in the South of France, under an assumed name.

"On my failure to produce her, my bond made me liable to act as forfeit in her place, and as Copely-Syle held my bond it would be up to him to enforce it. I could not hope to escape him by taking a plane to the United States or Australia; because with me he has occult links which would enable him to find and attack me on the astral, wherever I was; so I made up my mind to tell my office that I had gone abroad, then dig myself in here. Only here could I hope for the absolute privacy necessary to protect myself. The trap on the landing and the ape were designed to prevent Copely-Syle getting in to me in the flesh and us'ng the cunning that Lucifer has given him to wheedle out of me where I had hidden Ellen. The pentacle, as you evidently know, is my defence against his getting at me on the astral.

"He hasn't attempted to do either yet. That may be because he is occupied with other matters. Some while ago, you said that he was after Ellen's blood. As you know that, and why, you probably know what he has been up to this past week. I shut myself in here as soon as I returned from taking Ellen down to the Riviera; so about what has happened since you must be better informed than I am. Anyhow, I can give you no further information."

Suddenly Beddows' voice changed, rising to an hysterical note, as he added, "If I were a free agent I'd hand the two of you over to the police for having broken in here. As I am not, and you threatened to expose me to the most frightful peril, I've told you everything there is to tell about my awful situation. Everything, d'you understand? Everything! Now get out! And leave me unencumbered to fight my own battle."

Silence descended on the room like a curtain of draped black velvet.

Neither C. B. nor John had dared to interrupt Beddows' long monologue. Both of them had been acutely conscious that although he was definitely not possessed, he was, all the same, in a quite abnormal state. From the toneless voice in which he had spoken for most of the time it was clear that he was using them only as a focus at which to pour out his own story; and it was reasonable to suppose that in all the twenty-one years since he had made his pact with the Devil he had never told it to anyone before. To have cut in at any point with question, or even comment, might well have checked the flow and deprived them of hearing the all-important latter part of the revelations.

A good half minute elapsed before C. B. said, "We are very grateful to you for having been so frank with us; and I can only repeat that we are here as friends who want to help. We got drawn into this thing because John Fountain's mother lives in the villa next door to that which you rented for Ellen. I had better tell you what has happened since you left her there; then we shall better be able to decide between us on a plan of campaign for overcoming our mutual enemy."

"I can give you no help in that." Beddows' voice was sharp. "I'll have my work cut out to protect myself as it is, without inviting further trouble."

C. B. ignored the remark and proceeded to give him an account of the events centring round Ellen that had taken place in the South of France. When he had done, Beddows said thoughtfully:

"Copely-Syle must have smelt a rat as soon as he learned that I had gone abroad so near the date. The odds are that he came to The Grange in our absence and managed to get hold of some of the girl's personal belongings; an old hairbrush or anything she had used for her toilet would enable him to overlook her and find out where she had gone. Evidently the reason that he has so far made no move against me is because he has been too occupied with his attempts to have her kidnapped. I'm grateful to you for all you've done to keep her out of his clutches, and I quite understand now your reasons for breaking in here; but all the same I'd be glad if you would leave me."

"Oh come!" John protested. "Now you know the danger she is in surely you don't propose to ignore it?"

"Since you had this bright idea of having her arrested, she is no longer in danger. These crooks who are acting for the Canon will be far too scared of the police to attempt to abduct her from a French prison."

"You are forgetting the Canon," C. B. put in. "By using his occult powers he may be able to get her out; and it is as good as certain, now, that he will fly out there to-morrow morning. We know that he'll stick at nothing to get hold of Ellen and he still has over forty hours to work in."

"Well, there's nothing I can do about it."

"Yes there is. You and he must have been mixed up in all sorts of queer business. It's a sure thing that a thoroughly unscrupulous man like Copely-Syle has committed a number of criminal acts in order to carry on his sorcery and that you know of some of them. From time to time he must either have robbed churches or instigated others to do so, in order to get hold of Holy Communion wafers for desecration. We know, too, that he is having blood donors' gifts of blood stolen from hospitals to feed his homunculi. I want you to come with us to the police and make a statement. On that we'll get a warrant for his arrest, and even if he leaves for France in the morning I can get it executed there. That is the only way we can make absolutely certain of protecting Ellen until her maximum period of danger is past."

Beddows gave a short, harsh laugh. "What the hell d'you take me for? A lunatic? Can't you see that now you've queered his pitch with Ellen by having her imprisoned, the odds are that he will round on me? As long as I remain in this pentacle I've good hopes of cheating Lucifer yet; but the moment I move out of it I'm liable at any time to have my soul snatched, and my body will spend the rest of its days in an asylum. No thank you!"

"You got Ellen into this!" cried John angrily. "The very least you can do is to run some risk to get her out of it."

"She's safe enough where she is! A darned sight safer than I am, anyway! I did my best for her by taking the risk that I'm running already, instead of handing her over in accordance with my bond; and I'll do no more. Nothing you or anyone else can say is going to get me out of this pentacle within the next forty-eight hours."

"What is to prevent our smashing it up?"

"I can't; and if you do I'll be in hideous danger for a while. But better that than the far worse risk of going with you now and committing myself to having to face Copely-Syle in open court as a witness against him to-morrow. If you do bust the electric current, I can use candles instead, and the moment you've gone I'll make another pentacle. Besides, I've already paid your price for not interfering with this one by telling you what you came here to find out."

For a further twenty minutes they argued and pleaded with Beddows, but in vain. Nothing would move him, and when C. B. found that they were repeating themselves over and over again he said at last:

"It's no good, John. We must do what we can on our own. Let's get out of this and back to Colchester."

With a curt good-night to Beddows, they left him and, having eased the bonds of the ape a little, made their way downstairs. On slipping out of the window by which they had come in they found that it was no longer raining, and with heartfelt relief at leaving the dank, dark house, they gratefully breathed in the cool night air.

As they turned into the drive, John muttered, "The callous swine! I would have liked to strangle him."

C. B. shrugged. "After having had the luck to run him to earth like that it was damnably disappointing that he should refuse to help us; but he's far from being a hundred per cent evil, otherwise he would not have tried to hide Ellen and be facing the music himself. Just think what an ordeal he undertook when he decided to coop himself up in that grim room for days on end and wait for some frightful thing to come and attempt to get him! It can hardly be wondered at that he is half crazy from fear already."

"All the same, he might at least have given us some pointer which would help us to lay the Canon by the heels. The very idea of a father selling his child to the Devil in the beginning is almost unbelievable, and for him to refuse to utter a word that might help to save her from being murdered now is fantastic."

"Fantastic is the word for this whole horrible business, partner. What could be more so than the thought of Henry Beddows, a down-to-earth inventor of motor engines, who has constantly to deal with Trade Union officials, and is a power in the commercial world of Britain, sitting up there in a magic pentacle preparing to wrestle with demons for his soul; or a man who was, apparently, once a Canon of the Church of England planning to murder a girl in order to give a semblance of human life to a monster of his own creation? Nevertheless, we know these things to be actually happening."

"I know, I know! But what are we going to do now?"

"Get some sleep. I can do with it."

It was getting on for three o'clock in the morning by the time they reached their hotel. By then they were too tired even to tip the night porter to get them a drink. On reaching their rooms they pulled off their clothes, flopped into bed and within a few moments were in the deep sleep of exhaustion.

Next morning they had their breakfasts sent up to C. B.'s room and while they ate them discussed the position to date. During the previous evening and night they had found out a great deal. They now knew more about Christina's past than she knew herself, and the reason for her queer behaviour. They knew why the Canon was so anxious to get hold of her, and that if he succeeded it would cost her not only her freedom, but her life. They had traced her father and learned his reason for taking her to the South of France and abandoning her there; but he had positively refused to give them the aid they had expected from him. On the other hand it had been definitely verified that the danger in which she stood would be acute for only one day; since, should the Canon fail to carry out his abominable ritual on her twenty-first birthday, there would be no point whatever in his killing her afterwards. Therefore, their immediate problem boiled down to immobilizing the Canon for the next thirty-six hours.

Their prospects of doing so seemed exceedingly slender, as it was a foregone conclusion that either he was already, or would very soon be, on his way to France. The fact that Upson had arrived at The Priory the previous night made it certain he had come by air. C. B. thought it probable that during the war Upson had served in Coastal Command and had been stationed in that area. In any case, as it had been intended that he should fly Christina home, it was evident that he was familiar with the Essex coast and had already reconnoitred some of the many lonely creeks to select a good illicit landing-place. It was, therefore, long odds that when de Grasse had decided that his latest news was of too compromising a nature to convey by telephone, and sent it instead by personal messenger, Upson had travelled in his own seaplane and made a secret landing by last light somewhere along the coast, not far from Little Bentford.

If so, the Canon had a pilot and aircraft at his disposal, and could leave at any hour he chose. Obviously his only chance of getting hold of Christina now lay in flying south himself, so that he could exercise his occult powers on her jailers. However, there was one factor which might cause him to delay his departure for a few hours—namely that the Satanic writ did not run, as far as Christina's mind was concerned, except during the hours of darkness. Only during them could he influence her voluntarily to leave prison, should the way have been opened for her to do so. Having considered this, C. B. said:

"I had pretty well made up my mind that our best plan would be to make for Northolt right away, so as to catch the 10.30 plane for Nice, then bank on our being able to head him off from getting at Christina to-night. But an afternoon plane to Paris would still enable us to get down there by Air France or K.L.M. in time for that; so I think it would be worth-while making a bid against Copely-Syle's planning to leave before mid-day, and the sporting chance that we may then be able to prevent his leaving at all."

"I'm game to use force," John said quickly. "And if we manage to catch him, you have only to tell me what to do. But a charge of assault and battery would blot your official copy-book really badly, so——"

"Thanks, partner," C. B. cut him short with a smile, "but I don't think either of us need risk being hauled up before the beak on that count. I am proposing to lay an information against him for practising cruelty to animals, and request the police to apply for a search-warrant. They have only to see those poor brutes I saw in the crypt last night to issue a summons. It is illegal to leave the country with a summons pending against one, and I have enough pull with the police to get them to keep a watch on him. If he attempts to clear out after the summons has been served he will be prevented from doing so by the coppers."

"By Jove! That's a grand idea."

"I hope it may prove so; but it won't do us any good if he has gone before the police get out there. And they won't be able to secure a warrant until ten o'clock at the earliest, because the magistrates' court does not open until that hour."

"Well, if he *has* gone, I have another idea."

"Let's hear it."

John's dark eyes narrowed slightly. "The Canon can't do his final job on the homunculus without Christina; and Christina is no good to him without the homunculus. That's so, isn't it?"

"Yes. Unless he can bring her back here by to-morrow night he is sunk."

"Even if he does, it won't do him any good if his prize homunculus is no longer in a state to lap up Christina's blood. If we find that he has already left for France, I mean to go down into that crypt and destroy it."

"Good for you, John." C. B. laughed for the first time in

many hours. "I really am beginning to feel a bit more hopeful now. One way or the other I think we'll manage to spike his guns. As soon as we are dressed we'll go round and do our stuff with the police."

At the station, after the usual formalities, they were shown into the office of an elderly inspector named Fuller. To him C. B. produced his card and a small trinket that he carried, after which the inspector listened to all he had to say with considerable respect. Although C. B. refrained from giving more than a general indication of what lay behind the excuse on which he desired a search-warrant to be obtained, that was quite enough to have caused most people to show incredulity; but police officers of long experience have usually come up against so many extraordinary happenings that they are prepared to consider with an open mind every conceivable aberration possible to a diseased or criminal brain. In consequence Inspector Fuller took down C. B.'s formal deposition about the maimed animals without comment, and quietly agreed to put the matter in hand at once.

However, at the magistrates' court some delay was unavoidable, as no special priority attached to an application regarding cruelty to animals, and the lists had already been made out. So it was half-past ten before the application was granted, and after a quarter to eleven by the time the formalities of drawing the search-warrant were completed.

There was no hurrying the law, and John fumed with impatience in vain; but at last Inspector Fuller and a constable came out to join C. B. and himself in the car, and they set off.

Anxious as C. B. was to learn the results of his move, he felt that any attempt on his part to accompany the police into the house might be met by the Canon, if he was still there, with legal objections, or possibly even a false accusation of having broken in the previous night, which might have seriously complicated matters. So it was decided that he and John should wait in the car just down the lane until the inspector had carried out his search of the premises.

It was twenty-past eleven when they pulled up under the trees that fringed the road some fifty yards east of The Priory, and the two police officers got out. Both C. B. and John thought it almost certain that by this time the Canon would be on his way to France; so they had lost much of the optimism that had buoyed them up earlier that morning, and they found the wait before they would know the best or worst extremely trying. In anxious silence for the most part, they sat side by side smoking cigarette after cigarette while they watched the clock on the dashboard of the car tick away the minutes.

It was close on twelve before the inspector and the constable reappeared. Without a word C. B. and John got out of the car and walked with anxious faces to meet them.

The inspector smiled rather ruefully as he addressed C. B. "Canon Copely-Syle is there all right, sir, and he couldn't have been more helpful. But there is no one in the house answering your description of the airman. There are no animals either, or human-looking fish in big glass jars like you described. We visited the crypt and it has the appearance of being used as an ordinary laboratory; no curtains embroidered with pictures of the Devil, or anything of that sort. We went over the whole house from basement to attic, and there is nothing whatever in it on which we could ask for a summons."

John looked at C. B. in amazement and dismay. The Canon had completely outwitted them. He was still there, but free to leave at any time he chose; for he had anticipated the raid, and there was now no legal pretext on which he could be detained. Moreover, he had removed his homunculi; so it was no longer possible to go in and destroy them.

CHAPTER XX

THE SECRET BASE

THE police constable's face remained wooden, but C. B. felt sure that he was deriving a secret satisfaction from being in on a case where a plain-clothes high-hat from London had made a fool of himself. The inspector, on the other hand, knew that men like Colonel Verney did not apply for search-warrants without good reason, and he said:

"I'm sorry, sir. It looks as if they were tipped off that you were after them."

C. B. rubbed the side of his big nose. "That's about it, Inspector. We won't go into the source of my information, but you can take it from me that it was red-hot last night. They have destroyed most of the goods and unloaded the prize exhibit that I was after."

"Is there any other way in which we can help, sir?"

"Only by telephoning for a car to take you back to Colchester. I shan't be going back yet. Let's go along to the pub and have one while you are waiting for transport."

Getting into the car, they drove along to the Weavers Arms and went into the private bar. When C. B. had ordered a round of drinks and the constable had gone to telephone, he drew the inspector aside and said, "There is one thing you can do for me. Some time this morning a big crate or package, about four feet six high and three feet square, must have been removed from The Priory, either in a lorry or on a trailer. In such a quiet place as this it is a good bet that someone will have seen it being loaded up or passing along the road. Have a word with the landlord. The public bar is sure to be pretty full at this hour. Ask him to enquire of everyone there, and tell him there's a quid for himself and a quid for anyone who can give us any useful information."

The enquiry being made by a police inspector naturally

secured the immediate co-operation of the landlord with no questions asked. A few minutes later a lean, elderly man with a weather-beaten face was brought into the private bar. His name was Sims and he proved to be the gardener at The Vicarage. He had seen a crate of the size described and a number of smaller packages loaded on to a lorry outside The Priory about ten o'clock. The loading had been done by the coloured servant and a tall man with a fair, fluffy moustache, under the Canon's supervision. The lorry was owned by one Joe Cotton, a local character who was no better than he should be, and he had driven off in the direction of Weeley.

Having obtained as detailed a description of Cotton and his lorry as Sims could give, C. B. paid for the information and the drinks, took leave of Inspector Fuller and, accompanied by John, left the pub.

As John turned the car in the direction of Weeley he said, "Well done, C. B. If we can catch the fellow with the lorry we'll do in that filthy homunculus yet."

"Yes—if!" C. B. replied dubiously. "But he's got two and a half hours' start of us, and remember Copely-Syle runs a coven in these parts. The odds are that it has been stowed away in the cellars of a house belonging to one of his brother warlocks an hour or more ago."

At the village of Weeley they got out and made enquiries; but no one they asked had seen such a lorry, so they decided to go back to the last crossroads. On reaching them they took the road east to Thorpe-le-Soken, and there they had what they thought might turn out to be better luck. Soon after mid-day a woman had seen a lorry pass through and take the road north towards Great Oakley. It sounded like the one they were after, but as she was certain that there had been two men in its cabin there was a possibility that it was another. No one else they asked had noticed a lorry at all; so they drove on, now heading north.

They were still about five miles from the open sea, but approaching a great area of lakes, creeks and islands known as Hansford Water. To their left there were still occasional farms and coppices, but to their right was only an almost trackless waste of marshes. The road was straight, flat and empty; so they could see a considerable way along it, and about two miles out of Thorpe-le-Soken they sighted a lorry coming towards them. As it came nearer C. B. exclaimed:

"By Jove! I believe this is it. Pull into the centre of the road, John, and signal it to stop."

As the two vehicles pulled up within a few yards of one another, C. B. got out. A glance showed him that the lorry was empty, but it answered the description he had been given, as did also the small ferret-faced man who was the sole occupant of its cabin. Walking up to him, C. B. said:

"Good afternoon. You are Joe Cotton, aren't you?"

"Yes, guv'nor."

"I thought so." C. B.'s smile was a triumph of candid innocence. "You have done the job quicker than we expected. Canon Copely-Syle will be pleased about that, providing you've done it all right. But he is nervous as a cat on hot bricks about the safe delivery of his stuff, so he sent us after you to make certain the big crate had come to no harm."

Cotton gave C. B. a rather doubtful stare. "Why would 'e do that, when 'e sent the other gent wiv me so as 'e could help wiv the unloading 'isself?"

"Because that crate is very valuable. The Canon wanted confirmation that everything was O.K. as soon as possible."

"Well, I'm giving it you, ain't I?"

"All the same, I think you'd better turn round and come with us, so that we can vouch for it to him that we have seen that everything is all right for ourselves."

"What d'you want me to come wiv you for?" Cotton's close-set eyes showed sudden suspicion.

"He told us the road to take; but we are strangers in these parts, and we'll lose a lot of time if we miss our way across the marshes."

"So that's the lay, is it? You don't know where I bin an' want me ter take yer there. Nothin' doin', guv'nor." As Cotton spoke his ferrety face had become taut with something between fear and anger.

C. B. saw that his bluff had failed; but he showed no

resentment. As he had nothing on the man he decided that bullying would get him nowhere; so he shrugged and said with a smile:

"You're a fly one, Cotton. It didn't take you long to see through me, did it? Still, there's no harm done, and I've private reasons for wanting to know where you delivered that crate. How about a tenner to take us near enough to point out the house; and we won't let on afterwards that it was you who put us wise?"

"Not for ten quid, nor for twenty," came the prompt reply. "I ain't done nothin' wrong; but, all the same, I ain't tellin' no tales."

Starting up his engine, Cotton swung one wheel of his lorry on to the grass verge, scraped past the car and drove off down the road.

"Blast the fellow!" exclaimed John angrily. "That's the second trick we've lost to-day."

"We didn't lose it altogether," C. B. murmured more philosophically. "When a man like that says 'I ain't done nothin' wrong', you can be quite certain that he has. He wouldn't have refused a tenner without a good reason, either, and a suspicion that we might be connected with the police."

"Even if he knew what the crate contained, there is nothing illegal in delivering it to a house."

"No. You noticed, though, that the woman in Thorpe-le-Soken, who put us on his trail, was right about there having been two men in the cabin of the lorry when it passed her. Any guess who the other was?"

"Upson?" said John, after a second.

C. B. nodded. "Any guess where the crate has got to?"

"Hell's bells!" John exclaimed. "They've put it aboard that blasted seaplane."

"Well done, Watson! You see now why friend Cotton was too scared to take a bribe to say where he had off-loaded it. Seeing Upson's aircraft moored in some quiet creek miles from anywhere would have told him that it had come down there to evade the authorities, and he would know darn' well

309

that to help load anything into it that had not been passed by the Customs was a serious offence."

"Of course! But let's get on. We may be able to find the seaplane and stop it before it takes off."

"Not much hope of that, I'm afraid. This group of creeks covers an area more than twice the size of Birmingham, and Cotton was over two hours ahead of us; so he may have taken the crate to a stretch of water miles from here."

"What filthy luck!" Exasperation made John almost spit with rage. "Then that swinish Canon has got the best of us again! He's put it out of our power to get hold of his homunculus and destroy it, anyhow for the next twenty-four hours. What a cunning move to have Upson fly it out to the Riviera, then bring it back in time for the ceremony, with Christina if they get her. But let's pray to God they won't. The only bright spot so far to-day has been finding that he is still here, instead of having gone to France to work his filthy spells on her jailers."

"That is one thing that has been puzzling me," C. B. said as he got back into the car. "The creation of fully-functioning homunculi is Copely-Syle's life-work; so you can be certain that up to the very last moment he will strive to seize this chance of pulling it off. When I told him that Christina was in prison he immediately decided that he must go out there, and he changed his mind only when I persuaded him that I could do the necessary for him. His discovery that I was an impostor ruled that out; so why hasn't he gone himself? I can't believe for one second that he's chucked his hand in."

"No; but think of the work involved in getting that private hell of his cleared up in anticipation of a possible visit. It must have taken him all night and probably well into the morning to burn or bury all his animals and those awful deformed creatures he created. Obviously his first concern would be with that and getting his prize homunculus out of danger."

"That's true; and it gives me a nasty thought. As he was so fully occupied himself he may have decided to get somebody else to do what I offered to do for him. Since he is head of a coven he might have got in touch with one of his pals during the night. If so, they could have gone up to London first thing this morning and caught an aircraft from Northolt to Nice."

John groaned. "I never thought of that. If you're right, and they caught the earliest one, they will be in Nice by now."

"It's a possibility; so we can't ignore it, although I think it would take a pretty high-grade Black to use effectively what amounts to hypnotism at a distance on several people he has never seen, with only their soiled garments as a medium. Anyway, we still have a choice of strong cards left. Earlier on you were arguing that we could save Christina by depriving the Canon of his homunculus. That is true, of course, but not the best way of expressing the core of the matter. To put it in a nutshell, we win out on the big issue if we can prevent any one of those three factors from joining up with the other two for the next thirty-six hours. Our object in trying to get a summons against the Canon was to keep him from going to Nice. We failed to get the summons; but as it turns out he has remained here of his own accord. The homunculus will be brought back here, and possibly Christina. By keeping a watch on the Canon we should be able to cut in at the last moment and prevent their reaching him. Alternatively, by making full speed for London, we can still get on a Paris plane and be in Nice late this evening. We could then get Malouet to try to find out where Upson has brought his seaplane down, with the object of destroying the homunculus; and, should we fail in that, we might anyhow lend a hand in preventing Christina from being whisked out of prison. My own feeling is that our chances are pretty good either way; but this is really your party, John; so I'm going to leave the choice to you."

After a moment's thought, John said, "It will be dark before we can get to Nice; so if Copely-Syle has sent a brother wizard down there, he may get Christina out before we arrive on the scene; and Malouet's chances of finding out at short notice where Upson comes down seems pretty problematical. Of course, that is taking the worst view. All the same, a bird in the hand is worth two in the bush; so I think our best bet would be to remain here and concentrate on isolating the Canon."

"That seems sound to me. We'll return to Colchester, then collect our bags from the Red Lion and transfer to the Weavers Arms at Little Bentford. By making that our new H.Q. we will be able to maintain a twenty-four-hour turn and turn about watch on The Priory, with only half a mile's walk to relieve one another, and between watches get food and sleep. Let's go."

John drove on till he found a suitable place to reverse the car, then they drove through fourteen miles of twisting lanes back to Colchester. By two o'clock they had packed, paid their bill, and left. Half an hour later they took up their new quarters at Little Bentford and tossed to decide which of them should do the first two-hour spell of duty. John lost, and went out to take up a position in the coppice from which he could keep an eye on The Priory without being seen. As he did so he thanked his stars that throughout the day the weather had taken a turn for the better; so it seemed unlikely that the dreary vigils he and C. B. proposed to keep would be made additionally unpleasant by rain.

He need not have concerned himself about the weather prospects for the night. At a quarter past three he came racing back to the inn and burst into its small parlour. C. B. was just sitting down to an early tea, which he had hoped would make up a little for the lunch he had missed. He looked up to hear John shout:

"Didn't you see that car go by? It was he, driven by his black servant. They've taken the road the lorry took this morning."

With a sigh, C. B. abandoned his untasted tea and followed John out to the yard, where they had parked the car under a lean-to. Three minutes later they were on the road to Weeley. The Canon's car was out of sight; so they had to take a chance at the crossroads and, instead of continuing south, turned off to Thorpe-le-Soken. There they took another chance and turned north towards Great Oakley. They passed the place where they had met Joe Cotton in his lorry two and a half hours earlier, and still they had not picked up the Canon's car. It was not until they had covered another three miles that C. B. spotted a low moving blob that he thought must be it, far away to their right in the midst of the apparently trackless marshes.

A quarter of a mile farther on they found a narrow track that led seaward, and took it. A few minutes later, after passing a patch of tall reeds, they caught sight of the car again, and some way beyond it the upper structure of the seaplane.

"Look!" cried John bitterly. "I've been expecting this ever since I saw the road the Canon took out of Little Bentford. Upson didn't leave for France early this afternoon, as we thought. If only we had looked around a bit we might have caught him in his lair, and made a darn' good bid to sink his aircraft."

"Once the horse was out of the stable, and one saw the direction it was taking, it was easy enough to guess where it would pull up," C. B. agreed. "But we might have hunted this wilderness for a couple of days without catching sight of Upson's plane. Given a nice straight piece of Nile it would have been easier to find Moses among the bulrushes."

Within a few hundred yards of leaving the road, it became clear that they were not on the same track as the Canon's car had taken; but it also led towards the sheet of open water upon which the seaplane sat motionless.

"Stop, John!" C. B. cried. "We must go back! This way we'll be cut off by the water from getting at him."

At that moment they came out from behind another wide patch of tall reeds and could again see the Canon's car. It had halted about four hundred yards away. Near it, on the water's edge, rose the roof of a low boat-house. John had already put on the brake, but as the car continued to run forward at a slower pace they saw that the track curved round in the direction they wanted to go. Assuming that it joined the other further on, John took off the brake. Gathering speed again they covered another hundred yards, once more behind a screen of reeds. When they could next see the water, the Canon was out of his car and down by the boat-house. Beside it lay a broad duck-punt. In the punt stood a countryman holding a tall pole.

The track had now become a narrow causeway and was

very bumpy. As they bucketed along they could see the Canon looking in their direction. Only two hundred yards separated them from him. Stooping down, he made the gesture of picking up something from the ground. Raising his arm he appeared to throw it at them.

John jerked his head aside. The car swerved violently.

"Look where you're going—not at him!" yelled C. B. But his shout of warning came too late. The near front wheel had gone over the edge of the low bank. The stiff reeds made a sharp rustling sound as they scraped along the coachwork of the car. Heaving on the steering-wheel, John strove to right it; but the bank was too steep. The car heeled over sideways, ran on for a dozen yards, then lurched to a stop, both its near wheels axle-deep in mud and water.

"You idiot!" snapped C. B. "Why the hell didn't you keep your eyes on the track?"

"I couldn't help ducking when he threw that stone," John protested angrily. "It was instinct."

"He made the motion of throwing, but he didn't throw anything."

"Yes he did; a damn' great stone. It came hurtling straight at the windscreen."

"He didn't, I tell you. He couldn't have thrown anything that distance."

"I saw it."

"No you didn't," C. B. said bitterly. "But I don't doubt you thought you did. It just shows what a powerful Black he is to have been able to cast the thought into your mind so successfully."

While they were speaking they had scrambled out of the car and started to run down the track. It curved again round another island of reeds, then came to an abrupt ending at a rough wooden landing-stage.

With a curse John made to plunge into the water. Grabbing his coat collar, C. B. pulled him back, and cried, "Don't be a fool! The mud in these marshes is yards deep in places, and there are under-water reeds as well. You would drown for a certainty."

To have run all the way back to the road, then down the other track which followed the far side of the creek on which they were standing, would have taken at least twenty minutes. Impotent and furious, they could only remain where they were, watching the final scene of their enemy's triumph.

The coloured servant had already turned the Canon's car and was driving it back towards the road. The Canon was now in the punt and being poled out to the seaplane. They could see now that, although small and tubby, it was a powerful twin-engined affair. Upson came to its door and helped his passenger aboard.

As the labourer in the punt pushed off C. B. cupped his hands and yelled to him to come and pick them up, offering him treble the money he had received for ferrying out his last passenger if he would do so. He made the bid only as a forlorn hope and, as he expected, it proved futile. Either from fear of the Canon, or because he knew that he had been assisting an illegal emigration, the fellow ignored C. B.'s shouts, poled the punt back into the boat-house, then disappeared among the reeds. By that time Upson had the seaplane's engines running. Two minutes later it turned into the wind and ran forward. A double sheet of spray hissed up from beneath its stern and a quarter of a mile down the creek it sailed gracefully into the air.

Returning to the car, they spent twenty minutes trying to get it unditched; but there was no brushwood, or anything else of that kind in the vicinity that they could stuff under the wheels to give them a grip; so they were forced to abandon their efforts.

C. B. glanced at his watch and said, "This is not so good, John. It is a quarter-past four and we are miles from anywhere. If we had the use of the car we could have reached London before dark and, perhaps, managed to hire a plane to fly us out to Nice; but that is ruled out now. It must be a good hour's tramp to the nearest village and in these little places they don't run to hire cars. By the time we've telephoned to Colchester and got a car to pick us up, then done the seventy miles to Northolt, it will be getting on for eight o'clock; and the aircraft of the private companies are not equipped for night flying."

John looked a little puzzled as he replied, "But we decided to stay here."

"That was when we thought the Canon meant to stay here too, and we could keep a watch on him."

"I know; and the fact that he will now be down on the Riviera by about nine o'clock naturally adds to the chances of his being able to get Christina out of prison. After your visit last night he is certain to have telephoned de Grasse to make all the preliminary arrangements for his attempt; and now he'll have the whole of the night to work in. But all the same, it seems to me that we still have a good hope of spiking his guns at the last moment."

"You mean if the prison authorities do their stuff? I agree about that. From the moment the idea of putting her inside was mooted I felt that we were on a winner. And in spite of what the old so-and-so said to me last night I'd still lay three to one against his or any other Black Magician succeeding in getting her out at such short notice."

"No, I didn't mean that, C. B. I meant in the worst event—saying that he does succeed. He has still got to bring her and the homunculus back here to-morrow. Seaplanes can't just land anywhere. At least, this one can't if it is to fulfil its purpose of putting the Canon, Christina—either unwilling or unconscious—and that heavy crate safely ashore. And I should think the odds are very much against his having another prepared base in this neighbourhood, because he could hardly have foreseen that we should discover this one. Now that we have, you can go to the police, report his unauthorized departure from the country, and have it watched for their return. We'll relieve him of Christina as he lands, and have him and Upson arrested."

C. B. looked at John and his face was troubled. "It's a good idea, laddie; but I'm afraid it won't work out. Now he knows we know his base he is much too crafty to return to it. And there is more to it than that. You remember what we were saying a while ago; about our being certain of winning out on the big issue only if we could prevent one of the three factors—Canon, homunculus and Christina—from joining up with the other two? Well, that is now beyond our power. In a few hours' time all three of them will be in Nice. You know the story of Mahomet when he couldn't get the mountain to come to him? In this case Christina is the mountain; and so far the Canon has failed to budge her. Since we have made things so hot for him here, and the time in which to get her back is now so short, it is my bet that he decided this morning to do the job out there. That is why he had the homunculus put on the seaplane instead of hiding it in the house of a pal. And now Mahomet has gone to the mountain."

CHAPTER XXI

THE PACT WITH SATAN

"Oh God!" muttered John. "So far that fiend has won
every trick, and soon there will be only a few locked doors
between him and Christina. Is there nothing we can do to
help in preventing him from getting at her?"

"We can send a telegram warning Malouet that the Canon
is on his way," C. B. suggested. "There is just a chance that
the French police might pick him up on landing. If so, he
could be arrested for illegal entry. But you can be sure that
he has been in communication with de Grasse about flying
out; so the seaplane will not come down at the Ile de Port Cros.
De Grasse would not risk that. He will appreciate that since
our visit to it yesterday morning Malouet may have got the
police to keep it under observation; so he will have instructed
Upson to land at one of his other haunts, where there is little
chance of his being spotted. I'm afraid, John, that for to-
night you'll have to pin your faith on the French prison
system; and believe me, it's a pretty good one."

"I only hope you're right. Anyhow, the sooner we send
that telegram, the better." Leaning through the window of
the car, John pulled a map from the pocket next to the driver's
seat. A glance at it showed that the nearest village was probably
Great Oakley. They could not be certain of their exact position
among the tangled creeks of Hansford Water, but judged the
village to be between three and five miles distant. Having
locked the car they set off there.

The sky was a uniform grey, but somewhere in the west
the sun was now getting down towards the horizon, and as
they began to trudge in that direction John wondered miserably how fate would deal with Christina during this last
critical night before her birthday. He would have given a great
deal to be with her or, that being out of the question, at least

able to keep watch outside her prison; and his impotence riled him all the more from the fact that it was he who had taken the decision to remain in England to watch the Canon. C. B. had given him the choice early that afternoon, and had he chosen the alternative they could have been well on their way to Nice by now. Yet he knew that it was silly to blame himself for his blunder, as it had seemed the best course to take at the time.

It was half-past five when they reached Great Oakley and the light was fading. From the village pub they telephoned their telegram to Malouet, then put through a call to a garage in Colchester for a breakdown van with a searchlight. It picked them up at a quarter-past six and they returned to the marshes. They lost twenty minutes searching along several tracks for the point at which C. B.'s car had become ditched, but once they found it there was little difficulty in hauling the car out. Both of them now thought it unlikely that the seaplane would bring the Canon back and land again on the same stretch of water next day, but that possibility could not be ignored; so they intended asking the police to keep a watch on it. To do so meant going in to Colchester and, with the Canon gone, there no longer seemed any point in their sleeping at Little Bentford. In consequence, in the car with John at the wheel once more, they collected their bags from the Weavers Arms and drove to the market town. There John dropped C. B. off at the police station and went on to book rooms and order dinner at the Red Lion.

By then it was getting on for eight o'clock. Soon afterwards C. B. came in and they sat down to dine. While they ate, in low voices they reviewed the situation, and could not escape the fact that they had far graver grounds for depression than they had had when dining there the night before. Then, their only cause for gloom had been that their journey appeared to have been rendered futile by their failure to locate Beddows through his office. Now they had found him, but he had refused them his help. They had also found out a great deal about the Canon; above all, that he was not merely seeking to corrupt Christina but, if he could get hold of her, meant to kill her.

The thought of the night to come, and his utter helplessness during it, to which he must attempt to reconcile himself, had now been preying on John's mind for four hours. He seemed obsessed with the idea that if only they could think of it, there must be some way in which they could either foil the Canon in his bid to get at Christina, or strengthen her mind to resist his influence.

C. B. could only suggest that they should rout out a parson, beg the keys of his church and pray for her in it. John said he would willingly spend the night on his knees, but had always believed that God helped those who helped themselves; and felt sure that there must be some active measure which might bring about more definite results. Yet it was the suggestion of prayer that gave him an idea, and after a moment he said:

"I am still convinced that something could be done through Beddows. After all, he is much more than Christina's physical father. As it was he who sold her to the Devil, he is her godfather as well—and not just in the modern sense of buying her a christening-mug and trying to remember to give her a quid on her birthdays. By inducting him as a Satanist the Canon took spiritual responsibility for him, and he in turn took spiritual responsibility for Christina. If we could only persuade *him* to pray to Jesus Christ for her to-night I believe we would achieve something really worth while."

"I get the idea," murmured C. B. dubiously. "As he admitted to us that it was having her baptized into the Satanic faith which makes her subject to evil influences during the hours of darkness, your theory is that if we could get him to recant she would no longer be subject to those influences."

"Exactly! Then, whatever success the Canon may have in casting spells on her jailers to-night, when it comes to willing her to leave her cell she would reject the thought and sit tight there."

C. B. rubbed his big nose. "Your reasoning seems sound enough; but I'd as soon hope to jump Becher's Brook on a donkey as get Beddows to do as you suggest. Do you realize that after all these years of battening on the fruits of evil he would have to abjure his Master? It isn't even as if he really cares very deeply what happens to Christina. And the risk! If he forswears Satan now, it wouldn't surprise me to see him struck dead by some form of seizure."

"Well, he has had his fling; and if he lives on he will be lucky if he escapes being hounded into a madhouse by the Canon. Providing he abjures, even if he does die, we shall have achieved our object, and I wouldn't allow his life to weigh with me for one moment against Christina's. I agree that it is a thousand to one against our being able to persuade him to rely on God's mercy, but there is that one chance; and to make the attempt is a thousand times better than spending the night doing nothing."

"O.K., partner." C. B. finished his port. "We'll pay him another visit."

Soon after ten they were again approaching The Grange. Now that they knew its owner was there they were indifferent to the possibility of the Jutsons hearing them and coming on the scene; so they drove straight up to the front door. But, knowing that their ring would not be answered, on getting out they walked round to the yard. No chinks of light showed between the curtains of the windows above the stable, and with no more than a glance at them they entered the house through the staircase window, the catch of which C. B. had forced the night before.

By the light of C. B.'s torch they proceeded through the baize door, across the hall and up the stairs. The atmosphere of the house was still chill and eerie, but to-night it did not fill them with the fears that had racked their nerves during their previous visit. Swinging themselves across the gap in the floorboards of the landing, they approached the upper flight of stairs. The clanking of the ape's chain came clearly, telling that it had been freed—no doubt by Jutson when he had come up to give it fresh food and water that morning—so they expected to have to catch and bind it again. That proved unnecessary. The creature had evidently learnt its lesson, for the moment C. B. shone his torch it cowered away, chattering with fright, into the farthest corner of the upper landing. Keeping a wary eye on it, they climbed the stairs and sidled past to the door of the great attic. Its lock had not been repaired and the door opened at a touch.

Beyond it the scene was the same almost unbelievable one that would for ever remain engraved upon their memories. There sat the twentieth-century business man cross-legged on his blankets, his back propped against the tea-chest, surrounded by the paraphernalia of mediaeval witchcraft, his form dimly lit by the unflickering blue light given off from the glass tubes of the pentacle that enclosed him.

This time he showed no fear of his visitors. Their approach had roused him from a doze, and after giving himself a little shake he said, none too cordially, "So it's you two again. What d'you want now?"

C. B. felt that this was John's party; so he waited for him to speak, and John, having decided on the way there that a tactful approach was essential to any hope of success, replied quietly:

"A lot has happened since we saw you last night, Mr. Beddows; so we thought we ought to come and report."

"Why? I'm not employing you." Beddows gave him a chilly stare.

"No; but I'm sure you are not indifferent to Chris . . . to Ellen's fate; otherwise you would not have gone to such trouble to hide her in the South of France. What is more, you are vitally concerned in the outcome of this affair yourself."

"I can't stop you talking, if you want to," came the ungracious reply; "but if you think you are going to wheedle me into taking any action you might as well save your breath."

"We've come to you partly because we want your advice."

"All right." Beddows' voice sounded as though he was slightly reassured. "Advice costs nothing. Go ahead."

"Thanks." Feeling a trifle awkward standing there, John took a step forward and sat down on the floor as near as he could get to Beddows while remaining outside the pentacle. As C. B. followed his example, he began to give an account of all that had happened that day. When he had done, he went on:

"Now! One of the things we wanted to ask you, Mr.

Beddows, is can the Canon perform his ritual with the homunculus and Ellen anywhere, or will he have to bring them back to do the job to-morrow night in his own crypt?"

"He needn't bring them back, but he can't do it anywhere. The ceremony must be performed on an altar that has been properly dedicated to the Lord Satan."

"We feared as much. Are there many such altars in the South of France?"

"A certain number. There is at least one in every big city in the world. All over Europe they are scattered in the country parts too; mostly in ruined abbeys, old castles and such."

"Do you know the whereabouts of any of those on the Riviera?"

Beddows shook his head. "No; I've never attended a ceremony outside England."

After a moment John asked, "What do you really think of the Canon's prospects of getting Ellen out of prison?"

"It is difficult to say. To do so he has got to temporarily paralyse a system. That is a far more formidable undertaking than enforcing sleep on the members of an ordinary household. No one of average powers would even attempt it; but he is an Ipsissimus, and there are few things impossible to a Mage of that highest grade. There is, too, one thing in his favour. If he can succeed in bemusing the jailers into unlocking the right doors, he will have no difficulty with Ellen. He will have only to call her on the astral, and she will walk out."

"Yes; that is just what we fear. Can you suggest any means by which we might cause her to resist his will?"

"Only a White Magician who has greater power than Copely-Syle could cause her to do that."

"Do you know of one?"

"No. I've naturally kept clear of anyone I believed to be working on the Right Hand side."

Again John paused, then he said, "I take it from what you were telling us last night that Ellen's subservience to evil during the dark hours is not a part of her nature, but entirely due to the fact that you . . . you had her baptized into the Satanic faith?"

"That's so."

"If she were re-baptized into the Christian faith, would that destroy the influence that the Dark Powers have over her?"

"No. There is no point in hiding the truth. It was I who sold her to the Devil; so only I can redeem her."

"How would you do that?"

Beddows gave a harsh laugh. "I wouldn't! Is it likely? It would mean my abjuring Satan."

"But if you did? Say you abjured Satan here and now, on her behalf and on your own, would that take immediate effect? Would it result in her resisting when the Canon calls her to-night on the astral, and remaining in her cell?"

"Yes. The effect would be instantaneous. Of course, she would still be subject to hypnotic suggestion, like her jailers or anyone else, in normal circumstances in the future; but not to-night. Such an act would restore the powers of her Guardian Angel, who has been chained all these years. Once freed, he would give her everything he'd got, and throw an aura round her which would protect her from every harmful thought."

Beddows ceased speaking for a moment, then added suddenly in an aggressive voice, "But don't think what I've told you is going to get you anywhere. If you've come here to try to get me to abjure, you've backed the wrong horse. I've no intention of being struck dead by an apoplectic fit and frying for all Eternity."

"Is that what it would mean for you?"

"Yes. Hell is real! Don't you believe these modern parsons who are fools enough to tell their congregations otherwise. I know, because I've seen it. Copely-Syle showed it to me the night that he initiated me as a Neophyte of the Left Hand Path. And it is gaping wide with great tongues of flame for anyone like me—should I betray the Master."

"The mercy of God is infinite," said John quietly.

"Maybe," sneered Beddows. "But not till after one has paid the price for what one has taken at Satan's hands. God would leave me to burn for a thousand years before He even had a look at me. If you think I'd give a blank cheque of that kind to save Ellen you must be crazy."

John remained silent long enough for Beddows to cool down, then he said, "There is another thing we wanted to ask you about. Last night you told us that for a time you gave up your engineering studies on account of a personal attachment. Would you tell us about that?"

"Why? It has nothing whatever to do with this business of Copely-Syle and Ellen."

"I'm not so sure. I think it might have. Every major emotional experience in your life must have had some bearing on your present situation. Please tell us about it."

Beddows shrugged. "Very well. Since I've told you the rest of the story, I may as well fill in the gap. When I first came here as chauffeur old Mrs. Durnsford had a companion. She was a girl named Isobel—a frail, gentle little thing, but very beautiful and the sort that is too good for this world. The old girl made her life hell, but she had to grin and bear it. You see, she was a poor relation, with no other relatives to go to, and neither the training nor the stamina to take any other job; so she had no alternative to staying on here.

"When I had been here for a bit Mrs. Durnsford had the idea that I should teach Isobel to drive the car. She didn't want to, and I didn't want to teach her, as I thought it might result in my being given the sack; but it was an order. Things being like that, Isobel's progress was not very fast; so I had plenty of opportunity to get to know her. At first she was very shy, but gradually we got to confiding in one another. I found then that behind her timid manner lay a wonderful mind, filled with courage, unselfishness and an infallible understanding of all the things that really matter.

"She held that money, birth and position counted for nothing; that real happiness could be gained only by giving happiness to others; that God always provided for His children if they did the right thing; that one should never strive to pile up possessions, but only to make people kinder to one another; and that one should live from day to day, so that if death came unexpectedly one could face it with the certainty that one's heart would weigh no more in the scales of judgment than the feather of truth.

"I fell in love with her; and, although I have never understood why, she fell in love with me. When she had got the hang of driving the car sufficient for there to be no excuse to give her further lessons, we continued to meet, but in secret, at any odd times we could snatch. Naturally I had told her all about my engineering ambitions, but she wasn't in favour of that. Partly because it would have meant living in a town, but more, really, because I had frankly admitted that my object in taking it up was solely to make money out of it.

"She had money coming to her: not a lot, but enough. Under a trust Mrs. Durnsford enjoyed the income on condition that she gave Isobel a home until she was twenty-five. It could not be touched before that, but then the capital had to be handed over with no strings attached. We had eighteen months to go, but we were content to wait. Isobel wanted to start a small school for crippled and backward children. She would have given them the indoor lessons and I was to teach them gardening, carpentry, and a bit about the inside of cars, and generally run the place. That may sound very different from what I have made of my life, but I would have been far happier doing that. With those kiddies to look after there would have been more new interests every day than I get out of all my businesses: and no man could have been unhappy with Isobel for a wife."

Beddows sighed heavily. "But it was not to be. Before Isobel was twenty-four she fell ill. She was so frail that I think she must always have had it in her, but she caught a chill and soon afterwards T.B. developed. After a bit they sent her to Switzerland, and I was distraught. But I managed to see her alone before she left. We swore we would love one another always and, of course, we promised to write frequently.

"We did; and for the first few weeks I received her letters quite regular. They told me about the place, and the other patients; about the nice young doctor who was looking after her, and how she was sure she would be well enough to come home in time for Christmas. Then her letters grew more infrequent, and after two intervals of ten days they stopped altogether. If I'd been a town chap I suppose I would have telegraphed her to know what was wrong, but sending cables to foreign countries was away over the head of a young country feller like I was in those days. I put her silence down to the young doctor. You see, I'd never been able to convince myself that I was good enough for her; so I didn't even write and ask her to let me know if she had changed her mind about marrying me. I just let my misery have free reign, and decided to stop writing till I heard from her again.

"About three weeks went by like that; then one day, as Mrs. Durnsford was getting into the car, she told me quite casual that Isobel was dead. It was a dirty, wicked lie—may her soul rot! But I never found that out until years later; in fact not until after she was dead herself. She had no near relatives, and when she died her executors sold off the whole contents of the house as well as the place. I had my own furniture, and I didn't want any of hers; but I thought the shelves in the study would look a bit bare without some books, so I bought those at the sale. Naturally, the executors removed her private papers, but there was one lot they overlooked. I came on them soon after I moved in. They were with a pack of Tarot cards and a collection of witch's-brew recipes in what was left of a big old family Bible that had had its middle cut out to form a box. Among them was a score of letters from Isobel to me that I had never had.

"It was quite clear then what had happened. My post had always been delivered to the house with the rest of the letters before being brought across the yard to me by one of the maids. The old bitch must have seen a letter with Swiss stamps on addressed to me in Isobel's writing, steamed it open and read it. In our letters we naturally wrote of our love for one another and of our future plans. The thought of people being happy and making life better for a lot of crippled kids would have been poison to old Mother Durnsford. I bet she got no end of a kick out of sabotaging all our hopes. It would have been easy for her to intercept Isobel's letters—a few at first, then all of them later on. That's what she had done; and when she judged that she had got me really worried she both provided an explanation why I had not received any letters from Isobel for the past few weeks and gave me the knock out; because the inference was that for some time before her death Isobel had been too ill to write. Mother Durnsford had rounded the affair off nice and neatly the other end too. The envelope of Isobel's last letter was marked 'to await collection' and I saw from it that the old woman had written her saying that I'd gone away and left no address.

"Even that was not the full measure of her malice. Naturally, after I thought Isobel was dead I went all to pieces for a bit. But I was young and healthy, and next spring I started to tumble Hettie evenings in the barn. I've told you how she got in the family way with Ellen and spilled the beans about it. That must have given Mother Durnsford a fine old laugh. I didn't know it then, but she had learned from Isobel's letters how anxious I was to educate and improve myself. Nothing could have been more likely to scotch that than to tie me up to a brainless little working-class slut who was going to have a kid, and would probably go on producing them like rabbits.

"Well, it didn't work out that way. But she succeeded in robbing me of Isobel; and you are quite right in your idea that losing her altered my whole life. I still don't see, though, what that has to do with the Canon and Ellen."

John had listened to Beddows' love-story with intense interest, and now he asked, "Did you ever find out what happened to Isobel?"

"Yes. After I found those letters I had enquiries made. There had been a world war in between, but they succeeded in tracing her up. She did die, but not till nearly a year after I believed her dead; and ever since I learned that I've been tortured by the belief that she just let herself die of a broken heart."

"Say she had lived, Mr. Beddows, and you had found out sooner that she was still alive—would you have married her after your first wife died?"

"Of course I would."

"But you couldn't possibly have married a person as fine as she was, unless you had first forsworn the Devil. To have continued secretly as a Satanist would have robbed your marriage with her of all the genuine happiness you expected to derive from it."

"Yes; I see that," Beddows admitted slowly. "Still, love is the greatest protective force in existence. I think hers would have proved strong enough to shield me from all but loss of my worldly wealth. Anyhow, it's true that I should have had to abjure in order to put myself right with her; and for her sake I would have risked anything."

"You must have loved her very deeply."

"More than anything in this world or the next."

"Then you will be able to understand how I feel, Mr. Beddows, when I tell you that I love your daughter."

Beddows raised his eyebrows. "Is that so? You haven't known her very long, have you?"

"No; but in the hours we have spent together much more has happened than during an ordinary courtship. We are already engaged to be married."

For the first time a glint of humour showed in Beddows' brown eyes as he asked, "Am I to take it that you've come here to-night to ask my consent?"

"We should be glad to have your blessing," John answered seriously. "But first we need the help that only you can give. And you know how desperately we need it."

"I'm sorry. Indeed I am. But it's no good harking back to that."

"Mr. Beddows, you have just said that you loved Isobel more than anything in this world or the next. That implies that you still love her spirit. If it were here in this room to-night—as it well may be—and could speak to you, what would it say? You know as well as I do that it would beg you to become again the person it knew and loved. It would urge you to defy Satan in order to save your daughter and make possible the happiness of another pair of lovers."

"Yes," Beddows muttered. "That's what it would say."

"Then if you still love her, do this for her sake."

The eyes of the man in the pentacle suddenly blazed, and he

shouted, "Damn you, stop torturing me! I can't! I won't! Get to hell out of here!"

After his long and skilful guidance of their talk, John had felt that he was almost on the verge of victory; so Beddows' outburst came as a bitter disappointment. For a moment he remained silent, searching his mind for some last card that might yet win him over. To his distress he could think of nothing approaching the potency of the arguments he had already used; so he could only fall back upon what he felt to be a frail piece of reasoning, unlikely to alter a mind so evidently fixed by terror in its determination. Nevertheless he threw out the suggestion with no lessening of persistence.

"You were saying a little while ago that if Isobel had still been alive and you had abjured to put yourself right with her, you thought that her love would have protected you from all but the loss of your worldly wealth. Surely, although she is now a spirit, her love would continue to protect you?"

"No." Beddows' voice was firm. "For all I know, during those last months she may have believed that I had deliberately jilted her, and died hating me. I can't afford to chance that. There is one thing and one thing only that could protect me. That is to cheat Satan by getting back the Pact I signed with him."

John's muscles tensed. "D'you know where it is?"

"Copely-Syle has it."

"I naturally supposed so; but he wouldn't carry it about on him. I mean, do you know where he keeps it?"

"I don't know for certain, but I can give a good guess. It is a hundred to one that after offering it up he would place a document of that kind under the Satanic altar in his crypt."

"Then . . ." John hesitated.

Beddows flung out his hands in a violent gesture of protest. "No, no! Don't think of it. Forget what I said! You're young and healthy! You should have many years of happiness ahead of you. There are plenty of other girls in the world besides Ellen. You would be crazy to try to raise that altar. You would be blasted where you stood. If you did survive you would be found as a gibbering idiot in the morning. I wouldn't let my worst enemy attempt to get that Pact."

Slowly John stood up. "If I do get it, and give it to you to destroy, will you swear to me by your love for Isobel immediately to abjure Satan?"

A shudder ran through Beddows. With eyes distended by horror he stared up at John. For a moment he was silent, then he gasped, "All right! I swear. But I warned you: I warned you! You'll be going to your death."

CHAPTER XXII

THE DEVIL'S ALTAR

THE palms of John's hands were already sweating. His memory of the impotence and fear he had felt when in the crypt twenty-four hours earlier was still vivid in his mind; yet he had made his decision the moment Beddows had spoken of the Pact as the price on which he must insist for his co-operation.

John had come there determined to secure that co-operation somehow; not only because it could bring to nought the Canon's attempt to get Christina out of prison during the night that was already upon them, but also because on that depended her whole future. To save her from an abominable death at the hands of Copely-Syle was the overriding consideration for the moment, but even success in that could later prove a barren victory if she were to continue to be the nightly victim of evil cravings which, now she was out in the world, must soon lead her to become cynically immoral, decadent, unscrupulous and, perhaps, criminal. Only her father could save her from that by ratting on his bargain with the Devil. Since his price for that was the Pact, he must have it.

The mere idea of going into the crypt again filled John with terrifying qualms. He felt that to argue the matter further could only weaken his resolution, and that in immediate action lay his sole hope of maintaining it long enough to force himself to enter that Satanic stronghold when he got there; so he said abruptly:

"Perhaps you are right, and I'll be dead in an hour. If not, I'll be back here." Then he turned towards the door.

"Hi!" C. B. called after him. "If we've got to do this thing, we had better take some weapons with us."

"You are not in this!" John's voice was made surly by fear. "This is my show. You stay where you are."

"Is it likely?" C. B. grunted. "I've never liked anything less in my life; but how could I ever face your mother if I let you go alone?" Turning to Beddows, he said, "These cups in the valleys of the pentacle have Holy water in them, haven't they? Where's the rest of it?"

Reaching behind him into the tea-chest, Beddows produced a quart bottle half full. As he handed it over, C. B. asked:

"Have you any spare horse-shoes?"

"No. I'm afraid not."

"That's a pity," muttered C. B. "And I daren't deprive you of any of your defences, in case something gets at you while we are away. I suppose you haven't got a crucifix in the house?"

Beddows shook his head. "Of course not! I could hardly bear to look at one, and it would burn me if I touched it. As it was I had to be mighty careful when I poured the Holy water out: if I had spilt any on my hands it would have scalded me."

John was already at the door. Without another glance at Beddows, C. B. joined him and they hurried downstairs. When they reached the hall John made for the baize door, but C. B. called after him:

"Hold your horses! We've got to forge a few astral weapons before we leave here. I wish to goodness we had a little time to make proper preparations. We ought to have necklaces of garlic and asafoetida grass, not to mention purifying ourselves with the smoke of sweet herbs and putting on clean underclothes. Still, we must do the best we can."

As he spoke he led the way through the breakfast room to the pantry, and began to pull open its rows of drawers one after another. In one he found string and scissors, in another a bundle of firewood. Handing them to John, he said:

"Here, take these. Use four of the sticks to make two crosses. Bind them together with the string and attach long loops to them so that we can hang them round our necks."

In a corner of the room were stacked several crates. The top ones contained quart bottles of beer, but underneath he

333

found one holding small bottles of lemonade. Taking two of them, he opened and emptied them at the sink, then re-filled them with Holy water and corked them roughly with tight wads of screwed-up newspaper.

"Put this in your pocket," he said, handing one of them to John. "And don't use it until I tell you to." The other he pocketed himself.

Picking up a broom that stood behind the door, he wrenched out the long handle, then laid it over a Windsor chair and snapped it in two pieces about one third of the way up. With another length of string he lashed them together, so that they formed a large cross to carry in the hand. After a quick look round, he went to the further door that led to the rear quarters of the house, opened it and said:

"I am going to hunt round for something with which to prise up the altar slab. In the meantime pull down some curtains, soak them with water and carry them out to the car. Unbolt the front door and go out by that. It will save time."

John did as he was told, and he was still piling the sopping mess on the floor in front of the back seat when C. B. rejoined him, carrying a steel case-opener. As he held it out, he remarked, "This is not much bigger than my own jemmy, but the best thing I could find. You take it, and I'll carry the cross."

As they got in the car and he started up the engine, John said, "I take it the wet things are for throwing down the furnace chimney?"

"Yes. We've been lucky here in finding that the Jutsons go to bed early; but it's only just eleven o'clock; so that coloured servant of the Canon's may still be up. I had thought of going to the front door and knocking him out as soon as he answered it. We would be almost sure of having the free run of the place then, as it is most unlikely that anyone who performs the Canon's tricks would have any other servants living in; but the door to the crypt is of iron and has a Chubb lock. As Copely-Syle keeps the key to it on him we wouldn't be able to get in that way; so I think we would do better to ignore the Egyptian and go straight in down the chimney."

A few minutes' drive brought them to The Priory. Pulling up a hundred yards short of it, John parked the car under the trees that overhung the road, and they got out. A light wind had risen, keeping off more rain, but the sky was four-fifths scudding cloud and it was only when the moon broke through at intervals for a minute or two that there was enough light for them to see their way at all clearly.

Carrying the sopping curtains between them, they broke through the hedge into the coppice and approached the house by the route that John had taken the previous night. On reaching the crypt they dumped their burden and made a brief reconnaissance round the house and back. No light showed in any of the windows; so it looked as if the Egyptian had gone to bed. C. B., as the taller, gave John a leg up, passed him the bundle of curtains, and scrambled on to the roof after him. In single file they crossed it to the chimney.

"Now," said C. B. in a low voice, "I needn't stress the fact that we are going into great danger. We must kneel down and pray."

Side by side they went down on their knees, and remained so in silence for a few minutes. As they got up, C. B. murmured, "I wish I could remember the Twenty-third Psalm. It is said to be exceptionally potent as a protection against demons. Do you recall how it goes?"

John shook his head. "I think it is the one that has in it 'though I walk through the valley of the shadow of death, I will fear no evil'; but I can't say for certain."

"Then we had better stick to the Lord's Prayer. Keep on repeating it to yourself; and if anything nasty comes at you cry aloud, 'In the name of Jesus Christ I defy thee, Satan.'"

John dropped the curtains down the wide chimney mouth. As they fell on the furnace at its bottom with a faint thud, he made to follow them; but C. B. pushed him firmly aside. "No, John. I am carrying the cross; so you must let me be the leader of this party. What is more, if at any time I tell you to get out, you will *get out*, and not stop to argue about it. By doing so you will not only save yourself, but will be able to bring help, with at least some chance of saving me later. Is that clear?"

As John nodded, C. B. swung his long legs over the chimney lip, found the first rungs inside and disappeared down it. Dropping the last few feet, he landed on the wet curtains. Beneath them the coke made a crunching sound, but the fire was dull and he scarcely felt its heat as he jumped off it.

The crypt was in darkness. Holding the cross in his left hand, he pulled his torch from his pocket with his right and switched it on. The instant he could see his way, he ran up the steps that led to the iron door and brushed down all the switches beside it, flooding the central aisle of the crypt with light. Pushing the torch back in his pocket he turned, planted his back firmly against the door, and only then let his glance rove round the vaulted chamber.

There was less change in it than he had expected from what Inspector Fuller had implied. The curtains at the far end, embroidered with the Goat of Mendes and the Woman with Seven Breasts, were gone; so were the sorcerer's robes, the altar cloth, the black candle, and the broken crucifix with the bat nailed upside down on it: but the sword, the chalice and the book still reposed upon the altar slab, looking not inappropriate in the rôle of harmless ornaments. The skeleton still dangled grotesquely from its wire and the mummy-case lay undisturbed beneath the nearest table; but both were the sort of exhibits that might be found in the museum-workshop of any amateur scientist. That also applied to the astrolabe, the six out of the seven great glass jars that had contained the homunculi, and the bottles, measures, balances and retorts that loaded the four long refectory tables.

One sweeping glance was enough for C. B. to take that much in, and he had hardly had time to register it before John thumped down on the furnace, sprang off it and pulled the now steaming curtains after him. Neither had the least intention of staying there one moment longer than they had to, and both simultaneously started forward towards the altar. They had taken only two steps when a cock crowed.

The cock's raucous challenge, seeming unnaturally loud

as it echoed from the stone arches overhead, sounded like the voice of doom. The two men halted in their tracks. The blood rushed to their hearts. Fearfully they jerked white faces round towards the left-hand aisle and the shadowy tier of cages behind the row of pillars, from which the crowing came.

There was nothing really terrifying about the sound itself—it was hearing it so unexpectedly in those surroundings. They had forgotten that although, according to the inspector's account, the Canon had disposed of all his maimed animals, he had not removed the chickens, doves and other fowl which he used for sacrifices. In the darkness they had all been silently sleeping, till the sudden switching on of the lights had aroused them to chirp and flutter in a false dawn.

As realization dawned upon the two intruders, that this was no demon giving tongue in the likeness of a bird, they let go their breath and breathed again; but only for a moment. Something moved swiftly behind one of the pillars. Both of them glimpsed the quick, furtive jump of a shadowy body, but neither could have said what it was. Instead of advancing further, they remained there, staring apprehensively at the base of the pillar behind which it had disappeared.

Before they could make up their minds to leave it un-accounted for in their rear, their attention was distracted to the roof. A faint squeaking sounded up in the shadows above the row of lights. There was a sudden movement up there too, then the squeaking ceased.

"Come on!" said John. "We're wasting time."

As he spoke the thing behind the pillar moved again. It sprang out into the open, a yard ahead of them, right in their path. Their gasps merged into sighs of relief. It was an obscene and ugly creature, but appeared to be no more than an exceptionally large toad.

John took another step forward. His foot had not reached the ground when something hurtled at his head from above, like a small dive-bomber. He gave a cry of fear and ducked, but caught a swift sight of the thing as it streaked downward between his upturned face and the nearest light. As he did so he upbraided himself for showing such funk, when the

337

squeaking should have told him that the creatures above the lights were only bats.

Next moment he had cause for real terror. The toad had been watching him with bright, jewel-like, unwinking eyes. Suddenly its mouth opened and it laughed.

That deep unholy chuckle, coming from a reptile, sent chills rippling down both their spines. Instinctively they backed towards the steps.

"We've got to go forward," said C. B. hoarsely. "If we lose our nerve now, we're finished."

In two paces they recovered their lost ground; but the toad held his. Then an extraordinary thing happened. Its outline blurred and it crepitated until it turned into a yellowish-green ball of gaseous matter. An instant later there were two toads squatting where there had been only one before.

With unbelieving eyes they stared at the twin creatures begotten so mysteriously. As they did so they heard a swish in the air above them, and this time two bats came hurtling at their heads. Both of them ducked; the two toads laughed, wobbled into whirling balls and became four.

It was at that moment that the lights went out.

For a few seconds they were blinded by the darkness; then they became conscious of a glow behind them. Swinging round they saw that the door had opened, and the Canon's coloured servant stood framed in it.

It occurred to them only then that he must have a key to the door in order to keep the furnace going and feed the birds. What had brought him on the scene they could not guess. They had been in the crypt for about two minutes. It was possible that he had heard the cock crow, or seen a line of light below the door, or simply come to stoke the furnace up for the night, or perhaps been summoned as the guardian of the place by some occult signal. They could only be certain that it was he who had turned out the lights; for, as they swung upon him, he still had his dark hand on the two lowest switches.

After the unnerving episode of the toad a human enemy held few terrors for the nocturnal intruders. The Egyptian was as tall as C. B. and the flowing white burnous which concealed

338

his limbs gave him the appearance of being considerably more powerful; yet without a second's hesitation John tensed his muscles to spring up the steps towards him.

C. B. did likewise, then swiftly averted his gaze and shouted a warning. "Don't look at his eyes! Don't look at his eyes!"

It came too late. John was already staring straight into the coloured man's white-rimmed eyeballs. The reason why he had switched out the lights instantly became clear. It was to prevent them dazzling him and to enable his eyes to become luminous in the semi-darkness. In his coffee-coloured face they now showed up brilliantly. They held John's gaze so that he could not draw it away, and seemed to increase in size with extraordinary swiftness. To his fury and amazement his body made a futile jerk, but he was incapable of launching himself up the stone stairway. The eyes that bored into his grew bigger and bigger, until they merged and became one great blinding circle of light. An intolerable pain shot through his head, his knees gave under him and he crumpled up on the lowest step

The Egyptian had overcome him in a matter of seconds by catching his glance as he was about to jump. But C. B., after one glimpse of the baleful light in the coloured man's eyes, had torn his own away. Riveting his gaze on the stone flags of the floor for a moment, he concentrated both his mental and physical strength. Swiftly, he muttered a short prayer; then, without raising his glance, he hurled himself at the Egyptian's legs.

John had at that second collapsed. Having dealt successfully with one intruder, the Egyptian turned on the other. But he had time only to kick C. B. in the chest. The force of the kick would have broken C. B.'s breast-bone had the man been wearing boots, but he had on only soft leather sandals. The jolt was no worse than a punch from a pugilist wearing boxing gloves; yet that was bad enough. It shook C. B. sufficiently to make him gasp and boggle his tackle. Instead of getting the man beneath the knees, he succeeded in grasping him only by one ankle. Tightening his grip, he drew a deep breath, then threw his weight backward.

The Egyptian's foot flew from beneath him and he crashed to the ground. Without losing a second he kicked out with his other foot. It caught C. B. on the head and sent him reeling down the steps. But John, now freed for a few seconds from the paralysing effect of that hypnotic stare, was on his feet again. He still grasped in his right hand the steel case-opener that he had been holding when he came down the chimney. Rushing up the steps he beat wildly at the coloured man with it just as he was struggling back on to his feet. One blow caught him on the shoulder, and he let out a yell of pain. The second landed on his forehead. Without another sound, he went down like a pole-axed bullock.

C. B. came panting up the steps into the doorway. Seeing the look on John's face he muttered, "Don't worry! These Arab types have heads like cannon balls. You haven't killed him. But he'll be out long enough not to bother us again. Help me to get him back into the passage."

Grasping the unconscious man by the legs and shoulders, they pulled him from the stairhead and clear of the door; then for a second they stood in it side by side, staring down into the crypt.

It was lit now only by the glow coming from the passage behind them, and was no longer silent. From all sides of it came weird discordant noises, as though it was filled with horrible, half-human, half-animal life. A lunatic-like chuckling mingled with the bleating of a goat. The cock was crowing again, the bats squeaked as though they were now legion, a pig grunted, and as a background to it all there came a low rhythmical throbbing of Voodoo drums.

"We've got to go in at the charge this time," said C. B. urgently. "The longer we wait, the worse it will get. They can't harm us as long as we remain defiant and trust in the Lord. To tackle the Gippy I had to drop my cross at the bottom of the steps. I've got to get that; so you must give me a moment to snatch it up. I'm going in now. As I grab it I'll give a shout. Switch on all the lights, then come hell for leather after me."

As he finished speaking, he ran down the steps. Stooping, he seized the broomstick cross, lifted it on high and cried,

"Oh Lord be with us!" The lights flashed on. John leapt down beside him. Together they dashed forward.

They had fifty feet to cover. In the brief space that the lights had been out the huge toads had multiplied exceedingly. A company of them, dozens strong, now barred the way between the tables and either side of them. From the roof a cloud of bats streaked down.

The first rush carried them fifteen paces. They were half-way along the crypt, but there they lost momentum and their footsteps faltered. The bats thudded into their bodies and dashed themselves against their faces. The toads spat venom which turned into clouds of greenish vapour. It had the awful stench of rotting corpses. In a few moments it had formed a thick barrier through which the altar could no longer be seen. The poisonous fumes it carried stung their eyes and made their throats feel raw.

"Satan, I defy thee!" cried C. B. "Satan, I defy thee!" And John chimed in, "Oh God, destroy our enemies! Dear God, destroy our enemies!"

Suddenly the babble of sound subsided to a muted, angry muttering. The clouds of poisonous vapour dissolved. The bats flopped helplessly upon the floor, and the toads wilted into weak, flabby, grovelling creatures.

Again C. B. and John ran forward; but a new terror arose to halt them. The lights flickered twice, then dimmed almost to extinction. Ahead of them the floor began to glow with a dull, reddish light, and to heave like the swell of an oily pond. It seemed to be imbued with some weird malevolent life of its own. With the next steps they took they could feel its heat through the soles of their shoes, and wisps of smoke curled up from the leather. The flagstones had become red hot, and those in front of the altar were molten.

For a moment they remained half crouching, shoulder to shoulder, their eyes nearly dazzled by the glare that came from the shimmering crucible that threatened to engulf them if they advanced another few steps. A blast of intense heat hit against their hands and faces; so that in another few seconds the sweat was streaming from them.

"Have faith, John! Have faith!" whispered C. B. "If we trust in the Lord we can walk unharmed through this fiery furnace. We must go forward boldly."

Simultaneously they began to recite the Lord's Prayer and walk steadily towards the altar. Their shoes ceased to char and, although the stones about them continued to appear white hot, they no longer felt any heat on the soles of their feet.

As they reached the altar the glow of the stones faded. Only then did they become aware that some awful thing was materializing on the altar itself. The lights remained dimmed and out of the shadows immediately in front of them emerged a monster that made them blanch with fear. It had a woman's face set in the middle of a round, fleshy body. The face was beautiful, yet incredibly evil: the body was covered with filthy suppurating sores and from it eight writhing, octopus-like tentacles reached out to seize them.

Terror again gripped them as they sprang back to evade the groping tentacles. Then, recovering himself, C. B. pulled the small bottle of Holy water from his pocket. Holding the cross aloft in his left hand, he tore the paper stopper from the bottle with his teeth and flung its contents at the demon.

The red lips of the woman's mouth opened and emitted a piercing scream. The tentacles threshed wildly. The leprous body suddenly exploded in a great puff of magenta-coloured smoke. Its stench was so nauseating that both C. B. and John were seized with a fit of retching. When they could raise their heads again no trace of the awful thing remained upon the altar. They had just time for that one glance; then the dim lights flickered and went out, plunging that end of the crypt in total darkness.

Instantly they became aware that with the darkness had come a cessation of all sound. The Voodoo drums, the horrid laughter, the snarling pandemonium made by the denizens of the Pit had given way, as at an order, to utter silence. There was something more frightening about the eerie stillness than the hideous noises that had preceded it. Quite suddenly, too, the crypt had become as cold as the interior of an ice-house.

With every nerve alert they waited, as though a paralysis

had descended on them, riveting them there unable to move hand or foot. Then out of the blackness behind them came a clear silvery voice. It said:

"I have always admired courage. You have proved yours; so I will give you that for which you came. You no longer have cause to be afraid. I have here the Pact which Henry Beddows signed with my servant Copely-Syle. Turn round and you shall receive it as a free gift from me."

"Don't look, John!" gasped C. B. "For God's sake don't turn round! Shut your ears to everything you hear and prise up the altar slab."

As he spoke he lugged his torch from his pocket and shone it on the flat piece of stone. At that moment the voice came again, low and persuasive:

"You foolish men. The Pact is not there. I have it here in my hand. For those who are not prepared to serve me willingly I have no use; and no one has ever accused me of meanness. I am not one to hold a man to his word when he regrets having given it. You may take the Pact back to Beddows and tell him that I release him from his bond."

Ignoring the honeyed words, John forced the edge of the case-opener under the slab and heaved upon it. The four-foot-long stone lifted a little. Another heave and a gap of a few inches showed below it. John dropped the heavy jemmy, got the fingers of both hands under the slab and prepared to exert all his strength in lifting it back like the lid of a great box.

Again the voice came, but its tone had changed. It now rang out like the clash of cold steel and was vibrant with menace.

"Stop!" it commanded. "I have allowed you to trifle with me long enough. I give you two minutes to leave my temple. Remain and I will make Hell gape open to receive you."

With the sweat pouring from him in spite of the icy cold, John strove with all his might to raise the stone. It would not budge, and C. B. could not help him as he was holding the torch with one hand and the cross in the other.

Without warning, there came an ear-splitting crash of

343

thunder. The floor of the crypt heaved; its walls rocked. Throwing the arm with the hand that held the torch round John's shoulders, C. B. raised the cross high above both their heads and cried:

"Oh Lord, defend us!"

There was a blinding flash. A fork of light streaked down through the roof striking, not them, but the centre of the altar slab, shattering it into a hundred fragments. God had intervened. Instantly a deafening din broke out. Cries, screams, moans and groans sounded from every direction, as the minions of Hell fled back into the dark underworld.

Still dazed, C. B. shone his torch down into the cavity now gaping where the altar stone had been. Among its fragments reposed a small, brass-bound coffer. John pulled it out, snatched up his jemmy from the floor, and broke it open. It contained about twenty pieces of parchment. On all of them were several lines of writing in dried blood. Hastily John shuffled through them until he came on one signed 'Henry Beddows'; then, with a sigh of relief, he crammed the whole lot into his pocket.

In the frightful stress and excitement of the last few moments they had scarcely been conscious that all the lights had come on again, or that big drops of rain were splashing upon them. Turning now, they saw that the crypt was as peaceful and empty as when they had entered it; then, on glancing up, they noticed that a three-foot-wide hole had been torn in the roof above the altar by the thunderbolt that had smashed it.

"Let's get out this way," C. B. suggested, and, clambering up on the altar, they wriggled through the hole.

Outside the rain was sheeting down, and by the time they reached the car their outer garments were almost soaked through with it; but for the time being they could think of nothing except their delivery from the awful perils they had so recently encountered.

The car swiftly covered the mile back to The Grange. As they got out C. B. looked at his watch and said, "How long do you think we have been?"

"Goodness knows," John muttered. "Two hours—three perhaps."

"No. It is now nineteen minutes past eleven. Allowing for going and coming back, and our reconnaissance round the house before we went in, we could not have been in the crypt much more than seven minutes."

Two minutes later they were upstairs with Beddows. Until John showed him the Pact he could not believe that they had got it. At first he was overcome by astonishment at their success; then, as he looked at their haggard faces and realized what they had been through, his gratitude was pathetic.

C. B. took the rest of the papers from John with the remark, "I'll turn these in to Scotland Yard. They may be of use in tracing up some of the Canon's associates; although I doubt if any of them could be persuaded to give evidence against him. Still, the people who signed these other Pacts will be informed that they have now been freed."

He then stepped into the pentacle, removed the contents of the tea-chest, turned it upside down, leant his broomstick cross upright against its back and set two of the unlit candles upon it, thus transforming it into a temporary altar. Having lit the candles, he said to Beddows:

"Now, take the Pact in your right hand and burn it; then say these words after me."

Beddows took the Pact, lit one corner of it, and repeated sentence by sentence as C. B. pronounced the abjuration:

"By this act I, Henry Beddows, renounce Satan and all his Works, now and for evermore, both on my own behalf and on that of my daughter Ellen. I have sinned grievously; but, trusting in the Divine Mercy promised by our Lord Jesus Christ to sinners who repent, I beg to be received back into God's grace. In the name of Christ I now call upon the Archangel Michael and his Host to protect my daughter, Ellen, this night; to guard her from all harmful thoughts and to deliver her from evil. Blessed be the names of the Father, the Son and the Holy Ghost for evermore. Amen."

John and C. B. then knelt down beside Beddows and

prayed, giving thanks for the courage they had been granted and their safe delivery from the Valley of the Shadow.

When they all stood up, and Beddows stepped from the pentacle, they saw with amazement that an extraordinary change had taken place in his appearance. He seemed to have aged twenty years. His broad shoulders slumped, his hair and the bristles of his beard had turned white; and he had the look of an old man. Yet, after thanking his rescuers, he said firmly:

"I shall leave for the South of France first thing in the morning. Ellen should be safe now; but I mean to hunt Copely-Syle down, and see to it that he goes to the Hell to which he has led so many others."

C. B. endeavoured to hide his surprise at the transformation in Beddows, which was evidently the first sign of the payment he would now have to make for the twenty-one years of favour he had secured by unholy means: then he said to John, "The outside chance of the Canon's coming back tomorrow is taken care of by the police. They will pinch him if he lands illegally in the marshes. There is nothing more we can do here now; so we'll go South too."

Glancing again at Beddows, he added, "I think it would be best if you accompanied us back to Colchester, as we must make a very early start. They will find you a room at the Red Lion, then we can all drive up to London together."

"That suits me," Beddows agreed. "But I'll have to get into some clothes and pack a bag. I am feeling very weak, too, from my long semi-fast. While I am getting dressed perhaps you would go down to the larder. Jutson asked me through the door this morning if I was all right, as he had seen that somebody had been up here; but he doesn't know why I locked myself in, or anything about this business. He is very well paid to ask no questions; but all the same, the less he knows, the better; so I'd rather not have him routed out. It would save time, too, if you'd open up a tin or two for me yourselves, and I'll leave a note for him before we go. You will find quite a selection of tinned stuff down there, but anything will do."

Together they descended to the first floor. Beddows went

into his bedroom and the others continued on downstairs to prepare a picnic meal. A quarter of an hour later, when he joined them in the dining-room, they had ready a spread of sardines, cold ham and tinned peaches. After their ordeal C. B. and John also felt hungry; so they sat down with him and, while he ate ravenously, kept him company.

Soon after midnight they left the table and went out to the car. As Beddows stowed his suitcase in the back he said, "I've never done the Government down more than I've had to; but this is a case in which I have no scruples. It may need big money to finance bringing Copely-Syle to book; so we can't afford to observe currency restrictions. Fortunately, I've always kept a tidy sum in my wall-safe against an emergency; so I was able to pack the best part of three thousand pounds in fivers into a couple of pairs of shoes."

C. B. smiled a little wryly. "I'd rather you hadn't told me that; but since you have, how about it if the emigration authorities search your baggage?"

Beddows smiled. "They might if I went to and fro regular. But the odds are all on my getting away with it once."

At twenty-five past twelve the night porter let them into the Red Lion. He booked Beddows a room on the same floor as the others, and entered an order from C. B. to call them all at a quarter to five. Before they went upstairs C. B. telephoned his office and asked the night duty officer to ring Northolt, and use all the pull he could to secure three seats on the plane leaving for Nice at 7.16. Then they went up to their rooms, got the worst of the dirt off themselves with a quick wash, and, mentally exhausted from the strain of the past few hours, fell asleep as soon as their heads touched their pillows.

When C. B.'s bedside telephone rang, he roused out of a deep sleep and picked up the receiver. It was the night porter, who said:

"Your call, sir. It's a quarter to five and about half an hour ago I took a telephone message from your office. It was to report a telegram which reads '*Special stop Despatched from Police Headquarters Nice at nought hours twenty stop Christina removed*

*from prison without authority twenty-three hours fifteen stop Has
since disappeared without trace stop Signed Malouet.'*"

"Thank you," said C. B. quietly; but as he hung up, his
face was grim. In a few minutes he would have to break it to
John that, although they had braved such fearful perils during
the earlier part of the night they had, after all, failed to save
Christina. Beddows had abjured Satan at a little after half-past
eleven. By about eighteen minutes the Canon had beaten them
to it again.

CHAPTER XXIII

THE CAVE OF THE BATS

OVER the cups of coffee that the night porter had made for them and on the long drive to the airport, John and his two companions spoke little. After learning the contents of Malouet's telegram they could only hope that by the time they got to Nice the police would have succeeded in tracing the vanished prisoner: in the meantime all speculation on their chances of rescuing Christina was futile.

At Northolt a young man from C. B.'s office met them to take over his car, and told him that only by luck had it been possible to get three passages for Nice by the first plane that morning. The Riviera season was still at its height and the aircraft booked to capacity; but one travel agency had rung up the previous afternoon to charter a special plane for ten; so B.E.A. had decided to put an additional Viking on the run, which would carry Colonel Verney's party. C. B. then asked him to send a telegram to Molly, to let her know that they were on the plane and ask her to meet them at Nice.

The regular plane left on scheduled time, but there was some delay in its relief getting off, as it was held for two of the party of ten who, it transpired, were motoring down from Scotland. The others all appeared to know one another and were all middle-aged or elderly people. Their clothes and hand baggage suggested that they were all very well off, which was borne out by a remark that John heard exchanged between two of the three women in the party, to the effect that they had decided to make the trip at the last moment only to attend a wedding.

While in the waiting-room he had ample time to study their fellow passengers, but his thoughts being otherwise occupied he took little notice of them, except to remark that they seemed an exceptionally ugly lot. He reminded himself then that most fellow travellers seen at airports, railway stations and boarding liners appeared unprepossessing until one got to know them; yet his impression was strengthened on the arrival of the couple who had been motoring through the night from Scotland. The man was very tall and so lean that his skin seemed stretched over the bones of his face to a degree that made it almost corpse-like, while the woman had the most disconcerting squint that he ever remembered seeing.

In spite of the delay, which held up the take-off until twenty minutes to eight, the flying conditions were so good that the aircraft made up most of the lost time, and they came down in the brilliant sunshine of Nice at ten past one. Molly and Malouet were both there to meet them and, after Beddows had been introduced, the elderly ex-inspector said:

"I regret to say I have no news for you; but one gets as good a lunch at the airport restaurant here as anywhere in Nice; so I have booked a table. While we eat I will tell you all that is known of the most extraordinary occurrence last night."

The meal justified his recommendation, but John scarcely noticed the wonderful selection of *hors-d'œuvres*, or the point at which he passed from eating *Loup flambé* to *Escalope de Veau Milanese*—he was too intent on Malouet's report and the discussion that followed.

Apparently getting Christina out of prison had proved a much easier matter for the Canon than her friends had supposed would be the case, as he had found it necessary to exert his occult powers on only one person.

Three nights before, a murder had occurred in Nice. At a *bistrot* in the old part of the town a sailor had been mortally wounded by a knife-thrust during a brawl in which several men were concerned. There was some doubt which of two men had delivered the fatal stab, and the *patron* of the place declared that a girl called Marie Courcelle must know the truth, because the quarrel had been over her and she had been within an arm's length of the victim when the stabbing took place. The two suspects were Marie's lover and her brother, and both were under arrest, but she, evidently reluctant to give evidence against either, had promptly disappeared. However, the police had picked her up the previous morning in Marseilles, taken her into custody as a material witness, brought her back to Nice in the afternoon and lodged her in the women's prison which also held Christina.

In accordance with French police practice, the *Juge d'Instruction* had ordered a re-enactment of the affair at the scene of the crime with all the principal participants present; and that no time might be lost he had ordered it for that evening at approximately the same hour as the stabbing had taken place two evenings earlier. It was at this point that the Canon must have entered the game.

The assumption was that he had learnt of the affair when, on his arrival, he had discussed ways and means with the de Grasses and had decided to make use of the *Juge d'Instruction*. In any case, for some reason which this examining magistrate was afterwards utterly unable to explain, he had written Christina's name instead of Marie's on the form authorizing the release of prisoners under guard for questioning. A Black Maria had picked up the two men then called for Christina. The head wardress on duty knew nothing of the enquiry the magistrate was conducting and had acted on the instruction to hand over Christina, simply assuming that she was required for questioning about her own case at the *Préfecture*.

On the arrival of the Black Maria at the *bistrot* the mistake had at once become apparent. The magistrate, still presumably under the influence of the Canon, had then decided that the Black Maria should remain outside for the time being with the two men in it, while Christina was sent back to prison in a taxi and Marie brought there instead. A single *gendarme* had, quite reasonably, been considered an adequate escort for one young woman, and as a taxi driver, who had been having a drink at the *bistrot* when it was temporarily cleared by the police, was still outside among the little crowd that had collected they set off in his cab.

In the light of what had then occurred it seemed certain that the taxi driver was one of de Grasse's people, and had been deliberately planted in the *bistrot*. After driving a few hundred yards he had turned into a dark alley-way, pulled up and opened the door of his cab. He had told the *gendarme* that he had stopped only to slip into his lodgings to pick up the thermos of hot coffee his wife would have ready for him for his night's work. While he was talking, another man opened the other door of the cab and, as the *gendarme* turned, squirted a water pistol in his eyes. The driver had then hit him on the back of the head, rendering him unconscious. He had come round to find himself bound, gagged and face down among some bushes. Later he had recovered sufficiently to squirm his way on to a path near the gate of a private garden, and to attract the attention of a passer-by. He had been dumped in the grounds of a villa on the road to Villefranche and he naturally had no idea what had become of the taxi or Christina.

When Malouet had finished his report, C. B. asked, "How about Upson's seaplane? Is it known where he landed the Canon?"

"We think so;" Malouet pulled at his grey moustache; "but we cannot be absolutely certain. Last night there was a strange occurrence out at the great reservoir from which Nice draws her water supply. It is situated some miles inland from the city, up a broad valley in which few people live, other than scattered market-garden cultivators. Soon after dark a car drove up to the quarters of the Superintendent. The men who work there had gone for the day; so he was alone except for his wife and son and the night watchman, who has a small office in the building. Four armed men got out of the car, entered the place, herded its inmates into the boiler-room and kept them there for three-quarters of an hour. There was no attempt at robbery and no damage done, other than the disconnecting of the telephone.

"When the intruders had gone the Superintendent reported this apparently pointless hold-up to the police. They could offer no theory to account for it then; but further enquiries in the neighbourhood this morning elicited the information that a seaplane was seen to come down on the reservoir about an hour after sunset. It would not have been visible from any considerable distance, but several people saw it land, and take off again about twenty minutes later. A woman living nearby states that a covered lorry with powerful headlights had been stationary on the road alongside the reservoir for some time before the plane came down. Such a large sheet of water would, of course, be easy to pick up as long as there was any light at all; so the headlights near it were probably used not only to help guide it in, but also as a signal to the pilot that all preparations had been made for his landing. Evidently, too, the men who held up the Superintendent and night watchman did so to ensure that they should know nothing of this illegal proceeding until after it had been completed; so they would be unable to interfere or communicate with the police."

"I take it the police have not succeeded in tracing the lorry?" C. B. asked.

Malouet made a negative gesture. "One could hardly expect them to. Its presence there was not reported till this morning, and the description given of it was only of the vaguest."

"Then the Canon has got away with the game again," John commented bitterly. "It is a hundred to one on that having been Upson's seaplane. And how darned clever of them to have planned the timing of the job so well. By delaying his departure till the afternoon, Copely-Syle was able to fly practically straight in to Nice, yet give Upson the benefit of last light for crossing the mountains. He must have worked fast, though, to have pulled that one over the *Juge d'Instruction* so soon after his arrival."

C. B. shrugged. "Two and a half hours should have been ample if the de Grasses had the job already planned and everything prepared for him. Then there is always the possibility that it proved unnecessary to resort to a magical operation. Not all law officers would be above taking a bribe to alter a name in an official document."

"This man is, I think, an honourable magistrate," Malouet said. "But one can never be certain of such things. There is, too, the fact that Satanism is world-wide in its ramifications; so it is even possible that he is a secret associate of the Canon's, and acted as he did on a simple request."

"Have you reason to suppose that Black Magic is widely practised down here?" C. B. enquired.

"I would not say that. Among the peasants up in the hill villages sorcery has played its part from time immemorial, and still does so. On the coast there is some sorcery, too, of a quite different type, which is resorted to by people who live here only for the gambling. Inveterate gamblers are always superstitious and easily become the dupes of occultists who promise them aid to win money at the tables. But activities which suggest the presence of genuine Satanists are no more frequent here than in Paris or Marseilles."

"I asked because I think it very unlikely that the Canon will attempt to tackle this business to-night on his own. Even if he doesn't assemble a full coven, he will almost certainly need a few brother warlocks to assist him with the homunculus. It occurred to me that if there are certain people in these parts whom you suspect of being practitioners of the Black Art, we might trace him through them."

"You have been thinking on the same lines as myself," Malouet nodded. "There is an antique dealer in Cannes, a Polish countess living here in Nice, and one or two others who may be worth investigating. I was going to suggest that this afternoon we should see if we could pick up a lead from one of them."

"What about the de Grasses?" John demanded. "They are up to their ears in this."

The ex-inspector gave him a pitying look. "Is it likely that we should have neglected them, Monsieur; or that they are such fools as to have exposed themselves? M. le Marquis is still laid up with his wound and Count Jules has an alibi covering him from seven o'clock till past midnight."

"But they must know the whole story. Upson is their man and the Canon travelled by his seaplane."

"There is no proof whatever, Monsieur, that the seaplane that landed on the reservoir was Upson's."

"Who can doubt it; or that the de Grasses did all the spade work for getting Christina out of prison?"

"Let us accept that," agreed Malouet. "The police are endeavouring to trace the lorry which presumably drove away the Canon and the homunculus, and the taxi in which Mademoiselle Christina was carried off. But in both cases they have very little to go on, and nothing at all that links either up with the de Grasses."

"They know the truth! We must get it out of them!" exclaimed John impatiently.

Molly laid a hand on his arm. "Johnny dear, don't be unreasonable. Since there is nothing with which they can be charged, the police have no excuse for questioning them; and they certainly won't give anything away to us."

"But, Mumsie, we've got to make them, somehow," he protested. "It is our only chance to find out what has been done with Christina."

"There is still a chance that we may get a line through one of these occultists whom Monsieur Malouet suggests that we should investigate this afternoon," C. B. put in quietly.

"Perhaps! But we have only this afternoon left to work in," John argued desperately. "So we can't possibly afford to ignore the only people we are all convinced could give us the facts if they liked. I am going to ring up Jules and make him give me an appointment."

"Just as you like." C. B. gave a little shrug. "But I'm afraid you will be knocking your head up against a brick wall."

John jumped up and left the table to telephone. When he returned a few minutes later he said, "I got on to Jules at the Capricorn, and he has agreed to see me at four o'clock. Mumsie, you'll drive me over, won't you? And I'd like Mr. Beddows to come with us. He has certain arguments which I think might induce Jules to talk."

Beddows had taken very little part in the conversation, but he now gave a quick nod and said, "I get the idea: it's O.K. by me."

C. B. had also got it, and turned a serious glance on John.

"It's worth trying, though I doubt if Jules will prove willing to make any admissions, whatever you offer. Still, I can guess how you must be feeling; so good luck."

As they left the table Malouet said, "Colonel Verney and I will maintain contact with the police in case they pick up any information about the lorry or the cab, and will spend the afternoon ourselves making enquiries in other quarters. If you wish to get in touch with us, ring up Inspector Drouet at the *Préfecture* in Nice. I will see to it that he knows from time to time where to get hold of us."

Outside the airport they separated, C. B. and Malouet taking a taxi into the city, while Molly took the road to St. Tropez with John and Beddows as her passengers. At her villa they made a brief halt to drop their suitcases, but out of his Beddows took the bulk of his bank-notes and stuffed them in his pockets. They reached the Capricorn soon after four, and as they drove up to the hotel Molly said to John:

"I don't think I'll come in with you, Johnny. I'll just wait in the car and say a little prayer that things may go the way you want them to."

"Thanks, Mumsie." He leaned over and gave her a quick kiss. "Keep on praying till we come out, please. This means an awful lot to me."

On giving his name he was shown up at once to the de Grasses' suite. Jules let them in and John introduced Beddows to him. The young Frenchman gave Christina's father a swift, appraising look, then led them into the sitting-room. When they were settled there John said:

"I'd like to come straight to the point. A few days ago you offered to double-cross Canon Copely-Syle if I would make it worth your while to do so. Is that offer still open?"

Jules' eyebrows rose in evident amusement. "A lot has happened since then; and things are rather different now, aren't they?"

"You mean that I caused you a lot of trouble, and that it was largely owing to my having taken a hand in the game that your father was wounded?"

To John's surprise, Jules replied, "No; I wasn't thinking

of that. You made yourself a nuisance, of course, but even if you hadn't been with us at the château that hell-cat might have got hold of Upson's pistol and run amok as she did; so I reckon that what we lost on the swings owing to your intervention we more than made up for on the roundabouts. I saw you knock the gun up when she was about to shoot my father through the heart. I am very fond of my father, and it was your having saved his life that decided me to hear anything you had to say this afternoon."

John smiled a little awkwardly. "I'm afraid I can't take any great credit for that, as it's a natural instinct not to want to see murder done. But of what were you thinking, when you said things are different now?"

"Simply that as we have already handed over the goods I don't think there is much that we can do."

"You could put us on to the men who met the Canon, and those who later kidnapped Christina."

"Perhaps; but that would mean laying certain friends of mine open to criminal proceedings; and that I am naturally not prepared to do."

"I'm ready to ante-up handsome, Count," Beddows put in. "I've quite a tidy sum on me, and if more is needed I don't doubt I could fix passing it through the Tangier International Zone."

"Thank you, sir," said Jules, with a frigid little bow. "But it is not in the tradition of my family to sell our servants."

John was tempted to make a swift retort to the effect that it was even more shameful to traffic in dope, arms and women; but he checked himself in time, and said, "May I ask you a question?"

"By all means." Jules snapped a gold, pocket gas-lighter to the Gitane cigarette that was hanging from his lips.

"Do you know where Christina is now?"

"I haven't an idea."

"Then do you know where the Canon plans to hold this abominable ceremony to-night?"

With a genuinely puzzled look Jules asked, "What ceremony?"

"Surely you are aware of the reason why he has been trying to get hold of Christina?"

"No. I thought he just had a yen for her. Old boys do get that sort of thing for young girls, you know; and are often willing to part with a lot of money for a chance to gratify it."

"This is something very different. He wants to use her in what, for lack of a better name, we will call a Black Mass."

"Really!" Jules' plump face showed only cynical interest. "That sounds very intriguing. Ellen, or Christina, or whatever you like to call her, would look pretty good stretched out naked on an altar. I think I must try to muscle in on that."

John fought down an impulse to hit him, and said, "If you did, as the culminating point of the ritual consists in cutting her throat, you might find yourself later being charged as an accessory to murder."

Letting out a low whistle, Jules stood up. "So it's not just fun and games, eh? Well, I don't wish her any harm, even if she is half off her nut; but I'm afraid there is not much I can do about it."

"You said that you might muscle in on the ceremony. Could you do that? Or, at all events, find out where it is to take place?"

"I might, but it would not be easy. We did all that was required of us last night and were paid well for our trouble; but, to be honest, I don't think my own people could help much. What you have just told me explains a lot. You must already have a pretty shrewd idea how the two jobs were done; so there's no point in my concealing from you what happened afterwards. The Canon and the big crate he brought with him were taken to a villa on the outskirts of the town. Some three hours later Christina, doped and concealed in a large trunk, was delivered at what I imagine to have been the same place; but of that I can't be certain. You see, when the men who did these jobs reported to me this morning, none of them had anything but the vaguest idea where they had been. They couldn't even recall the district in which the villa lay."

"Oh hell!" John groaned, at the thought that his last hope was slipping away. "Then that swine of a Canon pulled

358

a fast one on you too, and hypnotized your men into forgetting where they had driven."

Jules nodded. "That's about it. I couldn't understand what had come over my chaps this morning; but now you tell me that he is contemplating murder, the reason why he went to such lengths to cover up his tracks is obvious."

"All the same," Beddows put in, "you said just now that you might be able to find out where the ceremony is going to take place."

"I could try; but it would mean putting a lot of people on the job, and they would have to work fast. You see, by this time the Canon may have carted Christina off to anywhere between Mentone and Marseilles, to have her handy to some devil-ridden spot suitable for doing her in; so we shall have to cast a very wide net."

"Then get to it! Money is no object."

Giving Beddows an unfriendly stare Jules remarked, "If I do anything at all it will be for John, because he prevented that crazy daughter of yours from killing my father." Then, as an afterthought, he added, "Still, we may as well look after the old firm as far as expenses are concerned. How much are you willing to pay?"

"I'll give you a thousand pounds down, and another thousand if you get results."

"Good. I'll have my people get a line on all the queers along the coast. There is an old priest at Cagnes who has a pretty gruesome reputation, and a fortune-teller in Monte Carlo who does not stick to telling the cards. There is one man in Nice, too, who might know something—if only we can persuade him to talk. He is an elderly cabaret singer with a husky bass voice, and he does his act at a dirty little dive off the Place Massena. One of his stunts is to intone the *Paternoster* backwards. However, the telephoning I am about to do is strictly private; so I must ask you to leave me now. I may be unlucky; in any case it will be a couple of hours or more before I am likely to have anything to tell you; so you had better make yourselves as comfortable as you can in the lounge down-stairs."

Beddows produced the thousand pounds; and John, now blessing the impulse which had caused him to save the Marquis from a bullet in the heart, thanked Jules for what he was about to do. Then they went down, collected Molly from the car, and ordered tea in the lounge as a means of killing a little time, although none of the three felt like drinking it.

John never remembered a longer hour than the one that followed. From time to time one of them endeavoured to start a conversation, but it inevitably tailed off into silence after the exchange of a few sentences; and, now that he had the leisure to con the cold, hard facts, the slenderness of their chance of saving Christina became more and more apparent to him. He had pinned his faith on either bribing or bullying Jules into giving them the information that they needed so desperately; but it had turned out that he had not got it to give. He had, through a strange freak of fate, become friendly instead of hostile; but, in the event, all that he had actually done was cynically to accept a thousand pounds to institute the same sort of enquiry as Malouet was already engaged upon gratuitously.

John knew that on the Riviera there must be more people than anywhere else in the world who, having once been rich, had through wars, revolutions or gambling lost all but a pittance, and so were peculiarly susceptible to the temptation to attempt to regain something of their past affluence by trafficking with the supernatural; yet it seemed beyond all reason to hope that, in a matter of a few hours, one such could be found who was not only in the Canon's confidence, but prepared to betray him.

Outside, the sun was shining. Through the broad windows could be seen the lovely prospect of the blue, unruffled bay; with, in the foreground, two mimosa trees in blossom, a row of striped yellow cactus, and some brilliant scarlet geraniums in pots. Inside, there was the constant passing of well-dressed men and women, laughing and carefree, all intent on the enjoyment of a summer holiday snatched from the grim winter in northern lands whence most of them came.

The contrast between the scene and the thoughts of the

little party at the tea-table made the long wait all the more intolerable. The minutes crawled by. For John each of them brought a new vision of Christina—as she might be now, locked in some cellar; or in an attic room with barred windows; or with her clothes removed so that she could not escape, lying in bed half drugged—as she would be to-night, carried away again, stifling in a trunk, to some secret place; fighting on her release until she was beaten into submission; stripped and cowering among a group of ghouls excited to a frenzy by unnatural lusts; screaming as the sharp sacrificial knife severed the muscles of her throat; still and dead with the blood gushing from her neck.

At half-past five John ordered a round of drinks. In the next hour he knocked back five double Martinis. As he ordered a sixth Molly laid a hand on his arm and said:

"Johnny, haven't you had enough—anyhow for the time being?"

He turned and gave her a weak semblance of his old familiar grin. "Don't worry, Mumsie. People can't get drunk when they feel as wretched as I do."

It was a quarter to seven when a page came to their table and said that Count Jules de Grasse would like to see them upstairs. Molly went out to the car; the two men hurried over to the lift. As soon as Jules had let them into the suite he said:

"I think I have the information you want; but there is one proviso that I must make before I go any further. I require you both to give me your word of honour that you will not inform the police, either directly, or indirectly through your friends who brought them to the Ile de Port Cros, if I enable you to make use of the tip-off I have secured."

"Why?" asked John.

"Because you will need guides to take you to the place where the ceremony is to be performed; and the only guides with which I can provide you at such short notice are two smugglers who are wanted by the police. They are key men in our organization for exchanging goods across the Italian frontier. What is more, they trust me; so I cannot allow their safety to be jeopardized by the police being brought to the scene by other guides at round about the same time as they arrive there with you."

"The Canon will probably have a number of people with him," Beddows pointed out uneasily. "Last night I . . . I was subjected to a shock that seems to have aged me greatly; so I'm afraid I wouldn't prove the man I was, in a fight. With only my help John Fountain might not be able to overcome them. In fact, instead of rescuing Ellen the two of us may be knocked on the head."

Jules shrugged. "You must take your chance of that. In an affair of this kind the participants are certain to be nervy. If you use your wits you should be able to succeed in breaking the meeting up. Once my friends have taken you to the place and left you, I naturally have no objection to your getting help from wherever you like; but I will not have you telephone to the police in advance any information likely to lead them to the place to which you will be taken. Now, what do you say?"

Glancing at one another, Beddows and John nodded; so the latter said, "All right; we both promise."

"Good! I accept your promises; but even so it is unnecessary that you should know your final destination for the next hour or two. It is enough for me to tell you that the job is to be done up in the hills behind Nice. Drive back towards the city, but do not enter it. Across the Var and about two kilometres past the airport you will come to a turning that leads inland up to the little town of St. Pancrace. Outside the church there you will find two men waiting for you. The taller of the two has a red beard. They are your guides, and will take you to the spot where the Canon and his friends are meeting. But I should warn you that you have none too much time. The meeting is due to start at nine o'clock."

"It would be," Beddows muttered. "Christina's birth hour is nine forty-five, and they would want to perform the . . . the actual sacrifice as near that time as possible."

"And it is nearly seven already!" exclaimed John. "Come on! We must not waste a second!"

Beddows threw the second thousand pounds worth of bank-notes on the table; and with brief good-byes to Jules they ran from the room. As they came hurrying out of the hotel Molly saw them and started up the car. John took the wheel, and within three minutes of leaving Jules' suite they were on their way back to Nice.

It was still light, but there was a sharp chill in the air and the end of the sunny day was fast approaching. There was quite a lot of traffic on the road—auto-buses taking work-people home and bringing less well-off holiday-makers back from day excursions, many motor-cycles, and the cars of the wealthy carrying couples and foursomes to neighbouring towns to dinner—but John snaked his way through it at high speed without taking too many risks that might have brought them to grief.

Before they had gone far he said, "It would save a little time if we could stick to N.7. and cut across inland from Fréjus to Cannes, instead of going round by the coast road; but now we have to tackle the Canon's crowd on our own I think it's more important that we should call at the villa to collect some weapons."

"No," replied Molly promptly. "I thought this afternoon that we might need the armaments before we were through; so you can go by N.7. While you were dropping your bags at the villa on our way out I picked up some things. C. B. has still got my big gun, but I have the small one in my bag, and I've two heavy truncheons, knuckle-dusters and knives in the back of the car for you. I put in a couple of extra torches and a bottle of brandy as well."

"Good old Mumsie! You've thought of everything. I wish you'd let me have your gun, though."

"No, darling. I'm hanging on to that. This is a chance in a life-time to see how it works."

The streets of St. Maxime and Fréjus hardly caused John a check, but he had to slow down to go through Cannes, and by then the sun was setting. When they passed Antibes the sky behind them was a rich glow of orange and salmon pink which by the time they crossed the River Var had faded to a

363

few streaks. It was half-past eight and the light had gone as they wound their way up the hill into St. Pancrace.

The sweep of their headlights picked out a man who was standing on the steps of the church. As John pulled up he came forward. He was tall and bearded. Leaning down to the car window he asked in a low voice:

"Has Monsieur come from St. Tropez?"

"Yes," replied John. "We are the friends of Monsieur le Comte."

"Good!" nodded the man, and went on, "Monsieur will excuse me if I do not introduce myself. It will serve if you call me Number One and my companion, who you will meet later, Number Two. Do you know the road to Falicon?"

John shook his head.

"It is through Gairaut and no great distance; but perhaps it would be best if Madame would allow me to occupy the front seat next to Monsieur."

The rearrangement was soon made by Molly getting out and joining Beddows in the back. As they set off along the twisting road up hill again, John asked:

"May we know where we are going?"

"Monsieur has given his word to M. le Comte not to communicate with the police until I and my friend have left him?"

"Yes; we won't let you down about that."

"Then I am about to take you to the Cave of the Bats."

Into John's mind there flashed a memory of the first time he had been in the crypt at The Priory, and had seen the bat nailed upside down to the broken crucifix on the altar. He suppressed a shudder as Beddows asked, in French that had an appalling accent but was just comprehensible:

"What sort of place is it?"

"A very unusual cave, Monsieur. Most caves are natural fissures in the rock and run more or less level for some distance into a mountainside; but this is not at all like that. It is entered by dropping through a hole high up on the side of a hill and was made by man, or at least has been much adapted by him, as it has several passages of uniform size and one quite large vaulted chamber. Even the archaeologists who visit it at times cannot say what race of men first used it. There is a legend that the Phoenicians offered up human sacrifices to their god, Moloch, there; but many think that long before that prehistoric man had hewed the little temple nearly a hundred metres below the surface of the hillside as a place to perform his secret rites with doves and virgins."

John felt the palms of his hands go damp upon the wheel. He had expected that he might have to break into some little wayside chapel which was being desecrated, or stumble his way through the ruins of a long-since-abandoned monastery; but this underground warren which had been the scene of countless ritual murders through the centuries sounded infinitely more terrifying. He began to pray that they would catch up with the Satanists before the latter reached their horrible rendezvous.

After they had covered another five kilometres up the winding hill road they approached a group of houses, and Number One said, "This is the hamlet of St. Michael. It is here that we leave the car. To the left of the crossroads there is an inn. You can park your car in the open space alongside it."

As they pulled up and got out, a figure emerged from the shadow of some trees and gave a low whistle. Number One replied to it and the figure approached. It was Number Two. In a husky voice he made his report:

"The tip-off that M. le Comte got about the meeting being here was a right one. The party arrived in five cars nearly an hour ago. There were thirteen of them; nine men and four women. Out of the cars they unloaded a packing-case, a big trunk, two stretchers to carry them on and some suitcases; then they sent all the cars away. One of the men led the way as guide and the other eight carried the loads on the stretchers. It was all very orderly with everything evidently arranged beforehand, as none of them uttered a word. They just formed a little procession and set off up the hill."

John drew a quick breath. "Then they are nearly an hour ahead of us! I was told that the meeting was not due to start till

365

nine o'clock. It can't be much more than twenty-to, and they may have started already."

"No, Monsieur." Number One shook his head. "They should be punctual, but not much in advance of the time set. They cannot have yet reached the cave. With burdens to carry over rough ground and uphill all the way they will find it a good hour's walk."

Beddows swore, then apologized to Molly. Like John, he felt that the fact that they should be able to catch up a little through having nothing to carry was small consolation. He, too, had had an eye on the time, but had not realized that a long, hard walk lay ahead of them; so he had believed that there was a good hope of their coming up with the Canon's party before it reached the cave. Now that hope was dashed and they would have no alternative but to go down into it.

"There are times when I become profane myself," Molly replied a little grimly; then she added to John, "I shan't keep you a moment, but I'm just going into the inn."

"Would it not be as well if Madame remained there?" suggested Number One.

"Yes, Mumsie," said John quickly, "you must. You can't come up to this place with us."

"Of course I'm coming," she retorted, as she turned away.

"No, you are not," he called after her. "I won't let you! And, anyhow, we can't possibly wait."

"If you don't I'll get lost trying to follow you and probably fall down a precipice," she called back. "I tell you I won't keep you a moment; but I've been out all day and I simply must pop in here before I start climbing that hill."

As she disappeared through the lighted doorway of the inn, John and Beddows got the weapons and torches out of the back of the car and distributed them in various pockets. Molly was as good as her word and rejoined them after a few minutes. Then, with Number Two leading the way, they set off in Indian file up a track that curved round behind some outhouses and chicken runs.

Within a few minutes they were out on the bare hillside and began to appreciate how rough the walking was going to be. The path was barely a foot wide and in places disappeared entirely. It wound in and out among knee-high boulders between which grew myrtle, wild thyme and a low leafless shrub that had sharp prickles. Before they had covered two hundred yards they had barked their ankles half a dozen times stumbling over rocks and Molly's nylons were ruined.

"The Canon and his crew must have had the hell of a job getting up here with loaded stretchers," John muttered.

"They were using torches, and that would have made keeping to the track much easier for them," replied Number Two. "But we dare not do so, in case one of them is acting as a sentry on the hilltop and spots us following them."

The path zigzagged diagonally along the slope of the hill and on their left its crest was visible against a starlit sky. After twenty minutes' gruelling tramp they reached a sparse belt of low trees, and Molly stopped to ask breathlessly:

"How much further is it?"

"We are not half-way yet, Madame," Number One told her. "But higher up you will find the going a little less difficult."

"Why not wait for us here, Mumsie?" John pleaded.

"No." She shook her head. "I shall manage, somehow." Panting, they stumbled on through the trees until they came to a series of low terraces, which suggested that the hilltop had once been a Roman fort. Now they had to scramble up the rough stone walls of each terrace. Even with help Molly was sobbing for breath, and upon mounting the second she panted:

"Is . . . is the entrance to the cave . . . on the hilltop here?"

"No, Madame." Number Two shook his head. "We have to go up this way; but when we reach the top we have another half-mile to do along the crest of the ridge."

Gamely she struggled on up the last terraces, where there were again some trees and the low walls of ruins that might have been the remains of a few cottages. The men were all conscious that she was delaying the pace of the party, and John was half crazy with exasperation, but had not the heart to insist on leaving her behind.

Coming out from among the scattered trees they had to

scramble down a further series of terraces, which proved nearly as arduous as getting up those they had scaled five minutes earlier. As they reached the last, Number Two halted. From their elevation they could now see the moon just over the crest of a much higher ridge to the east, and its light faintly lit the scene. Pointing along the ridge on which they stood he said:

"Can you see that blob of white ahead of us and a little way down the slope to our right? That is a small pyramid of rough stone, erected no one knows when, to mark the entrance to the cave."

They could just make it out; but Molly had sunk sobbing and exhausted on to a large flat rock.

"I'm sorry!" she gasped, as the others again moved forward. "I can't go on yet! And I'm holding you up. You must leave me. I . . . I'll follow you when I've had a few minutes' rest."

"Hard luck, Mumsie," John muttered, but they did not stop to argue with her. Every moment was now vital, and having brought her with them had already cost them most of the gain they might have made on the Satanists through having nothing to carry.

Below the terrace they struck another path, which Number Two told them was a smugglers' track, centuries old, leading in a dead straight line over the mountains to a point on the Rhine only forty kilometres from Strasbourg. John asked him then if he could tell them anything about the interior of the cave, and he replied:

"Yes; I went down into it once as a boy. When one is older one has no stomach for such places, but youngsters have no fear of them. The air in it is good; so those who made it must have provided some system of ventilation, and it is always bone dry in there. As far as I recall it, from the entrance there is a sheer drop of about six metres. At the bottom one finds a flat space and a few shallow steps; then comes a steep slope downwards for some fifty metres. Where it ends there are three passages. Two of them are *culs-de-sac*, but I cannot remember which. The third is roughly ninety metres long and runs back under the hill here. At its end is what is called the sacrificial chamber."

Still panting and stumbling, they advanced among the rocks until they were within forty feet of the pyramid. No one was on guard near it, and after the constant rustling made by their feet their coming to a halt brought a sudden eerie silence. They could see now by the moonlight that it was built with small uneven pieces of stone fitted skilfully together, and must originally have been about twenty feet in height; but its point and uppermost six feet of stones had been broken away, leaving it truncated, with its top an irregular platform. Its base was about thirty feet square and the side they were facing curved slightly inward to disappear into a black, gaping hole.

"Here, Messieurs, we will leave you," said Number One. "It remains only for us to wish you good fortune."

"Come with us," said Beddows in his atrocious French. "I'll make it well worth your while. I'll pay you a hundred thousand francs apiece to come in with us."

"I would not for a million, Monsieur," replied Number One quickly; while Number Two shook his head, crossed himself and muttered, "We have only our suspicions of what has led thirteen people to go down there together to-night; but that is enough. I wish to die shriven; not of a fit from coming face to face with the Devil."

Seeing that it would be useless to attempt to persuade them to change their minds John said, "Then pray for us, please."

"We will, Monsieur! We will!" they answered readily. Then both of them swung about and hastened away, taking a much more precipitous route across rocks between which no path could be seen.

Within a few moments John and Beddows reached the pyramid. Beside it lay the two stretchers. At its base yawned the big hole, about ten feet in length, four feet across and roughly oval in shape. Dug firmly into its nearest lip were two strong steel hooks, and, suspended from them, the upper few feet of a rope ladder could be faintly discerned. Below that lay impenetrable darkness.

John shone his torch, and they could then see the bottom of the ladder trailing loose on a rough floor of stone twenty feet down. He was about to get on his knees when Beddows pushed him aside and said gruffly:

"You keep your torch on. I got the girl into this; so I'm going first. Pray God we'll be in time, and that we manage to get her out."

All day he had walked with a stoop, and shown signs of the new feebleness that had descended on him; but he seemed to have managed the climb up the hill without suffering the exhaustion one might have expected, and now both his voice and movements gave evidence of a sudden return of rugged strength.

Swinging himself over the edge, he got his feet on one of the rungs of the ladder and began to descend. John held the torch steady and took a quick look at his watch. Having been handicapped by Molly, the two-mile climb had taken them a full three-quarters of an hour. The margin left them was now reduced to a bare thirteen minutes. His heart began to hammer wildly.

The instant Beddows reached the floor of the shaft John followed him down. Each holding his truncheon in his right hand and torch in his left they went forward. There were five shallow steps, then came the long steep slope leading into the bowels of the earth. As they slithered down it both were thinking of the countless gruesome companies of priests and victims which must have preceded them along it. For perhaps as much as ten thousand years, to mark the changing seasons, youths and maidens selected for their strength and beauty had been dragged down that slope by brutal witch-doctors and demon-ridden magicians; so that, by the infliction of a horrible death, their blood might appease Satan in the form of many monstrous, evil gods.

At the bottom of the slope they came upon the big trunk in which Christina had been brought there, and the packing-case—now empty but for great masses of cotton-wool that had been used to protect the glass jar containing the homunculus. Beside them were several suitcases, a pile of cloaks and several soft hats. Quickly now, they ran down the nearest passage. It was only four feet wide and after about thirty paces they found that it ended in a blank wall. Hurrying back, they tried the next. Some eighty feet from its entrance it curved slightly and in the distance they suddenly saw a faint light. Beddows was still leading and again broke into a run. John tapped him sharply on the shoulder and whispered urgently:

"For God's sake go easy! Our only chance is to surprise them! Put out your torch, and make as little noise as possible."

"You're right," Beddows whispered back, and he dropped into a swift padding trot.

When they had covered another hundred feet, they could see a part of the chamber. It was lit only by a red glow from a brazier that was burning in its centre. Grotesque shadows were thrown up by people congregated round it. The murmur of voices reached them, and a thin discordant music, like a violin string being twanged at random, helped to cover the noise of their approach. On tip-toe now, they advanced another sixty feet. As they did so they were able to make out more clearly what was going on in the temple. Only its central section, framed in the four-feet-wide and six-feet-high doorway, was visible to them; but that was enough for them to see that the ritual had already started.

The Canon was standing with his back to them, intoning Hebrew from a large book. On either side of him stood another man. One of them was making the discordant music on a stringed instrument; the other was swinging a censer to and fro, from which issued wisps of evil-smelling smoke. All three were clad in Satanic vestments in which they must have come to the cave, wearing over them the cast-off cloaks that had been left in the little chamber where the long slope ended. Facing them stood Christina.

With the Canon practically blocking the line of vision it was difficult to catch more than glimpses of her from the passage; but John and Beddows could see that her eyes were closed and that she appeared to be fully dressed still. Turned towards her on either side, two women were holding her arms, but she looked as if she was standing without their support.

Her hair was tousled, an ugly bruise disfigured one of her cheeks and she had a cut lip, from which a trickle of blood was running. The other members of this evil congregation were shut off from sight by the sides of the passage, as was also the jar containing the homunculus.

Beddows now had less than forty feet to go to reach the doorway. He had taken four more swift, cautious paces when the Canon stopped intoning and closed his book. Christina opened her eyes. Over the Canon's shoulder she saw her father, his face now lit by the glow from the brazier, advancing towards the entrance to the chamber. The mingled emotions of shock and hope proved too much for her. Unable to control herself, she let out a sudden scream.

As though they had been waiting for some such signal, Beddows and John rushed in. Brandishing their cudgels, they raced down the last thirty feet of passage and fell upon the Satanists. Taken completely by surprise, the devilish crew were seized by panic and cowered into groups for mutual protection. Beddows cracked in the head of one, and John delivered a swipe which smashed the face of another. Christina broke free from the two women, and threw the smaller of them to the floor.

For a moment it looked as if the champions of Light were to be granted an easy triumph; but only for a moment. Beddows felled another man with a glancing blow, but a black-haired woman with feverish eyes threw herself upon him like a tiger cat. Burying her teeth in his chin, she flung her arms about him, rendering abortive his further attempts to strike out. John's truncheon came whizzing down on a fourth man's shoulder, causing him to reel away with a scream of pain; but next second his arm was seized and he was flung back against the wall.

In two groups the remaining Satanists then hurled themselves on the intruders and bore them kicking to the ground. By then Christina had smashed her fist into the face of the second woman who had been holding her, and made a dash for the doorway; but there she was caught and dragged back by the Canon.

After some few moments of confusion a semblance of order was restored. Two of the Devil's congregation lay senseless and three others were groaning from their injuries; but eight remained unharmed, and between them they now held John, Beddows and Christina with their arms firmly grasped behind their backs. Still panting, and slobbering with rage, the Canon addressed his evil flock:

"Brothers and Sisters in Satan! Do not for one moment allow this interruption to our ceremony to lessen your faith in the protection of our Master. That some of our number should have been injured is most regrettable; but Prince Lucifer must have willed it so. I know these men. One is the girl Ellen's father and the other her would-be lover. Take notice that they come here alone, unsupported by the slaves of the Christian Law. They have been sent here and given into our hands for a purpose. Beyond doubt it is the Proud One's intention that they should witness the sacrifice, and be made fully aware of His greatness by also witnessing the miracle which will follow from it. Afterwards they too shall know the coldness of the altar slab upon their bare backs and feel the sharpness of the sacrificial knife as it cuts through their throats. But we have not a moment to lose. Temporarily we must ignore the hurts of our brethren. The fateful hour approaches. We must allow nothing to prevent us from completing the ritual while the woman's birth star is at the zenith. The time has come to strip her."

At this clarion call new heart entered into the Satanists. The men had nothing handy with which to bind John and Beddows; so they forced them to their knees and held them there. The women fell upon Christina like a pack of furies. She struggled wildly, until one of them hit her a savage blow under the chin, rendering her half unconscious. But, even then, instead of removing her clothes garment by garment they tore them from her body shred by shred, till she stood swaying among them stark naked except for her shoes and stockings.

Beddows was giving vent to an unending flow of curses. John ground his teeth in silent agony. He knew now that their hope of saving Christina was gone. They had made their last desperate bid and failed. He tried to pray, but the words would not come.

Christina, still struggling, was forced back against the altar and stretched out upon it. John could see her long, silk-stockinged legs dangling over the right-hand end of the altar; but he could not see the upper half of her body or her face, as they were hidden from him by one of the acolytes. The Canon again began to recite, this time in Latin, saying the Mass backwards. Parodying the motions of a priest, he bobbed and gestured to his assistants, who from time to time made hoarse responses to his muttering. A chalice was produced and Copely-Syle spat into it several times, then again he muttered feverishly and genuflected while breaking Holy wafers, stolen from some church, into it. Then he picked it up and carried it to each member of the congregation in turn, for them to sup up some of the horrid, sodden mess.

As he reached the men who were holding Beddows, they relaxed their grip on him slightly, and he strove desperately to knock the chalice from Copely-Syle's hands; but the Canon managed to protect his vile sacrament and enable Beddows' captors to partake of it. When all the members of his coven, except the two who were still unconscious, had done so, he carried it back to the altar, held it above Christina and swallowed what remained himself.

Setting the chalice down, he took from one of his assistants a small metal box that appeared to contain soot, and dipping his finger in it began to draw black symbols on each of Christina's limbs. As he did so he chanted unintelligible words in a high, excited voice. The sweat was now pouring down his flabby face and, as he proceeded with this new ritual, a frenzy seized upon his congregation, causing them to give vent to hideous animal noises and those who were free to do so pulled up their robes, exposing themselves.

With distended eyes John stared at the frightful spectacle being enacted before him. Already he had become vaguely conscious that some of the faces about him were familiar.

Suddenly he realized where he had seen them before. Ten of them were those of the party who had flown out with him from Northolt that morning. Before leaving England the previous afternoon the Canon must have sent an S O S to ten of the leading Satanists of Britain to join him in Nice for the ceremony. The mention of a wedding he had overheard must have been a covert reference to the spiritual union of Christina with the homunculus. He could only guess that the two others, making up the coven of thirteen, were French Satanists who had selected the Cave of the Bats as an appropriate setting for this unholy marriage.

John's distraught glance switched to the homunculus. He had been given a description of it by C. B., but had never seen it. The big glass jar that contained it had been placed by the left-hand end of a low altar, hewn from the living rock, at the far end of the small chamber. In the jar the squat, repulsive travesty of a female figure undulated gently, its arms and legs moving with the same apparent aimlessness as the tentacles of an octopus. Slowly the red-rimmed eyes swivelled from side to side, while the mouth opened and shut with a fish-like motion. As John gazed at it his flesh began to creep, and he felt that for sheer unadulterated filthiness the reality utterly beggared the description.

Suddenly the ritual of the symbols ended. The acolytes threw themselves on Christina, hauled her, now only half conscious, from the altar and stood her upright. One of the women near her produced a sack-like robe with strange designs upon it. The garment was thrown over her and her arms were then pulled through slits in its sides. Another of the witches put a pointed fool's cap on her head and tied it there by a ribbon beneath her chin. Into John's mind came a picture of heretics on their way to the stake, to be burnt at the order of the Spanish Inquisition. The costume was evidently designed with the same intent, but had the symbols of the Devil instead of those of Christ figured upon it. A third witch tied Christina's hands in front of her with a strip from her torn dress. Next moment the three of them had flung her down again on her back along the altar. Her head now rested on the top of the jar that held the homunculus. The black-haired witch removed its big round stopper. Sick with horror, John closed his eyes and again strove to pray.

When he opened them the Canon had begun another incantation. In a frenzy of excitement he mouthed and postured, while the witches held Christina down. The congregation screamed responses. Beddows shouted and cursed, and strove to break away; but he could not get up from his knees or shake off the men who held him. The Canon drew a long curved knife from his girdle and waved it aloft. Breaking into English he shrieked in a high falsetto:

"The hour has come! The great hour has come! I, Augustus Copely-Syle, Prince of the Bats and High Priest of the Lord Satan, by this act give a soul to my creation."

"Stop!" John's yell cut through the hideous din. "Stop, I say! Your ceremony is useless. She is no longer a virgin! I took her virginity that night we were together on the Ile de Port Cros."

A sudden deathly silence descended on the vaulted chamber. The Canon swung upon him, his face livid with ungovernable fury.

"It is not true!" he gasped. "It cannot be true."

"It is! I swear it!" cried John desperately.

Copely-Syle's eyes bulged, and he groaned. For a moment he remained silent and motionless, then he muttered, "Oh, I feared it! I feared it from the moment I saw you with her in the Casino!"

Again, for the space of a dozen heart-beats, he stood glaring but seemingly paralysed. It was Beddows who broke the spell by suddenly emitting a harsh, unnatural laugh.

It seemed to electrify the Canon. With blazing eyes he leapt towards John, brandishing the knife on high and screaming, "My life-work is ruined. I will cut out your heart. I will cut out your heart!"

The knife cleaved the air with a swish. It was aimed at John's neck above the collar-bone. Another second and it would have cleaved his jugular vein. Of the two men holding him on his knees one was the tall, gaunt-faced individual who had come from Scotland. At the penultimate instant he struck the blade aside and cried:

"No, Prince of the Bats, no! You cannot sully the sacred knife dedicated to the sacrifice of offerings on the altar. Do your will upon him, but not in blind anger. We are not here to witness common murder. I demand that he be sacrificed in due form, so that his blood may mingle with hers and the altar be deprived of neither."

"Yes! Yes!" chorused the others, and the squint-eyed witch who had also come from Scotland screamed above the rest, "But the woman first. She is ready for you, and we are waiting."

Slowly Copely-Syle turned about. His anger seemed suddenly to have drained from him, and he muttered to himself, "The incantation may yet work. It is her birth hour and she is twenty-one."

Again he approached the altar, and this time raised his knife with quiet deliberation. John felt as if his heart was about to burst from impotence and distress. For a moment hope had sprung wildly in his breast, but now he knew that final defeat was rushing upon him. Only seconds of life remained to Christina.

Suddenly, on an unbidden impulse, he found himself shouting with all the power of his lungs, "Christina, darling! I love you! I love you!"

As his voice rang through the chamber Christina's whole body tensed. With a violent jerk her wrists snapped the strip of fabric that bound them. From the impetus, her freed hands were flung out and backward. At the end of its swing her left hand struck the jar that contained the homunculus. John's ring hit it with a loud clang. The inch-thick glass shivered and broke as though it had been paper-thin crystal. As the jar fell to pieces the liquid in it gushed out. For a moment the naked and obscene homunculus stood among the falling fragments; then she leapt straight at the Canon.

With a piercing shriek he staggered back under the impact. Her taloned hands dug into his shoulders; her claw-like feet fixed themselves in his legs above the knees. For a few seconds her slimy, dripping face was pressed against his in an awful mockery of a kiss; then, her eyes goggling with her hunger for blood, she lowered it and fixed her teeth fiercely in his neck.

The rushing water from the jar swirled against the low brazier. The coals in it hissed and dulled, reducing the glow of light in the chamber to a glimmer. Pandemonium broke loose. Screaming, the Canon fell to the floor with the homunculus on top of him. Two of the men holding Beddows and John left them to run to his aid. By violent efforts both succeeded in throwing the others off. Beddows groped for his knuckle-duster and pulled it from his pocket. John whipped out his knife. Savagely and indiscriminatingly they laid about them. Shrieks and curses told how their weapons were finding their marks.

Rushing forward, Beddows kicked over the brazier. The remainder of the live coals hissed in the water and swiftly dulled. Near darkness engulfed the awful *mêlée*. Beddows shouted to John:

"Get the girl out! I'll keep these bastards busy."

John had already reached Christina and pulled her to her feet. The squint-eyed witch barred their path. Without hesitation John knifed her in the breast. With a filthy imprecation she clutched at the wound and staggered sideways. Jumping the still-hissing coals, John and Christina dashed towards the doorway. As they did so, by the dying light they glimpsed the tall bony-faced man charging at them. Evading his clutch by inches they gained the passage and sped down it.

Before they were half-way to the foot of the slope John knew that Christina's strength was failing. With one hand he had thrust his knife into his pocket and pulled out his torch, so that he could light the way ahead of them: the other he had round her waist and, as they ran on, he could feel her flagging. From behind them came the sounds of pounding feet, telling that they were very far from being out of danger. A veritable madness had seized upon the remaining Satanists, and those not occupied in endeavouring to overcome Beddows were in full pursuit, headed by the lean man from Scotland.

Gasping and reeling, the flying couple reached the slope,

but after a few steps up it Christina staggered and fell. This last effort after her terrible ordeal had proved too much for her; she had fainted. She was nearly as tall as John, yet, temporarily granted superhuman strength, he pulled her arm across the back of his neck, heaved her up in a fireman's lift across his shoulders and continued the steep ascent.

Bent nearly double, he lurched a dozen steps; then he knew that he could never make it. He had still a hundred and twenty feet of slope to mount, and at its top he would have to get her up the twenty-foot-long rope ladder. Even a Hercules could not accomplish such a feat in time to escape the fiends who were now coming up the slope behind him, howling for vengeance.

Then for a moment he was given fresh hope by hearing Beddows' voice mingled with the rest, shouting, "Go on, John! Stick to it! I'll stop them following!"

That cheering sound told him that Beddows had either dealt with, or escaped from, the Satanists remaining in the temple, and was now attacking the others at the bottom of the slope. It meant a brief respite and he did his utmost to make the best of it. Holding his torch in one hand and grasping Christina's wrist with the other, he dragged his feet yard by yard upward. Yet he was barely half-way to the top when he fell to his knees, weighed down by Christina's limp body, and mentally crushed by the knowledge that he was at the end of his tether. In vain he tried to rise. He could not. He could only pray, and mutter over and over again:

"Oh Lord, help us! Oh Lord, help us!"

And then indeed help came. There was the sound of slithering footsteps above him, and the light of torches shone in his eyes. Echoing back from the stone walls C. B.'s voice reached him:

"John! John! Thank God we are in time!"

Willing hands lifted Christina off him. Still gasping for breath he staggered up the last half of the awful slope. At its top, C. B. and another man got Christina up the ladder. A third helped him to climb it.

Half-dazed, he stepped out into the moonlight. His mother

was there and flung her arms about him. Beside C. B. stood old Malouet, and with them were several *gendarmes*. It was they who carried Christina to one of the stretchers and covered her sacking garment with warm cloaks.

John was still standing on the edge of the hole when he again caught the clamour of the surviving Satanists. They had reached the platform immediately below the opening. Molly and C. B. ran to it. The latter shone his torch downwards. It lit a group of wild upturned faces. That of Beddows was among them. It was covered with blood, but he was still striking out at the nearest of the enemy. In the darkness and confusion they had failed to identify and overcome him.

What John took to be a stone fell into their midst. Next second there came a blinding flash of light and a shattering explosion. C. B. swore and pulled Molly back. Two of the *gendarmes* came running up to ask what had happened. No one could say. It could only be assumed that one of the Satanists had been carrying a package of explosives, and a blow upon it during the *mêlée* had set it off. When C. B. shone his torch down the hole again it revealed a tangle of dead and dying men and women.

Leaving all but two of the police, who had already picked up the stretcher on which Christina lay, to perform such rescue work as might still be possible, the others set off down the hill. When John had recovered a little he asked C. B.:

"How did you manage to come on the scene like this and save us at the very last moment?"

"It was your mother, my boy," C. B. replied. "She is a woman in a million."

"Nonsense!" cut in Molly, who was walking just ahead of them. "I did no more than use my common sense. Your having promised Count Jules that you would not communicate with the police was not binding on me."

"No," said John slowly. "I suppose not. But how on earth did you manage to do it?"

"I didn't go into the inn for the reason you thought I did. It was to write a brief message. I gave it with a five-hundred-franc note to the woman I found behind the bar, in exchange for a promise that she would telephone it at once to Inspector Drouet. I knew that would bring our friends to St. Michael as soon as they received it. But I thought I ought to make certain of being able to find you as well; so I went up to the top of the hill with you, then threw a weak woman act as soon as the smugglers had pointed out the entrance to the cave. Immediately you were out of sight I hurried back to the inn, so that when the police arrived there I was able to lead them straight up to it."

"Bless you, Mumsie; you really are a wonder." John laughed. "And if it is true that you are not still on the secret list as Molly Polloffski the beautiful spy, that's a great loss to the nation."

The arrival of the police at the inn an hour before had resulted in the good woman who ran it keeping it open a little later than usual, and it was still not yet eleven o'clock when the stretcher party arrived there. In the public room a warm fire was glowing in the stove, and Christina, now fully conscious again, was made comfortable in borrowed wraps beside it. C. B. ordered coffee laced with cognac for them all to warm them up, and when John carried two cups over to the corner where Christina was sitting the others discreetly took theirs to the far end of the room.

When John had settled himself beside Christina, he told her how Jules had enabled him to trace her to the Cave of the Bats, and how his mother's quick wits had brought the police on the scene in time to save them; but she smilingly shook her head.

"It was clever of you to think of making use of Jules, and wonderful of your mother to think of a way of getting help to us; but your first attempt to rescue me failed, and the police would have arrived too late if it hadn't been for your eleventh-hour inspiration."

"What do you mean by that?" he asked with a puzzled look.

"Why, that frightful lie you told about my no longer being a virgin."

"By Jove!" he grinned. "D'you know, I'd already forgotten about that. It was a whopper, wasn't it? What's more I swore it, and that is perjury, or something. Do you think I'll be forgiven?"

"I'm sure you will. It must have gained us the best part of five minutes, and so saved my life. But that is not all. It was your ring that really saved us both."

"Yes. There must have been some blessed magic in it for a single tap from it to have shattered that thick glass. Would you like to keep it?"

"Do you want me to?"

He hesitated, then asked, "Do you know that your father is dead?"

"No," she replied calmly. "I was absolutely staggered to see him there. How did he come to be with you?"

"That is a long story, and I'll tell it to you to-morrow. For the present it is enough to say that just after we got out of the cave there was an explosion and I saw him with his head half . . . well, so badly injured that he couldn't possibly recover."

"Poor Father," she sighed. "It is sad to hear that; but he never loved me or I him; and you haven't told me yet how you induced him to come in with you."

"Up to last night he was a Satanist himself. He sold you to the Devil when you were a baby. That was what made you so unlike your real self during the hours of darkness. But last night he repented and released you."

"That would explain, then, why I felt so different soon after I was taken out of the prison, and again this evening after sunset."

"Yes. He abjured Satan and all his works on your behalf; then he came back here with us to help try to rescue you. But he is dead now. I am certain of it, and I have a reason for telling you so at once, instead of waiting until later. Before he died he had no chance to alter his will; so nobody can yet know how he has left his money."

"I don't quite see what you are driving at," she murmured.

"Simply that I would like to ask you to marry me before it is known whether you are a great heiress or a pauper."

"Oh John," she smiled. "What has money got to do with